BEFORE I
WAKE

Also by Steven Spruill
Painkiller

BEFORE I
WAKE

STEVEN SPRUILL

ST. MARTIN'S PRESS   NEW YORK

Design by Glen M. Edelstein

Library of Congress Cataloging-in-Publication Data
Spruill, Steven G.
    Before I wake / Steven Spruill.
      p. cm.
    ISBN 0-312-06910-3
    I. Title.
  PS3569.P733B4 1992
  813'.54—dc20   91-41808
                           CIP

First Edition: April 1992
10 9 8 7 6 5 4 3 2 1

To Mom
For all your love and caring

And for bearing a son
with one eye green
the other brown

ACKNOWLEDGMENTS

My thanks to Dr. Tom Stair, Professor of Emergency Medicine, and Dr. Russell Nauta, Chief of General Surgery, at the Georgetown University Medical Center, and to Dr. Lowell Weiss, Associate Clinical Professor of Medicine at the George Washington University Medical Center, for their kind help in making the medical aspects of this novel as accurate as possible. Any errors are mine.

I am grateful to Claire Cockrell, Richard B. Setton, F. Paul Wilson, Jeanne Kamensky, William Carney, Gary Edwards, Harris Eisenhardt, Jocelyn Knowles, and Bill and Marcia Eggleston for their invaluable feedback on the story.

My special gratitude to Maureen Baron, Executive Editor at St. Martin's Press, without whose professional skill and insights I could not have written this book.

From the bottom of my heart, I thank Al Zuckerman for all his wise counsel.

And, as always, my love and gratitude to Nancy Lyon Spruill for her constant editorial help and support as I wrote *Before I Wake*.

BEFORE I WAKE

1

Dr. Amy St. Clair eyed the stack of paperwork on her desk and groaned. When she'd made Chief of Emergency Medicine at Hudson General Hospital she'd expected it to be a *big* job. Actually, it was an endless avalanche of small ones. Most of them she enjoyed, but this . . .

She sighed and picked up the pile, sorting through it, doing a quick triage. Not so bad, no ugly surprises—except possibly for this letter from the law firm. In truth, the whole stack could wait until morning.

But that, she thought, was not how you made chief.

She picked up the letter: ". . . do hereby request all relevant records pursuant to the death from cardiac arrest of Richard Jameson III while in the care of Hudson General's emergency staff . . ." The type blurred and Amy set the letter down. Lawyers trying to sniff out a suit? This one could definitely wait until morning. She rubbed gently at her eyelids, feeling the answering burn of spent adrenaline. What a day— on at seven and still here. A Con Ed cave-in, two cab wrecks, and another gang fight. I must be tired, she thought. A dull ache chewed at the small of her back—punishment for three straight hours standing on thirty-nine-year-old feet in ER's surgery bay. She could feel the tangles in her hair clear down to the roots. She probably smelled like iodine.

If Tom Hart walked in right now, she thought, would he still think I look like a young Blair Brown? She pictured the actress's face—the intelligent eyes, the glamorous expressive mouth, the thick auburn hair. Terrific Tom—a silver tongue in a golden body.

She found herself wishing he would walk in, no matter how she looked. But it was Monday. His afternoon and evening were blocked solid with the cancer group and private patients.

Besides, she'd told the girls she'd be home for dinner.

Some of her weariness vanished at the thought of sitting and talking with Denise and Ellie, finding out about their day. And, if Denise wanted her to, she would help her with her science homework, then she'd watch "Night Court" with Ellie. After the girls were in bed, she'd talk to Joyce, make sure they hadn't given their nanny any static after school . . .

And then?

Up to bed, Amy thought. I'll page through the new journals, then see if there's a nature show on PBS . . .

And then?

She felt the small familiar dread, knowing that in the last hour of her day she would no longer be able to pretend she was not alone. The prospect made her chest feel hollow, her heart ache in the sudden emptiness. She took a deep breath, holding it, easing it out. Come on, life was good again. She adored her daughters, loved her work—except for the mountains of paper—and her relationship with Tom Hart was shaping up nicely. It was enough!

Amy glanced at the clock above her computer. Six-twenty! The paperwork would have to wait until morning after all.

She hurried out the back way, resisting the temptation to stick her head into ER one last time, knowing she'd get sucked in for another hour. Exiting Hudson General at Forty-third Street, she walked into a warm haze of exhaust and tar fumes. The warmth surprised her. It must be seventy out, a heat wave for early April. Unbuttoning her coat, she headed up Third Avenue. The tail end of rush hour crept along, cabs and buses darting and stopping like frenzied fish in the liquid blue shadow of the Chrysler Building. She scanned the street for an empty cab, knowing it was useless. At Fifty-first Street she gave it up and walked over to the Lexington Avenue subway. A train came almost at once, standing room only. Finding a pole near the door, Amy held on, bumping and swaying uptown, trying not to feel the press of bodies all around her. Between the heads of two people, she noticed a tall man in a denim jacket. The man was staring at her. There was something unhealthy in his gaze—beyond the obvious fact that one did not look, much less stare, at people on subways. Amy looked away, annoyed.

A moment later she found his reflection in the dark glass. He was still staring at her, unaware, now, that she was watching him too. He had close-set eyes, a mean, pinched mouth. His dark hair was greasy, slicked back.

The train stopped with a series of rude jerks. Amy checked the station. Fifty-ninth. Two more stops and she could get off. Relax, she told herself. There are plenty of people on the train. Maybe he's from out of town, someplace where everyone watches everyone else.

But she knew that a gaze like that was not polite anywhere in the world. Memories crowded in, of the rape victims she'd treated at Hudson General—good, innocent women and girls full of a hurt she could not take away. She felt her jaw clenching. She realized with a shock that the man was staring back at her through the reflection now, smiling intrusively. She looked away. A chill ran up her spine. He wants to hurt me, she thought.

She drew a slow, even breath and looked for a transit cop. No luck. Maybe she could work her way into the next car . . .

The train began to slow. Good, it would be Seventy-seventh—her stop. She braced her feet as the train decelerated with a sharp screech. As soon as the doors opened, the crowd waiting on the platform started to surge in. She pushed through them in a burst of determination, tucking her elbows in and lowering her head, projecting an image of herself as a charging lion. She hurried up the steps, glancing back, scanning the crowd for the man in the denim jacket. She could not see him. When she reached the street, she saw with dismay that it was getting dark. There still wasn't a free cab in sight, and she didn't want to just stand here. Should she head up the long blocks between avenues now, or keep to the more populated short blocks?

She checked behind her. No Denim Jacket.

Relieved, she headed up Lexington, passing Jams, where Bud had liked to go on Friday nights. The fragrance of mesquite and roasting beef filled the lowering dusk, starting her mouth watering. Salad and cottage cheese, she told herself sternly.

Looking back as she waited for a chance to cross, she saw the man in the denim jacket walking toward her. Her heart leaped and began to pound. Even from this distance she could see that he was staring at her, openly aggressive, not caring if she saw him. She felt a surge of anger at him. Hurrying across Lexington up Seventy-ninth Street, she caught up with two men in business suits. She kept pace close behind them. Glancing over her shoulder, she saw Denim Jacket tailing her, half a block behind. The tops of her lungs burned; her knees felt spongy. She forced herself to calmness. He wouldn't try anything with the two men so close.

The men turned in at a restaurant.

Amy's heart sank. Follow them in? She glanced back. Denim Jacket was nowhere in sight. Where had he gone? Never mind. She was almost home now. She felt a rush of exasperation—at the man for spooking her, and at herself for letting him. This was what she got for allowing herself a moment of loneliness. It made her feel vulnerable too, and that was nonsense. She could take care of herself. The creep from the subway was real, a possible danger, but she was not helpless. She could deal with it, like she dealt with everything else.

Amy turned onto Eighty-first Street, feeling more confident as she sighted her town house at the other end of the long block. Beyond it, across Fifth Avenue, a rosy twilight found its way through the lacy, budding trees in Central Park. Amy felt her shoulders relaxing. She'd had a little scare but she was all right now—

Denim Jacket stepped out of a service alley right in front of her.

She stopped, stifling a gasp. Her mind flooded with all the advice, the articles, the talk shows: Don't display fear, project a positive, forceful image. Don't look like a victim.

She willed herself to step forward, stride past him.

He caught her arm. "Got a match?"

His hand clamped her upper arm with a force just below pain.

"Let go of me." She was astonished at how firm and strong her voice sounded. His grip lessened a fraction, but he did not let go.

"What's the matter, pretty lady? I scare you?" His voice was light, derisive. He looked at her more closely, staring into her eyes. "So that's it. I knew there was something different about you the minute I saw you on the train."

Amy tried to twist away, but he held her arm tightly.

"Don't get mad," he said. "A green eye and a brown eye—I like it. It's wild, you know? Sexy."

Amy jerked her arm free and tried to step around him. He blocked her way. Her mind screamed at her to run across the street, try to get to her town house—

No, he would be right on her heels, and if he got inside, he might hurt Denise and Ellie. The thought terrified her. She must not let him know she was close to home.

Run to Fifth Avenue, Amy thought desperately. There will be people up there, buses and cabs.

She said, "Let me pass, please."

"You haven't given me a light." The man reached for her blouse. "Is it maybe in here?"

She jerked back from him, knocking his hand away.

"Hey, bitch! I don't like that."

She felt the heat of his breath on her face. Her lungs filled with a scream. Behind her, she heard the scuff of footsteps. The man's gaze slipped up over her shoulder; his confident leer faded.

She turned and ran, feeling a thrill of pure relief as she saw the man walking toward her, walking his dog, a big German shepherd. Beautiful! The dog growled at her and the man stopped, giving her an inquiring look. He was about sixty, fit looking, dressed in linen white ducks and a designer sweater.

"Yes?" he inquired.

"I'm having trouble with that man back there," Amy said. "I wonder if I might walk with you a minute." She looked over her shoulder and saw that Denim Jacket was gone. He must have run back down the service alley. She turned back, agitated, trying to explain, but the man held up a hand.

"I saw him. General Schwarzkopf and I would be happy to walk with you, young lady."

Amy laughed, delighted with the man, the dog, her escape, the whole world. "General Schwarzkopf? Who could ask for more?"

After the girls were tucked into bed, Amy sat at her bedroom desk, writing checks to Visa and MasterCard. Her hand shook a little, and she had to bear down to hold the pen steady. She wondered if she should have told Joyce about the man in the denim jacket. No. It would only alarm her needlessly. Joyce was already careful when she went out, and, like all first-rate nannies, very watchful with the girls. The man was probably miles away by now, riding the subway, trolling for some other victim. The police had taken her description over the phone— not that it would do any good. The NYPD had better things to do than chase after a man who, technically, had only asked her for a match. Forget it. She'd done what she could. Now she must put it from her mind.

Amy sorted through the rest of the mail, finding the *New England Journal of Medicine*. She pored over it for a while, seeing the man's greasy face, his hard eyes staring at her from behind the columns of print.

She put the *Journal* aside and went to draw a hot bath. She soaked in the tub for half an hour, letting the wonderful, steamy heat relax the tense muscles in her neck and shoulders. When her fingertips began to crinkle, she got out, dried off, and slipped into her nightgown. In the bedroom she went to the window, but as she reached for the drape, she hesitated. What if she peeked through the curtain and Denim Jacket was out there on the street, staring up at her? A chill shot up her spine. *Stop it!*

She jerked the curtain aside and stared defiantly down at the street. The sidewalk glowed empty in pools of streetlight. She shut the curtain again and climbed into bed. If Bud were here, she thought, I could tell him about the man. I could get rid of some of it. Bud would know just what to say . . .

She felt the emptiness coming and blanked her mind for a second. Good, now start over. Keep the memories but lose the pain—a hard trick, but she was going to learn it yet. She practiced, relaxing, letting her mind go back to him without pain, to that last hour of the day, when they had talked and relaxed alone in the cozy sanctuary of the bedroom. Bud letting her lean on him if she needed to after a day of everyone leaning on her. And the little things: Bud reading the art reviews in *The New Yorker* to her in a hilarious parody of prissy arrogance. Bud lying behind her, smelling faintly of linseed oil, cradling her cheek on his big arm until she drifted off—

The longing grew too sharp. Amy eased Bud back behind the curtain in her mind.

Picking up the remote control on her night table, she channel-hopped until she found a PBS special on owls. The narrator had a wonderful low voice, soothing and hypnotic. The screen swam before her eyes and faded, leaving only the soothing voice, and then it dwindled away too.

The TV switching off woke her. Joyce at the doorway, fingers giving a good-night wriggle. Room light going off, leaving only the soft, reassuring night light from the hall.

Faint thirst. Get up?

Considering it, Amy drifted off again.

For an indeterminate time there was nothing.

Then she found herself in some woods. It was dark. She was small, a child again, the dirt of the path cool against her bare feet. Ahead of her a shape swirled in midnight mists, looming closer among the trees. Fear ran up her spine in a cold, prickling wave.

"You see the shape," a voice murmured in her ear. "Tell me what it is."

She tried to see who had said it, but could find no one.

"Look at the shape," commanded the low voice.

She didn't want to look. She wanted to get away.

Amy turned to run but the shape swung around so it was centered in front of her. She mustn't look! She jerked her head to the side. Dangerous—she could feel it. If she let herself see the shape, *recognize* it, something dreadful would happen. Fighting panic, she spun back the other way and there it was again, wavering among foggy trees, still in front of her. She tried to scream for Mommy, but her voice came out in a tiny whisper.

Suddenly a hopeful thought broke through: Maybe this wasn't real, like a story in her brother's comic books. How else could that awful shape keep swinging in front of her?

Or maybe she was dreaming it.

A nightmare, yes.

Shape and woods melted away. She could feel that she was on her back in bed, her adult self again. She did not feel asleep any longer, but knew, somehow, that she was not quite awake, either. She must open her eyes, but they resisted, the eyelids sticking together. Her arms felt as heavy as lead. Sit up, she commanded herself. She squirmed and pushed with her elbows, but could not rise. She had the sudden, panicky sensation of lying on the bottom of a dark pool, pressed down by water, feeling the air going stale in her lungs. *Wake up WAKE UP.*

Amy broke through at last, opening her eyes, blinking in the darkness of her bedroom. The streetlights glowed on her curtains. She felt terribly groggy, and yet she could feel her heart pounding. Her nightgown, drenched with sweat, stuck to her back and legs. A smell lingered in her nostrils—sweet but cloying, like lilacs that had started to rot.

A nightmare, only a nightmare.

The nightmare, the same one she'd had a few nights ago.

A vague alarm penetrated the haze in her mind. This wasn't right. She never dreamed—at least never remembered her dreams. And now she'd had the same one twice?

She gazed dully at the glowing red numerals of her bedside clock: 2:40. Her mouth was parched. She should get up, get a glass of water. She tried to swing a leg out of bed. The muscles tensed, then went slack again. She felt herself slipping back toward sleep.

No, I've got to stay awake. Something isn't right.

Rolling her head to the side, she saw that her door was closed. A yellow glow lapped under the sill from the night light in the hall. She felt another dull surge of alarm. That door

should not be closed—she never closed it, in case Denise or
Ellie cried out for her in the night.

Someone was in here!

Holding her breath, she listened. Her heart thudded between her eardrum and the pillow, a grainy sound, like feet
treading across sand. She imagined the man in the denim jacket
lying under the bed, or maybe on the floor beside her, his
mouth open to still his breath, staring up at the edge of her bed,
ready to spring up and strike if she moved . . .

She thought of the hammer she'd put under the bed after
Bud had died. It had made her feel safer those first months
alone in the bed, but now that she really needed it, it was back
in the kitchen drawer. What was she going to do? Denise and
Ellie were sleeping just across the hall.

God, please, don't let him hurt them.

She listened for a long time. Her heartbeat slowed and
faded in her ear. Against all reason, she felt her body relaxing
again, sinking into the bed. She tried to fight it, but her mind
kept fading back along the edge of sleep. Despite everything,
her eyes closed.

Light surged gently on her eyelids. Mustering all her will,
she forced her eyes open a slit. Through the blur of her
eyelashes she saw that her bedroom door was open now.

She felt a distant, dreamlike anxiety.

The stairway outside her bedroom creaked and she knew
without question that someone was creeping down the stairs.
It seemed oddly distant, as though it were happening to someone else.

She really must think, do something, but she could not
seem to keep her mind focused. The bed swirled under her.

She heard a soft click from downstairs, the front door
opening and closing, and then it all slipped away.

2

. . . a car horn, blaring on and on, *somebody please stop it*
   Alarm clock.
   Amy rolled over and groped for it, her fingers clumsy on
the snooze button. Got it—ahhhh. She slipped back toward
sleep.
   No, get up, NOW!
   Pushing up with an effort, she sat woozily on the edge of
her bed. On the curtains, the first glimmer of dawn boosted the
light from the street. She felt exhausted, as if she hadn't slept.
   Something happened last night, she thought.
   The memory crept back: She had awakened from the
nightmare, barely able to move. Then she'd sensed someone
in the room. Her door had been closed, then open. Amy shuddered. So eerie . . .
   She heard a muffled giggle from Ellie's bedroom, the clink
of pans downstairs in the kitchen. The warm sounds failed to
reassure her.
   Amy got up. Her knees buckled; she grabbed the bedpost
in alarm, steadying herself. What was wrong with her? Nothing,
she thought determinedly. I'm tired, that's all.
   After yesterday and last night, who wouldn't be?
   Taking a deep breath cleared her head a little. She shuffled

to her bathroom, leaning on the vanity, gazing at herself in the mirror. Her face bore the ridged imprint of the blanket; her neck itched. She started to scratch it, then held back, seeing a faint reddish patch high on her neck, near her earlobe. She probed it. Hives? Unlikely, since there was no swelling. It might be some kind of contact dermatitis.

Making a mental note to check it again later, she turned on a cool shower and stepped in, gasping as the water shocked her skin. She leaned against the tiles, feeling the blood surge in her veins. She toweled off briskly, blew her hair dry, and dressed in a red skirt and the white silk blouse her mother had given her. A little makeup, and she felt better, ready to run ER for another day.

Joyce called up from the kitchen—breakfast in five minutes. As Amy reached the bottom of the stairs she caught the wonderful smell of brewing coffee. In the kitchen, Joyce stood at the stove, stirring a pot of oatmeal. She turned and smiled. "Good morning."

"Morning." Amy smiled back, pleased at the extra brightness she was seeing in Joyce these days. Part of it must be her new trimness, emphasized by the dark slacks and turtleneck she was wearing this morning. With her rosy cheeks, her blond hair plaited on her head, she looked like an elegant Swiss cosmetician. Would she start dating again now that she'd finally got the twenty pounds off? Amy hoped she would find a nice guy or two and get back into circulation—even if it meant having to look for another nanny. Three years was too long to mourn a divorce.

Or widowhood, chided a small voice inside her.

Amy poured herself a cup from the Norelco and settled at the table. The first sip of coffee slid down her throat hot and wonderful. Ellie trudged into the kitchen, still dressed in her Wonder Woman PJs. Holding out an arm, Amy clotheslined her into a hug. "Why aren't you dressed?"

"Denise isn't dressed."

"Ah. That explains everything." Looking into her daughter's deep brown eyes, Amy felt a sweet sense of wonder. Ellie had grown five inches in the past two years, and her face had changed too, losing its babyish roundness, taking on intriguing new expressions. But for all that, she was still a child, and would be one a while longer. Amy found the knowledge heartening.

"Morning, Mom." Denise ambled in, tall and graceful, straight hair still tangled from sleep.

"Good morning. And you know you're not supposed to hack on the computer until you've dressed, eaten breakfast, and are completely ready for school."

Denise gave her a startled look.

Amy almost laughed. "You've got a diskette in your hand," she said.

"Oh."

"Now go on, get dressed, both of you." Amy sipped the cooling dregs of her coffee. Her mind turned back to last night. In her worry about the door, she had given scant thought to the nightmare. So strange—walking in the woods, hearing the insistent, disembodied voice, the questions. She tried to remember theories about recurrent nightmares from her R-1 rotation on psychiatry. But that had been ten years ago and she hadn't paid much attention, convinced that psychiatry—and especially the theories of the unconscious and dream interpretation—were basically mumbo-jumbo.

Maybe I should talk to Tom about it, she thought.

The idea brought a flush to her face. No way. Things were at a very nice place with Tom. They could chill out fast if she made him start thinking of her as one of his patients.

Joyce set a bowl of oatmeal in front of her.

"Did you close my door last night for some reason?" Amy asked.

Joyce glanced at her. "No. Why would I do that?"

Ellie and Denise came back down, dressed this time, and settled at the kitchen table.

"I hear Randy Niswander wants to be your boyfriend," Ellie said to Denise.

"Don't make me zuke. He's totally buttly—"

"Girls, listen," Amy said, a little too sharply.

They looked at her, eyes wide.

"Relax. I just want to know if either of you closed and then opened my door last night."

They shook their heads. Denise paled a little. "Why do

you ask?" Her voice was suddenly low and guarded, not at all the voice of a twelve-year-old. The adult tone did not quite mask her anxiety. Had she heard something too? Amy saw Ellie looking nervously at Denise and realized this was not the time to ask.

"I guess I dreamed it," Amy said. "Eat your cereal now. You'll be late for school."

For a moment no one moved. Joyce gave her a thoughtful look from the other end of the table. Amy forced a smile, doling out a reassurance she could not feel. *Something* happened last night, she thought. Something more dangerous than a nightmare.

On her way out, Amy asked Joyce to get all the outside locks changed.

Amy rubbed at the small of her back and looked around the emergency room, surveying the situation. A madhouse. It had been the usual "full day." What an understatement! Phones rang; a baby squalled in the pediatric room. A crazed chirping sound swelled beyond the entrance—someone pushing the gurney with the bad wheel. Turning in a circle, Amy scanned the thirty curtained examination "rooms" that lined the perimeter of the big ward, hoping some of them had emptied out during the afternoon. No such luck. In contrast, the staff station in the center of the ward was all but empty, the nurses and doctors drawn off by the crush in the patient rooms. Only Kathy DiGenova stood on the nurses' side of the long counter, dark hair swinging down, her pretty, tanned face set in a frown of concentration as she measured out medication. On the other side of the counter, Harry and Jerry Anderson, New York City's only redheaded identical-twin ER doctors, sat at two of the five small phone carrels, receivers shouldered against their freckled ears as they scribbled in charts. One of them—God only knew which—stood, still talking into the phone, and handed a chart across to Kathy, who made a face at him. Amy felt a proprietary pride. Too busy, too noisy, and too crowded, but it was all hers.

Amy headed for room sixteen, a new arrival. The girl was fourteen, slim and tall, wearing a rugby shirt and shorts that flopped like tents around the lean muscles of her thighs. She had bruised an eye playing racquetball. Looking at her and seeing Denise, Amy felt a hand clutching her heart. *My girls could have been hurt last night,* she thought. *Who was in my house? That creep from the subway?*

Holding the girl's eyelids apart with a thumb and forefinger, Amy started to squeeze bacitracin onto the reddened sclera. The girl blinked, flinging a blob of ointment onto Amy's face.

"I'm sorry, Doctor." The girl blushed furiously.

"No problem. That's the best stuff anyone's thrown on me all day." Amy tried again, and succeeded this time. She handed the tube to the girl. "Take this home and do what I just did every four hours."

The girl nodded, looking worried.

Amy patted her shoulder. "You're going to be fine. The pain and blurriness should be gone in a few days. Just wear goggles from now on when you play racquetball."

"Thanks. Uh, how long did you have to go to school for this?"

"Four years," Amy said, knowing where the question came from. Girls that age often asked it, usually while looking away, shy, afraid she might snub them. What they really wanted to know was if she thought they might be able to be like her. "Plus a four-year residency," she added. "But it goes by real fast if it's what you're meant to do. Are you thinking about becoming a doctor?"

The girl nodded, looking at her now.

Amy scribbled on the back of a prescription form. "This is a book about it you might like. It's in most libraries."

The girl took the note eagerly. "Thanks!"

"Good luck."

Amy followed the girl out of the curtained booth and headed for the station. Elaine Sikma, the second-shift head nurse, hurried up to the far end, staring down at the printer, shifting from foot to foot. Amy watched, amused. Elaine's small, compact form bristled with impatience as a lab workup jerked up line by line from the buzzing machine. Her blond brush cut looked ruffled, emphasizing her aura of frenetic energy. Amy walked over.

"How's it going?"

Elaine looked up in surprise. "How come you're still here?"

"Our esteemed Dr. Wickham is late."

Elaine checked her watch. "A whole hour. Poor you."

"I don't mind. Bernie's usually here early."

"We've got a chest pain coming in," Elaine said. "Man named VanKleeck. His doctor just called again. One of those snooty Upper East Side types—begging your pardon. Wanted to make sure we knew how rich and important his patient is."

"I guess we'd better give him a private bedpan, then."

Elaine smiled. "Better watch out for Kathy. She's already cranky from doing a long shift, and now she's steamed because I moved her seizure out of cardiac. She had to put him in the hall, and he's been griping."

"I don't blame him."

A distant wail reached up the corridor from the front entrance. "Let's go," Amy said. She led the way to the entry hall, her heart sinking as she saw it was still packed with overflow patients. What was the count now? Five—no, six—of them, cramming the tiled corridor. Their gurneys lined both walls, choking the corridor down to half its normal width. Amy felt a wave of frustration. This was getting out of hand. Two of the patients she recognized from yesterday. They'd had to stay in the hall overnight, grabbing whatever sleep they could on their gurneys without even a curtain for privacy. If ICU didn't clear some beds in the next few hours, ER would have to start rerouting ambulances to other hospitals. The thought made Amy's teeth clench. Most paramedics were pretty sharp, but ten extra minutes in an ambulance could still be a death sentence.

Stopping at the entrance, Amy looked out at the rush-hour traffic. Through the blare of cab horns, the siren surged closer. A catering truck tailgating a bus edged back grudgingly, allowing the long, boxy shape of a Park Ambulance to squeeze through into the bay. Amy waited impatiently while the paramedics lifted the gurney down from the back. The doors hissed open and a cool breeze rolled in with the gurney, peppering her face with grit.

The medic in the lead blinked at her as if he were just waking up. "Well, hel*lo.*" A big, handsome kid with one of those little pistol-butt ponytails Amy associated with Cajuns, even though the style had probably started in New York.

"Hey, Doc," he said, "when do you get off?"

"Rhythm strip," she said coolly, holding out her hand. Her stomach tightened as she scanned the EKG taken in the ambulance. He's on the edge of ventricular tachycardia, she thought, and catching Elaine's eye, she mouthed the word "Tachy." Aloud, she said, "Let's get Mr. VanKleeck down to his nice reserved room."

Elaine finished switching him from ambulance to ER oxygen and grabbed the front end of the gurney. The big paramedic, all business now, pushed the other end. Walking beside the gurney, Amy had her first chance to look at Owen Van-Kleeck. That name—vaguely familiar. Hadn't she gone to school with a girl named VanKleeck? She didn't recognize this man's face. It was tanned and craggy, dominated by a Roman nose and shaggy, Walter Cronkite eyebrows. His white hair was slick with sweat, a bad sign. Amy could smell it on him, not a sharp, locker room smell, but the subtler, sour odor you get with diaphoretic sweat. The smell of fear.

She took his hand. "Try to relax, Mr. VanKleeck. You're home free now." Amy held on a few seconds. His palm was warm, a point against congestive heart failure.

"Does this mean we're engaged?" he croaked.

"I believe someone else has already had that honor." Amy gave his wedding ring a twist as she let go. He managed a smile for her. It transformed his face, softening the cragginess and lighting up the eyes under the bushy eyebrows.

Amy heard heels clipping along the tiles. "One moment, please," said a stern voice behind them—Gladys Courtney, admitting supervisor. Amy turned too late to intercept her.

"Name?" Gladys asked VanKleeck, blocking the gurney with one brogaged foot.

With an effort, Amy checked her temper. "Give him a number, log him in, and get the rest later."

Gladys started to protest.

"Get out of the way, please." Amy motioned, and the medic shoved the gurney forward, narrowly missing Gladys's foot as she jumped back. Gladys sputtered something; Amy ignored it. Hurrying alongside the gurney, she put her stetho-

scope to VanKleeck's chest. "Breathe deeply." VanKleeck took
a huge breath and let it out. She could detect no crackling in the
lungs, no trace of the odd creaking you heard when the ventricles overfilled. The knowledge did nothing to cheer her. Ruling
out heart failure made it more likely that VanKleeck had suffered the swifter, more deadly myocardial infarction.

Amy helped Elaine steer her end of the gurney into the
cardiac bay and up to the EKG machine. Elaine attached the
twelve taped leads for an EKG in a corona on VanKleeck's
chest, then added an IV line to supplement the D-5 drip they'd
already hung in the ambulance. Amy held the EKG strip as it
curled from the machine. She felt a stab of alarm. Over a
hundred and sixty beats per minute, and the ventricular complex was starting to fall out of sync with the atrial.

"Lidocaine," she said to Elaine. "An eighty-milligram
bolus, then a four-per-minute drip."

Elaine injected the bolus into the IV line she'd just set up.

"Pain?" she asked VanKleeck.

"No, thanks, I've already got some."

Amy smiled, feeling a surge of warmth for him. He reminded her suddenly of her father. Whenever things were at
their blackest, Winnie found a way to laugh. Not many people
with pains in their chests could manage it. If the pains in his
chest hit full stride, the shock alone could kill him.

"BP?" Amy asked Elaine.

"High enough for nitro."

"Good. Let's try an inch."

Elaine nodded. She groped the red supply cart, then
frowned. "There's no nitro."

Amy had a sinking sensation. *Philip,* she thought. She
looked around, saw her brother pushing an empty wheelchair
back to Supply, his tall, athletic figure bent over the top of the
chair. Elaine called him and he hurried over. His eager expression tore at Amy's heart. *Like a lamb to the slaughter,* she
thought. As Philip bent down to turn his good ear toward the
nurse, Amy glimpsed the hearing aid coiled in his ear like a little
pink chameleon trying to hide. She felt sick, wanting desperately to intercede, but she knew she must not interfere. Philip
was the nurses' responsibility.

"Philip," Elaine said firmly, "I've told you before about the nitroglycerine paste. We've got to have some on this cart at all times."

Philip swallowed hard, and Amy saw tears welling in his eyes. She felt an answering pressure at the backs of her eyeballs. Philip was forty-one; it was wrong, tragic, that he could weep in a second like any child. Go get it, she thought. Now! Don't make her tell you. But Philip just stood there, his hands twisting together.

"Go get the paste, Philip," Elaine said firmly. "Hurry."

Philip stood a second longer as if mesmerized, then nodded and hurried off.

Elaine turned back to her, eyes filled with pity, and Amy felt a stinging warmth in her face. Elaine turned away quickly, fussing with the cuffs of her rubber gloves. "You know, with his hair longer like that, he's really so handsome."

Amy appreciated the attempt, but understood too well the sentiment behind it: At least he *looks* normal.

Better than normal, yes, he always had.

He never handles anything important, she reminded herself. And he's doing better all the time. It's up to him—he'll make it or he won't.

Philip raced back with the paste. Elaine dried VanKleeck's sweating arm with a piece of gauze and squeezed the nitroglycerine paste on quickly, rubbing it into his skin.

Amy checked the EKG monitor and felt a small measure of relief. Mr. VanKleeck's heart had slowed to eighty-five beats per minute and the ventricles were now in proper sync with the atria.

"Mr. VanKleeck, you're looking good now."

"Thanks, but how's my heart?"

"Better than your jokes."

"That good!" His voice was shaky with relief.

Amy patted his shoulder, then took Elaine aside a few steps, speaking in a low voice. "I'm going to get someone from cardiology down here so they can do an angio, see if we can find a thrombus. Go ahead and get some blood. Let me know the minute the cardiac enzymes come back from lab."

"Dr. Wickham should be in by then."

"Oh, that's right. Well, whoever."

Amy made the call to cardiology, then dialed CCU. They

didn't have a bed, but hoped to before the day was over. Amy did not like it, but it would have to do. VanKleeck could stay in cardiac bay for now—unless another heart attack came in. She stepped back to VanKleeck, taking a brief medical history. As he answered her questions about diet, family history, and exercise, Amy felt more and more perplexed. Here was a guy who played tennis regularly, was close to his ideal weight, watched his diet and fat intake, never smoked, and had no family history of diabetes or heart disease. No way should he be having a heart attack.

At the station, Amy scribbled her notes onto the chart. With the immediate crisis past, she could feel the energy draining out of her. Her body suddenly craved a hit of caffeine. Where was her mug? Walking back to the cardiac bay, she saw it on the corner of the red crash cart. She gulped the coffee. It was cold. The scum of oil on top bit her tongue, but she could feel the caffeine prickling through her. She gave VanKleeck's ankle an encouraging pat and glanced up at the videocam in the corner of the ceiling, making sure the red light was on. The nurses' station would have to keep a close eye on Mr. Van-Kleeck until he could be moved to CCU—

"Hiya, pardner. Sorry I'm late."

She turned to find Bernie Wickham standing outside the cardiac bay. "Good to see you."

"The IRT had a power failure," Bernie explained, "and we were trapped in a tunnel for over an hour." He seemed unfazed by the ordeal. His round face smiled at her, scrubbed and cherubic. His coat was a pristine, starched white, his bald pate dulled with powder; a fresh stress jockey, raring to ride.

Amy walked him around ER, briefing him on her patients, stressing VanKleeck. When she was through, she felt a huge burden had been rolled from her shoulders. The responsibility was now Bernie's. The long shift was over.

Time to head for home, make sure the girls and Joyce were all right—

Wait—she could not go home yet. This was her night to sit in on Philip's therapy session. Her mind rebelled at the thought. Normally she was happy to sit in with Philip, glad to see Tom. But tonight she felt a strong need to get home, make sure the girls were all right. Amy rubbed at the back of her neck, forcing the stiff muscles to relax. She mustn't overreact to last night. Whatever had happened, the girls had come through it fine, and by now Joyce would have the new locks in.

Whereas Philip definitely needed her tonight. After his blunder with the nitro paste today, he would be anxious and depressed. Tom would be gentle, but it would not be pleasant for him.

Amy started for her office to call the girls.

"Dr. St. Clair!" Elaine's voice, sharp with urgency.

Amy turned, seeing Elaine waving at her from the cardiac bay. Her face was white and strained. Bernie was there too, bent over VanKleeck, his shoulders thrusting down in a measured cadence.

VanKleeck had gone into cardiac arrest.

A shock of adrenaline kicked into Amy's legs. She ran to the cardiac bay, filled with grim determination. Owen Van-Kleeck was *not* going to die on her. The cardiac monitor showed the ugly flat line of asystole. Grabbing an endotracheal tube off the crash cart, she brute-forced it down VanKleeck's throat—no time to feel her way gently. Elaine anointed the pads with the gritty contact paste and handed them to her.

"Okay, Bernie," Amy said, and he stood back. She shoved one pad as far under the shoulder blade as she could and set the other on VanKleeck's chest. "Now," she said, and the current surged through VanKleeck. His body went rigid, then flopped back against the table as the charge cut off. The line on the cardiac monitor stayed flat.

"Epinephrine," Amy said. "He weighs one-eighty."

Elaine grabbed an intracardiac needle, measured the dose, and banged it into VanKleeck's chest. As soon as she jerked the needle out, Amy shocked him again. His body went thump-thump against the table.

"Amp of bicarb," she said. Elaine shot it into VanKleeck's IV line.

Amy stared at the monitor, Come on, *come on,* willing peaks and valleys to pull out from the flat lines. Bernie went back to CPR, pushing at VanKleeck's breastbone while Elaine squeezed the bag, forcing oxygen into VanKleeck's lungs.

The line stayed flat.

Amy felt sweat rolling down her nose, dripping onto the

gurney beside VanKleeck. A strange fury filled her. "Again," she said.

Bernie stood back, looking at her. "I don't know . . ."

She pushed the pads tight and hit Mr. VanKleeck again and the line stayed flat.

"Ten minutes," Elaine said softly.

Amy stared at her, amazed. No. It wasn't possible. How could that much time have passed? Ten minutes without a heartbeat. The angry, frantic energy drained from her. She swallowed, tasting acid in the back of her throat. They could keep on working if it made them feel better, but it wasn't going to make VanKleeck feel better—or feel anything, ever again.

Amy saw that Bernie was still looking at her. He gave his head a slight shake. She took VanKleeck's limp hand in hers and squeezed, hoping that it could somehow get through to him, knowing he was gone.

What she did not know was *why*.

But I will, she thought.

3

The receptionist for Psychology Services was gone for the day, and Philip had not arrived for his session yet. Amy paced around the empty waiting room, trying to burn off her lingering frustration over Owen VanKleeck. Too sudden, always too sudden. One minute fighting for VanKleeck's life, her brain in overdrive, shouting orders, snatching the trache tube, the shock paddles. Then he was dead. How could it be? He still looked the same, his body lying as it had, waiting for her next move. She wanted to go on, needed it. Part of her could still not accept that it was over.

It's not, she thought. Not until I know why.

She chose a chair and sat down, determined to relax. Emptying her mind, she became aware of the gardenias, realized she had been smelling them since she walked in. She looked around, locating the plant on the receptionist's counter. The honeyed fragrance of the blossoms rushed to her head in a sweet sting of *déjà vu*. Oh, Bud, she thought, remembering how, every spring, he would bring home a raggedy young gardenia plant. Every winter, when the gardenia had flourished and grown perfect under his attentive eye, he'd lose interest and give it away to whoever he thought would take good care of it. But for six months it would be theirs. One April day each year, there it would be, waiting on the Victorian marble stand in the foyer when she walked in from work. Amy closed her eyes, smelling those other gardenias now, ten happy springs of them. Hurry, hurry, up the two flights to Bud's studio, feel the pine-needle prickle of his beard on her cheek, smell the turpentine from where he'd rubbed his hands on his jeans and T-shirt. She felt a small pang.

I miss you. But I need someone else now. You *do* understand, don't you?

She waited for a sense of his assurance inside her. Instead, the question came, Do you mean Tom? Bud's growly bass voice speaking in her mind, but the question was hers, she knew.

Yes, why not?

Amy gazed at Tom's door, the glowing brass letters: Thomas J. Hart, Ph.D., Clinical Psychologist. She noticed for the first time how close to the floor the door was cut. Tom was in there with someone now, but not a murmur leaked past the solid oak. In there, it was safe to let go—shouts, sobs, secrets, all safely sealed away.

All at once, Amy found herself envying Tom's patients. Exasperated, she hauled herself up from the soft chair and stalked across to the magazine rack, jerking out a copy of *People* and fanning through photos of actors and actresses running on beaches and laughing together in restaurants.

Tom's door opened. A woman appeared in the doorway, head and shoulders turned back toward Tom, lingering as she talked to him. She was good looking, Amy decided—about thirty, trim and sharply dressed, with a full mane of black hair.

"—want to thank you again, Dr. Hart," she was saying. "I really have a good feeling about this session. You always seem to know just what to say."

Oh, please, Amy thought. Then: What the heck, it's true.

Tom's voice floated from behind the door, muffled, mellow with reassurance. The woman protested that he was being entirely too modest. Clearly she thought she was still alone with him. Amy had the uncomfortable feeling of being a voyeur—*come on, turn around, will you?*—but the woman was immersed in Tom, determined not to take her eyes off him until she absolutely had to. I know the feeling, Amy thought.

She coughed softly. The woman started a little, then said good-bye to Tom in a brisk voice. She nodded at Amy, spots of color flaming high on her cheeks, and hurried out.

Tom appeared in his doorway, saw her and leaned a shoulder against the doorpost, hands in his pockets. He said nothing, but looked at her with a hunger that made her breath catch. God, he was handsome—a wild, angelic beauty that his staid, herringbone jacket and sedate dark slacks could not tame. Alexander the Great might have looked like that, the same finely chiseled face, the golden hair, the startling blue eyes, crackling with purpose and drive. Amy knew exactly how Tom's mouth would taste right now, could almost smell the smooth, sandalwood scent of his cheek.

As if reading her mind, he stepped forward and took her hands, leaning into her for a kiss. Rising on her toes, she found his mouth, tasting the heat of his tongue. His arms closed around her, and awareness flamed down her body—the hard planes of his chest, his flat stomach pressed against hers. She felt the magazine slip from her fingers and plop down against her ankle. Tom let her loose; dizzied, she put a hand against his chest to steady herself.

"If a picture is worth a thousand words," he said, "then your kiss is worth a thousand pictures."

She looked at him, flattered and a little amused. There was poetry somewhere inside Tom, but it kept getting crossed up with algebra. Maybe that went along with being a psychologist. "Let's see," she said. "That would make my kiss worth a million words. And you get paid, what, a hundred dollars an hour for talking?"

"A hundred and twenty," he corrected. "And that's for listening. My talk is free."

"But never cheap."

"Certainly not." Putting a hand on her shoulder, he traced a finger along her collarbone, sending a delicious shiver up her neck. "You're early today."

"Mm-hmm. Usually I go home, then come back for Philip's session, but there wasn't time today."

Tom looked at her sharply. "Your shift ran over?"

"Two hours. Bernie—Dr. Wickham—got tied up in a sub-way breakdown."

Tom studied her. "That's not all, is it?"

Amy shrugged. "I lost one. Cardiac arrest."

His expression turned sympathetic. "Rough."

"A lot rougher for him than for me. Thing is, there's no way he should have died."

Tom cocked his head, intent. "And why is that?"

"His risk factors were way low. The man was a walking ad for cardiovascular fitness. We got him stabilized and then—pow—a second attack. I was right there, Tom—Bernie, too. I had the paddle on him in seconds. But there was no bringing him back. I don't understand that. And I don't like it." She realized she had raised her voice. She burned with frustration.

"I don't blame you," Tom said. He slipped his hand outward to her shoulder, giving it a comforting squeeze. "Want to talk about it?"

"No thanks. Losing patients is part of medicine." Talk was no good now. She did not want to feel better about VanKleeck. She wanted to know why he had died.

"We tough, we tough," Tom said, his tone half playful, half goading.

"I don't like anyone dying on me, but yes, 'we tough.' "

Tom sighed. Stooping, he retrieved the magazine she had dropped when she kissed him and tucked it neatly back in its rack. He said, "Since we have a minute before Philip gets here, let me give you a quick preview of what's next for him—I think it's about time he started dating."

Amy struggled to switch mental gears, feeling faintly shocked. Philip dating, kissing, making love to a woman?

And why not? Why should Philip go through life deprived of love, sexual love, just because he'd become mentally handicapped? Amy found herself considering the incredible idea. Through the last part of Choate and his years at Harvard, Philip had always had at least one girlfriend. But what kind of woman would go out with Philip as he was now? A mentally handicapped woman would be least likely to find Philip dull. But what if it were some young schemer with her sights set on the St. Clair fortune? And what about children? Philip's genes were unimpaired, but if the woman *were* mentally deficient . . .

Amy realized she was getting way ahead of herself. Philip

hadn't even had a date yet. "So when do you plan to bring this up with him?"

"Soon," Tom said. "As soon as he's feeling sure of himself on the job."

Amy tried to dismiss her discomfort, but failed. Philip was so vulnerable, so easily hurt. Was this really a good idea? "I don't think he *is* very sure of himself yet, Tom. He'll do quite well for a while, and then he'll stumble. Like today. He—"

Tom held up a hand. "Wait. Let's hold that until he gets here. If he messed up, I want to see if he'll tell me himself. And if he does, I don't want him to sense that I already know."

"Do you think he's that perceptive?"

"Don't you?"

Amy considered it. Sometimes she thought she saw eerie flashes of the old Philip, resources and insights that no one believed he could have anymore. But she had assumed it was only her imagination—wishful thinking. It was easy for her to romanticize Philip, see more in him than could be there, because physically there was no sign of the damage inside him. He was tall, good looking, the kind of man who drew second looks on the street. At some things he was incongruously good—chess, for example. But if you observed him for a few minutes, or listened to him speak, you realized that an earnest child lived behind the handsome face.

"No," Amy said. "I'm afraid I don't think he's that perceptive."

The door opened and Philip walked in, and she felt a twinge of guilt.

"Hi, Sissy," he said. "What's wrong?"

Amy almost laughed. So much for Philip's lack of perceptiveness. She glanced at Tom, who raised an eyebrow, giving her no help. "I was just talking about you behind your back to Tom," she said to Philip. "So then, when you walked in, I felt embarrassed."

Philip nodded. "What did you say about me?"

Amy suppressed a groan. "I was wondering how perceptive you are."

Philip cocked his head, turning the hearing aid in the better ear toward her. "Per expect . . .?"

"Perceptive. It means you can sometimes tell what people are feeling," Tom said.

Philip's brow furrowed in concentration. "Per septive, per septive, per septive."

Amy felt a pang at his effort, knowing that he would not remember the word, though he had undoubtedly known it once. As soon as it left his echoic memory, it would be gone, along with its meaning. She was struck by a sudden memory of sitting by Philip's hospital bed one night—it must have been the third or fourth day of the coma—and Winnie coming in and joking with Philip, acting as if his son could hear and understand him and they could laugh together, even though Winnie's heart had to have been breaking. The memory slid through her numbly, like a finger tracing a scar.

"Shall we?" Tom said, indicating the inner office.

Philip walked over to him and pulled him into a hug. "Hi, Dr. Tom." His voice was drawn out and overloud, the way it got when he felt a strong emotion. Tom patted his back, letting Philip cling until he was ready to let go. Amy was touched by Philip's show of love for Tom. Tom deserved it, no doubt about that. Almost twenty years, half a dozen other therapists, none of them able to budge Philip from his slack, mumbling stagnation. Then Tom. The changes in Philip in just two years were incredible. He was holding down a job. He had his own place. He had *pride*.

Inside the office the two men sat in their usual places on the big couch. Settling into the wingback chair across from them, Amy noticed something new—Tom had installed a spotlight to illuminate the Mexican rug he'd hung behind the couch. It made the colors even brighter, more cheerful. Letting her gaze roam over the rug's blazing yellows, blues, and reds, she listened to Tom and Philip warm up. Philip still wanted to talk about the Mets opener that Tom had taken him to more than two weeks ago. As he talked, Philip stroked his fists together, pantomiming Kevin McReynolds's home-run swing, then made a high arc with his hand to reproduce the path of the ball. Leaning way back on the couch, Tom held up his glove hand and watched the ball sail over his head. They horsed around another few minutes and then Tom said, "Philip, let's work now. How's it going in ER?"

Philip's face turned grim. "I goofed," he said. He sat tight-lipped, a sudden gloss of tears on his eyes. Amy felt the weight of his sorrow and frustration settling over her. He wanted so badly to do well.

"Tell me about it," Tom said.

Philip did, his voice harsh with stress. "I remember to check the carts, but it's so hard to see what's missing, so hard, so *hard*. How can I do it better?"

"You just asked the right question," Tom said. "That's a good start. Now think about it. See if you have an idea."

Philip sat, staring across the room, hands clasped at his knees, shoulders hunched. Amy found herself trying to think for him, to conjure up some way to help him. A minute passed; the time grated on her nerves. She started to say something, but Tom warned her off with a quick shake of the head. Philip closed his eyes; his lips moved in some private inner dialogue.

"Maybe I could . . ."

Another minute passed. Amy could feel Philip's tension jumping the gap between them, jittering along her own nerves.

Philip said, "Maybe I could take some pictures of the carts the way they're supposed to be. Then I could look at the pictures and look at the carts and see what's missing."

Amy looked at Tom, surprised and delighted. Tom gave her a triumphant look, then clasped Philip by the shoulders. "That's wonderful."

A look of joy dawned on Philip's face. "It is?"

"Your idea is very good, Philip."

Philip grinned and thrust his hand out. Tom slapped his palm and reversed, taking Philip's soft pat.

"Amy, do you have a camera," Tom asked, "so you could help Philip with this?"

"Yes," she said eagerly. "I can help you take the pictures and we can blow them up big so they'll be easy to see."

"Think of this, now, Philip," Tom said. "You did make a mistake today, but you learned from it. You decided, *by your-self,* how you could do better. Some people let their mistakes beat them, but you didn't. I'm impressed."

Philip laughed with exhilaration. "So am I!" he said.

Amy leaned across and threw an arm around Philip's neck, hugging him. After a second he squeezed back. She felt him starting to squirm and broke off, surprised at his bashful grin. It made her remember what Tom had said earlier, about Philip dating. Maybe it *was* time.

Amy followed along as Tom and Philip discussed other problem areas at work, the back of her mind still perking on Philip's solution to the cart-stocking problem. The photo idea wasn't cold fusion, but it *was* clever, better than anything she'd been able to come up with off the top of her head.

Tom and Philip stood, and she realized the session was over. She started out with Philip, but Tom caught her arm.

"Stay a minute."

She felt a flush of premonition, a pleasant stir in the pit of her stomach. She said good-bye to Philip, then turned as Tom pulled his door closed against her back. He leaned into her, his tongue sliding along her lips, finding its way inside, hot and quick with excitement. He pinned her against the door, his hand stroking down her flank. She felt her heart plunge and begin pounding between them as the skin of her face heated and tingled. She tried to draw a breath, but his tongue and mouth blocked her, his cheek sealing off her nose in a dizzying onslaught. Using the door as a springboard, she bounced him away a little and gasped a breath.

He took her head in both hands and gazed at her, his blue eyes electrified and somehow dangerous, as though downed power lines hummed in their depths. Amy found it tremendously exciting. She wanted him now, wanted to take him on the cool glass of his desktop, fight him for position, grapple her way to a blinding climax on his strong alabaster body. She could smell the homey wool of his herringbone jacket. Slipping her hands around his waist, she felt the cool silk of the lining against her knuckles.

"I love your eyes," he said. "Green and brown, stop and go." His voice was husky.

She saw that his gaze was focused on her brown eye. "You're looking at 'stop.' "

"Yes."

She looked down at the bulge in his pants. "But that says 'go.' "

He looked down with her and flushed. "With you, what else could it say?"

"Mmmmm." She pulled him to her, feeling him against her thigh. He nuzzled her ear, sending a thrill up her spine. I have to go home, she thought. Check on the girls. Reluctantly she stepped back and straightened her skirt. "You wouldn't, perchance, have a cold shower in your office, would you?"

He smiled. "It might look suspicious, a shrink having a shower in his office."

"I don't know. I think it would be kind of sweet."

Tom checked his watch. "Seven-forty-five. Let me take you to dinner."

"I have to get home, check on the girls."

"Isn't Joyce there?"

"Of course, but . . ." Amy told him about the creep following her from the subway, the strange business with her door last night.

Tom's face paled. "You should have told me this right away. Do you think the man who followed you was in your room?"

"I don't know. I can't even be sure there *was* a man in my room. It's just that I can't explain the door. Anyway, I've had the outdoor locks changed, just in case he saw where I live. The windows all have grilles, so we should be fine. But I still want to check up on the kids."

Tom pulled her to him, hugged her tight. Her stomach felt tied in knots, hungry, but not for food.

"We'll stop by," Tom said, "make sure everything's all right before we go anywhere."

"Yes."

Amy hung at the edge of climax, looking up into Tom's face. Oh God, hurry! She thought, but she could tell from his eyes that he meant to hold back longer. He sat, straddling her waist, his muscled buttocks riding her hips. Both of his arms plunged straight down out of sight behind his back as if bound there; one of his hands caressed her, a finger inside, barely moving, keeping her just at the edge. She could feel his thighs along her ribs, his knees in her armpits, his hardness a hot weight along her stomach. She wanted to rear up and look at it, but a thread of shyness held her back.

She ran her hands up his thighs, letting a hand stray in toward him, feeling a little shock in her fingers at the way he strained, hot and eager. And then she did look down, between her own breasts, at the red hardness in her hand. A giddy pleasure filled her. She was doing this to him, making him swell, commanding the blood to plunge through his body to this place. He wanted her, oh yes, and she wanted to make him come now, to feel and stroke the part of him that wanted her so much and watch his face as it happened. She glanced up at him and saw that he was looking at her. His eyes were hot, blue as methane flames.

"Do it," he said.

She looked down briefly, scratching him delicately with her fingernails, stroking him, watching it begin, breathless with wonder. His own hand moved more urgently along her and she felt a ball of golden fire blazing up through her belly—*no, wait*—stroking him harder, seeing the contraction begin and then looking up to drink in the ecstatic look on his face, his mouth open wide in a silent gasp as it happened to him, then inside her, too. She kept her eyes on his face to the last, bucking wildly under him.

He dried her stomach and breasts with the soft blanket, then fitted his hands to her ribs, stroking her, rubbing slowly up the ridges of ribs to her breasts, his palms hot and damp with sweat, as slippery as heated body lotion, giving her a lingering massage that made her shudder even as she loved it.

He stretched out beside her and lay for a long time. She felt him stroking her as she floated in a delicious haze. "Next time," he said, "let's do it standing up."

"Do we have to wait until next time?" she said.

Later, in the cab, she kept her face toward the window, afraid the cabbie might see in his mirror the lust still burning in her. The cab pulled away from Tom's apartment, passing Hudson General next door. Half dazed, she watched the trendy stores and restaurants of Third Avenue slide by, their facades lit sedately against the night. She could feel her heart still pounding. Now that she was out of Tom's presence, her wantonness shocked her a little. She was a widow, with two children waiting for her at home. She did not do this kind of thing. She liked to fall asleep in her own bed, alone, watching nature specials on PBS, for God's sake.

Listen to yourself!

Okay, she didn't like falling asleep alone, she liked what had happened tonight. How could Tom make her feel this way? She had never known sex could be so fantastic, so imaginative—different every time. Tonight he had pretended his hands were tied behind him, as if he were completely under her power. A euphoric fantasy, faster in the blood than a hit of cocaine: Amy makes a man helpless with her beauty, commands his gorgeous, muscular body. So wonderful to be desired. She shivered with delight in the backseat of the cab. She could feel goosebumps beneath her blouse and jacket. How had he known to open that door in her when she hadn't even known about it herself? He had seen straight into her with those blazing blue eyes.

What would it be like to have that every night?

But, of course, if she married Tom, they would *not* have it every night—which was probably just as well, since it would kill her.

Amy remembered making love with Bud—long, dreamy episodes that built slowly and finished with a warm glow. God, how she had loved him. But some nights they had just watched nature specials together, Bud falling asleep to the deep, soothing voice of the narrator. There was a place for that, too.

Would she and Tom do that?

She was getting ahead of herself. She needed someone, yes. Someone who could be in *her* bed, not every so often, but every night. Someone to hold and love, who loved her back.

Did she love Tom?

A skilled healer of minds, a savior to Philip, fantastic looking, a wickedly good lover. She liked him a lot, respected him—in a way, even adored him. He thrilled her, took her breath away . . .

But no, she could not say that she *loved* him, not yet.

Maybe she would. Maybe it was still too soon after Bud. Maybe if Tom would just tell her that *he* loved *her*.

A fair number of men had said that to her, but only two had meant it—actually, one man and one boy. The man was Bud, and the boy had disappeared many years ago in the jungles of Vietnam.

If Tom would say those magical words . . . and she could feel that he meant it . . .

But she wasn't going to ask.

Amy saw her face reflected in the cab window, superimposed now on a cortege of darkened town houses. Their vacant, barred windows gave her an empty feeling. I'm too proud, she thought.

And too alone.

4

Scared, Amy tried to run away, but the tall shape got in her way again. She could see the moon shining down through the trees like those searchlight beams at the circus. The beams seemed to shiver around the shape. The air was a nasty gray color, and poured the way it did when Cook opened the door to the big freezer room. Amy felt so scared she could hardly breathe. Go away, she tried to say, but nothing came out.

Tell me what you see, Amy.

"No," she whispered. She tried to shut her eyes. They would not close. She twisted to the side, gazing down her nightgown at her feet.

Tell me.

"I don't *want* to."

An owl hooted, making her shiver. She didn't like owls— in her picture books they were fuzzy and wise, but Philip said they ate little rabbits and mice.

Don't be afraid. Just tell me.

"NO!" An odd sensation crept through her, a soft pressure along her back, as though she were lying in her bed instead of standing. The woods tilted around her and faded; the voice dwindled. She heard a distant curse, then nothing more.

* * *

Amy got to work forty minutes early, the chill of the nightmare still clinging to her. She paused in the ambulance bay,
confronting her reflection in the smoked-glass doors. Two ambulances waited in the bay; ghost figures flitted urgently behind the glass. All she had to do was walk through those doors
and she could blow her anxiety off in the final flurry of the
night shift. Exactly what she needed right now.

No. What I need right now is to face this.

She walked around to Forty-third Street, using the side
entrance. As she'd hoped, the cafeteria was deserted, the orange tables becalmed like life rafts on a smooth green sea of
tile. Amy got a coffee from the Macke vending machine and
took a table in the corner. Cradling the paper cup, she let the
heat of the coffee soak into the icy skin of her palms.

Why was she so anxious? It was only a nightmare.

Amy held a sip of coffee in her mouth, savoring its heat
on her tongue, letting her mind ease back over last night.
She'd come home, checked on the girls, then gone to bed,
kicking off her shoes, slipping out of her clothes and col-
lapsing in her slip on top of the covers. Lying there in a
dreamy postcoital haze, she'd wished Tom were lying in the
bed beside her. She longed for the comforting weight of his
arm across her waist, knowing even as she wished it that she
could not yet have Tom up to her bedroom, not with Denise
and Ellie just across the hall . . .

Sleep.

And then the nightmare, invading her mind when she
could not resist, running its bizarre, frightening course. If there
were just some way to control it—feel it coming, head it off
some way. But no. That was not the way nightmares worked.
Three times now, the same exact dream. What did it mean?
Amy tried to sort out the images, find some sense in them. The
fear intensified, icing her mind.

She became aware of muffled voices, punctuated by the
faint clack of the cafeteria's plastic dishes. Behind the thick
vinyl curtains that sealed off the steam counters, the kitchen
staff was preparing breakfast trays for patients. The friendly

murmur soothed her. A year ago, those curtains would have been rolled back along their tracks by now, the cafeteria bustling to life as people from the morning shift dropped by for a quick, cheap breakfast. But that was over now, another victim of Eric Kraft's long-knived accountants.

Too bad she couldn't get Eric to declare her nightmares over budget. They'd be gone in a flash.

Amy got up and wandered to the bank of windows along the south wall of the cafeteria, staring out at the gray side of the SkyTek Building six feet away. Sometime in the distant past, these windows had looked out on a lovely shade garden with trellises, a fountain, and an intricate maze of trimmed hedges. Now they shared the sad fate of a thousand other old windows in Manhattan, gazing at nothing, ancient eyes dimmed over by cataracts of progress.

Amy heard a foot scuff behind her. Turning, she saw a man about twenty feet away. The man stood utterly still, gazing at her. He was tall and muscular, his green surgical scrubs darkened at the chest with spots of sweat.

"Amy?" His voice was low, a little hoarse. She did not recognize it, and yet it sounded familiar.

"You're even more beautiful than I imagined," he said.

For a second she was annoyed, and then he smiled and she recognized him—*My God!* "Campy?"

He nodded.

Campy, oh God, Campy. A scar marred his chin. His boyish features had matured into a strong, impressive face. He'd been leaner as a boy, but he was still trim, an inch or two taller, with brawny shoulders. The glorious mop of sandy hair had receded and thinned, replaced by a neat, masculine brush cut.

Amy felt her heart pounding. Her weariness fled, replaced by a feeling of agitation. The pit of her stomach ached suddenly. How many times had she imagined this during the years she'd waited for him, until at last her hope and her will to hope had run out. And now here he stood. Miraculous, incomprehensible!

And cruel.

She struggled for something to say. What came out was, "Where the hell have you *been?*"

"Surgery."

"For the past twenty years?"

He gave her a thin smile. "I was afraid that was what you meant. I know I have a lot of explaining to do. If you will listen, if you'll try to understand, I . . . need that more than anything."

Her paralysis broke; she felt herself walking toward him, looking at him, filling her eyes with him. She stopped at arm's length, glancing at his left hand. No wedding ring. He held out his right. After a second, she took it. It was very hard. That scar across his chin—how had that happened? She'd seen a wound like that once in ER, a casualty from a gang fight. Campy must have gotten it in Vietnam. So many things she had wondered about over the years. She'd come to doubt, even, that he was alive, despite the army's original assurances. And now here he stood, and she definitely wasn't ready for it.

"What on earth are you doing here?" she said.

"I meant to see you," he said, "a month ago, when I flew out for my interview. I was going to let you know then. But you were on vacation in the Virgin Islands, and I had to fly back to Ann Arbor that night. I thought of writing, but I'm not so good at that."

Amy swallowed a laugh, feeling it burn in her throat. "Oh, I don't know. Sixty letters from Saigon. Of course, they ended just like that, and I never heard from you again. But if you average sixty letters over twenty years, it's still not bad . . ."

He gave her a ghost of a smile.

"Campy, what happened? When you stopped writing, I was worried sick. I tried to find out if you were alive. At first the army didn't want to tell me anything, but then my father called Uncle Jake, and a general came and saw us."

"Uncle Jake?"

"Senator Javits."

Campy grinned knowingly and she felt herself flushing. "The general was very diplomatic, very nice. He talked a lot and said very little. What it all boiled down to was that you were alive and still in the army. That you were in good health and good standing but that you could not be contacted for a while. That was it."

Campy looked grim. "That was all they told you? They wouldn't let us write, but I was told you'd be fully informed."

"Informed of what?"

His eyes were distant. He did not seem to hear her. "And the other thing was, I thought it would be over in a few months. But I was wrong."

"Thought *what* would be over?"

His eyes focused on her again. "Amy, this isn't something I can explain in five minutes or an hour. We have to find a place and time to talk, really talk."

Amy felt a mixture of sadness and indignation. "Twenty years of nothing, and *now* you want to talk. When they said you were alive and well, I decided you weren't writing because you didn't want to. That you'd forgotten about me." She hesitated, but went on. "By that time I was at Vassar and I'd met Bud. He'd been asking me for dates . . . I . . . ."

"You did exactly right," Campy said.

"Yes, I did."

He didn't flinch. "I'm so sorry I hurt you."

"Hurt me? I stopped hurting when I married Bud."

"I know."

"Is that so? And just how is that?"

"I met him."

Amy stared at him, incredulous. Met Bud? Bud had never mentioned that. Why wouldn't he have told her? Dear God, she must slow this down somehow.

Amy realized Campy still had hold of her hand, his fingers as motionless and careful as if he were defusing a bomb. She pulled her hand back. "I'm sorry—I'm not being very nice, am I? It's just such a shock." She forced a smile. "So. What's the story with the scrubs?"

"Say hello to Hudson's newest general surgeon."

Amy felt her jaw drop. The Campy she had known was smart and good with his hands—*oh, yes*—but had never borne down on a book in his life. She remembered cutting class and sneaking away from Miss Porter's to meet him outside Hartford High after school. Holding hands with him at a table in Frenchie's, seeing the traces of auto grease he hadn't been able to scrub out.

"So you switched from cars to people," she said.

"And you gave up your white gloves for rubber ones."

"Touché. I'm impressed, Campy. I mean it."

"Good. I'll take any edge I can get with you."

She felt the heat in her face again. Campy, she thought, you can't just walk in the door and start pressing me like this. Back off and back up.

"So when did you start?" She kept her voice cool.

"Today's my first day. I finished my residency five years ago. I stayed on in Ann Arbor until I heard . . ." He stopped, his eyes clouding briefly. "Anyway, as you no doubt know, Dr. Halvorson is retiring. I've bought out his practice, and Hudson General has given me a contract to take over for him here."

"Until you heard what?" Amy said.

"That your husband had died. I'm very sorry."

His voice, the husky man's voice, held the same absolute sincerity that she had never questioned in the boy—until it was too late and he was gone beyond reach. She wanted to question it now, and found, perversely, that she could not. He *was* sorry about Bud.

Or he had gone from a boy who could hide nothing from her to the world's greatest liar.

Which was possible.

She nodded, her neck feeling stiff. The air between them seemed to crackle with unasked questions. "How did you 'hear' about Bud?"

"I went into a gallery in Ann Arbor," he said, "and saw *Echo Valley*. They wanted ten thousand for it—worth every penny. But I'd seen others of his paintings over the years, always priced in the high hundreds. When I asked the dealer why, he told me that the artist had died a couple of years ago. I was stunned. I had no idea."

Amy was conscious of how careful he was suddenly being, of all that he was not saying. *Bud died and I knew you were single again, so I came back at last.* Her stomach churned. She did not know how to feel. From what he'd said, Campy had come back once before, met Bud . . . and left again without seeing her. Why? For her?

Or for himself, because he felt her marriage to Bud got him off a very old hook.

But if *that* was true, why come back now?

"I know this is terribly sudden," Campy said, "and you go on duty in a few minutes. I have so much I need to say to you. Could we have dinner?"

She groped for an answer. Dinner? No, she couldn't do that. She needed time to think. "Campy, you're right, this *is* terribly sudden. I . . ."

The pager at her waist beeped. She gave him a wry smile, hiding her relief at the interruption. There was a house phone on a nearby column. She walked over to it and called in, glancing at Campy while she waited to be patched through to ER. Campy walked to the table where she'd left her coffee. He pulled out a chair, planting one hand on the back of it. He sat slowly, biceps bulging. Something about the careful way he did it raised alarms in the back of her mind.

". . . you there?"

Daisy McCann, third-shift charge nurse in ER. Amy collected herself. "Yes. Hi, Daisy, What's up?"

"Cynthia VanKleeck called in," Daisy said.

VanKleeck? Oh yes. His daughter. Snap out of it, Amy!

"Good," Amy said. "I left our number on her answering machine."

"She didn't know what it was about," Daisy said. "From the evening report, I figured it was about her dad, so I went ahead and told her."

Amy felt a rush of relief, tinged with guilt. The woeful task shouldn't have fallen to Daisy. By rights, the family doctor should take care of notification. But the VanKleecks' Park Avenue doctor had taken off on some family crisis of his own. Which left me, Amy thought.

On the other hand, Daisy was a veteran ER nurse, a kindly woman with three young grandkids and lots of experience telling people the bad news.

"Thanks for handling it, Daisy. How did she take it?"

"Not too well. She's in California now—she said something about getting a deposition, so I gather she's a lawyer. She says she'll get the first plane and will be here this afternoon to claim the body."

"I should still be on shift," Amy said. "I'll meet her and go down to the holding room with her." The thought oppressed her, but she shoved the feeling aside. "Thanks for letting me know, Daisy."

"Sure."

After Daisy hung up, Amy kept the phone against her ear,

looking at Campy, trying desperately to think. After twenty years, Otis Camp walks back into her life and asks her to dinner. Did she want to go?

Yes, oh yes—if only to hear what he had to say.

But it wasn't that simple. Where was this going to lead? She had a serious relationship going with Tom now—a very serious relationship. If Campy had shown up six months ago . . . but he had stayed away thinking her still happily married to Bud.

And what about those years before Bud? Those years I waited for you, Campy?

Amy felt totally confused. Bud had helped her get over Campy. How could she still be angry?

Amy realized that the confusion wasn't going to go away. She would just have to muddle through this somehow. Hanging up, she walked over to the table. Campy started to get up, but she waved him down, picking up her coffee. It was cold. She drained it anyway for the caffeine. He looked up at her, saying nothing, waiting.

"I'm dating someone now, Campy."

"I know."

She felt a surge of irritation that he knew so much about her when she still knew nothing about him. "This is your first day, and you already know I'm dating?"

"I found that out from some of the surgeons when I came for the interview. Not surprisingly, you are the subject of much admiration in this hospital, including that of the unattached males up in surgery. Thomas Hart has been a lucky man."

"Has been?" she said sharply.

"Is. *Is* a lucky man." Campy sighed. "Just dinner, Amy. Two old friends."

There was pain in his voice, well covered, but she could hear it all the same. She softened. "Could we make it lunch instead?"

"Lunch would be fine." His shoulders sagged a little, and she realized how tense he had been.

"I'm not sure when," she added. "I'll check my calendar."

"Good." He got up more smoothly than he'd sat, but he still leaned forward just a bit too far, keeping one hand on the table.

Amy felt a twinge of foreboding. "Your foot?"

"Left one. Just above the ankle." He sounded a little vexed that she'd noticed it. "It's one of those Du Pont feet. It's quite good, actually. And never an ingrown toenail." He managed a smile for her.

Amy felt a pressure of tears at the backs of her eyes. Fiercely she suppressed them. "You're very good. I'd never have known it from seeing you walk." She found herself standing close to him, though she was not aware of moving. She could smell him, suddenly—the same clean piney scent he'd had in high school. Something green and sloshy that you could buy at a drugstore for three bucks—all he could afford then— and it still smelled good on him.

So he'd lost a foot in Vietnam. Maybe that was why he hadn't come back to her. If so, it made a difference—a big difference. But not enough of one.

"It's taken a lot of years," Campy said, "far too many. But I want you to know that I—"

"Campy, don't."

"I *have* to, Amy. Call it a warning or a promise, whichever way it feels to you. But I've come back for you."

She looked at him, unable to reply, feeling a terrible sadness: You got your war and then I got Bud. And when I needed you again, you were not here. Now I've got Tom. Don't you see, Campy? It's too late for us.

Amy slipped through the streams of people filling the hospital corridors from the shift change, responding automatically to those who greeted her. She needed to clear her mind for work, but Campy lingered like a hit of adrenaline. After twenty years, she'd thought she was past him, past all the questions.

Damn!

Seventeen years since that final letter. He'd "lucked through" a big firefight north of Saigon. His captain had "gotten the totally false idea that he was some kind of hero." They'd promoted him to sergeant and sent him off to a new outfit that was going on some mysterious new assignment he wasn't allowed to explain in the letter.

Then nothing more.

Where *had* he been? The foot—how had it happened? And what had made him decide to go to med school? He'd joined up right after high school, so he'd have needed four years of college first. What had that been like for him, a veteran, years older than the average student, a man among the boys?

She remembered the first time he'd kissed her. He'd still been every inch a boy, then. She'd known he was going to kiss her before he had: The drive-in outside Hartford, Campy sitting mute beside her in the back seat of his father's rickety Fairlane, his arm suddenly tensing on the seat behind her shoulders. Dustin Hoffman on the big screen, frantically brushing his teeth for an amused Mrs. Robinson. Campy turning to her, smiling, and then his smile had faded and he'd cupped her chin in his hand, leaning slowly to her . . .

The memory was so sweet, so vivid, that she felt a tingle of expectancy in her face. How would Campy's cheek feel against hers now? Not the smooth cheek of a boy anymore.

Those days are gone, she thought. You know nothing about him now. And foot or no foot, he could have come back!

She strode down the narrow back hall to her office, realizing with surprise that the fear from the nightmare was all but gone. Her mind was sharp, ready to go. As shock therapy, Campy was an instant success.

Walking into her outer office, Amy saw that Doris was already at her desk, surrounded by her hanging ferns, her fingers fretting at the word processor. Amy started to say good morning, then blinked, startled: Doris's hair had turned dark brown overnight. Actually, it wasn't bad, compared to last week's monotone red. Doris was on the stocky side, but she would be pretty if her sister would just stop practicing her beautician-school techniques on her.

Doris glanced up, continuing with her typing. *"There* you are . . ." She squinted at Amy. "You look strange."

I look strange? Amy thought.

"Plus you have a rash behind your ear."

Reminded, Amy felt it itch. It seemed worse today. Maybe she should treat it with some Valisone cream. "Doris?"

"Uh-huh?"

"How do you do that?"

"Do what?"

"Type while you're looking at me and talking?"

"It's easy if you don't sweat the typos."

"Uh-huh." Amy read through her messages, made a few call-backs, then turned to her wall calendar. The first day she'd have time for lunch was Saturday. She called Campy and he said that would be fine. She hung up, her stomach in turmoil again. But she headed out to the ward to lead rounds, clearing Campy from her mind with a torrent of work.

At ten after four, the call came from the hospital morgue. Kathy DiGenova took it, relaying the message to Amy: Owen VanKleeck's daughter was down in pathology.

"Whereabouts in pathology?" Amy asked.

"Your friend Chris's office," Kathy said with a smile, clearly enjoying her little bomb.

Amy's heart sank. Christine Hunt was the best pathologist at Hudson, but one look at grieving relatives and she broke out in hives. Amy hurried through the warren of basement hall-ways, feeling the tension that had been lying in wait all through her shift knot fiercely in her stomach. At Chris's office, Amy knocked once and entered, surprised and pleased to see Tom sitting on the corner of Chris's desk. Chris must have called Psychology and then made her escape. Good, Amy thought. I can use the help. Tom's face held her gaze an extra second. He looked pale and somber, his blond hair gleaming blue-white under the fluorescents. It unsettled her a little. Who was this grim stranger? Where was the Greek god, face flushed and glowing, who had poised above her last night?

Cynthia VanKleeck was sitting in Chris's extra chair. The pretty face was drawn now, more mature than the underclass-man at Miss Porter's but Amy recognized her at once. Still slim, she'd have to be around thirty-seven, but looked younger. She wore a gray pin-striped suit, rather severe, but had yielded to flounces of lace at the neck of her blouse. Her eyes were her father's, red-rimmed in misery now. The pain she was fighting to contain bound her back straight against the chair, convulsed her throat as she swallowed.

"Ms. VanKleeck? I'm Amy St. Clair. I treated your father. I'm very sorry."

Cynthia looked at her closely. "Amy St. Clair," she said

with slow wonder. "President of the science club."

Amy permitted herself a small smile. "And you were captain of the sophomore debate team." From the corner of her
eye, Amy was aware of Tom looking at them. Cynthia stood
and offered her hand. Amy found herself looking up a little.
Cynthia had grown—she must be around five-ten. Amy was
glad to feel strength in her grip.

"I'd like to see him now, please."

"Of course. If you'll come with me."

Tom took Cynthia's arm as Amy led the way to the Pathology holding room. Amy smelled fresh paint as she walked in.
Someone had redone the walls in a soft yellow. But it was still
a place of the dead. VanKleeck had been taken from the
morgue drawer and placed on a gurney, a sheet drawn up to
his chin. His hair was still mussed, his face composed as if in
sleep. Cynthia stared down at her father, biting her lower lip.
Amy was painfully aware, suddenly, of her heart beating, the
air tingling in her lungs. A whiff of formaldehyde stung her
nostrils. She heard a distant phone chirring over and over, like
a greedy chick demanding to be fed. I'm alive, she thought, and
shivered, conscious of how fragile life was.

"Doctor," Tom prompted, "I believe it was over very
quickly, wasn't it?"

"Yes," Amy said. "I'm sure your father felt very little pain."
She hoped Cynthia would believe it, wishing she could be sure
of it herself.

Tom moved around beside Cynthia and gazed down with
her at the dead man. Amy was surprised to see a sudden glaze
of tears in Tom's eyes. Cynthia saw it too, and, as if released,
broke into sobs. Amy put an arm across her shoulders; Cynthia
stiffened, then leaned into her, pressing her face into Amy's
shoulder. After a minute, she stood back and dried her tears.

"Dr. St. Clair, Dad was perfectly healthy. He had a complete physical just a month ago. How could this happen?"

Amy realized Cynthia had handed her the opening she
was hoping for. "We can't be sure—not without an autopsy."

Cynthia winced. "An autopsy?"

From the corner of her eye, Amy saw Tom shake his head.
She pretended to miss it. "Some heart defects are hard to detect
on physicals. Your father's arteries might have been clogged.

Perhaps he had an inherited predisposition to a heart attack . . .
If you would authorize an autopsy, we can tell you much
more."

"An autopsy," Cynthia said, frowning. "I don't know."

Quickly Amy said, "If you tell the funeral home you *may*
want one, they can keep your options open for a day or so."

"I have to think about it. Mother will want her say in
anything like that." Cynthia hesitated. "Doctor—Amy, what I
want to know has nothing to do with an autopsy. I want to
know why you couldn't save him. I thought you could *force* a
person's heart to beat, put him on machines, keep him alive."

"We tried everything we could to get his heart started
again," Amy said gently. "But it wouldn't respond."

"Isn't that unusual?"

"Yes, it is."

Cynthia's eyes, red-rimmed, seemed to burn into Amy; she
fought the urge to look away from the woman's pain. She knew
exactly what the woman was feeling. Shock, grief—and the
anger that was only a neuron-flash away from anguish in the
human psyche. Amy felt a tightness in her chest, remembering
how furious she herself had been at the nurses, the cardiac
specialist who'd "lost" Bud.

Finally, Cynthia looked down at her father again. "I'm sure
you did all you could," she said in a low voice. "I . . . want to
thank you."

Tom patted her shoulder, and glanced meaningfully at
Amy. "Ms. VanKleeck, I imagine you'd like to be alone with
your father now. I have to keep an appointment back in my
office, but please call me at any time if there's anything further
we can do." He turned, hesitating when Amy did not join him.
She felt a strange reluctance to leave. She had dreaded this, but
she sensed now that Cynthia did not really want her to leave.

Tom cleared his throat, and Amy was afraid he'd take her
arm and try to steer her out. But he didn't. When he was out the
door, Any touched Cynthia's shoulder. "I'm very sorry about
your father."

The contact seemed to thaw Cynthia a little. "He was
going to retire from the bank tomorrow," she said. "He has—
had—a boat that he loved. He planned to take Mom and sail

around the Caribbean for a year. I was going to join them for the first two weeks."

Tears poured from her eyes again, running down her cheeks, but she did not give in to them, keeping her face composed. The little token of bravery touched Amy. "I'm so sorry. I didn't know your father long, but I liked him."

Cynthia nodded. She pulled some tissues from an inside pocket of her jacket and blotted at her face. Amy saw that she wasn't carrying a purse, and felt her bond to the woman strengthen, remembering how she too had weaned herself down to a pocketful of essentials a few years back. Cynthia VanKleeck knew how to travel light, to choose what she really needed and let the rest go.

And she had loved and needed her father very much.

Amy thought of her own father. Winnie controlled a huge fortune, just as Owen VanKleeck had. Despite their money, both men went to work every day—both of them in banking. And it was uncanny how much she had in common with Cynthia herself. Same exclusive prep school—and they'd both defied their privileged and genteel upbringing to pursue careers in rough-and-tumble professions. Almost too close, the similarities. What would she do if something happened to Winnie? The thought sent a chill of foreboding through her. Nothing is going to happen to Winnie, she told herself firmly. She found Cynthia's hand and squeezed. "Do you have someone to be with right now?"

Cynthia gave a little shrug. "I'll be meeting Mother at Kennedy in about three hours."

Amy had the distinct impression that Cynthia dreaded the prospect. "Would you like to go for coffee?"

"I appreciate your concern. But I'll be fine."

There was an edge of rebuff in her voice. Amy nodded, stung, but hiding it. I couldn't do anything for your father, she thought, and now you won't let me do anything for you. "I understand."

Cynthia's expression softened. "Actually, I could use a coffee. I don't know if I should leave Dad, though."

"There's a canteen just down the hall."

The canteen, hardly bigger than a walk-in closet, was

empty. Amy got two black coffees and seated herself across from Cynthia at one of the little Formica tables. Cynthia cradled her cup in her hands, looking down at it.

"It hurts," Amy said. "I know."

Cynthia looked up. "Do you?"

"My husband," Amy said. "A little over two years ago . . . a fatal heart attack."

"I'm sorry." Cynthia's eyes filmed over with tears. She blinked them away. "What will I do?"

"One day at a time," Amy said. "A cliché, I know. But it's also the only way. You *will* feel all right again. In the meantime, you get mad when you have to get mad and cry when you have to cry. The rest of the time you act like you're all right. Finally the act becomes real."

Cynthia blotted at her eyes with a napkin. "The thing is, I had a feeling something bad was going to happen. I even kept dreaming it."

Amy looked at her, startled. "*Kept* dreaming it?"

She nodded. "A nightmare, two or three times, just before I went out west. The same one, over and over. I didn't exactly dream that Dad was going to . . . die. It was more vague, the way dreams are. I dreamed I was a little girl, walking in the woods out behind our estate . . . Are you all right?"

Amy took a deep breath, and felt the shock recede. No, she thought. It's impossible. "What else did you dream?"

Cynthia frowned, her eyes going distant. "Someone's trying to tell me something awful, but I can't see him."

Amy's scalp prickled. She said, "You see a large, threatening shape ahead of you in the woods."

Cynthia's eyes widened.

"You can't make the shape out. You try to turn away, but it keeps swinging around in front of you."

Cynthia stood, bumping the table, knocking her coffee to the floor. "How in *hell* did you know that?"

Amy looked at her, shaken, unable to believe it. And yet, clearly, it was true. "I know it," she said, "because I've been having the same nightmare."

5

In the staff women's room, Amy flipped her hair back and frowned at the mirror. The red splotch on her neck was about the size and shape of a penny, high up on the left side, near her earlobe. It bothered her not to know what had caused it. Too many strange things were happening, things she could not explain. Compared to the weirdness of her having the same nightmare as Cynthia VanKleeck, however, the red spot wasn't much. Still, it was peculiar. Leaning closer to the mirror, Amy made out the red traces of broken capillaries in the middle of the splotch. And there—another, more faded spot, farther around toward the back of her neck.

Vampires, she said, and bared her teeth at the mirror.

The door opened, and she dropped the ghoulish grin, leaning over, embarrassed, to wash her hands. She heard a soft click, the door's button lock sliding in. Odd. She glanced over—

A man, tall, wearing a ski mask.

She felt a cold instant of shock, then her heart knocking inside her. Her brain screamed at her to run, even as she realized she was trapped. He held his hand out toward her as though offering her something, and she saw that it was a knife. The blade was long and shiny. It looked very sharp.

"Don't scream," the man growled.

She heard a rushing in her ears. Backing up, she felt the edge of the sink bite into her hip. She watched the man, terrified, waiting for him to move—

Denim Jacket! The man who'd followed her from the subway.

"Don't touch me." Her voice seemed very loud.

His mouth smiled horribly inside the black, knit circle of the mask. "How you gonna stop me?"

Yes, she recognized his voice from last time.

"Nobody's back here, Doc. You scream, nobody's gonna hear."

She realized it was true. With half an hour left until the morning shift change, everyone would be busy out front, finishing up.

"No guys with dogs in here, either."

Her fear deepened. Either he was very stupid, or he didn't care if she knew it was him. Then why the ski mask? In case someone did break in on them before he'd finished with her. Amy's scalp prickled. *He's going to kill me.*

He advanced another step.

She needed a weapon. But there was nothing in here—

Suddenly she thought of the bottle of alcohol she'd used to clean her stethescope. She could feel it in her pocket. She slipped a hand around it.

"You got a gun in there, Doc? Somehow I don't think so. Get your hand out."

With a sinking feeling, she took her hand from her pocket.

"Good." He brought the knife to her throat. "Now take that nice white coat off."

She did it, holding her head still, feeling the cold blade along her chin. She laid the medical coat on the sink counter, the pocket with the alcohol close to her hand.

"Now your blouse."

"No."

He flicked the knife point, nicking the skin. She felt a tiny burn. Her vision grayed out at the edges.

Please, God, let someone come.

"Do it, bitch."

His breath stank. She jerked back, twisting her head away, feeling the spine of the knife rake her jaw. She kicked up,

getting him on the bent knee, missing the crotch. He jumped
back in reflex, swearing as she went for the coat pocket. She
ripped the top off the alcohol, holding it out in front of her.
"Acid!" she said. She saw the black-rimmed eyes focus on the
bottle.

"Naw," he said. "Why would you be carrying acid
around?"

"I was bringing it back from the lab. It'll melt that ski mask
right off you, and your eyes, too."

His lips drew back, revealing a yellow grimace. She could
feel the heat of his rage on her skin.

"You bitch, I should have killed you right away."

"Stay back!"

He hesitated. "You're lying."

She could see the door over his shoulder, only five feet
away, but she had to get around him first. If she could just—

He lunged with the knife. She dashed the bottle at him,
watching the silvery arc of alcohol hit him in the eyes. He
screamed and spun away, grabbing at the mask. She pushed
past him, hand slippery on the doorknob, wrenching it open at
last, and then she was running down the hall, screaming at the
top of her lungs.

"That was very clever of you," Tom said, "telling him it
was acid."

She was stretched out on his couch, the muscles of her
arms and legs still trembling in tiny, annoying jerks. She found
that she wanted to breathe more deeply than she needed. The
air tasted very sweet.

"It preyed on his mind," Tom went on with obvious relish.
"When the alcohol stung him, he panicked and that saved you.
You did very well. Not many people have such presence of
mind." His voice was low, soothing, but she could hear the
undercurrent of anger in it. That made her feel better than all
of his professional techniques put together.

She sat up. "Thanks for all your help, Tom. I'm all right
now. I've got to get back to ER."

"What's the rush? No less than the chief administrator sent

you up here. I've cleared my desk for as long as you need me. You've got Anderson covering for you."

"It's his day off. I don't want to keep him here any longer than necessary."

"This *is* necessary." Tom put a hand on her shoulder, easing her back down on the couch. There was nothing intimate in the contact. It was the firm touch of the therapist. Somehow it made her uncomfortable. She couldn't seem to tell from one minute to the next whether she was dealing with Dr. Hart or Tom. Why should that bother her so much? It was good just to be here with him, to feel safe.

Tom said, "I know that you handle scares and crises every day of your life. If part of you didn't actually *like* stress, you wouldn't be working in Hudson's ER, let alone heading it up. But what you've got to understand is, no matter how mentally tough and resilient you are, you *have* just suffered a trauma, as surely as if that bastard had actually managed to beat or cut you." Tom hesitated, eyeing her. "And this trauma happened just when you were already in something of a state."

She sat up again. "What?"

"Come on, Amy. You hide it well, but not from me. Something's been weighing on you."

She gazed into his eyes. "Tom, go lock your door."

"Already locked."

"Then hold me."

He settled beside her on the couch, hugging her tight, rocking her back and forth. "Now tell me what else is bothering you."

She pulled back and looked at him.

"There's no better time than right now," he said. "Whatever it is, I want you to leave it in here when you go."

He sounded so sure she could do that. She wanted badly to believe him. "I've been having a bad dream," she said. "The same one over and over. But that's not the worst part."

"Tell me."

She described the nightmare.

"And the worst part?" he said gently.

"Cynthia VanKleeck is having the same nightmare."

Tom blinked. He sat back in the couch, lacing his hands behind his head.

"Incredible, right?" she said.

"Unusual."

The subtle distinction encouraged her. Had he encountered this kind of thing before? She felt a sudden lift of hope. A rational explanation—that was all she wanted. A professional opinion that this was not so bad.

"Only unusual?" she prompted.

"First, you're probably *not* having the exact same dream. It may not even have been all that similar."

"Tom, we discussed it. It was the same dream."

"Sure, after you'd gotten your heads together. Listen, the minute you wake from a dream, it's already fading. That's because the mental images of a dream are actually quite incoherent if not entirely nonsensical. To remember a dream at all, you've got to go over it in your mind within a very few minutes of waking—sort of like rehearsing. As you rehearse the dream, you unknowingly discard parts and add others as your mind struggles to fill in the blanks."

"Fine," Amy said, "so why did Cynthia and I both fill in the blanks in exactly the same way?"

Tom got up and went to his desk. He dug into a drawer and held up a card with an inkblot on it. "What does this look like to you?"

"An inkblot."

Tom did not smile. "There are two diagnoses associated with that response. One is resistance and the other is brain damage."

Amy looked at the Rorschach blot. "All right, it looks like two bears slapping hands."

"A nice creative response," Tom said approvingly.

She saw where he was heading. "And you get the exact same response from a lot of different patients."

"Exactly. People impose their own order on these incoherent blots—an order dictated by their nagging preoccupations, conscious or unconscious. Same with you and Cynthia and your dreams." He flipped the card onto his desk. "Some of these blots are very chaotic, quite unlike anything people have seen before. And yet very few responses are truly unique."

Amy realized that she was relaxing at last. The little muscles in her legs had stopped hopping. The narrow escape from the washroom had receded emotionally. It had happened and she didn't like it, but she was going to be all right.

Was Tom this good with all his patients?

I am *not* his patient, she thought crossly.

"When I was with you and Cynthia in the morgue, didn't I hear you talking about high school?"

"We went to the same one."

"Hmmm. And did you notice she doesn't carry a purse?"

"Yes," Amy said.

"I'll bet you have a lot more in common, too."

"A great deal, right down to both of us having big woods behind the houses where we grew up."

Tom gave a satisfied smile. "There you are, then. Same school, and you no doubt grew up reading the same books, watching the same movies. How many times have you seen the situation in your dream—a young girl traipsing through a deep dark woods with scary things all around her. It's right out of the Brothers Grimm."

Strangely, Amy felt her tension going up again. "You make it sound so simple," she said. "So . . . *harmless.*"

Tom studied her. "You feel there is harm in the dream?"

She hesitated, looking down inside herself, finding the small edge of fear that would not recede. "Somehow," she said, "yes, I do."

"Of course, you've just had a bad scare."

"Even before that."

Tom nodded soberly. "Forget Cynthia. What does the nightmare mean to *you?*"

"Nothing."

"Are you sure?"

She felt the fear sharpening, slicing along the nerves of her stomach. "No," she said. She found herself thinking suddenly of Campy. Had he felt the blade or maybe a wire garrote slicing across his chin? Did he have nightmares? Did he wake up in the morning with the fear thick in his throat? What would it be like to talk to Campy about her nightmares?

She realized she was being unfair, comparing Tom and Campy. She must not do that. Her loyalty was to Tom now.

She looked at her watch. "I really have to get back to ER. I feel much better now."

"You did a few minutes ago. Now you're avoiding."

"Maybe. But I still have to get back." She stood.

For a minute he looked as though he wanted to argue. Then he stood too. "How about coming back when you get off at four? I can have an hour free then."

"Thanks, but today's a running day. As soon as I can get loose from ER, I'll be loping through Central Park, graceful as a gazelle."

Tom looked surprised. "Central Park?"

"Look, I can't let this bully screw up my whole life. The police are looking for him now. And I never run in the park unless there are plenty of people around. It's at least as safe as the staff rest room in this hospital."

Tom gave a half hearted smile. "I guess I've done a better job curing your fear than I intended."

Amy looked at him, wondering if he realized what he'd just said. It was meant as a joke, but the other meaning was there, too, unavoidably: *You're my patient, Amy.* How could he see so much else and yet not see how that grated on her? "You were marvelous," she said. "Thank you." She kissed him on the cheek and walked out.

Dr. Otis Camp sat in the doctors' lounge, alone with his fear. Quite a few years since he'd felt it like this, a monkey sitting in the back of his brain, cold, twitchy paws snared in the neurons. Years, but you never forgot. Above the DMZ, fear had been a friend, keeping him alive. He must find a way to use it now, too.

What was I doing out there last night?

It still would not come. He got up and walked to the low table in the corner across from him, switching the light up a notch. Standing at the staff bulletin board, he gazed at the scrawled messages and memos, trying to immerse himself in this new place, lose himself in the mundane, comforting cross-talk of Hudson General's hospital life. He could not focus on the words. His eyes and throat were dry, the tips of his fingers greasy with sweat. In exactly twenty minutes he had a surgery to perform.

What if I go blank again?

He rolled his head and shoulders, forcing the tight muscles to loosen. All right, try again: Last night, half past midnight. He'd been sitting at his living room window overlooking Seventy-seventh Street, a *Times* review on his lap, a Glenkinchie on the end table—

Could the scotch have caused it?

No. The Glenkinchie had been only his second drink of the night. He never drank until after six, and he'd lost a minute here and there in the mornings and afternoons back in Ann Arbor, when he'd been getting ready to move east—blank periods so brief he hadn't been sure he wasn't just daydreaming.

Until now.

All right, he'd been reading the *Times,* that review of the latest Gulf War book. Then—snap—walking down Third Avenue, twenty blocks from his apartment. Two-fifteen in the morning. A skinhead asking him for a light in front of the electronics store, the guy's buddy pretending to lounge against the wide mesh of the security screen, hands in the pockets of his black leather jacket. An obvious setup, so Campy had given each of them a look and told them to buzz off, and they had, their faces suddenly afraid.

Twelve-thirty to two-fifteen. Not just a few daydreaming minutes this time. Almost two hours, vanished without a trace. Where had he gone? What had he done? I need help, he thought. Maybe one of the psychiatrists here?

He groaned. Great way to start off at Hudson General.

All right, go someplace else, where they don't know you—Newark, Philly. Campy tried to imagine himself telling a psychiatrist—any psychiatrist. The first thing they'd try to do was medicate him. A little Valium, maybe, or some Xanax to shut up the monkey in the back of his brain. Campy rejected the idea at once. He hated the fear, but shutting it up wasn't the answer.

And if he went to someone and they found out he was a surgeon, they'd try to pull his license. If things got worse, they might even want to put him on a locked ward. He could hear the words now: *For your own protection, Dr. Camp—in case you go somewhere dangerous during one of your blank periods.*

A cold sweat broke out on Campy's forehead. Easy. You won't let them do that. No more cages.

Static crackled on the lounge intercom. "Dr. Camp, Dr. Camp." Angela Pinckney's voice, throaty and firm, tunneling into his brain from a great distance.

"Yo, Dr. Camp, you there?"

He walked over and pushed the button on the wall box. "I think so. And everyone calls me Campy."

"We are ready for you, Campy."

As Campy turned into the corridor toward OR, he felt a phantom twinge, his missing toes curling down to hold him in balance. The brief, sweet reincarnation lifted him like an omen. He had a date with Amy on Saturday. Only lunch, but it would be the start. Nothing was ever totally lost—not his foot, not those missing hours last night.

Maybe not even Amy.

Angela was standing by the scrub sink, finishing off a carton of chocolate milk. She was a tall woman with beautiful, chocolate-hued skin. The cuffs of her scrubs clung tight around her biceps. One of the surgeons had said that Angela had been a sergeant in the marines. She finished off the chocolate milk and made a show of crushing the carton, beer-can-style, in one hand.

"You've got some on your lip," he said.

"How can you tell?"

Campy smiled and went to the big stainless-steel sink and scrubbed slowly and carefully, making sure he lathered up to his elbows. The harsh smell of the soap reached far up his nostrils, soothing in its familiarity. When he pushed through into OR, the scrub nurse was waiting. What was her name? Betsy Findlay. She helped him gown and glove and tied his mask for him.

Campy moved to the table, pleased to see that Angela had put his stool in the proper place on the patient's right side. He cranked the seat up a little, so that he could lean his rump against the stool with his legs almost straight, more standing than sitting. That would take enough weight off the artificial foot so that he could hang in for hours if need be.

He looked at the patient. Mr. Trang, a recent Vietnamese emigré, intubated and asleep. Betsy was done with the Betadine paint—the guy's chest and abdomen glowed a sickly orange under the surgery light.

Campy draped four sterilized towels across the painted area, narrowing down the field and framing it for his incision. Betsy had already pulled up the sheet at the patient's chest, clipping it up to make a low wall behind which Campy could see the anesthesiologist's face—long nose, burnished skin, dark eyes, glossy black hair hidden under her cap. Dr. Mary Makepeace, a Sioux who'd done anesthesia at a reservation hospital for ten years before coming to the big city. Campy relaxed a little more. At the interview walkaround, Mary had impressed him as being very smart and very steady. The team looks good, Campy thought. And *I'm* good. Nothing is going to happen.

"Say," Angela said from her station against the wall, "did you hear that they're gonna be replacing laboratory rats with lawyers?"

Campy sighed through the mask. "I'll bite. Why?"

"Because the lab technicians were getting too attached to the rats."

Betsy laughed. "It's nice to have one group left you can tell jokes about."

"What's that supposed to mean?" Angela asked.

"Now, now, people," Mary soothed. "Let's try and make a good impression on the new doctor."

"Mary, have you got Mr. Trang nice and relaxed for me?"

"He gets any limper, he'll need new bones."

"Fine. Now let's see about this ulcer. We got your basic vagotomy and antrectomy here. With the vagus cut and the antrum of his stomach gone, Mr. Trang will have a lot less acid eating him up. I'm gonna finish with a Billroth II if that's all right with you guys, and even if it's not."

"Guess we know who's in charge here," Angela mumbled.

"The people with the knives and the gas," Campy agreed, holding out his hand. Betsy planted the haft of the scalpel firmly in his palm. He ran the finger of his left hand down the patient's breastbone, finding the spongy tip of the xiphoid process. Just below that, he placed the blade point against the skin. He hesitated, struck by how small the man was—no bigger than a twelve-year-old American child.

Campy's eyes felt dry again—he could feel the laminar flow of OR's air dragging across his pupils. A choking sensation began to build in his throat. He breathed evenly, and the pressure eased. Pushing the point of the knife in, he drew it down in a steady, firm motion to just above the umbilicus, the point trailing a wake of welling blood. Betsy swabbed it away and brought the retractors into position, helping him set the curved grips into the wound. He cranked the two sides back, drawing the incision open. The muscle and connective tissue resisted fiercely, and he threw his arm into it until the two sides of the long cut were several inches apart. He shifted the retractors up along their support track above the table, pulling the widest part of the incision up toward the rib line, giving himself room to work. He could hear Betsy and Angela bantering in the background. It irritated him, and he almost snapped at them before he caught himself. He had never snapped at team members back in Ann Arbor, no matter how irritated he got, and he wasn't going to start doing it here.

Looking through the incision, he searched the exterior of the stomach for signs of ulceration. Sweat ran into his eyes. Damn it, too dark, he couldn't see. "Angela, get that light down here a little closer, would you please?"

" 'Please'? I think I'm going to like you, Campy." Angela pushed a button on the wall, and the light buzzed down on its track. He could feel the extra heat on his neck. More sweat coursed into his eyes, and then Betsy mopped it away and there it was, the ugly, dark stippling of the ulcer's perforation—not too bad yet, but on its way. Campy inspected the abdominal cavity around the stomach for signs of soilage. Minimal—good. Another few weeks and Mr. Trang would have been leaking his lunch clear down to his bladder.

Campy wondered what had caused Trang's ulcer. There must be a lot of pressures in his life. Mr. Trang had come from a village in the south. Campy remembered the ones he had seen, and felt a bond of sympathy for Mr. Trang at having to leave it. Trang was a farmer, raised on the ripe smell of oxen, the sight of rice paddies sparkling in the sun, green sweeps of jungle. Now Mr. Trang's air smelled of exhaust. He spent all day sitting in a parking lot booth, from which he could see about forty feet to the greasy spoon across the street.

Then there were the Vietnamese gangs, American slum-lords, and guys like me, Campy thought. Men in their forties, black, white, Hispanic, who come into your parking garage and give you that look. We all got something out of that war, didn't we, Mr. Trang? I got a short leg and you got a new country that writes in blood on the walls of your stomach.

Campy slipped a hand into the incision, feeling his way along the slippery edge of the liver to the left lobe. When he pulled it out again, dark blood smeared across his knuckles from the edge of the incision. Betsy handed him the scissors without being asked. He gave her a smile of approval, then reminded himself that she couldn't see it through the mask. "I'll bet you could do this yourself."

"If the price was right," Betsy agreed.

Campy took the left lobe of the liver between two fingers of his left hand, pulling it down, cutting across the top of his fingers at the filmy ligaments that stuck the liver to the dia-phragm. He pulled the lobe down as he cut until he got into the center and could feel his way above it to where the esophagus pierced its way down through the diaphragm. He probed for the distinctive, guitar-string feel of the vagus nerves, easily finding the one that ran down the front of the esophagus. Working his fingers around to the rear of the esophagus, he tried to find the other branch of the vagus.

He remembered his bloody hand, a smear across his knuckles that glistened black in the moonlight.

He was deep in the woods, squatting in a small clearing beside Gordon Silvestre. Gordo wasn't dead yet, but he was going to be. The VC bastard had ripped across his belly with a machete, then jabbed upward a few times, nicking the heart. God, so much blood, pouring out of Gordo. His face was bone white in the moonlight, the eyes sunken and dark. Dying. Campy was sick with rage.

"He went that way, Top," Gordo whispered, jerking his head northeast, blood frothing on his lips. "I'll be fine. Go get him."

"Gordo . . ." Campy's voice choked off. He felt the fury

boiling up in him, blinding him, putting Gordon Silvestre's face at the far end of a long, dark tunnel.

"Top, you . . . bring me his ears. I'll . . . wait right here."

Leaping up, pulling out the K-bar and setting the blade between his teeth, so he could fend off the branches with both hands. Running in the moon-dappled darkness, hearing only the swish of palm fronds across his shoulders, feeling the thin tin insets in his sneakers flexing against his soles. He was not afraid of sharpened pungi sticks, afraid of nothing, high on rage. He would catch the VC and rip his belly, make him die slowly—

"—r. Camp?"

Campy realized he was standing, frozen, his hand in Mr. Trang's belly. He felt an icy plunge of fear in his gut. How long? He'd been feeling for the vagus nerve and then—

Nothing. A blank spot, as bare of memory as a stone.

"Dr. Camp, are you all right?" Dr. Makepeace asked, the barest edge on her voice.

"Can't find the rear branch." He tried to sound gruff.

"You were just standing there. I didn't . . ."

"You forget, Doctor, we get paid by the hour."

Her eyes crinkled a little. Betsy Findlay dabbed at his forehead, and he realized he was drenched with sweat.

How long?

It couldn't have been too long, or Mary Makepeace would have been more alarmed. It was all right now, nothing had happened.

Had it?

Campy tuned in on his fingers, realizing that he was no longer touching the front branch of the vagus nerve. Instead he had a grip on a larger, slicker surface—*the hepatic vein!*

Campy felt sick. The hepatic vein, pouring into the inferior vena cava, biggest vein in the body—one pull, and if it tore, Mr. Trang would have hemorrhaged to death.

Everything's all right. Now get on with it.

Campy released the vein and located the vagus nerve again, probing until he'd found the rear branch too. He cut them both, feeling strangely detached. He worked his way mechanically through the rest of the operation—clamping the blood vessels along the greater and lesser curvatures of the stomach. Stapling around the antrum, cutting it away, and then the Billroth II—sectioning a piece of intestine into the gap. Unclamping, stitching Mr. Trang back up, hearing the chatter of Angela and Betsy as a distant murmur of total strangers, the words meaningless. Remote, his head high above it all and yet still, somehow, able to see.

"Good job, Doctor," Betsy said.

"But of course," he managed to reply.

Back in the doctor's lounge, Campy went into the toilet and threw up.

6

Amy woke up alert, listening. The grandfather clock tapped patiently downstairs. Her nightstand clock said one-thirty.

What had she heard? A soft thump downstairs, like someone bumping into something.

A board creaked in the ceiling above her head. Amy felt her heart compress, a chill aftershock flooding her face, rushing along her arms. No one should be up there at this time of night. Was it the man from the subway? If he could track her to the hospital, he could track her home . . . Amy thought of the girls sleeping across the hall and felt another surge of alarm. She swung out of bed and pulled on her robe. Kneeling, she fished out the hammer she had put back under the bed. Its weight in her hand reassured her only a little. She slipped into the hall and crept up the steps to the third floor. The door to Bud's studio stood ajar, spilling blue light from the computer monitor—Denise!

But that still did not explain the sound downstairs.

"Mom, is that you?" Denise called softly. There was fear in her voice.

"Yes," Amy whispered. She set the hammer by the door and hurried in. Denise sat at the console, her back unnaturally straight with alarm. Amy padded across the bare oak to her, smelling the lingering ghosts of linseed oil and turpentine,

sensing Bud's paintings in the shadows. Denise turned her
cheek up. Amy kissed her and glanced at the words glimmering
on the computer screen—the first paragraph of a theme paper
about George Washington Goethals and the building of the
Panama Canal.

"Homework?" she said, surprised.

Denise nodded. "This is due tomorrow—uh, today, actually. I woke up and couldn't get back to sleep."

A memory flitted through Amy's mind—herself in med
school, drinking coffee, rubbing ice cubes on her face and
cramming until 4:00 A.M. without fail before every test. "I
thought we agreed you were to stop procrastinating."

"I'll do it soon." Denise laughed a little too softly, her gaze
darting over Amy's shoulder at the door.

"Honey . . . why did you wake up? Did you hear something?"

"I'm not sure."

"How about a minute ago? Did you hear a sound from all
the way downstairs?"

Denise's eyes were very round. "Stop it, Mom. You're
scaring me."

Amy gave her shoulder a squeeze. "I'm sorry. I don't want
to do that. But I need to know."

"I thought I did, but sometimes the house creaks—oh!"

Amy heard it too, a click, faint but definite, from far down
in the house. Goosebumps prickled along her arms. "That
sounded like a door latch," she whispered.

Denise gave a brittle nod.

Amy put a finger to her lips. Tiptoeing to the door, she
retrieved the hammer and backed into the studio again, keeping her eyes on the stairway. She motioned for Denise to shut
off the computer. The blue light winked out. For a second the
room seemed pitch black, then the computer station and the
peaked outlines of Bud's circle of easels swam from the darkness. The big bank of south windows, through which Bud's
precious daylight had streamed, glimmered as black as oil
slicks. Amy found Denise's hand in the darkness. "It's probably
nothing," she whispered. "But let's get out of sight a little
more."

Denise gripped her hand so hard it hurt. Amy led her

through a gap in the shadowy circle of easels and pulled her down with her to a kneeling position.

"Mom, I'm scared."

Amy squeezed her hand. "It's all right. Let's listen." She closed her eyes, feeling her hearing sharpen, fetching the clack of the grandfather clock up the stairwell to her. Denise's nightgown rustled and a board creaked softly as she eased into a sitting position. Minutes passed. There was no sound from below except the faint pacing of the pendulum. The goosebumps faded along Amy's arms. Should she go down and check? No, wait a little longer. The circle of easels made a flimsy fortress, and yet it comforted her. Six paintings. How could he have worked on so many at one time? His mind had been so full, and he'd rushed, like a great bear foraging to the edge of an early winter, as if he'd known what was going to happen to him.

She reached forward in the darkness until her fingertips found the slick-textured surface of her favorite painting. She could see it in her mind now, the man on the ocean, sitting on his armchair surrounded by waves, a gibbous moon streaking the sea around him. Like so many of Bud's paintings, set in the night, but radiating soft, peaceful light. Bud had done it right after *Echo Valley,* the painting that had eventually brought Campy back from Ann Arbor—scarred, one-footed Campy, the marks of war all over him. *Amy, I've come back for you.*

Actually, I could use a guy like you right now, she thought. She imagined Campy here with her and Denise, walking confidently downstairs to confront whoever was down there. Missing foot or not, he could handle the man with the knife. In Vietnam he had done harder things, over and over. She did not know how she knew that, but she knew it.

"Remember how Dad used to get up in the middle of the night and go down and eat the Cool Whip?" Denise whispered.

"He did what?" Amy said, surprised.

Denise gave a soft, nervous laugh. "So we *did* fool you. Sometimes I'd hear him and go down with him. We'd stick our fingers in the middle of the bowl and lick them off. You must sleep like a log—or you used to, before Daddy died."

Amy gazed at Denise in the darkness, filled with wonder at this unsuspected snippet of Bud—and the revelation about herself: She's right. I used to sleep through anything. Not any-more.

"That's what woke me up tonight," Denise whispered. "I dreamed I heard him creeping down the stairs like we used to do so we wouldn't wake you up. It was so real. I dreamed I got up and went to the top of the stairs, and there he was down at the bottom. I just got a peek at his back as he turned into the parlor."

Amy felt the room close in around them. "Honey," she whispered, "are you sure you were dreaming?"

Denise crept against her. Amy felt her daughter's arms clinging to her. "I . . . I woke up at the top of the stairs looking down," Denise said. "I think I was sleepwalking—God, I *hope* I was. But I'm not sure."

The hairs on Amy's neck prickled. "I used to walk in my sleep when I was a kid," she whispered.

"Really? Did you ever wake up and not be sure if you'd dreamed something or really done it?"

"I don't remember." I have to go down now, Amy thought. If he's down there and he comes upstairs, it will wake Ellie. I have to get to him before he can come up. "Denise, you stay right here."

"No, Mom, don't leave me—"

"I have to, honey, just for a minute." Amy pulled away gently, telling Denise to stay hidden among the easels and to keep still. She crept down the two flights, clutching the ham-mer, holding the head level with her shoulder. If it's him, she thought, he'll have his knife. I'll smash his wrist, smash it hard. She projected the thought, feeling her teeth clenching with fear and determination. She eased into the parlor, holding her breath. The front curtains were still, milky with light from the street. Her eyes felt huge and prickly, straining in the dimness. No windows open, no glass broken—good. She scanned the room, seeing the big things, the shapes a man could hide behind. The dropleaf table against the window, the two wing-back chairs. She circled between them.

Nothing.

She slipped through to the kitchen. The refrigerator hummed, masking any other sound. The pantry was still. Amy swallowed hard. She really did not want to look in there. But if she didn't, she would not rest when she got back upstairs. Pulling the door open, she darted her head in. Smell of Pine-Sol, jars and cans, the vacuum and brooms.

She searched the rest of the downstairs. The chairs, the dining room table, the humpbacked davenport in the living room seemed to tingle with suppressed information. She caught fleeting smells—the grease scent of hair, a hint of sweat—trailing through the rooms like a ghost wake. But the downstairs was empty.

Check the doors.

Locked, back and front.

Amy blew a breath out, feeling a huge relief.

As she turned from the door, her bare foot settled on something snakelike. She gasped, kicking it from the rug, hearing it skitter across the slate. She clamped a hand to her chest, feeling her heart hammer. Turning on the chandelier to a low glow, she bent over the thing—an electrical wire about three feet long. The black insulation had been stripped away from the middle foot but left intact on either end. Those ends had been looped back, their tips stripped and twisted onto the bare copper of the center section. What *was* it?

A garrote.

A chill shot up Amy's spine. That's what the loops were for—handles. She stared at it, her heart pounding. Someone *had* been in here. Either coming in or going out, he'd dropped this without knowing—it wouldn't be heavy enough to make much sound on the thick Persian carpet. In the low light, its twisting shape would have been disguised by the rug's patterns.

Good God, what was happening? How could someone get in here with the bars on the windows and the deadbolts locked? Even if she'd left a key lying around somewhere over the years, the locks were all new now. Whoever had dropped the garrote must be a master at picking locks.

Amy heard hesitant footsteps descending the stairs. Denise! She scooped the garrote up by the middle section and jammed it into a pocket of her robe, turning just as Denise came into sight.

"Mom?"

"Shh. Everything's all right. There's nobody here." Whispering, she was able to keep her fear from her voice. Ellie! she thought. What if—

Amy hurried up the stairs past Denise, her stomach clenching. Ellie was lying on her back, scrunched in the middle of a tortured pile of sheets and blankets. Her Wonder Woman pajamas had hiked up to her knees, and her brown curls lay straight up like rabbit ears along the pillow above her head. In the glow of the night light, Amy could not be sure her chest was moving. She hurried to her daughter, putting a hand lightly on her little chest, thanking God as she felt its regular rise and fall.

Joyce.

Amy patted Denise's shoulder and walked to Joyce's room, easing the door open a crack. A sliver of light from the hall fell across Joyce's face. She mumbled something in her sleep and rolled over.

Amy walked Denise back to her room.

"I think you should go back to bed," she whispered.

Denise gazed up at her with scared, knowing eyes. "Everything's not all right, is it?"

Amy felt her daughter's fear tearing at her. She took her hands. "Don't worry. I'm not going to let anything happen to you. I need you to be brave now and help me. There might have been someone in here, but he's gone now. I'm going to have the police come and look things over. If they wake Ellie, I'll want you to help Joyce keep her calm. Can you do that for me?"

Denise's face was white, but she nodded. "Just let me stay with you now, okay?"

"I really think—"

"*Please.* You're all I have."

Her throat full, Amy pulled Denise into a hug. "Don't worry. I'm not going to let anything happen to *me,* either." If I can help it, she added silently.

7

Amy sat at her desk, peering at the door to her office. I locked it, she thought. I never do that when I'm in here. The fear behind the little act disturbed her. Seven-thirty in the morning, the sun shining outside, and she had locked her door. True, the man with the ski mask had cornered her in the staff rest room around this time. But hospital security was now keeping a much better eye on this area—she'd seen a guard on her way in. She *hated* feeling intimidated. She must not let this creep destroy her life.

Amy thought of last night, the police detective and two patrolmen. Odd, the small but persistent anger she'd felt at them as they'd foraged through her house, dusting for finger-prints, checking the locks, writing things in their notebooks. Her real anger had been at the intruder she had not been able to see, who had brought these other men here, and it had spilled over onto the police. Even their unfailing solicitude had left a bad taste in her mouth. What if she had not been a St. Clair, daughter of *the* Winston St. Clair—the one who'd given hundreds of thousands to the police widows' and orphans' fund? Would they have offered to station uniformed officers inside the house with the lights on and the shades open, day and night, for as long as it took?

Amy shuddered, imagining strangers sitting downstairs in

her house while she tried to sleep. The girls would have no
chance to forget that they were in danger. And she would hear
every clink of a coffee cup, every murmur in the night, no
matter how hushed.

Besides, she wanted the bastard *caught,* not scared away
until some reporter got wind of the preferential treatment and
embarrassed the police commissioner into pulling the men off.

In the end, they had accepted her solution gracefully: The
police would keep a close eye on her town house during the
day. At night they would have an unmarked car outside. For
how long, no one talked about.

Once again Amy felt anger at the intruder, and cold fear at
what he had left on her floor. What did he *want*? If it was the
creep from the subway, why a garrote instead of a knife? And
why, after trying to attack her in the hospital restroom, would
he prowl silently around her house, taking nothing, touching
no one?

Amy started the coffeemaker beside Doris's desk and retreated to her inner office again. With the door shut, the place
seemed unnaturally hushed. Even the clattering and squeaking
Doris made with her file drawers and chair would be welcome,
but Doris wasn't due for another forty-five minutes—

Someone knocked at her door. She jumped. Annoyed
with herself, she got up and walked to the door. The handle
turned slightly. She stopped, her neck prickling.

"Amy?"

Campy's voice. She pulled the door open, relieved and
more pleased than she wanted to be.

He gave her a questioning smile. "Hope I'm not disturbing you."

"Not at all." She sensed his real question, but ignored it.
The locked door was her business. "Come on in. Help yourself
to the coffee."

Leaning against the doorjamb, she watched him at the
coffeemaker. He tucked a large X-ray envelope under one arm,
bending to pour two cups. She was impressed at how well he
balanced on the artificial foot. He looked good in dark pants,
perfectly creased, and a spotless medical coat. No surgical
scrubs this morning.

"You still like it black?"

She nodded. He handed her a coffee and sat on the corner of her desk. "Remember when you used to sneak away from school and meet me for coffee at Frenchie's?"

"Yeah? So?"

He laughed, and she joined in. In her mind she saw the dark, high-backed booths, the aging wood wrinkled with the carved initials of generations of Hartford High students. A flood of memories warmed her: Sitting there across from Campy, feeling grown up and sophisticated as they gazed into each other's eyes. Then Campy would make her laugh—whip out a pack of candy cigarettes or show her a fake tattoo he'd inked onto his wrist. One time it was "Born to Lube," in honor of his father's oil-and-grease-hungry rustbucket. Another time it was a very good caricature of her mother, with the word "Mothra" beneath. That was after Campy had made an Easter visit to the estate on Long Island. Mother had been politely monstrous to him. Back on safe ground in Hartford, Campy had done the "tattoo," inking Mother's hair out to the side in wings to make her look like the Japanese movie monster. Amy smiled at the memory. I laughed so hard I got the hiccups, she thought.

Does one of those booths still say "Campy Loves Amy"?

Looking at him, she found the past in his eyes, too. Time to change the subject. "Whatcha got there?" She pointed at the envelope.

He shook out a transparency from a CT scan. "Take a look, would you? I'd like your opinion."

His fingers touched hers as she took it. She waited longer than she liked for her mind to focus. The slide showed the right motor cortex. She could see a lighter area where the blood flow had been cut off, probably by a blood clot—a "pale" stroke. "So what do you want to know?" she asked.

"Is that a brain or a stomach?"

Laughter burst from her. "Oh, you're cute, you are."

Taking the transparencies back, he gazed at her. She felt it like a touch on her face. "I know you've got to get to work. Will I see you at the Waldorf tonight?"

Amy searched her mind. The Waldorf? Oh yes—tonight was the annual benefit for the hospital. Canapes and cocktails with the money barons of New York. Notices were up all over the hospital, but she'd been trying not to think about it. Tom couldn't come—he had night sessions with patients. It promised to be a very dull evening.

"I haven't much choice," she said. "My dad runs it."

Campy's eyebrows rose. "Winston?"

"Don't look so surprised. Winnie's put on a benefit for Hudson General every year for twenty-two years now."

"I knew he was a philanthropist, but to organize it himself is a lot of work for a man as busy as he must be."

"Yes." Amy wondered if Campy had seen Philip yet, learned what had happened to him, how Hudson General had saved his life. Apparently not, or he wouldn't wonder how Winnie could do all that work.

"I'm glad you're coming," Campy said. "See you tonight."

"Good." Amy had a twinge of misgiving. It would be nice to see Campy tonight, but seeing would have to be all. Slipping off to lunch with him on Saturday was one thing, starting the hospital rumor mill quite another. Relax, she told herself. Whatever develops, you can handle it.

Campy slid off the desk and headed for the door, turning as he reached it. "I went back to our booth at Frenchie's," he said. "Our names are still there."

"But *we* aren't." At once, she wished she had not said it. It had sounded cruel and hadn't been necessary. But he did not flinch, and she liked him better for it.

"No," he said softly. "But I wish we could be, just for an hour." He gave her a little wave and walked out as easily as a man with two good feet.

She was surprised to feel a lump in her throat. *Just for an hour.* It suddenly did not seem so much to ask: To be back at Frenchie's, with Philip whole, her parents together, everyone she loved still alive, and no problem worse than a pop quiz in algebra. To sit there in her young, tireless girl's body, half dizzy with the pure, pixilated rapture of first love. Amy felt a yearning so deep it shocked her. Campy had tapped into something she hadn't realized was there, a time she rarely let herself think about. How sweet it was. But now she *was* grown up, and adulthood meant a certain amount of pain and loss. It was your job to get over each blow and go on with your life.

Dear Campy, she thought. We can't go back to Frenchie's—

She saw the CT scan envelope and grinned.

But you can still make me laugh.

She realized he had not only made her laugh, he'd made her feel better. The danger was still there, but the fear that had bitten at her since last night was dulled, at least for the moment. She took advantage of it, sitting at her desk, sorting through memos. On top was the note she'd scribbled to herself yesterday: "VanK aut.—call Cynthia for permis." Amy checked the clock. Seven-fifty. Too early to call someone in mourning. She set the alarm on her watch for ten. As she stood to head out to the ward, her phone rang. She glanced at Doris's empty desk and picked up. "Dr. St. Clair."

"Ah, Amy—good. Eric Kraft here."

I can tell, Amy thought. The phone just turned greasy.

"I know this is short notice," Eric said, "but I need to see you in my office right away."

Amy felt herself bristling. "Eric, my shift is about to start. We're jammed down here."

"Not to worry—I've already called in Dr. Thompson to cover you."

Amy's annoyance deepened. *She* was in charge of ER. If there was any covering to be done, she should be the one to arrange it. "Dr. Thompson is not an ER specialist—"

"He was stitching up cuts and pumping stomachs when you were in diapers," Kraft said smoothly. "Relax, will you? I'm sure if anything requires your personal attention, ER will call us. I'll expect you in five minutes, all right?" Eric hung up before she could answer.

The elevator shivered up slowly through the heart of the hospital, stopping at each floor. Amy used the time to compose herself. Don't let Eric get to you. He's going to whine about money again. Whatever his latest scheme is, just nod and take notes. If he wants you to bring your own soap for the staff bathroom, ask him what kind.

Stepping off the elevator, Amy arranged her face into a pleasant expression. Dominique, the administrator's new secretary, was just settling behind her desk. She waved Amy through with a glance, bouncy blond hair gleaming under the soft, recessed lights. Passing, Amy noticed that her desktop was clean and wondered how much sweet young Dominique got paid. Forget it, Amy told herself. Therein lies madness.

She knocked as she entered Eric Kraft's office. Eric was sitting at his desk, working on some papers. The desk was enormous, but anything smaller would have been dwarfed by the spacious, high-ceilinged room.

"Amy." He rose and walked around the desk toward her, gently tugging down the sleeves of his suit jacket, as if he wanted her to notice it. The suit *was* gorgeous—Savile Row, no doubt, and beautifully tailored to Eric's sleek form. Objectively, she could appreciate that he looked quite smashing in it; he was health-club fit, a tanned, sleek man with a salon haircut and fox-bright eyes. He gave her one of his oddly shy smiles. It might have worked if she hadn't known that Eric Kraft was sly, not shy, hungry for the kind of power you didn't get by working out.

"I'm going to have to get back to ER as quickly as I can," Amy said.

"As quickly as we can," Eric agreed. "Meanwhile, come on in and take a load off your feet."

Amy saw that Eric was pointing her to a new couch, arranged catty-corner to his desk. Resigned, she settled into one of the crimson cushions, reflexively smoothing a hand along the lustrous satin.

"Just got it," Eric said proudly. "Brunschwig & Fils. You like?"

"Beautiful."

He made a deprecating gesture, but clearly he was pleased. Amy swallowed what she would like to say: Beautiful, yes, but she *didn't* like it—not here. This office already reeked of excess, from the huge antique sarouk spread across the oak floor, to the crimson drapes of Chinese silk bracing the windows, to the wall behind Eric's desk, faced in white marble. Too rich for a hospital, all of it. Every week, some of Hudson General's sick and wounded bled out their life savings beneath this lavish room.

But, to be fair, most of the Marie Antoinette excesses were not Eric's doing. They dated back to the last century, when

Hudson had catered exclusively to the richest families of Manhattan, people like the VanKleecks—and, all right, the St. Clairs. On the other hand, ever since his ascension to this office, Eric had kept adding little touches, like the sofa. Two grand at least. It was his own money—surely it must be—but why get so at home with an era of Hudson that was long and well dead?

"So," Eric said. "Things pretty busy down in ER, then?" He glanced toward the door.

Amy realized that he was killing time, waiting for someone else to show up. She felt a surge of annoyance. "You said five minutes, Eric. Here I am. Who are we waiting for?"

He hesitated, then looked toward the door again. "Ah, here he is now."

Amy turned and felt a little shock as Burton Fairchild, chairman of the hospital board, walked in. He was wearing a dark suit buttoned over his paunch, making her think of the plump banker on the Monopoly cards. But despite his jovial exterior, Burton Fairchild was a man to be reckoned with, wielding just the kind of power Eric craved. In his time, Burton had made and broken plenty of doctors—and a few administrators, too.

What was he doing here?

Amy felt a sudden tension in her neck and shoulders. This wasn't just a drop-by-my-office meeting, this was serious, and Eric had given her zero warning.

"Eric," Burton boomed. "And Amy, radiant as ever. How nice to see you, my dear."

"Sit, sit, both of you," Eric said. "Coffee?"

Amy shook her head, though she wanted a cup very much.

"Cream and two sugars, if you please," Burton said.

The discreet tink of Crown Renaissance china accompanied Eric's movements at the bar. He made up identical creamed and sugared coffees for himself and the chairman. Something in the careful mimicry alerted Amy; she recalled suddenly that she had seen Eric around the halls with Burton lately, Eric pointing here and there, the chairman nodding his snowy head gravely. Hospital politics—she loathed it, but it was time she paid more attention. Eric had been at the hospital over seven years now, and in all that time Burton had kept a polite and proper distance. Now they were getting chummy.

What did the two of them want with her?

Burton settled next to her, too close for her comfort. Eric pulled up a big wingback chair, his knees stopping a foot from hers, making her feel cornered.

Eric glanced at Burton, then homed in on her, his expression sober. "Burton and I both wanted to meet with you, Amy, in your capacity as head of ER." He hesitated. "Truth is, I have something difficult to tell you. You sure you wouldn't like a coffee? Some tea, perhaps?"

She shook her head and waited, feeling a faint flutter in her stomach.

"As you know," Eric said, "Emergency has been running in the red for some time now. I'm afraid it's starting to pull the rest of the hospital down with it."

"Surely it's not that bad."

Eric glanced at Burton. "I'm afraid it is. As you know, ER is the principal route into the hospital for people with no insurance. Almost forty percent of our ER admissions lately fall into that category. Now, your public hospitals in this city can stay open while the city borrows, issues bonds, and juggles its debts. We, on the other hand, can't float on that kind of red ink. Does this stop the city from dumping more and more of its problems on us? Hell, no. Aside from the insurance question, we're facing an increasing caseload of drug addicts and AIDS patients. As you know, your ER services are among the most expensive Hudson provides and yet, for the reasons I've outlined, ER patients consistently have the worst record for paying bills. We're already at the hilt of what we can charge the paying customers to make up for the nonpayers. We have to do something, soon. If I let emergency services drag us into bankruptcy, no one will get treated at Hudson.

"That's why I'm going to close ER down."

Amy felt a cold shock in her stomach. Eric had no idea what he was saying. Hudson's ER was one of the biggest and best equipped in the city. Manhattan's other hospitals were chronically near capacity. They'd never be able to handle the overflow.

Alarm spread through Amy in a slow, chilling wave. She remembered the last crisis. Near the end of November, they'd got an overload like they had now, patients lined up on gurneys in the hall. At one point they'd simply had no more room or staff coverage. Just for a couple of hours, but during the first of those hours, in a tenement on the Lower West Side, a woman named Rosie Hernandez had gone into premature labor. She'd had the presence of mind to call an ambulance. The paramedics bundled Rosie aboard and started calling hospitals. The four closest ERs were full; the medic in back had tried to deliver the child, but then Rosie had started to hemorrhage. Desperate, the driver had called Hudson, halfway across town, and Hudson's ER was overflowing too.

Except that Amy happened to be at triage when the call came in. She'd told the medics to get Rosie over here. They'd driven like Jehu, and Amy had met them at the door.

Amy closed her eyes now, not wanting to remember any more, but Rosie's exsanguinated face, as pale as candlewax, burned on her eyelids. She'd lost too much blood—hemorrhaging much faster than the frantic attendant could pump in plasma. There had been no chance for her child, but she should have lived. The delay had killed her.

How many more people would die if Hudson closed its ER? Die in ambulances circling around the city, while desperate paramedics called ER after ER and were turned away. Amy shuddered. She should have seen this coming, should have guessed that a man like Eric Kraft wouldn't stop with canceling staff breakfasts in the cafeteria.

But not ER, she thought, appalled. You can't take ER.

Amy forced herself to calmness. "Eric, I see your point, but—"

"Yes? If you have a solution, I'd love to hear it."

She tried to marshal her thoughts. "More fund drives and charity balls. We'll probably pull in a million in pledges at the Waldorf tonight. Why not do it every six months instead of once a year?"

Burton gave her a condescending little smile. "Because the contributors would scale back their donations accordingly. Your father is already doing all that can be done there, bless his heart. He's been a tremendous help over the years. Don't know what we'd have done without him. Not just the fund drives, but his own very generous personal contributions."

"But the point is," Eric cut in, "you can only squeeze out so much that way, and it's not enough. Your father *has* helped, but the truth is, he's hurt us too. If he hadn't used his position on the board to fight me tooth and nail, I'd have shut ER down two years ago, the public hospitals would be handling the public, and Hudson General would be in the black."

Amy stared at Eric, stunned. Two years ago? Winnie had already fought this out with Eric once? Why hadn't he told her?

Because he knew what Hudson's ER meant to her. Not just a job, oh no. Twenty-two years ago, in the long nights by Philip's bedside, Hudson had turned her from a girl to a woman, changed the whole course of her life. She had been reborn here. It was *home.*

Suddenly Eric's criticism—*his bloody nerve*—sank in and Amy felt her temper slipping. "I don't appreciate your remarks about my father." The words sliced out of her, sharper than she'd intended.

"Now, Amy," Burton said, "let's just stay calm here. I'm sure Eric didn't mean to criticize Winston. It's just that we *do* have quite a problem, and the old ways may not be enough to solve it. This hospital needs entirely new sources of revenue. Important new areas of medicine are opening up, where we can provide vital services without sinking into crippling debt."

"What are you talking about?"

"A clinic on preventive medicine, for example. A vital area being spotlighted nationally by the Secretary of Health and Human Services."

Burton's voice, always a bit pontifical, was waxing pompous now, and she wondered what he was hiding with the high-sounding talk. How would a clinic on preventive medicine work, when most insurance companies wouldn't even pay for routine medical checkups? "That sounds fine, Burton," she said, "but there's no way it could take the place of a well-equipped and well-staffed Emergency Service. I'm sure my staff would work hard with you to keep ER open. I could talk to them about a pay or benefits cut. They might be willing if they saw people up here on the top floor cutting themselves back too."

Eric flushed. Amy felt Burton Fairchild stir uncomfortably on the couch beside her. "A noble sentiment, Amy, but it wouldn't work out in the long run. There'd be resentment. You can't ask the good people who work so hard here to go backward."

"And with all due respect, Amy," Eric said, "not everyone has the St. Clair family fortune backing them up."

The spite in his voice made her face sting. Why would he say such a thing to her? She realized suddenly that he envied her. The thought seemed incredible.

What about my family misfortune, Eric? Would you envy us that, too?

With an effort, Amy controlled her voice. "We can turn ER around," she said firmly. "Make it, if not profitable, at least less unprofitable. What about that glowing article on our emergency cardiac services in *The Wall Street Journal* last week? The people who will read that are potential paying 'customers,' as you so warmly put it, Eric, and a lot of them are in the high-risk group for heart attacks. We could whip our publicity department into gear, try for more of that sort of thing—outreach, letting people know we're here and that we give top-quality care—"

Eric gave a cynical grunt. "You've certainly been effective at getting that message out to the wrong people."

"What 'wrong people,' Eric?"

He leaned toward her, an aggressive light in his eyes. "You want an example? How about last week, when you spirited that bag lady in past admitting and donated half an hour of ER time to her?"

Amy felt a quick, hot sense of betrayal. "Gladys."

"Never mind who told me. And you should be thankful you have Gladys to run your admitting procedures. If she hadn't been paying attention to the bottom line down there, we'd have had to close long ago."

"Gladys does her best," Amy agreed, "and we need her down there. By the same token, one old lady with no money getting a free moment of my time is hardly something to get upset about." Amy tried to control her temper. She had skipped lunch to see that woman. And the only supplies she'd dispensed were two Tylenol tablets from her desk and a referral note to the free dental clinic in the Village.

"Good Christ, Amy, there are others, don't deny it. And that bag lady might have had no money when she came in, but she went out clutching a ten-dollar bill."

Amy wondered what he was talking about, then remembered she'd given the woman cab fare because her warty feet, in their cast-off size-twelve tennis shoes, wouldn't have carried her two blocks, let alone to the Village.

"What do you think she tells her street cronies?" Eric said. " 'You gots a toothache, go to Hudson General. They gives you free pills and free money.' Terrific!"

Amy felt a rush of adrenaline. Eric hadn't even seen the woman and he thought he knew her, but he didn't and he didn't want to.

Eric said, "There's something you need to understand— we have done everything we could for this city. But now it's sink or swim for us. Ensuring that there are enough ER beds in New York is the city's responsibility, not ours."

Burton gave her hand a conciliatory pat. "Amy, I know this hits you hard, but there will be time to adjust. No one's talking about closing Emergency tomorrow—"

"How long?"

"Well, the plan hasn't been put before the whole board, of course—"

"Eric?" Amy asked.

"Six weeks. If we don't see some turnaround, I'm going to close ER."

She stared at him, feeling as if she'd been punched in the stomach. She turned on Burton. "And you're here out of deference to my father, to make sure Eric gives me fair warning, is that it? And to serve notice that this time you won't be on my father's side." Burton didn't say anything, but she could tell from his face that she was right on both counts. "Then may I let *you* know this—if you try to close ER, my father and I will fight you with everything we have."

The two men looked at each other, a glance of secret deals and smug power, shutting her out.

Amy felt suddenly weary, sick of the two men and their schemes. She stood. "If that's all—"

"Not quite," Eric said. "Sit down, Amy."

She remained standing, staring down at him.

"About three weeks ago," Eric said, "a man by the name of Richard Jameson died in ER."

"Eric," Burton said, "now may not be the best time."

"We'll keep it short. Are you familiar with that case, Amy?"

She tried to think. That letter, a day or two ago from the law firm. Hadn't that been about Jameson? Amy felt a twinge of foreboding. "I'm not familiar with the case. It must have been handled by one of the other doctors."

"Mr. Jameson came into ER with chest pains. Tests were run. While still in ER, he arrested and died."

"It happens," Amy said, thinking of Owen VanKleeck.

"Not to guys like Jameson, it doesn't. He was as fit as a marine sergeant. We played racquetball a few times. Every time, he trounced me—and he has a good twenty years on me. We had lunch once or twice at his club; hell, the man wouldn't touch red meat or put butter on his bread." Eric paused, eyeing her. "I can't believe you don't know him. He happened to be one of the wealthiest men in this city—right up there in your father's class. He's a banker, too—vice-president of New York National."

Amy tried to concentrate on what Eric was saying. This was VanKleeck all over again, a virtual carbon copy. But how could Eric drop the ER bomb and then expect her to think about this case? She saw that Eric was gazing at her, waiting for an answer. "People do die in ER, despite everything we can do."

"Let it go, Eric," Burton said.

"What's this about?" Amy asked.

The two men looked at each other. Neither spoke. Amy realized suddenly that Eric wouldn't have pressed the subject over Burton's mild objections unless he was actually speaking for Burton. What was behind this? Were these two desk jockeys accusing her or her staff of incompetence? Amy felt a surge of anger. "If you'll excuse me, gentlemen, I've got patients to look after. They might not be members of your club, but they count." She walked out, half-hearing Eric shout something after her. Bypassing the elevators, she plunged into the stairwell, dimly conscious of the rattle of her feet down the steps, the musty smell of dust. She felt sick. If Eric won this fight, she would survive. There wasn't an ER in the city that didn't need more doctors. But if the city lost Hudson General's ER, what had happened to Rosie Hernandez would be multiplied many times over.

Amy felt a distant pain in her hand and realized she was standing at the bottom of the stairwell, squeezing the bar of the exit handle with all her strength. She let go, flexing her palm. Eric's last words, called after her as she left his office, came back to her: *It's not my club, Amy. It's yours.* She felt her face burning. You're wrong, Eric. I don't have a club. All I've got is ER, and I'm not going to let you take it away.

8

Amy watched her father work the crowd in the grand ballroom, pleased at how healthy he looked. Grins and quick
laughter animated Winnie's face. The blazing chandeliers made
his thick white hair shine like the pelt of a polar bear.

Did he know Eric was planning to shut down ER?

If so, he looked completely unworried. Unbuttoning his
tux jacket, Winston St. Clair made his way through the crowd
at the edge of the dance floor. He shook hands with men and
women alike, hugging some, trailing a buoyant wake of movement and talk. Amy saw the mayor working his way through
another part of the crowd, heading toward Winnie. They made
her think of two powerful trains chugging toward each other
on the same tracks. Eric Kraft trailed in the mayor's wake, his
face falling when he saw where His Honor was headed. Good,
Amy thought. Watch and learn, Eric.

Meeting Winnie in the middle, the mayor put an arm
across his shoulder for a newspaper photographer. Winnie
grinned and faced the camera too. It reminded Amy of an old
World War II photograph of Winnie in his major's uniform,
striking a comradely pose with a fellow battalion commander.
He'd probably still fit into that old uniform, she thought, then
remembered what Eric had said about the dead Mr. Jameson:
fit as a marine sergeant. Dead all the same, just as Owen

VanKleeck was dead of cardiac arrest in *her* ER. Amy's palms ached suddenly, the nervous feeling she used to get during her first-year rotation on surgery, right before she had to cut.

I need that autopsy on VanKleeck, she thought.

Amy saw a gold-coated waiter offer the mayor and Winnie a tray of little bacon quiches. She winced—heart-attack food. The mayor took one. Amy beamed a mental warning. Winnie waved the waiter off. She felt absurdly relieved.

Stop it! He's fine.

She turned away, looking for Campy. He should be here by now; the benefit had been going strong for an hour and a half. His absence irritated her. With Tom unable to come, she'd counted on Campy—more, apparently, than she'd realized.

The orchestra started up a Strauss waltz, propelling a dozen couples around the floor in graceful sweeps. Amy watched the twosomes, trying not to feel envious of their closeness. The women were dazzling in their long, swirling gowns, icy diamonds or pearls gleaming at their throats. The men looked their best, too, stomachs flattened by cummerbunds, feet skating across the glowing parquet. The scene took her back to her childhood, Grandpa's estate near Amagansett. Grandpa liked his party guests to bring their kids. She'd tear around the halls with them, then slip into the ballroom, sweaty and breathless, to watch the grownups twirl each other around. The memory warmed her; for a second she had the old feeling, the warm comfort of being among her own kind.

Your club.

Her dreamy mood punctured, Amy turned away from the dancers. Time to do her duty. She knew she should pitch in and give Winnie a hand. Putting on a cordial smile, she waded into the crowd gathered around Winnie and the mayor, saying hello to her parents' old friends, making conversation with the men and women from Southampton and Central Park West and the Upper East Side. It went all right at first, but she quickly tired of it: *Missed you at the Cup, my dear; a physician, how . . . interesting; will we see you at Lyford Cay? . . .*

"Amy—there you are!"

Tom! Amy turned, surprised and pleased. He'd made it after all! She introduced him to the crystal magnate who had been pretending to disdain the fuss and bother Queen Elizabeth had caused by staying at his favorite resort. Once he learned that Tom was a psychologist, however, the crystal man took the first opportunity to glide away.

Relieved, Amy turned to Tom. "I thought you couldn't make it tonight."

"I had a couple of cancellations. I'll have to go back in an hour for a late-nighter."

"I'm glad you're here—and your timing was perfect!"

"I noticed."

Amy felt a small dismay. "I thought I was being very nice to him. How did you know?"

"He kept inching toward you and you kept inching back. Also, you were smiling like this." Tom bared his teeth.

Amy winced.

"Dance?" he said.

"Wonderful."

Tom led her through the crowd at the edge of the dance floor. Pretending to observe the dancers behind Tom, she glanced across his face. How handsome he was—and he looked stunning in a tux. An intoxicating whiff of his sandalwood cologne hit her and she leaned into him, savoring the shaved smoothness of his skin.

"You don't much like these people, do you?" he said.

She leaned back, looking him in the eye. "How long were you watching me?"

"It's my profession."

"I thought your profession was *listening* to people."

"Watching people is often the best way to 'hear' them. Your body language tells me two things: first, you don't like these people, and second, you're one of them."

Amy felt a twinge of annoyance. Eric and now Tom. "What makes you say that?"

"Come on, Amy. Aside from the fact that you're a St. Clair, you have the look. The way you do your makeup. Your clothes, your sense of style, even the way you walk, as if the universe belonged to you."

"Rubbish. And I have nothing against these people. I was like them once, and it seemed like a good life at the time."

"You sound annoyed."

"If you don't mind, I'd prefer to talk about something

else—you, for example. I've known you for two years, dated you for, what, four months now, been to—" Amy glanced around. "Well, you know what I'm saying. All that, and I still don't have the faintest idea what your life was like before I met you."

"Boring."

"So bore me."

Tom looked exasperated. "Come on. You know a lot about me."

"Tons," Amy said dryly. "Let's see—I know you were an only child. I know you grew up in the Bronx. You worked your way through City College and got your Ph.D. at Maryland. You like baroque music and French restaurants—I have some nice firsthand evidence of that."

"See?" Tom said.

"Right. The kind of stuff I could read in your high school yearbook. What was growing up in the Bronx *like* for you?"

"I played a lot of stickball and ran around with other kids who thought they were tough."

"I think you said once that your father wasn't around when you were growing up. Did you know him at all?"

"He left Mom before I was born."

"That must have been rough on her."

"I'm sure. Rougher than she ever let on to me."

"Did she tell you anything about him?"

"Mom preferred not to talk about him. She didn't even keep any pictures. Instead, she did her best to make up for him. She was wonderful."

"Your mother died in an accident, right?"

Tom's steps slowed, losing some of their unconscious grace. "Yes. A subway accident. She was . . . mangled very badly."

Amy felt the pain in his voice. She gave his hand a little squeeze. "How awful."

"I was twelve. The city took me under its official wing. As you know, I spent a few years in a foster home. My foster parents were all right, but they weren't Mom."

"Tell me about her—she was from Venezuela. Was she dark? I've always wondered about that. You're so fair."

"I like to think so."

She nudged him in the ribs.

"I guess I must take after my father physically. But Mom was actually pretty fair-skinned herself, especially for a Venezuelan. She had light brown hair with a lot of red in it. Her maternal grandfather was a Scottish sailor who got drunk, missed his freighter in Caracas, and settled down in a tiny village inland. Her parents moved from there to Brazil when she was little. When she turned nineteen, she immigrated to the U.S.—illegally, as a matter of fact. That's where she met my father. After he took off, she worked as a maid and took in laundry. That's how she supported the two of us. An old neighbor woman, part of an underground community of illegals, took care of me during the days. But at night, *Madre* was always there. She'd tell me stories while she ironed, about the old days in her village and about the fine *yanqui* houses she was keeping clean here in Nueva York."

Amy could sense the sadness in him. "You loved her very much, didn't you?"

"Yes, I did." His voice was husky. She felt a little ashamed for pressing him so, but it was wonderful too, the way he was suddenly opening up to her. Maybe all he'd needed all along was a push.

The waltz ended; at that same moment, Campy's face materialized over Tom's shoulder. Amy stared at him, startled. He *was* here. Tom glanced at her and turned.

Campy held out his hand. "Dr. Hart, I presume."

"That's right . . ."

Amy found her voice. "Tom, this is Otis Camp, an old friend of mine. He just joined the Hudson staff as an attending in general surgery."

Tom shook Campy's hand. "Pleased to meet you."

"And I, you. I've heard great things about your work at Hudson."

Tom gave an embarrassed smile, and it struck Amy that he never knew what to do with compliments.

"May I have this dance?" Campy asked.

Amy looked at Campy, flustered, realizing the orchestra had started up again. *He dances?* "By all means," she said. Tom nodded a little stiffly.

Campy's arm slid round her waist; as he turned her neatly

into the center of the crowd, she checked back on Tom. His
nettled expression surprised her. Did he sense that Campy
might be more than an "old friend"?

"Sorry to be late," Campy said. "The time slipped away
from me." His voice sounded a little tense, but then he smiled.
"Coming in late seems to be the story of my life."

"It does indeed." Amy felt herself relaxing into his rhythm.
Amazing, how well he was doing. His movements were mea-
sured but not rigid. There was no sign he was missing a foot.
"Now I *am* impressed," she said.

"Thank you."

"Who have you been practicing with?"

"You, in my dreams."

She smiled. Campy had never been afraid to utter romantic nonsense. And she still liked it.

"Seriously, now. Was it a girlfriend back in Ann Arbor?"

"Actually, once you get the walking down, the dancing
comes too. You may have noticed I'm hanging on for dear life."

She felt the firmness of his grip then, and remembered it
from when she'd first taught him to dance, in his father's barn
outside Hartford. He'd wanted to be able to dance with her at
his senior prom. He was terrible at first, but by graduation he
was better at it than she was. For a second his arm across her
back felt exactly the way it had that night in the warm gym
under the crepe paper, the band playing "April Love," their
whole lives ahead of them together.

She waited to see if he'd put his cheek to hers. He did not,
and it told her something about him. Back in Hartford, beneath
his grease-monkey facade, his beat-up school jacket, and all the
poor-boy-meets-rich-girl jokes, Campy had always been perceptive. He might have lost a foot in the jungle, but he had not
lost his intuition. He'd known to tell her he'd come back for
her, and he knew now not to push it. It made her feel more
attracted to him, and he probably knew that, too. *Campy,
you're not going to make it easy for me to say no, are you?*

Against her will, she realized how good he looked. Not as
natural in a tux as Tom, but still striking. He held his head back
a little, looking into her eyes. She found she could not look
away, did not want to. His eyes were grayer than she remem-

bered, as if something had leached the color from them. You've seen terrible things, haven't you? she thought.

"You are so beautiful," he said.

"Just how long *have* you been out of the jungle?"

Campy laughed. "A handsome man, Thomas Hart."

"I suppose so," she said.

"You suppose?"

"All right. He's damned handsome."

"And intelligent too, no doubt. Well, I never thought winning you back would be easy."

"Good. Then you won't be disappointed."

"No," he said, "I won't be."

The dance ended, and Tom was right there. "May I cut in?"

Campy stepped back gracefully. Amy watched over Tom's shoulder until Campy had merged with the crowd beside the dance floor. Tom danced her around in silence for a few minutes, then said, "An old friend, eh?"

"I used to date him in high school," Amy said, surprising herself.

"Aha!"

"He was in the war. He lost a foot." Saying it, she felt a strange pride.

Tom looked startled. "You're kidding! And he dances better than I do. If he's that determined, I'll have to watch him, make sure he doesn't set his sights on you again."

"Like I said, he's just an old friend now."

"Mm-hmm," Tom said. "When Otis came along, I was about to ask you how it's going with the intruder alert."

Amy had a sudden hollow feeling in her stomach. "As well as can be expected. The unmarked car is there at night. Judging from where he dropped the garrote, he picked the front lock to get in. If he tries it again, they ought to be able to get him— unless they doze off."

"Did the police get back to you on the garrote yet?"

"Yes. The handles were too small for full prints. No partials either. He must've been wearing gloves."

Tom sighed. "I wish you'd let me move in with you until this is over. I'd sleep on the couch."

"Thanks, Tom. But I want things as normal as possible right now for Denise and Ellie."

"It's just that I worry about you." Tom gave her a little squeeze. "You've had a tough life lately, what with the nightmares and someone prowling around your house . . ."

Amy shivered against him.

"Maybe we shouldn't talk about it."

"Maybe not."

Tom held her closer. "I hope I didn't offend you with that business about growing up rich."

"Of course not. It's ancient history for me."

The waltz ended. Automatically, Amy turned toward the orchestra and applauded with the others, the way she'd been taught at Miss Porter's school. Tom gave her a knowing smile, and she felt quite annoyed with him.

"So how are you holding up?" Winnie asked.

"Fine!" Amy said. She looked through the thinning crowd for Campy, but apparently he'd gone even before Tom left to go back to the hospital. She turned back to her father. "You seem in top form tonight."

"I've been faking it the last hour," Winnie said with a weary smile. At close range, she could see the wrinkles around his eyes, the long rogue hairs straying up from his eyebrows. Victoria used to make sure he clipped those off, but with her gone he tended to forget. He did look tired now, his earlier energy gone. Of course, anyone would be drained by what he'd had to do this evening—getting an affair like this up and running would be a tall order for a man half his age. She noticed that he was rubbing absently at the crook of his arm. "Did you hurt your elbow?"

"What? Oh, this. I gave blood at Hudson this morning. Forgot to take the Band-Aid off."

"No wonder you're tired," Amy said, relieved.

"I popped down the hall to ER, but you weren't there."

Because I was in Eric's office, Amy thought. "Sorry to miss you . . ." Here was her chance to bring up the matter of the ER closing. Reluctance dragged at her. "So how did we do to-night?"

"Besides the two-hundred-a-head gate, we've topped a million in pledges."

"Fantastic!"

"Actually, I'd hoped for more. It's a drop in the bucket for these people."

She patted his shoulder. "Chin up, Dad. A million is a long way from nothing."

"Yes, of course. Feel like getting some air?"

"Sure."

Outside the ballroom, Winnie led her past the stairs for the lobby and street. Intrigued, she followed him around the mezzanine and deeper into the hotel, past darkened banquet rooms, into a murky elevator alcove that smelled of dust and old furniture polish.

"I don't know if you can still do this," he said, "but let's try." There was an odd light in his eyes. He cranked the doors of the service elevator back and ushered her into the small cage. "Hang on." He pulled the hand lever over. The cage jolted and whined upward slowly, cables clanking. Amy leaned back, enchanted by her father's boyish enthusiasm. He seemed suddenly to have recovered his energy. He gazed at her; she had the eerie feeling he was seeing someone else. How had he known about this old elevator? Some dizzy, romantic fling in the past? The idea made her oddly uncomfortable.

The elevator clanked to a stop automatically, and she realized they'd hit the top of the shaft. Winnie led her into a narrow hall. Ornate electric sconces shed a candle glow on faded carpet. She inhaled the thick smell of ancient plaster. At the end of the hall, Winnie opened a steel door. A cool breeze, tinged with river smells, swept her face.

"Come on," he said, his voice sharp with excitement.

He stepped onto a small apron of roof and she followed, feeling the grit of tarpaper through the soles of her shoes. The narrow, porchlike ledge was guarded by a stone parapet with elaborately carved balusters in the shape of vases. From the corners of her eyes she could sense the top of the Waldorf stretching up behind her another thirty yards. As she tipped her head up, the wall seemed, through some dizzying trick of perspective, to overhang her. Stars wheeled beyond the crest of the hotel, sparking in an impossibly black sky. Glancing down over the broad stone rail, she felt her stomach plunge. Far below, cars, as tiny as beetles, crawled along Park Avenue. Dizzied, she stepped back a little and looked out over the city, avidly searching out familiar landmarks. Below her, to the north, St. Bartholomew's brooded in dark Byzantine grandeur. Southward on Park Avenue, the tunneled base of the Helmsley building channeled streams of traffic around the towering Pan Am Building and Grand Central Station behind. All around her the lights of Manhattan blazed like a man-made galaxy.

"Breathtaking," she murmured.

"A long time ago, I brought your mother up here and promised her that one day I'd be a lord of this city."

Amy looked at him, pierced by the sadness in his voice. So it *was* romance that had brought him up here—romance with Mother. She pulled him to her side with a gentle hug. "You kept that promise."

He looked away. "I don't know."

"Yes, you do. You helped rebuild this city. When it almost went bankrupt, Chelsea Bank made a lot of loans it shouldn't have."

"I got rich—richer—on it," Winnie said. "Don't give me any medals."

"You took some very big chances."

"And I lost what I wanted most." He took a deep breath, squaring his shoulders. "Still, I'm a very fortunate man. I have you. The best daughter a man could want. I'm very proud of you, dear Amy."

Tears pressed behind her eyes. "You haven't lost Mother," she said softly. "She still loves you."

He looked at her with a mixture of hope and doubt. "You think so?"

"I know so," Amy said, but she didn't.

Winnie sighed. "She still blames me for Philip." He leaned forward into the wind, closing his eyes. "I'm worried about your mother," he said. "I can't imagine why she insisted on selling the town house and moving to that dingy little apartment on Central Park West."

Amy laughed in disbelief. "Dad, there are no dingy little apartments on Central Park West."

"Even so, it's a big step down from what she had. I still send her the full fifty K a month, of course. And she made a small fortune on the town house. But what is she doing with the money?"

"What do you mean?"

"This grand city of ours crawls with predators," he said in a low voice, his eyes still closed. "Young studs and con men ready to sell their 'affections' to women like your mother in return for everything they have."

Amy laughed, then saw that he was serious. Victoria, the iron lady, keeping some young stud? Losing her money to a con man? "I can't imagine it," she said.

"Have you seen her lately?"

"Last week. She took Denise and Ellie shopping."

"How did she seem to you?"

There was pathetic eagerness in his voice. "Fine, she seemed fine." Amy felt a twinge of anger at her mother for being so cold to Winnie. Was it really over Philip? That had happened so long ago, more than twenty years. It seemed incredible that she could let an old tragedy cause another one, the death of her marriage. Amy remembered when she'd first noticed that the marriage was falling apart. She'd been at Vassar by then. Each visit home had given her a single frame of the cruel drama—time-lapse images that flowed together, making the disintegration seem swifter than it was. I was all that held them together, she thought, remembering the guilt when first she'd realized it. But what could she have done? Stayed home forever?

"Look at us," Winnie said. "We're depressing each other. I should never have brought you up here."

"No, I'm glad you did," Amy said, meaning it. She inhaled deeply, savoring the bracing, cold fullness in her lungs.

Winnie straightened, making an obvious effort to perk up. "So how are you and my darling grandkids?"

"Fine, just fine," she said heartily, wishing he had not asked. She did not want to tell him about the intruder and the police watch. If he found out anyway, he'd be upset with her for not telling him. But if she did tell him, he'd try to fill her house with security guards or move her somewhere else. She didn't want either option. Before Winnie could pursue her home life, she said, "Have you heard about Eric's plan?"

Winnie grimaced. "That back-stabbing young son of a bitch—I beg your pardon."

He looked so flustered that she almost smiled. "We have to stop him," she said.

"Yes, we do."

"I think Burton's going to be on his side."

Winnie gave her a sharp, questioning look.

"He was there when Eric told me."

Winnie looked grim. "That will make it a lot tougher."

"Yes. Unless we pull a rabbit out of a hat, you're going to be outvoted. He tried it once already. You never told me that."

"I knew I could stop him. I didn't want to worry you. You don't tell your old papa everything either, do you?"

She felt herself flushing. "This time I want you to let me help."

"You have enough to do, just running ER."

"I'm serious. You can't take them on alone."

Winnie grunted. She saw a small muscle jumping in his jaw and knew he was furious at Eric and Burton, but was trying not to show it. His anger unnerved her. Before, he'd always had that rabbit up his sleeve. Not this time. We *are* going to lose, Amy thought. Sick at heart, she looked again over the dazzling spread of Manhattan beneath them. This was how Burton and Eric saw the city—from a height. From here you could not see its sickness, its blood. All you could see was its breathtaking beauty. "Philip would love this," she said, though she knew she shouldn't have.

"I meant to invite him to the benefit," Winnie said, looking away. "I thought about it. I call him every day."

"I know," Amy said quickly. "He appreciates it."

"I hope he realizes how much I love him. I just wish I'd tried half so hard to show it before . . . before."

"Let's go back and dance," Amy said.

As the service elevator crawled back down the shaft, Amy could see in Winnie's eyes that he was still thinking about Philip. Though it had been twenty years ago, the fateful moment was reborn every time he looked in his son's face, heard his childlike speech. Her heart went out to her father. Half a billion dollars, one of the four hundred richest men in America, the wealthy elect. And yet there had been nothing he could do.

Except what he was doing tonight.

You're a much better man than you know, she thought. What would I do without you?

She thought of Owen VanKleeck—of Cynthia losing the father that she had loved so much. Amy felt a lump swelling in her throat. Why haven't I called her? Not just about the autopsy, but to comfort her about her father.

Because I'm afraid. We're too much alike.

I *will* call her, Amy decided. First thing tomorrow.

9

In the nightmare, Cynthia VanKleeck walked in the woods behind her house. She was hot. She could feel her nightie sticking to her back and legs. Where were her shoes? The dirt felt warm and icky under her toes and Mama had told her never to go barefoot 'cause there were nasty bugs in the ground. What was she doing out here in the woods? She did not want to be out here now. She wanted to go home, crawl back in her bed. She wanted her Daddy to tuck her in. Cynthia hugged Snagglepuss and bit her lip, trying not to cry.

What do you see in the woods, Cynthia?

She jumped, frightened at the voice. Where did it come from? She looked around, trying to see through the dark leaves and branches. She couldn't see anybody. It was like magic. Scared, she hugged Snagglepuss tighter.

What do you see?

"Nothing!" she cried.

All right, who *do you see?*

She looked around again, but she still could not see anyone. Why wouldn't the voice leave her alone?

She wished Daddy were here to pick her up and carry her back to the house.

No, he's gone, she thought. Something had happened to

him—something terrible. Grief wracked her, her throat aching, hot tears pressing at her eyes. The woods wavered and faded, and she was floating in darkness.

Who do you see?

The woods molded themselves from the darkness again. Cynthia choked back a sob as she realized she was back in the nightmare.

WHO DO YOU SEE?

No one, please, why won't you believe me?

All right, Cynthia, this is your last chance: Look ahead. There is a shape there in the darkness. You can see it if you try. Look at it and tell me what it is.

Cynthia squinted, trying desperately to penetrate the syrupy darkness, to see what the speaker wanted her to see. The dreadful finality of the voice rang in her ears, filling her with terror: *Your last chance!*

But she could see nothing. "What do you want me to say?" She tried to scream it, but her voice leaked out in a strangled whisper.

Silence. She felt a distant adhesive tug behind her left ear, like a Band-Aid being pulled off.

The woods shimmered and faded. She was lying in soft darkness again. She opened her eyes and saw a man bending over her. He looked startled. Her head swam with confusion. Was she awake? Yes—and she knew this man. What was he doing here? Alarm surged in her.

"Wha . . . ?"

He put a hand under her arm, helping her sit up. "You fainted," he explained, his voice kind. "Here, drink this." He pressed the rim of a glass to her lips. She realized she was horribly thirsty. She drank deeply. The water was bitter and gritty, bringing a stab of nausea. She tried to think of the man's name. Her head felt thick and stupid.

She felt a dizzying tug on her arm, his hand pulling her up, and then she was standing, the soft carpet of her bedroom between her toes. She could not seem to shake off the grip of sleep. The man—what *was* his name?—seemed to be here to take care of her. But how had that happened? Her head spun. Her knees felt too weak to support her, but his strong hands clutched her under her armpits, held her upright. She saw that he was walking her to her bathroom. Then he veered off toward her window.

This isn't right!

Her legs stumbled along, carrying her toward the window, powerless to resist his strong grip.

Something hard jarred her knees—the windowsill, shocking her to full wakefulness. She heard a scraping sound and then a cool breeze fanned her stomach and she could feel the lace curtains fluttering like butterfly wings around her elbows.

"No," she cried.

The hands leaned her body forward. "I'm sorry, Cynthia, but you saw me."

Panic welled as she felt the window sash scrape the back of her head and shoulders. She saw the street, eighteen stories below. Terror kicked through her. *I'm going to fall!*

Cynthia gasped, her stomach clenching, and grappled for a hold on the sill behind her. The strong hands fought her. Her knuckles scraped the concrete of the sill; she felt a nail break, the pain sparking faintly, as the hands pushed the small of her back and she pitched outward and down.

Wind, battering her face and body. Her hair streaming out behind. The street rushing up, spinning over her head, then swooping under her feet, dizzy, *God, I'll die!*

She screamed, "DADD

10

The phone felt slick in Amy's hand. Her ear tingled from the pressure of the receiver. She relaxed her grip, trying to smooth the tension from her voice. "Can't you clear even one bed?"

"We've been trying," Dr. Royce said. He sounded young, harried. Royce—Amy tried to put a face with the name and couldn't. Staff turnover was getting out of control in ICU.

"We've got eight people in the hall," Amy said. And Eric Kraft wants to close us down, she thought. She felt a surge of anxiety. "What about mambas? Any chance there?" She shut her eyes, appalled. She couldn't believe she'd said that.

The silence stretched. "If you are referring to ICU patients who have no chance of making it—"

"Dr. Royce, I'm sorry. I didn't mean to sound callous. It's certainly not how I feel."

"It's all right," Royce said, but his voice was still cool. "As a matter of fact, we have three terminal patients riding it out on respirators and another one going. Would *you* like to come up and try to persuade their relatives that they aren't going to make it and we should unplug 'em so people in ER can have their beds?"

"No. As I said, I'm sorry."

Dr. Royce blew out a sigh. "Me too. I got a little too hot

there. Fact is, you're right and we both know it. I'll talk to family of the most hopeless cases. Maybe by tonight . . ."

"Thanks." Amy hung up, feeling frustrated. But she would not have Royce's job for anything. How could you look someone in the eye and say it? *I know your father looks like he's sleeping peacefully, fighting the disease, but that's the narcotic in his IV line to keep him from tearing the respirator out in his delirium. His lungs can't recover. We're at capacity on the respirator now. He is dying, period. It might take five days or two weeks, but he will die. So we want his bed for someone else.* Amy winced.

She looked at the clock. Four-thirty. The outer office was quiet, Doris long gone. Time to quit, and for once Amy was glad. There was still plenty of daylight—did she have time for her jog today? The idea sent a chill of foreboding through her. In her mind she saw the garrote, felt the blade's razor touch searing her throat. The house was guarded now, but the man could be watching her, waiting for his chance . . .

Amy felt the fear, cold at her neck, and mustered defiance. She would *not* be intimidated. If she didn't run, she'd fall out of shape and lose the stamina she needed for these long days in ER. Besides, she loved to run, needed it. There were always plenty of people in the park around quitting time—whole packs of joggers she could run with.

But if she ran now, it might make her late for dinner with Chris and Joyce tonight. Reluctantly, Amy decided to skip the run today. If she cabbed home now, she could have an hour with Denise and Ellie before Mother showed up to take over.

Amy felt herself smiling in anticipation. This evening would be just what she needed—and Joyce, too, though Joyce would never admit she needed time off from her nanny duties. Maybe they could go to a place with dancing, watch people doing the mambo instead of the mamba. What should she wear? Her flowered skirt from St. Thomas and that fancy blue blouse Mother had bought for her—make sure Mother saw her wearing it on the way out.

She stood to leave, then hesitated, knowing she was forgetting something . . . Cynthia! Amy felt a twinge of guilt. She'd had every intention of calling today, but then she'd been swept up in the ER crush.

No more excuses.

Amy picked up the phone and dialed, feeling a swell of anxiety in her stomach. Ironic—her feeling of closeness to Cynthia, all the similarities between them, had twisted together into a feeling of danger, as if even a phone call now might bring their lives into some final deadly convergence. Since talking to Cynthia in the morgue, she had lost Winnie a dozen times in her mind. Irrational, but that did not make it go away.

One ring . . . two . . . Amy felt a slim relief. Maybe Cynthia wasn't—

"Yes?" A woman's voice, tight with tension. Not Cynthia—older.

"Hello, this is Dr. St. Clair, calling for Cynthia VanKleeck." Amy heard a sharp intake of breath.

"You! You have a nerve calling here."

Amy blinked, startled and confused. "Who is this, please?"

"I am Mrs. Evelyn VanKleeck, Cynthia's mother." The voice was bitter.

"Is Cynthia there, Mrs. VanKleeck?"

"No," she said in her brittle voice. "My daughter is not here, Dr. St. Clair. My daughter is dead."

Amy's mind lurched with shock, incomprehension.

"First my Owen, and now my Cynthia."

"Mrs. VanKleeck! I . . . I'm so sorry. What happened?"

"Don't you read the papers, Doctor? It was there for the whole city to see. It was even on TV this morning, her lying under that sheet . . ." The woman broke into sobs.

Amy's knees went slack, dumping her into her chair. She felt slightly sick to her stomach. There had to be some mistake. "Mrs. VanKleeck—"

"She jumped, *Doctor* St. Clair. Jumped from her apartment window. In the middle of the night."

Amy closed her eyes, horrified. Distantly, she heard Mrs. VanKleeck sobbing, felt tears rising to her own eyes. Suicide. Dear God. She tried to pull back, steel herself, but the old defense mechanisms faltered. She was like me, Amy thought. We had the same dreams. And now she's dead. Pressing a fist against her forehead, Amy struggled for perspective. All right. You liked Cynthia. It hurts. But you can't let it be more than that.

Amy said,"Is someone there with you now?"

The sobs stopped and Amy heard her swallow. "Don't worry about me, Doctor. I have more spine. Did she think she loved him more than I did? But I'm going to live with this." Her voice was icy. Amy heard the anger and knew exactly how it felt. It was not altogether bad. Mrs. VanKleeck needed it now.

"I could come over—"

"You've done quite enough. Good-bye."

"Mrs. Van—" Amy winced as she heard the phone bang down. She replaced the receiver gently and gazed through her doorway into the outer office. Out in the secretary's office, Doris's hanging basket of ivy swayed gently in the wash from the ventilator duct. From far away, the thump-thump of swinging doors released a muted burst of laughter, as unreal as a laugh track.

Amy groped her desk for a tissue, blotting the unshed tears from her eyes. Suicide. She still could not quite believe it. Why would Cynthia jump? Her mother talked about "spine," but Cynthia VanKleeck *had* spine.

In the middle of the night?

The time of nightmares. Did that have anything to do with it? Amy wondered. She thought of the shape in the woods, the disembodied voice, and felt a slow, prickling fear.

Carney's was warm, hazy and crowded. Looking around as Chris and Joyce caught up on one another, Amy tried to get into the spirit of the place. On any other night, she'd have loved it. Ceiling fans hung from varnished beams, stirring the steamy air. Waitresses in jeans, suspenders, and plaid shirts circled the pine booths along the walls and wove between the center tables with pitchers of beer and huge trays of chili and pizza. The intoxicating, meaty aroma of the chili, with its hint of cinnamon, made Amy's mouth water even though she did not feel hungry. Above her head she could hear the dull beat of music from the dance floor upstairs.

Amy fought off an image of Cynthia's body, smashed on the sidewalk. It still seemed impossible that she was dead—

and so horribly. Had she been drinking or unwittingly taking some other drug that acted as a depressant?

Amy's throat felt suddenly dry. She gulped her beer, waiting for the numbness, the blessed defocusing it would bring. Across the table, Chris and Joyce were laughing and talking, hitting it off as usual. Their friendship pleased and amused Amy: Joyce was so much the serene nanny and Chris the intense pathologist.

Chris looked as if she'd had a rough day in the labs, her hair tousled, her red curls sticking out in frizzy tangles, glasses hanging on at the end of her nose. Even so, a man at the next table was stealing glances at her. Amy was not surprised. There was a magnetic energy in the way Chris moved, an attractiveness in her voice, in her quick laughter, that made men forget she wasn't a classic beauty.

Amy noticed that the man at the next table wasn't the only one stealing glances. Joyce, too, was scanning Carney's discreetly, her gaze lingering that extra beat on the best-looking men. Though she approved, Amy felt a sobering premonition of loss. Joyce would be moving out soon. All the signs had been there lately. How long since Joyce had gone out of the house in anything but those pinned-up braids? Yet here she sat, her hair spilling free in blond-bronze glory around her neck. She'd worked on her eyes, too, just the right touches of mascara and blue shadow. Sitting on the edge of her seat, gazing around, pulling deep breaths . . .

She's ready for life again, Amy thought with wonder. Ready for pain and joy, for risk, for *romance.* Still, it was hard for Amy to imagine home life without Joyce. Who would look after the girls those vital few hours after school? Who would run the household?

Who will I talk to?

Firmly, Amy pushed her anxiety aside. If the old Joyce was really coming back—or rather, the young one—it should be celebrated, not regretted. Amy recalled *that* Joyce—the exuberant high school version. The first time Amy had seen her was when she'd sneaked away to Frenchie's to meet Campy. It was a Saturday night, Amy remembered, and I found Campy sitting in *our* booth with this dazzling blonde. Amy had stood, frozen in the doorway, feeling herself shrink inside. Who was that girl, so cute in her plaid shirt, suspenders, and jeans, ponytail swinging as she laughed at Campy's joke?

Upset, Amy started to back out of Frenchie's—

Then got mad. No way was she going to slink away. She would walk by and say a cool hello and then, right in front of Campy, hit on the nearest good-looking guy.

Before she could move, Campy's buddy Jerry sashayed up to the booth with napkins and a sugar shaker. He slid in beside the blonde and she leaned against him, ruffling his hair. The scene snapped into bright new focus, lifting Amy's heart. In seconds she was at the table being introduced, so thrilled to be wrong that she wanted to hug Joyce. Joyce, who'd prepared herself to meet a snobby deb from Miss Porter's, was delighted at Amy's warmth. Joyce's sweet, open nature was a treat for Amy after the cliques and intrigues at Miss Porter's. That night they had begun a lifelong friendship. They hung out with each other as much as they could despite their different schools. Every summer, Joyce spent a few weeks at the St. Clair's Southampton estate. Even later, when she was swamped by classes and labs at Harvard med, Amy found time to drive to Hartford to see Joyce.

During Amy's first year in med school, Joyce got married—not to Jerry but to Dwight, a handsome fishing guide from New Hampshire. Amy was the maid of honor.

A few years later, Joyce and Dwight moved to Montauk, only hours away from the Hampton estate. After Bud and Amy married, they were a foursome, eating out in the island's weathered seafood places, vacationing together, letting Dwight talk them into rafting down the Colorado river or skiing in Vermont or hiking in the Catskills.

But there was always that part of Dwight you couldn't reach. When his charter business had begun to fail, he had faded with baffling swiftness, rejecting all social overtures. He'd started taking out his frustrations on Joyce, conjuring new ways to hurt her until he'd found the one that cut the deepest— her inability to have children.

Amy could not think about Joyce's shattered marriage without sadness, but there were warm spots in the memories, too. All the nights she and Joyce had spent at the kitchen table, long after Bud and the girls were asleep, growing closer than ever as they struggled to sort out what could not be sorted out. Joyce had been so strong, so determined to handle her misery. Losing her quick laugh, yes, putting on weight, her country-girl prettiness disappearing beneath loose, dark sweaters and slacks. But never giving in to bitterness.

What will I do without you?

No, Amy thought determinedly. Just because Joyce might move out doesn't mean I'll lose her. We've always been friends, and that's the way it will always be. Amy looked at Joyce with affection. Find someone wonderful, she urged silently. Not just a passing romance, but someone who will cherish you, treat you as you deserve.

A nudge at her shoulder startled Amy, and she leaned aside as the waitress served their steaming bowls of chili and a new pitcher of beer. Chris hunched over her bowl, inhaling deeply. When she looked up, her blissful grin and fogged glasses made Amy laugh.

"This is *hot*!" Joyce exclaimed. "Where are the beans?"

"Beans in authentic Texas chili?" Chris turned to Amy. "Where's your friend from, anyway? Minnesota?"

"No. She only looks like it." Amy spooned up a fiery mouthful of chili and washed it down with a swallow of beer, savoring the slide of heat and cold down her throat. Distracted, she wondered if her mother and the girls were all right. Victoria had accepted her explanation that the police were keeping an eye on the house with her usual flinty calm. She had more sense than to bring it up with the girls, but there would be questions later, and Amy wasn't looking forward to them.

Amy felt Joyce's hand briefly on top of hers. "You're hardly eating. What's the matter?"

Amy told them about Cynthia. Chris's face turned grim.

"Suicide," Joyce said softly. "Rough. Especially when it's an old schoolmate."

"I didn't know her that well—not as well as I would have liked."

"Do you buy that she jumped?" Chris said.

Amy considered it. "Actually, I guess I don't. But I have trouble believing that *anyone* could jump."

"When I found out I couldn't have children," Joyce said

softly, "and then Dwight left me, I thought about suicide. Not jumping, just taking some pills and going to sleep."

Amy looked at her, horrified. "I'm glad you didn't."

"Me too. Now I've got two great girls—I mean, they're yours, but I think of them as almost like my own, too." Joyce flushed.

Amy gave her a quick hug. "I wish I could see as much of them as you do. You're terrific for them, but sometimes I feel terrible that I'm not doing more—"

"You mustn't think that way. One of the best things a mother can do is give her daughters an example worth following. Ellie is already talking about being a doctor, you know that. The way you've raised them is why I love them so much . . ." Joyce's voice hitched a little. "Listen to me. All I can say is, Dwight did me a big favor when he divorced me."

"Men," Chris said with a trace of anger.

"Come on, you guys," Amy said. "Men aren't *all* bad."

Chris laughed. "Easy for you to say. You've got two great-looking ones chasing after you."

"What are you talking about?"

"Listen to her, Joyce—playing innocent. Let's just say that my source, a certain cafeteria worker who shall remain nameless, has you and the new surgeon at the hospital, Dr. Otis Camp, meeting as a cozy twosome for morning coffee in the dark and deserted hospital caf."

"That!" Amy said. "That was nothing."

"And then dancing with him at the benefit. I suppose that was nothing, too."

"How is Campy doing?" Joyce asked.

Chris looked surprised. "You know him, Joyce?"

"Sure, I went to high school with him. He's the one who introduced me to Amy. I thought he'd made the catch of a lifetime."

Amy felt herself flushing. "Thanks, but that was a long time ago."

Chris put a hand over her heart, let it thump a few times. Joyce smiled and nodded. Amy tried to act annoyed, but their teasing about Campy and Tom was perversely pleasing.

"Tom Hart's so gorgeous," Chris said. "What's he like? Is he stuck on himself?"

"The opposite, actually," Amy said. "Getting him to talk about himself is like pulling teeth. He always wants to know about you, how you're feeling, what you think of this and that. It gets a little tiresome."

Joyce groaned. "Poor baby."

Chris had sat back and was shaking her head. "Amy, do you realize how many women would kill for a man like that? Most of the guys *I* meet care what *I* think only if it's about them."

"What's Campy like these days?" Joyce asked.

Amy shrugged. "The same in some ways, different in others. I really haven't had much chance to find out."

"He's not as handsome as Tom Hart," Joyce mused. "No one is. But there's something about him. Rugged and strong. It's hard to believe he's missing a foot."

"What?" Chris looked shocked.

"He lost it in Vietnam," Amy said.

"Poor guy," Chris said.

Joyce eyed Amy slyly. "Of course, it doesn't take any feet to make good love."

"Then you've been doing it wrong," Chris said.

Joyce burst out laughing, and Amy was surprised to find herself laughing, too. It felt good, bubbling up from deep inside. She could not believe Joyce had said that. Were they all drinking too much? She looked at the pitcher. Yes. But so what? Suddenly the smoky air of Carney's seemed as rich and golden as nectar. Amy realized she was hungry after all. She ate the rest of her chili and drained another beer while Joyce and Chris chatted. Aware of a sudden silence, she looked up to find both women looking at her.

"The medical examiner owes me a favor," Chris said. "If Cynthia's family was as prominent as you say, they may have done her already. When we're through here, I'll call him if you like."

Amy felt a surge of gratitude. "Please," she said. "That's exactly what I'd like. Can we do it in my office? There's something else I'd like to check."

* * *

After waving down a cab for Joyce, the two doctors went back to the hospital. In her office, Amy pointed Chris to Doris's desk phone and walked into the inner office where she seated herself at her computer terminal. What was the name of that heart-attack fatality Eric Kraft had mentioned at his bombshell of a meeting? She could feel the beer sitting heavy in her stomach, fogging her brain. Jameson—that was it. His chart should still be stored in the mainframe as a hedge against possible legal action. She tapped the name in, and page one of the chart popped up on the screen.

Eric says you were as fit as a fiddle, Amy thought. But let's just take a look at your risk factors. She scrolled to the history and scanned it: Jameson had, indeed, been a healthy-seeming man, not overweight, a nonsmoker, no cardiac medicines. He'd had a recent stress test—with excellent results. No diabetes, hypertension, or heart attack in the history. At two hundred five, Jameson's total cholesterol was borderline high, but that was offset by an excellent HDL fraction.

Amy had a sinking feeling. Mr. Jameson should, in fact, not be dead—not if you went by the odds.

She split the screen and called up VanKleeck's chart, ordering the computer to do a regression analysis of heart-attack risk for both men. The two numbers were startlingly similar: only one man in eight with such a risk profile would be expected to suffer a heart attack. And only a third of those could be expected to die of the attack, further cutting the odds to one in twenty-four.

The odds of *two* such unlikely deaths within weeks in the same modern, well-equipped ER would be much lower still.

Amy felt her mind clearing, the last of the boozy fog evaporating, the room snapping into focus around her. Heart attack was the number-one killer in the country. It happened all the time in ER. There had probably been dozens of heart-attack deaths in Hudson's ER just in the past few weeks. But the overwhelming majority of them would have been people with moderate to high risk factors. Smokers, overweight people, diabetics, people with high cholesterol.

Amy was dimly aware of Chris murmuring into the phone in Doris's office.

Two low-risk men. Were there more? She asked the computer to cull heart-attack deaths in ER during the last three months. Oh, no, too many. She'd have to be a lot more specific. What was she *really* thinking?

It was nuts, but why not try it?

Wiping the screen, she turned to the biographical data in Mr. Jameson's chart. He had been sixty-one years old, six-foot-one, with blue eyes. So had Owen VanKleeck. According to the insurance forms, Mr. Jameson had been a vice-president at New York National, Owen VanKleeck at the Chemical Bank.

And what was *not* in the charts: both men had been rich.

Amy tapped in the restricting information: Men, early sixties, over six feet, blue eyes, bottom quartile for heart-attack risk. As she typed, she was uncomfortably aware of how perfectly her own father would fit this description. Was that why she was doing this? It was ridiculous, actually. No way would she find more heart-attack deaths in such an absurdly restricted field. During such a short time interval there should not have been two to begin with—except by wild coincidence.

She entered the search command. PLEASE WAIT appeared on the screen, then two more names: Robert Levesque and George Christiani. Amy pushed back from the screen, stunned. Not two men but *four,* virtual ringers for each other, dead in the last three months in Hudson General's ER—*her* ER. Dead in one of the most painful ways possible.

Gazing at the screen, Amy realized that she knew the name Christiani. One of the top men at Citicorp, he had also been one of the wealthiest men in the country. She was willing to bet that Levesque was rich, too . . .

Just like Winnie.

She felt a creeping dread in the pit of her stomach. What in God's name was going on here?

A tap on the shoulder made her jump.

"Sorry," Chris said. "You all right?"

"Uh-uh, but go ahead."

Chris gave her a long look. "They'd done the post on Cynthia, all right. The official verdict is suicide. But they *did* find a fair slug of scopolamine in her system."

"Scopolamine? Chris, that's a cerebral sedative. Someone drugged her—"

"Hold on. They also found some Ru-tuss tablets in her apartment."

"The nasal decongestant."

"Right. And as you probably know, one of the active ingredients of Ru-tuss is scopolamine."

"Were the other ingredients also in Cynthia's system?"

"Yup."

"That blows that theory. But wait—what better way to mask that you gave someone a hit of scopolamine? Did they check the prescription, make sure Cynthia is the one who had it filled?"

Chris looked at her. "They couldn't. The tablets were physician samples. She could have got them from any doctor—or some friend whose doctor likes to pass out samples."

"I don't like that. It's too neat."

"Only if you're already suspicious. Sometimes things are just the way they look. Maybe Cynthia knew that four or five or ten tablets would make her dopey. Maybe she took them to help her do the awful deed. You must have seen it enough times in ER. People who want to kill themselves scarfing down everything in the medicine cabinet, then cutting their wrists or jumping just to make sure. You've got to admit it's logical. And when the ME hears hoofbeats, he doesn't look for zebras."

"Maybe he should. Maybe he's in Africa and doesn't know it."

Chris gave a humorless laugh.

Scopolamine, Amy thought, chilled. A prescription drug, which meant it was harder to get hold of. And it was not the sort of drug people thought of giving to themselves. Cynthia, was someone else there with you? Were you *pushed?*

"Another thing," Chris said. "Antihistamines and decongestants can have funny effects. In some people they can aggravate preexisting depression. If anyone had a reason to be depressed, Cynthia did. Maybe she didn't plan to jump. Maybe she popped a few tablets, crossed the line between depressed and suicidal, and jumped out her window."

"Did they find any partially dissolved tablets in her stomach?"

Chris blinked. "No. Good point."

"Right. If the tablets had dissolved, she waited a good

while after taking them. Which meant she'd be too dopey to get
to the window."

"Not necessarily. She might have been able to crawl."

"Maybe. Or maybe someone who wanted to cover up the
fact that they'd given her a big hit of scop ground up the Ru-tuss
in water and got her to drink it after she was already out of it."

"Fine, but you're probably talking injection now, and they
didn't find any needle tracks on her body."

"I just don't think Cynthia would kill herself."

Chris shrugged. "You'd know that better than I." She
peered at the computer screen. "What have you got there?"

"I'm not sure. It's not logical and it's not likely. But it
happened anyway." Amy felt a chill touch on her throat and
realized it was her own hand, the fingertips as cold as ice.
"Chris, forget logic—at least, *our* logic. I have a feeling this all
makes very twisted sense to someone. I don't know who, or
even if he really exists. But if he does, he's a murderer—and the
four dead men on that computer screen may be only the most
obvious ones."

11

Amy stared at the computer with dread fascination. From the couch behind her, she could hear Chris's breathing loosening into sleep. It made her aware of her own weariness, the gritty, bloodshot feeling in her eyes. Time to go home—

No, just a little longer.

Tapping keys, Amy ordered the computer to list cardiac cases from January through the present. The screen scrolled up rapidly with the names of patients. During the same period that the four bank CEOs had died, one hundred eleven other people had been brought to ER with chest pains. She told the computer to list deaths. Twenty of the one hundred eleven had died too, including DOAs—less than one out of five. Amy was satisfied with that number. Hudson was saving more than its share.

She ordered a trend analysis by age on the twenty deaths. The victims ranged in age from forty-five to seventy-one. Two were sixty-five, two were eighty, and three of them had been sixty-seven—two men and a woman. Of the three, one man had been diabetic but the other hadn't. No trend there. All right, try height: a number of pairings among the twenty had been the same height, but pairs were too small to be called a trend. Four of the men had been five feet eleven. But there were no other similarities between them. Amy tried occupation: the only group with more than three was cabdrivers, at four deaths. Again, one was a woman. One of the male cabbies was six-four and obese. No trend. There were no subgroups within the twenty deaths that came close to the four bankers for similarity. All right, what about risk factors? Amy's fingers slipped on the keys. She rubbed her fingertips on her coat, removing the film of nervous sweat. She tapped in the command: *list: RF.* She scanned down the list of numbers. The risk factor for each of the twenty dead was either intermediate or high, just what you'd expect. Not only was there no other subgroup with low risk factors, there wasn't a single death. Not one.

The four bankers should not have died, Amy thought.

And why were they so alike in other ways?

She tried desperately to think of some innocent explanation for the four deaths—something besides murder. How about something that had happened in cardiac bay—some accident? The staff making some ingrained mistake; a batch of contaminated lidocaine; some other thing in the bay environment.

No. Anything like that would raise the overall death rate. In the same room where the four bankers had died, four out of five of the other heart-attack victims—most of them less healthy than the bankers—had been saved.

No matter how she analyzed it, she kept coming back to the same ugly possibility: someone had murdered those four men. Amy shuddered.

So what should she do?

She'd have no trouble interesting a biostatistician in these numbers. The police were another matter. Showing the police these numbers would be like handing a TV reporter sonar tracings of the Loch Ness monster—*Sure, Doc. So where are the photos?* Before the police would believe anyone had been murdered, they'd want physical evidence. A bullet hole, ligature marks on the neck . . .

An autopsy report showing a heart toxin.

Amy groaned and heard Chris stir behind her. I have to talk to Mrs. VanKleeck again, Amy thought. I have to ask a woman who is furious with me to let us cut up her husband.

Amy felt her weariness growing, her body turning heavy, dragging at her brain. On the blue ocean of screen, the numbers blurred into frothy whitecaps. She patted her cheeks and, when that didn't work, clenched her fists until her nails dug into her palms. Caffeine—that's what she needed. She leaned back in her chair to check the coffeemaker in Doris's office. Empty—not even any cold dregs. Which left the machines in the visitors' lounge off the main hallway.

Amy checked on Chris. She was sprawled all over the couch, sound asleep with her mouth open. Amy walked softly past her. The narrow office corridor was empty. Passing the blood bank, she stopped, struck by a vague sense of something being wrong. The lights were out. Backing up to the door, she stared at the frosted glass. Without its usual pearly glow it looked gray and dead. She tried the handle. Locked. That, at least, was as it should be at this time of night.

Amy unlocked the door and eased it open, feeling for the switch. The fluorescents flickered to life, revealing a row of small tables, each with a chair beside it, still set up from yesterday's blood drive. The counter along the wall held a couple of racks of ten-cc tubes and stacks of blood donor information forms. Everything in order—

Except the ID file. One drawer stood open.

Amy stared at it, feeling uneasy. That was the file with the coded information sheets that linked each numbered unit of blood back to its donor. It should be locked.

Amy swung the door all the way back so she could see the blood bank's walk-in cooler. The big, gleaming door looked closed, but from here she could not tell for sure.

She hesitated in the doorway, her uneasiness deepening. Should she close the file, check the cooler door? But what if the man with the knife had slipped in past security again?

Even if he got past hospital security, he'd have no reason to lie in wait for her here. Besides, the door to the blood bank had been locked.

Amy entered the blood bank and stuck her head through the inner door into the lab beyond. There was no sign of the night tech. Maybe the tech was in the cooler. From here she could see that the door was ajar an inch. Walking over, she pulled it open. The man in the ski mask turned toward her. She gasped, her insides freezing with fright. He was dressed in green surgeon's scrubs, the top tucked in, his hands as pale and smooth as wax in their rubber gloves. Neither hand gripped a knife, thank God; one held a blue donor sheet from the opened file. The other cradled a test tube of blood. Two racks of code-numbered tubes lined the shelf beside him, blood waiting to be screened; she could see the empty slot in one of them.

Amy shouted for the lab tech.

The man in the mask slipped the tube of blood down the neck of his scrubs and lunged at her. She screamed, wheeling backward, feeling his hand close around her wrist. She pounded him with her other fist, kicking out in wild panic. He whirled her around, clamping an arm across her throat and yanking her back against him. In the frigid air, a plume of his breath streamed past her face. She kicked backward with her heels, trying for his shins, and heard him grunt. He tightened his arm across her neck, choking off her air. She fought desperately, trying to twist away, but he was too strong. Her vision reddened, pinwheeling at the edges. She clawed at his arm, straining to breathe, forgetting everything else. Smoke seemed to swirl into her eyes, she was *passing out!* Desperate, she slammed an elbow into his gut, connecting with the test tube, feeling the fiery stab of shattered glass all the way to the bone. He gasped and jerked at her neck, increasing the pressure. Her body seemed to stretch out, the cold floor soft under her feet. She felt her knees buckle. Her vision slipped away and she . . .

drifted . . .

Pain in her throat.

Her lungs tore the air in, huge flaming gulps that racked her with coughing. She felt a sharp prickle in her eyes and then she could see again, a woman's leg flashing in front of her face. Chris, kicking at the man in the ski mask!

Amy lurched up, grabbing the man from behind, clinging as Chris yelled and pounded at his shoulders. Amy felt the heel of the man's palm butt her forehead. She sat down, stunned. The man tore free of Chris and ran from the cooler.

Chris started to go after him.

"No!" Amy shouted. It came out as a strangled gasp. Chris stopped, turning back to her.

"Get me . . . out!"

Chris pulled her up, helping her from the chill maw of the

cooler. Outside, Amy collapsed to her knees, dimly aware of Chris slamming the big cooler door behind her.

The night tech ran in from the lab and stopped, staring popeyed at them.

"Where the hell have *you* been?" Chris shouted.

"Up on maternity, drawing blood," the tech stammered.

"Call security, then ER, get them back here stat. Then call the police."

The tech nodded and ran out.

Chris turned back to her. Amy struggled to stand. Chris put a hand on her shoulder, forcing her back down. "Just take it easy."

"I'm all right," Amy croaked.

Chris gave a shaky laugh. "The hell you are."

Amy grabbed Chris's hands and clung. A terrible coldness swept her. She could feel herself trembling, quaking, losing it. With desperate strength she clung to control. I'm all right. He could have snapped my neck, but he didn't.

"The ID file," Amy whispered, pointing. "He was after someone's blood." When she tried again to push up from the floor, she felt a sharp pain in her elbow as her arm straightened. She stood and probed the spot, pulling out the nubbed end of a shard of glass.

"He didn't get it," Amy whispered. "I smashed the tube."

Chris nodded. "That explains the blood on his chest. But what would anyone want with ten cc's of blood?"

"I don't know. I don't know." Amy saw that Chris's hand was clenched around a scrap of paper. "What's that?"

"What?" Chris looked down, opening her fist, letting the torn scrap of paper flutter to the floor, then bending to snatch it up again. "I must have grabbed it in the fight and it tore."

"It's part of an ID sheet. Can you tell whose?"

Chris smoothed the fragment of paper and stared at it. "Just a second—yes, I got the top. Here it is . . ." Chris's face went chalky under the fluorescents. She looked up slowly, and Amy had a shuddering instant of premonition.

"Whose blood was he trying to steal?" Amy whispered.

"Your father's," Chris said.

12

But it makes no sense," Winnie said. "Why would someone want my blood?"

Amy gazed at him, trying to keep the fear from her face. He sat at his grand gold and ebony desk, the city spread out behind him, and all she could see was Owen VanKleeck dead on the gurney. Her stomach clenched with foreboding. She said, "Maybe he *didn't* want your blood. Maybe he wanted to *tamper* with it, frighten you."

Winnie was looking closely at her. She realized she was touching her throat, and dropped her hand at once. The mandarin collar hid the ugly bruise, and aspirin was taking care of the sore throat, but nothing could cover the rasp in her voice. Winnie seemed to have accepted that she had laryngitis, but if she wasn't careful, he'd guess the truth. If he realized she had been roughed up, he wouldn't hear another thing she said about his own danger.

Walking away from his probing gaze, she took a seat at the far end of his long conference table. Movement caught her eye at the panoramic window beside her, a pigeon strutting on the ledge, one iridescent shoulder brushing the glass. Across Park Avenue, the upper stories of the Philip Morris Building glowed in the morning sun. A beautiful Saturday morning, making last night seem like an aberration. But it wasn't. It was part of a growing pattern she needed to decipher but could not.

Winnie said, "All right, suppose he puts something in my blood and the lab calls me. I'd just go in for more tests and the truth would come out." His voice had that soothing sound she remembered from childhood.

She controlled her impatience. "Dad, imagine yourself getting that call. Suppose he'd put HIV antibodies in your blood. AIDS is a virtual death sentence. Hearing that you have the antibodies is a terrible shock, believe me."

Winnie's gaze lost focus, moving slightly past her. He cleared his throat softly, the way he did when he was nervous, and she knew she'd gotten through to him.

"How long since you've had a physical?" she asked.

"A few months. I see that all of my staff gets one every year, so I can hardly beg off myself. Waste of time. I'm perfectly healthy. Not an ounce of fat on me——"

"Do you happen to remember your cholesterol level?"

"Just a minute." He got up and walked out, returning a moment later with his medical file. Amy scanned the blood workup. Winnie's cholesterol was two hundred thirty with an HDL of forty-seven. She felt an odd relief. The total was too high, but it wasn't awful. Just bad enough to bump his risk factors up a notch.

"Pretty good, huh?" Winnie said.

"Not really."

"Then why do you look so pleased?"

"Because this workup makes you different from the four men who have died of cardiac arrest in my ER in the past three months. In other ways, each of them could have been your twin brother——but they all had excellent cholesterol and low risk factors for heart attack."

"What are you saying? You think someone might have murdered them?"

"Yes, I do."

Winnie said, "Did any of them give blood before their deaths?"

"Not at Hudson General."

"Then I don't see any connection. Unless you think this

guy wanted to scare me into a heart attack, which seems pretty farfetched. If someone wants to kill me, there are more direct— and foolproof—ways."

"If he's sane, yes—"

Amy looked at the cholesterol levels again. "You *do* have to do something about these. Your own doctor should have told you." Amy made some diet and exercise suggestions. Her father nodded, writing them down, and she felt a little better. Winnie was a very disciplined man; if he tackled the problem, he'd improve, she had no doubt.

If someone didn't kill him first.

She felt her jaw clenching. She was not going to let that happen. "How's security at the estate these days?" she asked.

"Same as always."

"I would bring more people in. Here at the bank, too. Be very careful about letting any stranger close to you. And tell the cook to be sure no one—"

"Amy, *Amy.*" He held up both hands.

"I'm serious, Dad." She felt a lump forming in her throat. "I don't want to lose you."

He got up and came around the desk to her, and put a hand on her shoulder. She stood and hugged him, feeling the familiar fuzzy comfort of tweed against her cheek. He patted her back. "Promise me you'll be careful—and don't say it if you don't mean it."

"I will be careful," he said. He held her away at arm's length, giving her a sober look. "And you must be careful, too. Whatever the man wanted in your blood bank, you took a risk confronting him. If he hadn't run . . . if he'd attacked you, hurt you—"

"I'm fine."

Winnie gave her another long look. "You look fine. But you're tired, I can tell. You don't get away enough. Now might be a good time."

For a moment, Amy was tempted. If she made it a condition, Winnie would probably come with her. The girls were still in school, but they could stay with Joyce or her mother.

It would get Winnie away from this, she thought. And me.

And then she saw that it wouldn't. If someone was out to

kill them, a little distance wouldn't stop him. She felt a stab of fear, and fiercely suppressed it. I won't run, she thought. Whoever you are. I'm going to fight you.

"Let me fly you down to our Palm Beach place," Winnie said.

"Maybe later," she said, "when I'm over my laryngitis."

Amy cabbed to Hudson General, hurrying in the back way to her office. Doris never worked on Saturdays, so she had the place to herself. She locked the outer office door and checked her clock—ten minutes until lunch with Campy. She hoped he wouldn't be early.

If she had her way, they would put off lunch anyway.

Sitting at her desk, Amy dialed the VanKleeck estate. Mrs. VanKleeck's secretary insisted on taking a message. Amy insisted harder on talking to Mrs. VanKleeck.

After a wait, a cold voice spoke into the phone. "Make this short, Doctor. I bury my husband in four hours."

"I know, Mrs. VanKleeck, and I'm very sorry, but that's why I need to talk to you right now. Earlier I asked your daughter about a possible autopsy on your husband—"

"Out of the question. Perhaps you didn't hear me. The funeral is today. My husband has been . . . the funeral home has already . . ."

The misery in the other woman's voice triggered a sympathetic pain in Amy's bruised throat. "I know what you're saying, Mrs. VanKleeck, but a lot can still be determined. We'd need only a short time. It could be done right there in the funeral home. The body wouldn't be disturbed for viewing, and the funeral could proceed on schedule."

Silence on the line. "Why do you want to put me through this? Are you saying it wasn't a heart attack?"

"No. But I have trouble understanding why a man in such good health should have a heart attack. That bothers me, Mrs. VanKleeck." *And your husband might have been murdered. That bothers me even more.*

"I'm afraid you're going to go on being bothered, Doctor. You said it yourself—my husband shouldn't have died. You're lucky I don't sue you and Hudson General for all you're worth, close down your miserable excuse for an emergency department. Now, if that is all?"

Amy felt the blood rushing to her face. With an effort, she controlled herself. "Mrs. VanKleeck, I know you are upset. Forgive me for disturbing you at such an awful time. My staff and I did all we could for your husband. I'm sorry it wasn't enough. But we can at least—"

Mrs. VanKleeck hung up on her.

Amy replaced the receiver with forced gentleness. She could feel her hands shaking, the small muscles in her arms jumping. "Damn!"

Someone knocked on her door.

She got up and opened it. Campy, looking good in wool slacks and a fisherman's sweater. He gave her a close look. "Troubles?"

"Always. That's why they call it 'emergency.' "

Campy raised an eyebrow. "Do you have a cold?"

"Maybe a little one." Amy felt a brief pain in her throat— not from the bruise, but from a feeling of loss that she could not do what she once would have done—pour out the whole story of how she was mugged in the blood bank last night and revel in his sympathy. She had not even done that with Tom, so she could not now with Campy. How odd that she would want to, after all these years. Clearly, something in her felt like she still knew him well, but it was only a feeling—quite possibly false.

"You need to sit down at a table," he said, "eat carbohydrates, and let me tell you how terrific you are."

"Sounds good, except for the carbohydrates. I'm not very hungry, I'm afraid."

"How about a walk in the park, then? It's beautiful out today. We could grab a hot dog."

"Fine." Still boiling with frustration, she knew she did not appear as calm as she wanted. She had to have that autopsy, and Mrs. VanKleeck wouldn't give it to her. She didn't want to go to lunch, she wanted a court order, but it was too late, and if she couldn't convince Winnie he was in danger, how could she hope to convince a judge that a heart attack might be murder?

"Come on," Campy said gently, holding out his hand. She

took it, letting him pull her up, feeling the weight and strength in his arm. He held on for just a second and she let him, the desk safely between them, feeling a little charge of him tingling up her arm.

On the other hand, she thought, maybe a walk in the park with Campy is just what I need.

The cab left them off at the Sixth Avenue entrance to the park. Stepping out eagerly, she lifted her face to the breeze, inhaling the familiar park smells of moist earth and greenery. It made her want to jog. Maybe later, she'd change and come back here and run for all she was worth. It wouldn't get Mr. VanKleeck autopsied, but it would blow off some of the frustration.

Campy stopped at a vendor's cart, then passed along a steaming hot dog wrapped in greasy paper. She held it uncertainly, still not hungry.

The sudden clatter of hooves behind her, startled Amy. Whirling, she saw a mounted policeman bearing down on her, the horse's white-rimmed eyes glaring, and the old panic sprang up inside her. She scrambled, terrified, across the sidewalk, tripping and sprawling into a bush. The hoofbeats thundered past and diminished, and her panic subsided. She got to her feet, mortified, as Campy hurried up, his face creased with concern.

"Are you all right?"

"I feel stupid. Otherwise, yes." Her face burned. "Stupid horse—why did he run at me like that?"

Campy looked a little uncomfortable. "Run at you? Uh, I think somebody snatched a purse over there. But the horse was actually quite a ways from you."

Amy shuddered. "I hate those ugly brutes."

He looked perplexed. "You used to love horses."

"Can we drop it?"

"Of course."

Still embarrassed, Amy led the way into the park. As they passed the statue of José Martí, she avoided looking at the bronze horse, high on its pedestal. Campy's sidelong glance told her he was still wondering what had happened, and she flushed again. Deeper in the park, she sneaked some slow, deep breaths, willing herself to forget the horse and relax. The

park glowed like an Impressionist painting, the sunlight tapping a pointillist dance through the brilliant young leaves of the
oaks and maples. Everything was green. She could smell the
nip of newly mown grass. All around her, people in shorts and
jeans ate from picnic baskets or sat on benches and rocks,
turning blissful, lidded eyes to the sun. Here and there in shel-
tered places, vagrants sprawled in the grass, brown bags hiding
the proof. Everyone seemed at peace with each other, mistrust
forgotten in the intoxicating promise of summer.

"I should explain, I guess," she said.

"Not if you don't want to."

Amy nodded.

"Shall I go back and get you another hot dog?"

She looked at her empty hand, mystified. "What happened to mine?"

"You threw it at the horse," he said in a carefully neutral
voice.

"What happened to *your* hot dog?"

"I threw it at the horse, too," Campy said. "I figured you
knew what you were doing."

She laughed.

"On the other hand," Campy said, "if you want to tell me,
I'd like to hear it."

She stopped, looking across the low fence at the broad,
sunny expanse of the Sheep Meadow. The meadow could have
been the field behind the family estate. She remembered every
moment of that day almost twenty years ago, and felt the old
ache of sadness, which she knew would never entirely leave
her as long as she lived.

"It has to do with Philip," she said.

"I was going to ask you about him. What's he up to these
days?"

Amy looked at Campy, realizing from his easy tone that he
didn't know. No reason he should, unless he'd happened to see
Philip in ER. She envied him his lack of knowledge. For Campy,
Philip was still her brilliant older brother whom he'd met so
long ago.

"Philip is . . . not as you remember him," Amy said.

Campy turned, his face growing serious at the tone of her
voice. "Tell me."

13

Let's find a place to sit," Amy said. Campy pointed at a bench by the Sheep Meadow—and too near the bridle path. She led the way back through some trees toward the statue of Robert Burns, finding some smooth boulders still in view of the meadow. The stone felt cool as she sat; billowy cumulus clouds had rolled in from nowhere, hiding the sun and turning the breeze damp against her face. Not like the day, so indecently bright, when the first Philip had died.

Amy closed her eyes, unsure that she wanted to talk about it. Putting it into words always brought back shadows of the old pain. As if he sensed her reluctance, Campy kept a sociable silence, gazing out at the park.

"I was eighteen," she said. "It was the summer after I had graduated from Miss Porter's. You were in Vietnam, but still writing to me. It was July eighteenth. I remember everything about that day, even what I was doing before Philip came in. I was up in Mother's powder room, making sure I looked all right for a picture I was going to send to you . . ."

In her memory, Amy gazed again into Mother's huge, gold-edged mirror, trying to get the look she wanted Campy to see—alluring but not seductive. July heat poured in through the bathroom window. She could hear a bee humming at the screen. Outside and below, Philip was still batting a tennis ball against the south wing—*thok-whump, thok-whump, thok-whump*—no doubt seeing how close he could come to the windows without hitting them. It felt strange but nice to have him around. Usually he hung out with his girlfriend on weekends, but his current one, Lorianne LeMay, was in Martha's Vineyard with some of her sorority sisters.

Amy adjusted the smile in the mirror, trying for Lorianne's college-woman look, but all she could see were her own non-matching eyes. Maybe she should turn her head to the side, give Campy just the green one . . .

The face in the mirror gave her a shifty, sidelong glance. Amy gave up in despair. Trying to plan a picture of herself was utterly tedious when what she really wanted was a picture of Campy. Him with a buddy or two, some buildings in the background for context. If she could just see him, even in a picture, she'd know he was all right. His letters were all cheerful, but there were little clues that he was changing. She remembered a passage from his most recent letter: "Went to the PX today. Got the new Peter, Paul and Mary tape. Listened to it later, wishing for just one look at your face." The short, compressed sentences made her uneasy. Where had the "I's" gone? Was he losing himself over there?

Amy shivered despite the heat. Campy, where are you right now? Are you all right?

The face in the mirror suddenly looked too pale. Amy rubbed some of her mother's blush into her cheeks and stood back. Better. Putting the blush back, she took care to leave it exactly as she'd found it. Her mother didn't like her to use her things.

"Hey, Sis."

Amy jumped and whirled. Philip, lounging in the doorway of her bathroom, twirling his tennis racket. One pocket of his shorts bulged with the ball. His thick, dark hair tumbled around his sweatband.

"You scared me!" she accused, her heart pounding.

"Sorry." He gave her a wry look, showing he meant it. "Ready for me to take your picture?"

"I guess."

"What's wrong?"

"I don't even know if Campy will get it."

"Why wouldn't he?"

"I don't know. What if he . . ." Amy trailed off, miserable.

"Amy, listen to me," Philip said firmly. "Campy will be fine. Vietnam isn't what you imagine. I talked to Stan Litchfield—you remember, he went right from the Point to Vietnam. He says the closest most guys over there ever get to combat is the sound of mortars miles away. Don't let the evening news upset you with all those bloody shots of combat and the ghoulish body counts."

Amy nodded. "I'm sure you're right. And thanks for not telling me I ought to forget Campy and date around this fall. Mother never stops."

"She just doesn't want you to be unhappy."

"You think so?" Amy said doubtfully. "I thought she just wanted me to date someone of 'our own kind.' " Amy imitated her mother's cool patrician voice.

Philip rolled his eyes sympathetically. "That, too. But don't listen to her. Campy's got guts. I should defy the old man and get myself over to Vietnam too. As soon as my 2-S is up, that's exactly what I'm going to do."

Amy looked at him, horrified. "Philip, no! You should go on to graduate school—"

"So I can do what? Teach Elizabethan lit to dozing sophomores? Meanwhile, the sons of poor men, like Campy, slog through the jungles for me and 'our kind,' taking all the risks."

"Oh, Philip, stop being so noble. What good will it do anyone if you go off and get killed in this hopelessly stupid war? You don't know how much like Campy you sound. What about your obligation to the people who need you and love you? All you guys think about is yourselves."

Philip looked annoyed. He started to say something, then closed his eyes for a second. "If you think I *want* to go crawling through the jungle in Southeast Asia, you're wrong. But I want it more than I want to skulk through life feeling like a rich parasite. If you call that thinking of myself, I can't argue. Anyway, you know one reason you love Campy is that he carries his share of the load. If he stopped doing that, if he ducked Vietnam because you asked him to, what would you gain? You wouldn't have to worry about him getting shot. He'd be here, with you. What would you lose? A part of Campy that you admired. The man you saved would no longer quite be the man you loved."

Amy said nothing. But worrying about Campy was already almost more than she could bear. If Philip went too . . .

"Look, I'm sorry," he said. "I didn't mean to depress you. I've got two years of college left. Maybe the war will be over by then."

"Somehow I doubt it."

"Come on," he said penitently, "we have to cheer you up. Let's *do* something—shake off the blues."

"Like what?" She tried to sound grumpy even as she felt her dark mood lift a little. "There's nothing to do around here."

He gave her a wicked smile. "Perihelion."

Her enthusiasm died. "Winnie said we're not to ride him."

"No," Philip said. "He said *I* wasn't to ride him. He never said anything about you."

"That's because he knows I'd never dare. Philip, that horse is out of our league. He came in second at the Derby. He's way too fast, and you have to know how to ride him."

"The Derby is ancient history. Perihelion's retired. And how will we know how to ride him if we never try it?"

"Winnie will be mad if he finds out."

"Winnie," Philip said. "What's he going to do, cut off our allowances? I know it hasn't sunk in yet, but you're a college woman now, not his little girl. Besides, how's he going to find out?"

"The grooms—"

"Old Jacob's the only one down there today. I'll bet you twenty bucks Winston never told him I couldn't ride Perihelion." Philip drew out "Winston," saying the name as if it were a joke. Amy wished he wouldn't do that; she couldn't fathom why he did.

"So how about it?" Philip asked.

Amy hesitated, torn. She didn't like to defy Winnie. But Philip had never asked her to go riding before. He and his friends played polo out in the west meadow and he'd ask her along to watch. But this was something more. She wouldn't get too many chances like this.

Excitement surged through her. *Perihelion!*

"All right," she said.

"Good girl!"

"Woman," Amy corrected with a grin.

"Right you are." He gave her shoulder a squeeze. "Let's go."

Right then, she would have followed him anywhere.

Amy rode Ike through the meadow behind Philip and Perihelion. The wind whipped her face, streaming her hair out behind. She could feel Ike's muscles bunching under the saddle. Philip was at least three lengths ahead, and the gap was widening. Amy began to feel anxious. He'd promised he wouldn't go full out, but Perihelion seemed to have ideas of his own. Or maybe Philip just wanted to show off for her. Amy was flattered, but still nervous for him.

"Philip!" she yelled.

He gave no sign of hearing, pulling farther away. His shoulders were hunched now, and she could tell he was tensing up, starting to get a little nervous himself. The brown flanks of the racehorse rippled beneath him in the sunlight, muscles cording up. Amy realized with alarm that Philip was heading into the tall grass along the west end of the field. He must have lost control of Perihelion—the ground under that grass was uneven and rough, no place for a galloping horse—

Perihelion stumbled.

Amy's heart leapt into her throat. Time seemed to slow: the horse's head plunged down, Philip flew from the saddle, soaring forward over Perihelion's neck, suspended in the air ahead of the horse as Perihelion rolled onto his shoulder, hind hooves kicking in the air, then crashed down with a whinny of fright. An instant later Philip smashed to the ground headfirst, one leg kicking in the air, then flopping down as he crumpled into the tall grass.

"Philip!" Amy screamed. Sick with dread, she spurred Ike forward. When she got to Philip, he lay on his side, very still. His eyes were closed, his face bleached white under the short bill of his riding helmet. She dismounted, knelt down, and

grabbed his shoulder to shake it, crying his name over and over. His head lolled.

Oh God! Panic welled up in her, lapping at her vision, filling her chest so that she could barely breathe. What was she going to do? She sprang up and looked around the field, frantic, but no one was there, no, of course they weren't. A hundred yards away, Perihelion pranced and whinnied. Amy felt a spasm of hatred for the horse, swallowed up at once in her fear. She knelt again, trying to rouse Philip. He lay still and unresponsive, his mouth open, barely breathing. Her dread deepened. He was hurt bad. *No, please. He'll wake up, he has to.*

Maybe she could get him on her horse. Amy looked for Ike, but he had run away across the field too, spooked by her fear.

Besides, what if Philip's neck was broken? You weren't supposed to move people with broken necks—or even if other bones were broken.

She must get help. The house was just on the other side of those woods, less than half a mile if she ran straight through. By the time she could catch Ike and ride back around, running would probably be just as fast.

Amy closed her eyes, fighting the urge to scream and sob. "I'll be back," she said to Philip. As she plunged between the trees, she slowed in the sudden dimness, barely able to see the narrow footpath. She tried to look ahead for roots, but the ground swam on her eyes, dark and featureless. Branches slapped at her face, stinging her eyes. She stepped on a rock, twisting her ankle, and cried out in pain, but pressed on. The air was heavy with mildew and the stench of rotting leaves. Her fear sharpened, taking on a new cast. Damn these woods—she hated them. Why hadn't Winnie had them cleared out as he'd said for years he wanted?

"Is something wrong?" Campy said.

Amy blinked, feeling a wrenching sense of dislocation as her eyes focused on the present again—Central Park, the Sheep Meadow. Campy was looking at her with concern. The woods, she thought. I always hated the woods. And now they're in my nightmare!

"Amy?" Campy's voice was more insistent now.

"Sorry." She let out her breath. Her heart was pounding. "Where was I?"

"You said you ran through the woods to your house," Campy prompted.

"Yes. Mother was with her garden club. I ran in and fell over the tea table, scattering dishes everywhere. It was another minute before she and the other ladies could calm down enough to listen to me. Then Mother called an ambulance. It followed the horse trail back to Philip. They got him to the local hospital, but couldn't rouse him. They had a medevac chopper, so they flew him in and landed him on the roof of Hudson. Philip almost died in the emergency room of Hudson General. He had a contrecoup concussion and a heavy fluid buildup pressing on his brain stem. He stopped breathing. They got a team working on him and saved him. They wouldn't let me close, but I watched from a distance. After they got him stabilized, they transferred Philip to the intensive care unit. He stayed in a deep coma for nine days. Winnie brought in the finest specialists in the city. On the tenth day, Philip started coming to. We were overjoyed. Then, as the days passed, we realized he . . . wasn't right. Finally the doctors made it official—serious hearing loss and permanent, severe brain damage."

"It must have been terrible for all of you," Campy murmured.

"For us? For *Philip*. During the week, we lived at the Park Avenue apartment. I went in to Hudson every morning and hung around there as much as they'd let me. Six weeks. Even though he was awake, he was very passive. He didn't want to do the physical therapy or the speech exercises—it was torture for him. But I could usually coax him into it. He didn't want to eat, either, so I fed him. The rough part for me was that I kept wanting to bawl, and I knew for his sake I shouldn't. So I smiled and laughed, and Winnie came in and told him jokes. Mother would hold him for hours, telling him what was going on with the summer crowd in the Hamptons, stuff like that. When Mother or Winnie was there, it wasn't bad for me. But sometimes when I was alone with him, and he was trying to say something to me, laboring for simple words, I'd have to excuse myself, run out in the hall, cry my eyes out, then come back in and say, very brightly, 'Now what were you saying?' " Amy stopped, her voice raw—partly from the bruise and partly from talking.

Campy sat on the boulder, his knees drawn up within his arms, gazing at the ground. There was something pained and self-protective in the posture; Amy saw that he was feeling all this more deeply than she'd realized.

"I always liked Philip, admired him, really," he said. "I remember that dinner at your place at Easter, when your mother kept treating me like I'd stepped on something on the way in. Your father was being nice enough in a detached, faintly amused way, but it was Philip who treated me like a brother. He made me feel I might belong at that wonderful long table with the linen and silver. I never forgot that."

Amy was touched by the pain in Campy's voice. He'd held a place open in his heart for Philip all these years. Maybe he could still take Philip into it. She touched his hand. "There's a good chance Philip would remember you," she said softly. "And if he does, I know he'd be pleased to see you. He's working in ER, now. He has made tremendous strides in the past year and a half, since Tom Hart has been treating him. Before Tom, no one seemed able to do a thing for Philip. He could barely speak, never smiled, never did much of anything. His life was over. Now he's tremendously improved. He'll only go so far, but it's been wonderful to see."

"Tom Hart did that for him?"

"Yes."

"You must be very grateful to him."

"I am." Campy had sounded entirely sincere, but Amy felt suddenly uncomfortable. Had he meant, in one sentence, to so neatly touch the center of her dilemma with Tom? Philip aside, Tom Hart was a very sexy and exciting man. The trouble was, whenever she tried to decide exactly what she felt for Tom, she could never seem to put Philip—and gratitude—aside.

Campy looked at her. "When I . . . left, you were thinking about being an art history major. When I finally got back to New York and checked the phone book for you, I was surprised to find the M.D. after your name. But I guess now I know why."

"Actually," she said, "I always sort of liked the science

classes. I never told you, but I was president of the science club at Miss Porter's. The sort of thing you'd rather die than admit to the boys."

Campy grinned. "What are you talking about? You never acted dumb for anyone in your life."

"Uh, Campy, I hate to tell you this, but when you thought I was acting smart, I was actually playing dumb for you."

Campy tilted slowly, falling off the rock and curling into the fetal position. She laughed, and he clambered up, brushing himself off. She felt an unexpected delight at his silliness. How many forty-year-old men still had the psychic freedom to take a pratfall like that? Amazing that Vietnam had not crushed every ounce of the child from him. He gazed at her; it made her a little uncomfortable. In high school, she thought, we could look into each other's eyes for half an hour and it felt like the most natural thing in the world. Will I ever have that with anyone again?

All at once, something he'd said earlier registered. "You looked me up in the phone book?"

He nodded.

"What if I'd taken Bud's name—Thurman—when we married?"

"A fair number of women around that time were keeping their own names. You were the type. I figured I might as well take a shot at it." Campy shook his head wonderingly. "So you always harbored a secret love of science. What was med school like for you? I'll bet you finished at the head of your class."

"I worked my tail off."

Amy realized suddenly what was happening. From the moment they'd left the hospital, the focus had been on her. She'd done ninety percent of the talking. That was not why they were here. "Campy, when you asked me to lunch, you said there was a lot you needed to say to me."

He looked at her, folding his hands together, twisting the knuckles. "So much that it's hard to know where to start."

She felt a sudden anxiety. Did she really want to hear this? *Yes.* "Start anywhere you want," she said.

"I was the world's worst fool to leave you—and you are twice the woman now that you were then."

Her anxiety deepened.

Look at him. Don't flinch away.

She felt her heart beating, the blood swirling in her head. "We had a lot of time back then to talk about why you thought you had to go to Vietnam," she said. "What we never got to talk about was why you didn't come back. Why you suddenly stopped writing like that."

He looked away. She saw his shoulders heave in a deep breath. "Once we went on the mission, they wouldn't let us write. It wouldn't have mattered anyway—where we went, there was . . . no way to get letters out."

"Oh, come on," she heard the snap of anger in her voice and took a deep breath. "Sorry. But all armies have supply lines. They can't function without them. A letter a day for sixty days, then nothing. Don't tell me you went the whole rest of your hitch with no route to the rear."

He looked at her. "I went the whole rest of my hitch with no route to the rear."

She saw in his eyes that it was true. Her spine tingled with fear for him, feeling the danger twenty years gone.

"When I finally got back to Saigon," he said, "I was delirious. They had to take the foot. Next thing I knew, I was stateside. Even then, I was pretty out of it for a couple of months. The usual things amputees go through—as a doctor, you've seen it dozens of times. I thought I was tougher than that, but I guess I wasn't."

A strange, painful tension filled her. His tone, so dry and matter-of-fact, made it plain that he wanted no sympathy— dreaded it, in fact. And something in her seemed to dread it too, her compassion dammed up behind the question he still had not answered: What about after that? All those years? Are you going to make me ask?

She would *not* ask. Nine of those years had been with Bud, wonderful years. The hell with you, Campy, she thought. But she could not feel that, either. Her emotions swirled, she could not seem to come down anywhere.

"When I finally got it back together," Campy said, "the first thing I wanted was to come back to you."

"But you didn't."

He looked at her, unflinching. "There was something else I had to do first—the one thing in all of this that I can never apologize for."

She looked at him with dread fascination.

"I didn't get out of the jungle alone," he said. "I couldn't have. I was delirious, unable to walk. So my buddy carried me. He got me down to an LZ. Then he went back in, vanished . . ."

Campy stopped as a voice started yelling behind them. It was a man, his voice sharp and bullying. Campy swiveled on the rock and stared toward the sound. Amy did not look, hoping the interruption would go away. He must not stop talking now, she must hear the rest of it, but Campy was standing up. His face had hardened. Alarmed, she looked around at last and saw the cop, about fifty yards away. He was shouting at a bum who lay on the ground. Roughly, the cop grabbed the lapels of the man's jacket, yanking him to his feet.

"Excuse me," Campy said, and then he got up and ran toward the two men. Startled, she hesitated, then sprinted after him, closing up easily. His left shoulder dipped with each stride; she could hear him grunt each time the artificial foot hit the ground. Campy stopped a few steps from the two men. They stood, locked together by the cop's fists, oblivious of anything else. The bum's face had a ravaged look, broken capillaries in his cheeks, a shaggy brown beard laced with white. One shoulder of his filthy fatigue jacket sported a company patch, the other, corporal's stripes. He looked in his mid-fifties, but she knew from long experience in ER that he could be much younger.

The cop jerked on the bum's jacket, pulling the frowsy face close. "I told you to keep your ass out of the park."

The bum's head lolled forward, chin to chest. Drunk, Amy realized. Again the cop jerked the jacket sharply, snapping the man's head up. "You hear me?"

The man mumbled something.

"What seems to be the problem, officer?" Campy said.

The cop turned at last, red-faced, still hanging on. He had small, belligerent eyes and a pug nose. "Butt out."

Campy ignored his hard stare, looking instead at the bum's fatigue jacket, inspecting the patches. "Seventh Cav," he said. "Chu Pong?"

The bum's reddened eyes focused on Campy—a look of pained acknowledgment so intense it shocked Amy. "Yeah, with Custer's old outfit," he mumbled. "You?"

"First of the Ninth, then a transfer to Rangers after Ia Drang." Campy looked at the cop. "Let go of the corporal." His voice was suddenly very quiet.

"Corporal?" the cop sneered. "This ain't no corporal. This is a rum-dum who pisses on your sidewalk and gets in your face to panhandle you when you come out to your park for a stroll. Corporals take baths and shave. They don't harass honest, hardworking citizens."

"How old are you, officer?"

"What's that got to do with anything? You're butting in here, interfering with—"

"How old are you?" Campy's voice snapped like a whip. Amy looked at him, startled. Suddenly he was a stranger—Sergeant Otis Camp, U.S. Army.

"I'm old enough to run your ass in, pops."

"And too young to know what a real corporal is."

The cop put the end of his nightstick on Campy's chest, glancing at Amy, a gleam in his eye. In a flash she sensed his new objective—to humiliate Campy in front of her. Her heart sank. *Think! Do something.*

"Take the stick off me." Campy's voice was soft now.

The nightstick didn't move. The cop let go of the corporal and he staggered away and sat down, his head hanging. "You want a piece of me?" the cop said. "You old buggers kill me. Think you're so hot because you were in 'Nam. If you're so hot, whyn't you win that war? The guys *I* grew up with kicked ass in the Gulf."

"I don't think you grew up."

"Let's all just cool it," Amy said. "There's no need for this."

"The stick," Campy repeated.

The cop shoved hard with the nightstick. Campy fought for balance. Amy started to reach for him, and then the false ankle bent suddenly at a sharp angle, a strap popping loose. Campy fell hard on his back, the foot dangling by one strap from the stump of his leg.

Appalled, Amy reached down for him, but he waved her off. She whirled on the cop, furious, groping for words.

The young, puffy face went pale. He held up both hands. "Hey, lady, I'm sorry. How was I supposed to know? For cryin' out loud, he *ran* over here." Stepping to Campy, the cop offered a hand. Campy ignored it, working at the straps, getting the foot back on and securing it. He pushed to his feet with an effort. Amy turned back to the cop to say something, but he had vanished.

The drunk veteran sat on the ground, gazing at Campy.

"You all right?" Campy asked.

The veteran nodded mutely, his eyes shiny with tears.

Campy made a low sound, deep in his throat. He touched the man's shoulder, as if he could no longer trust himself to speak, then turned and stalked off. Amy hurried to catch up with him, feeling the wake of his pain and rage dragging around her. "Are *you* all right?"

He cleared his throat. "I apologize for losing my temper."

"But you didn't," Amy protested.

"I'm afraid I ruined our time together."

"Not at all."

She wanted to stop him, talk to him, but he kept walking. Out on Fifty-ninth Street, he hailed a cab, opened the door for her. After she slid in, he stood a moment in the open doorway, leaning down to look in at her, and she realized he wasn't going to join her.

"I'll call you," he said. "I want . . . so much, so much, to talk to you. To just *talk* to you." He closed the door and strode off. Amy grabbed the handle, hesitating in an agony of indecision. Get out, go after him?

No.

"Lady?"

The cabbie, peering over the seat at her.

"Hudson General," she said.

"And don't spare the horses, right?" he asked with a gap-toothed grin.

"To hell with the horses."

14

Amy jogged into the park, determined to stop worrying about Campy and enjoy her run. It was only six—another hour and a half of daylight—but the earlier beautiful weather had fled completely now, leaving the sky a leaden gray; she could smell the rain in the dark clouds, an odor like damp bark. The air felt heavy and chilly against her legs, seeming to resist her. She fought it, lengthening her stride, trying to find her normal pace. Seeing a knot of runners up ahead, she closed up, tagging along behind them—three men and a woman, haunches rippling, their spiffy red and blue Spandex outfits making her feel a bit shabby in her cotton shorts and sweatshirt.

Looking around, Amy wondered if Campy might still be in the park. Probably not. He'd probably just checked back briefly to make sure the corporal was all right.

Amy realized she was not just worried about Campy; she was annoyed with him. Admirable, the way he'd leaped to the defense of the vagrant. But the timing couldn't have been more frustrating—running off right in the middle of his explanation about why he hadn't come back to her. How many more years must she wait to hear it?

The Spandex quartet headed up toward the band shell, their pace dropping off. Amy surged past them, crossing the road and trotting down to take a turn around the fountain's circular terrace. As she made the circuit, she glanced around for another jogging escort and realized with a twinge of unease that she was alone. Well, not quite—four pigeons watched her from perches on the head and wings of the fountain's statue. At the north bulwark of the terrace, a green rowboat bumped, abandoned. The empty boat chilled her, adding to the sudden atmosphere of isolation. The clouds were really dense now, making it seem like dusk.

Time to get out of the park.

Then Amy spotted someone on the wooden footbridge that crossed to the upper east shore of the lake—a muscular young woman in shorts and a red sweatshirt. Amy closed up, following her along the lakeside, realizing with a pang that she had not run the lovely but secluded lake trail since the man had followed her from the subway. Resentment welled in her. Somehow she must end the fear. But how could she, when she could make no sense out of what was happening? Three times now the man had threatened her—four, if she counted his unseen presence in her house. Last night, in the blood bank, the threat had spread to her father. Winnie's resemblance to the four men who had already died in ER was too close to be a coincidence, but what did it mean? And how did Cynthia's death fit into this? If Cynthia was part of it, then so was the nightmare.

Which seemed impossible.

At least I haven't had the nightmare lately, Amy thought. Not since the police started watching the house at night.

Did the police really make her feel that much safer?

No, and yet the nightmare had stopped.

And finally, there was the garrote. The police were keeping watch in the first place because the intruder had left it behind. But why had he crept around her home with a weapon that killed in silence, then left without hurting anyone, when only a day before, in the staff rest room, he'd seemed bent on raping and killing her?

A sudden terrifying image struck her, of her own body lying inside a dark, airless drawer in the Hudson morgue. Her throat clenched, a feeling of pressure along the bruise, so powerful it nearly gagged her. With a fierce effort she forced her breathing back into rhythm.

The woman ahead of her turned onto a side path that rose
steeply away from the lake. Amy felt a stab of dismay. That was
the Ramble up there, a secluded hill overgrown with brush and
trees. She did not want to go up there. But if she did not, she
would lose her escort.

Amy realized she was letting the fear dictate to her again.
Dark clouds or not, it *was* still daytime. During the day, people
walked their dogs and went birdwatching in the Ramble; as
long as she stayed in sight of the other woman she should be
fine.

Putting on a burst of speed, Amy charged up the slope,
fighting it like an enemy, closing to within twenty yards of the
woman. The path leveled off, branching in several directions.
The woman loped off to the right. Amy followed as the path
wound back to the south. Trees and bushes lined the twists and
turns, making it hard to keep the woman in sight, but giving
Amy enough flashes of red sweatshirt to stay on track. Round-
ing a tree into a clear space, she stumbled to a stop, startled.
There, in her path, stood an old gazebo. It listed with age,
brassy in the dim, filtered light. Goosebumps rippled along
Amy's arms. She stared at the gazebo, baffled at her rush of
fright. Why did the thing look so . . . dangerous?

Of course, up here, it could be.

Amy imagined two lovers necking in the gazebo, unaware
of a man hunched down in the bushes, watching them, waiting
to move in—

She cut the dark fantasy off, amazed at herself. Where had
that come from? Suddenly her nerves were really playing up.
She looked ahead for the red sweatshirt, couldn't see it. She felt
an instant of wild alarm, then got hold of herself: You'll be all
right—just retrace your route, get back down to the lake.

A huge raindrop hit her face, startling her. She turned to
run back the way she had come, then stopped as she saw a
movement between the bushes that lined the path. She froze,
watching the near edge of the bushes. No one appeared. He'd
stopped back there.

He was waiting for her to come to him.

Amy felt a stab of fear in the pit of her stomach. The rain
poured down with a sudden rushing noise, rippling up the
path in thick swaths, shrouding the trees and bushes and sting-

ing into her eyes. She felt her heart pounding. *Get out of here—now!*

But how? If someone *was* waiting behind the bushes, she couldn't go back out that way, and she had no idea what lay ahead, past the gazebo—

Through the driving curtains of rain, she saw the man break between the bushes and run toward her. Terrified, she looked around. There!—a dirt path cutting away from the gazebo into some bushes. She sprinted into the bushes.

The path ended in a tangle of underbrush.

She tried to claw her way through. Footsteps squelched closer behind her; she broke through the bushes, but there was no path now, just thick clumps of underbrush like a maze. She could hear the man very clearly now. He was close behind her. Panicked, she foundered ahead, straining to see in the downpour.

She glanced over her shoulder, saw the rain-cloaked figure closing on her, heard his feet slapping in the mud.

"Help!" Her scream soaked into the muffling sheets of rain. *"Help, help!"* God, someone help me!

She muscled her way through a gap, but another bush blocked her way. She kicked at it, trying to find an opening. Her leg caught on a low branch, her other foot slipping to the side in the mud. She went down on one knee, scrambling up again, turning to see the man almost on top of her. He had his knife out. Terrified, Amy screamed and tried to run, feeling the root catch her ankle, powerless to stop her fall. She sprawled down, rolling over, kicking out with her legs, knowing he must be right there.

But he wasn't.

Through the downpour, she could see only a thick bush. Scrabbling backward through the mud, she managed to sit up. She heard a man scream, but the sound was choked off in a low gargle. Amy sat, stunned. What was happening? She heard the snap of bone, ugly and unmistakable, then nothing.

She sat still, not daring to move or make a sound. The rain streamed into her eyes, plastering her hair down along her face. She stared at the bush. There was no movement, no sound but the rushing torrents of rain.

Getting gingerly to her feet, Amy crept to where she'd last

seen the man. Through the branches of a bush, she made out
a sprawled leg, blue denim dark from the rain. She watched the
leg, counting to fifty. It did not move. Slowly she stood, then,
parting the wet branches of the bush, she stepped through and
looked down at the man. He lay on his back, arms outflung,
neck bent at a hopeless angle. His eyes stared up, unblinking,
into the driving rain. His knife lay in the leaves beside him, the
blade bright and bloodless.

She had only seen his face once before, but she would
never forget it now. It was the man from the subway. She could
not make herself touch him. She did not need to. She had seen
death often enough.

Amy felt herself shaking in relief. It was over. He was
dead, his neck broken—

By whom?

Amy stared around her, feeling the fear again, cold on her
neck, and then she began running, tearing at the branches until
she burst through into the open and saw the path back down
to the lake. She slipped and slid down the path, sprinting
around the north shore, breaking out of the park into the broad
avenue of Central Park West, dimly aware of headlights,
squealing tires, the angry blare of horns. Finally, on the far side
of the street, she stopped running.

15

Amy relaxed with her morning coffee and the Sunday *Times* from the day before. Her office door, wide open, let in the murmur of ER. She had not realized, having locked herself in the past week, how much she'd missed the reassuring sounds channeled back along the hall—the printer's squirrely chatter, ringing phones, the muted rumble of Philip's trash cart. Emergency sounded almost serene this morning—the overflow had cleared over the weekend, leaving ER merely at capacity. In a moment she'd head out, get a jump on the morning shift. First she wanted to read the *Times* article about the murder again. Each time through, it made her feel a little safer, a little freer. She looked at the headline—"Rapist Murdered in Park"—and felt only a slight lurch in her stomach. A rapist, yes, but he was *dead* now. She read on:

Police are investigating a murder that occurred Saturday afternoon in the region of Central Park known as the Ramble. The victim has been identified as Robert Strickney, of no fixed address. The murder was reported to police by a woman jogger who was being chased by the victim. Dense underbrush and Saturday's torrential rainstorm prevented the jogger from actually witnessing the murder. She has been cleared of suspicion by the police because of the extreme physical force used on the victim. According to the medical examiner, Mr. Strickney was killed by a single powerful blow to the back of the neck. The nature of the trauma indicated that the blow was struck by the attacker's hand, rather than by an object or weapon. Mr. Strickney's shoulder was also dislocated, which, the medical examiner said, indicated that his arm had been twisted up behind his back, probably to immobilize him for the fatal blow. The heavy rains washed away footprints and other clues that might have given the police a lead on the killer.

An opened switchblade knife was found beside the body. Records show that such a knife was used by Mr. Strickney in a case of rape and assault with a deadly weapon for which he was convicted twelve years ago. At that time, Mr. Strickney was sentenced to twenty years in the Attica Correctional Facility. He had been indicted for rape and assault three times previously, in cases that did not come to trial. Mr. Strickney was released on parole for good behavior in late March. Asked for their theories about who might have killed Mr. Strickney, the police declined to comment, saying only that the investigation will continue.

Friends and family of Mr. Strickney's earlier victims had petitioned the parole board not to release him. When asked if the investigation was centering on this group, the police again declined comment. The mother of the victim whose rape resulted in Mr. Strickney's single conviction said, "I'm glad. The man was scum. We all said he should never have been paroled in the first place. This will keep him from raping and maybe killing other women."

Women like me, Amy thought with a chill. She remembered Strickney's scream, the sound of his neck snapping, the rain splashing on his dead, staring eyes. She could take no pleasure from it. But she could not be sorry, either.

As for who had killed him, it was interesting that the police had not told the *Times* reporter what they'd let slip to her—that several people had made threats about Strickney. Two men, husbands of Strickney's victims, had been particularly vocal after his parole. Clearly, someone had been stalking Strickney as he stalked her. In keeping that from the *Times*, the NYPD was giving itself room not to press the case too hard.

Amy could not be sorry about that either. Whoever had killed Strickney, she owed him.

And just as surely, if he walked in here right now she'd be afraid of him. To stalk and kill a man in cold blood, a man you'd already subdued by tearing his shoulder apart . . .

Amy shuddered. She had no desire to meet a man with that much rage in him.

Firmly, she put the killer from her mind. He was the police's problem now. Strickney was dead, she and Winnie were
safe . . .

And the questions remained: Why had Strickney branched
out from rape to kill the four bankers? How had he done it?
What had he planned to do with Winnie's blood? Now she
would never know.

She could live with that. What counted was that there
would be no more suspicious heart-attack deaths. With Strickney dead, there was no point in pursuing it. An autopsy on
Owen VanKleeck might have turned up some hard evidence,
but he had been buried before his killer died.

Amy found herself paging through the *Times* to the article on the VanKleeck funeral. A grainy photo showed Mrs.
VanKleeck leaving St. Thomas's, her back straight, her face a
stoic mask. The high arched door behind her framed other
somber faces. Hundreds of the city's top business and community leaders had attended the funeral. The story noted the
heart attack and quoted several friends and associates, who
were "shocked" because VanKleeck had been in such good
health. The article raised no actual suspicions and made no
mention of the deaths of three other prominent New York
bankers.

Of course, that might happen yet.

Amy felt a twinge of unease. If she could ferret out the
baffling pattern, so could an aggressive reporter. It would be a
terrible irony if the papers got hold of it now. The *Post* would
have a field day: NEW YORK BANKERS DYING IN HUDSON
ER. All Eric would have to do was show a headline like that to
the board, and he'd get his wish. No one could stop him from
shutting down ER, even though the murderer was dead, the
threat past—

Amy dropped the paper in her wastebasket. Forget it.
There would be no headlines. Her life would go back to normal
now. She could look out her front window without seeing an
unmarked police car. She could go to the staff rest room, run
in the park, without worrying—

Any more than the average New York woman, she corrected herself with a grin.

"Dr. St. Clair?" Andrea Chase, head of the blood bank,

stood in her doorway. If she'd caught Amy's grin, her face gave no sign of it.

"Yes . . . ?" Amy bit back the "ma'am" she was about to add. Andrea really had the headmistress look down pat, especially today, with her severe straight skirt and herringbone jacket perfectly complementing her gray hair. A red scarf would have done wonders for the outfit, but Andrea never wore anything colorful.

"I hope I'm not disturbing you," Andrea said, "but we've just had another . . . incident in the blood bank, and since it involves your father . . ."

Amy felt herself tensing. *No, it's over.* "What happened?"

Andrea looked uncomfortable. "Well, we hadn't yet screened the sample of your father's blood when it was, ah, destroyed the other night. It couldn't be used if it wasn't screened, of course. Labs decided to thaw the full unit and screen a sample of that. At least that way the blood could be used if needed the next couple of days in surgery or ER. So a tech got it from the freezer last night and was soaking it in saline, you know, to get the glycerol off—"

"What happened?" Amy asked again.

Andrea seemed to gather herself. "The blood was there an hour ago, the tech is sure of that. He went to the rest room. When he came back, your father's blood was gone."

Amy's scalp crawled. She felt the fear rushing back, a cold fist turning in her stomach. It's *not* over, she thought.

16

Philip St. Clair was combing his hair for his session with Tom and Sissy when someone knocked at his door. He stared at himself in the mirror, feeling very excited and mixed up. Someone coming to see him? No one ever came to see him.

Maybe it was Dad!

Philip dropped his comb and headed for the door, grinning.

Wait! You want him to see your comb on the floor? What would Tom say? That a grown man always puts his things back in their proper place.

Turning around, Philip hurried back and looked for the comb. The knock came again, and he felt very anxious, hot and cold prickles running over his skin. "Just a minute!" he cried, searching the parquet under the hall mirror. Where was it? There, at the edge of the little rug from Persia that Mother had given him. He picked the comb up and shoved it in his hip pocket. Hurrying back to the door, he felt his head brush the foyer chandelier, messing his hair again. Forgot to duck, he told himself. He paused at the door, looking down at himself. Shirt untucked. Hurrying, he tucked it in, then pulled the door open, smiling.

The man outside was not Dad.

Philip felt all the lightness go out of him. With an effort, he

hid his disappointment and looked at the man. He was strong
looking and had a round face. His hair was thin; he'd combed
it across to hide that he was getting kind of bald. I've seen him,
Philip thought. Where did I see him? Never mind, he's wearing
a nice suit and tie, so he's probably all right. What would Tom
do? Be polite. Philip smiled at the man.

"Hello"—suddenly he knew who the man was—"Lieutenant!"

The man blinked. "Lieutenant?"

"You're the lieutenant, from 'Cagney and Lacey,' " Philip
said, proud that he'd remembered.

The man smiled. "No, but lots of people tell me I look like
him, except taller. My name is Martin Lenz. I know your father
and mother and your sister." He held out his hand.

Philip started to slap it, then remembered in time that he
only slapped when he and Tom were joking. Supposed to
shake. He shook the man's hand.

"May I come in?" the man asked.

"Sure!" Philip stood aside, pointing through the little foyer
to his living room. A friend of Mom, Dad, and Sissy. Coming to
see him, just him. This was neat!

The man walked in and looked around. He looked at the
carpet and touched the gold edge of the mirror. "Air ice ace
hoov god ear."

Philip realized he had his bad ear turned toward the man.
He moved his head the other way, so the hearing aid worked
better. "What?"

"Very nice place you've got here."

Philip felt himself flushing with pride. "Thank you. I think
it's nice, too. Dad found it for me. It has a doorman with a
uniform, Mr. Durand. Sometimes he watches TV with me. And
Mrs. Corbeil, the housekeeper, gets my groceries for me . . ."
Philip realized he was chattering.

Mr. Lenz didn't seem to mind. He walked over to the
window that looked out on Second Avenue. "You can see the
hospital from here."

"Yup, it's right across the street."

Mr. Lenz looked at the big chair by the window. "May I sit
down?"

"Sure!"

"hhnankoo." Wrong ear again. Philip shifted the good one toward Mr. Lenz, determined not to forget again.

"It's kind of funny, though, isn't it?" Mr. Lenz said as he sat down. "Your father having that great big mansion and all that money, and yet you staying in an apartment so far from him."

"Oh, Dad *wants* me at home. He argued and argued. But I really wanted my own place and this is real close to where I work. Tom thought it would be good so he helped me talk Dad into it."

"Tom?"

"My doctor," Philip explained. "And my best friend in all the world."

Mr. Lenz nodded. "I see."

What should I do now? Philip wondered. Tom never talks much about this, having someone into my apartment. Philip felt suddenly very nervous. He looked at the man, trying to remember his name. If he asked again, he'd look dumb. But he had to do *something*. Philip had a sudden inspiration: On TV, they usually offer people who visit a drink. "Can I get you something to drink?"

The man looked interested. "What have you got?"

"Water. It's right in the faucet in my kitchen. And I've got Dixie cups with dinosaurs on them."

The man looked a little disappointed, but he said, "That would be fine, Philip."

Philip got the man a cup of water and one for himself. The man just held his. Philip began to feel embarrassed. He wished he knew what to do next. "Would you like to play chess?"

The man's head jerked up. "You play chess?"

"Sure."

The man gave him a funny look, as if he didn't believe him. But he said, "Fine. Let's play."

Happy, Philip got the set from the armoire and set it on the marble table next to the man's chair. He pulled up the ottoman his mother had bought him, and sat down. His heart beating with excitement, he took the pieces from the wooden chest and set them up on the board. The man watched him as though he were doing something very important. It made him feel wonderful.

"This is a beautiful set," the man said. "Did your father give it to you?"

"Yup. He's got lots of nice things."

"I know. Do you by any chance remember the pre-Columbian statue?"

"Statue?"

The man looked at him without blinking. "A Mesoamerican funeral figure with elaborate gold—"

Philip felt a little anxious. Why was the man looking at him like that? "A statue—like the ones in the park?"

"Smaller. About this high." The man held his hands apart about ten inches. "And it was very unusual, made long ago by some people called Aztecs. It was very beautiful, and had gold on it, worth lots of money?" The man spoke slowly and seemed more patient.

But Philip did not remember Dad having any statue. Anyway, he didn't want to talk about it. He wanted to play chess. "I'll make you white," he said, "because you're my guest."

"Fine."

Philip watched the man move pawn to queen four. That was interesting. Most people went pawn to king four. At once, Philip moved his knight to king's bishop three. The man looked at the board for a minute, then moved his pawn to queen's bishop four. Philip moved his pawn to king three, freeing the king's bishop. The man stared at the board. "So," he said. "Do you remember that statue your father had?"

"No," Philip said, feeling cross but hiding it.

The man moved his knight forward. "It was back a long time ago. See, the interesting thing is, your father had this statue in a display case in his house, and then it was gone. It was right about the same time you fell from that horse and hurt yourself so bad. A real mystery."

Philip felt a small pain in his head. He moved his bishop and rubbed at the spot behind his ear, hoping it would not be a big headache. "I don't remember much from back then."

The man glanced at the board, then looked at it harder. He took a long time before he moved. Philip moved. The man castled on his king's side, the way Philip figured he would. Philip did the same thing.

"Not bad," the man said. "Not bad at all." He moved his knight to bishop three.

Philip moved his knight to king five, smiling, feeling warmed. "Thank you."

The man stared at the board. Philip tried not to look at his own knight, even though the man probably thought it was pretty harmless. After all, if it took the man's knight, the man could take it right back with his pawn. Oh-oh, the man was looking at it now. He didn't seem to like it there, smack up against his own knight and pawn. He moved his queen over to defend his knight, too. Philip took the knight anyway. The man looked up at him, then shrugged and took the knight back with his queen. Philip moved his pawn to queen three. The man looked at the board for a long time. He traded some more moves with Philip, getting his pawns out in a wedge. Philip took one with his bishop and the man smiled, moving his queen right up to take one of Philip's pawns.

Just like I wanted, Philip thought.

He forced the queen back with his knight, then moved his king's bishop one square. The man looked and looked at the board, frowning. Philip tried to guess what he was thinking. He probably saw that if he moved his pawn now, he would lose his queen's rook. But did he see the rest of it? Philip kept his face very straight, hoping not. The man made other moves, bringing his bishop up and attacking, putting Philip's king in check. Philip wiggled the king out of it and watched the man take his other knight and lose only a pawn—he thought!

This is going just right, Philip thought. He took the man's bishop, then pretended that he was trading his queen for the man's rook. The man looked disappointed in him. He took Philip's queen. Then Philip moved his bishop out and checked the man's king. The man blocked him with a rook. Philip captured the bishop the man had forgotten about.

"Yikes!" the man said. "But I still have my queen, and you don't."

"That's true," Philip said.

The man moved his king behind his rook.

Philip moved his queen's rook over so that both of his rooks commanded his king's file. The man's face turned a little red. He stared at the board for a long time, then moved a pawn

forward to threaten the front rook. No problem, Philip thought.
He just moved the rook up a row. The man wasted a couple of
moves while Philip got his queen's bishop ready on his own
back row. The man didn't seem to notice. Then Philip swung
his rook up to threaten the queen. This time the man took a
long while to move. He was stuck, oh he was! Finally he took
his queen back to defend his king on the back row. Dumb!
Philip moved his rook over, checking the king. He traded a
rook for the man's knight, and the man smiled. Philip realized
the man thought he was okay. Philip got him between the
bishops and the other rook, checking him again.

You can run, Philip thought, but you can't hide.

The man stared at the board some more, then tipped his
king over. "You've got me," he said. "I resign."

Philip wanted to jump up and clap his hands—no, that's
not what Tom would do. What did Tom say when he won their
games of chess, which he usually did? "Well," Philip said, "you
played a pretty good game there, partner. I was just lucky."

"Lucky? I'm pretty good at this game. I played my *best*.
And you still beat me." The man smiled, as though he were
really happy. He looked like he was the one who had won.
How come? Philip wondered.

"You know," the man said, "I'll bet you could remember
all about that statue if you tried."

Amy sat on the end of Tom's office couch, head dropped
forward, enjoying the gentle massage he was giving her neck
and shoulders. His fingers seemed to know just where to
touch, just how hard to press, unlocking the tension that
clung high up in her back. Warm waves of pleasure spread
down her spine and flowed in lulling rhythms through her
shoulders.

"How does that feel?" Tom asked.

"Wonderful. Don't stop. I was more tense than I realized."

"It's upsetting, bizarre."

"All day I've been worried sick about Winnie," she said.
"Since the first attempt to steal his blood, I've assumed he was
in danger."

"Why? I thought you said none of the four had given blood before they died."

"True. But if you assume the blood thief wants to harm Winnie, it's a good guess that the four dead men so very like Winnie were also his victims."

"A guess, yes. Nothing the police would buy."

"I know. With what I've got now, they wouldn't even buy that the other four had been murdered." Amy felt a bitter frustration. Just when she thought the danger was past, she could feel it closing in again. She was trained for life-and-death fights, but not like this. She longed for a danger she could see and understand, strike back at. "When Strickney was killed in the park," she said, "I thought it was over. I wondered why a rapist had expanded into murdering rich bankers, but with him dead there was no way to know. Then the blood bank thief struck again, proving that it wasn't Strickney the first time. The heart-attack killer is still out there, and he's much more dangerous than Strickney."

"At least you're safe now."

"Am I? What about Cynthia?"

"There's no proof that was anything but suicide."

"No proof, no."

Tom's hands rubbed gently at her neck. "Come on now, relax. You're getting all tense again."

"If I could just figure out what he wants with Winnie's blood."

"Maybe it's for some kind of ritual—voodoo is big on blood."

Amy shuddered.

"Come on—you don't *believe* in voodoo, do you?"

The way he tripped off the last three words made her smile in spite of herself. "No, I don't believe in voodoo. But I do believe in crazy."

"Oddly enough, so do I," Tom said dryly.

"Come on, Tom. This man *scares* me."

"Of course. I understand."

"Maybe we shouldn't talk about it right now," Amy said. "We'll waste this wonderful neck rub."

"Right now is just when you should talk about it," Tom

said. "It's impossible to feel relaxed and tense at the same time. So if I can help you relax while you're talking to me about it, you won't feel so tense later, when you talk to yourself about it. That's the whole point of the neck rub."

She turned her head halfway to glance at him from the corner of her eye. "And here I thought you were being affectionate."

"Nope. You can write this one off on your taxes."

"Oh, you're charging me, too?"

"Your father, actually. This is Philip's time. Speaking of which, I wonder what's keeping him. He's almost never late."

"Maybe we should walk over and check."

"Let's give him another minute." Tom stopped the massage, letting his hands rest on her shoulders. They felt good there, comforting.

"So what are you going to do now?" Tom asked.

"Try to find who's doing this. I missed my chance at an autopsy, but maybe I can find some other form of evidence, some hard proof I can take to the police that four men have been murdered."

"Any ideas?"

"Not really. Just this nagging feeling that I'm missing something."

"Really? Like what?"

"I don't know," she said, feeling the frustration build again. "But whatever it is, I've got to find it. Nobody can kill four men without leaving some kind of evidence behind."

She sat up, reluctantly pulling away from Tom's fingers. "It's a quarter after. Don't you think we ought to go over and check on Philip? We could call, but he often doesn't hear the phone."

"All right."

As they rode the elevator up to Philip's floor, Amy felt a twinge of worry. What if Philip had had an accident, had fallen and hurt himself, perhaps? It really wasn't like him to be late to see Tom. She began to wish Tom hadn't gotten her quite so relaxed. Hurrying ahead, she paused at the door, her hand raised to knock, but heard the mumble of voices inside— Philip's and another man's.

She turned to Tom, surprised. "He's got a visitor."

Tom raised an eyebrow. Stepping past her, he rang the doorbell insistently. A moment later the door swung open. Philip smiled out at them, then his smile faded.

"Oh, no. I was supposed to be at therapy!"

"Don't worry, Philip," Tom said. "Do you want to introduce us to your guest?"

"Uh, sure. Come in."

Amy followed Tom inside. A man was sitting in the chair by the window, Philip's prized chess set on the table beside him. With a shock, Amy recognized him. *Martin Lenz!* Lenz stood, gazing evenly at her.

Philip said, "This is Lieutenant—" He clapped a hand to his forehead, looking confused. "No, not lieutenant. I forgot."

"Martin Lenz," Amy said. The depth of her anger surprised her. She could feel her stomach clenching, the blood rushing to her face. In her mind, she saw Lenz stalking into Philip's hospital room, standing on the other side of the bed from her father and her, leaning over the comatose body of Winnie's son while he called Winnie a liar and a thief. Amy felt her teeth clenching. Lenz the sadist, Lenz the thug. He still looked the same, a little less hair, but he still had the powerful shoulders and those little ratty eyes.

"I'm flattered you remember me," Lenz said.

"Don't be." Amy saw Tom look at her in surprise.

"Your brother and I were just playing chess. He whipped me pretty good." Lenz looked at Tom. "And you would be . . . ?"

"Tom Hart." Tom started to move forward, then hesitated.

Don't you dare shake hands with that man, Amy thought, and he didn't.

"Hey, Philip," Lenz said in a jovial voice, "is this the good doctor you were telling me about?"

"Uh-huh," Philip bit his lip, looking at Tom.

Amy said, "What are you doing here, Lenz?"

"Just having a friendly little visit with your brother."

"You don't know Philip."

"No, but I always wanted to meet him. I didn't exactly have that pleasure before, if you remember." Lenz turned toward Tom. "Hey, congratulations, Dr. Hart. I'm really impressed with your work."

"Not my work," Tom said, "Philip's."

Amy felt a surge of impatience. "Are you still working for the insurance company?" she asked Lenz.

Lenz smiled without humor. "You'll be happy to know I finally made chief of investigations—despite the St. Clair case."

"Which is the real reason you're here. You're still looking for the statue."

"Statue?" Tom said. "What's this about, Amy?"

"A pre-Columbian funerary piece—an Aztec figure, very rare," she explained. "The Mexican government gave it to my father in appreciation for some big loans he made in the early sixties to help them build up their manufacturing capacity. Someone stole it from a display case in my father's den twenty years ago. The police—and Mr. Lenz here—were unable to find either the thief or the statue. Mr. Lenz's insurance company had to pay up." She turned back to Lenz. "The time limit on theft prosecution ran out years ago. Why don't you just give it up?"

Lenz looked at her. "I really must be going." He turned to Philip. "Maybe I could come again, we'll play some more chess."

Amy started to tell Lenz to go to hell. She felt Tom clasp her arm. With an effort, she held back.

Philip looked uncertainly from her to Lenz. "Well," he said, "I'll have to ask Sissy and Tom."

"Why is that?" Lenz asked.

"Philip," Tom said quickly, "would you excuse us a minute? Mr. Lenz and your sister and I would like to talk outside."

"I think we can talk right here," Lenz said.

"Outside," Amy said.

"Maybe you could put your chess set away," Tom said, "and we'll come in for you when we're ready to go for your session."

Philip looked chastened. "Okay. Good-bye, Mr. Lenz."

"You don't have to—"

"Good-bye, Mr. Lenz," Philip repeated, his voice high with stress.

Lenz shrugged and walked toward the door. "Good-bye, Philip. I really enjoyed our game. You owe me a chance to get even now, don't forget."

Taking Lenz's arm, Tom walked him out. Amy held back a second. "Philip, did he ask you about Dad's statue?"

Philip hung his head as if sure, now, that he had done something wrong. "Yes."

"That's all right," she said, furious, but keeping her voice gentle. "You wait here for Tom and me. We'll be back in a few minutes. Don't worry about it, it's fine."

She closed the door gently behind her. Lenz had started down the hall. Tom was looking after him, his expression uncertain.

"You," Amy snapped. "You wait. We're not finished."

Lenz turned, giving her a look of exaggerated patience.

"You are not going to start harassing my family again."

"Harassing?" he said mildly. "I was just doing my job."

"Your job wasn't to accuse my father of stealing."

Lenz grunted. "Give me a break. Was I really supposed to believe that some stranger somehow got keys to your house and knew exactly how to disable the alarms? That he slipped in and took the statue out of the display case, but left that stamp collection and all the coins? Then he locked the door again on his way out, and even the dog didn't hear him?"

Amy wanted to grab him by the shirt collar and shake him. She felt Tom's cautioning hand come to rest gently on her back. "Listen to me, Lenz," she said. "We told you all we knew at the time. None of us had anything to do with the theft. Why should my father, who had millions of dollars, steal his own statue just for the insurance?"

"Another million or so never hurts."

"He gave more than that to charity every year. You know what the police investigation showed as well as I do. A professional burglar—"

"The police," Lenz scoffed. "What did they care? Like you said, your father gave more than that to charity, which, by the way, included the police widows' fund."

Tom cleared his throat. "I think this has gone far enough——"

"Tom, let me. Mr. Lenz, what do you want with Philip?"

"Nothing. We had fun. He's a good chess player, your brother."

"You did ask him about the statue."

"So? Listen, Doc, I saw him at the ballgame with the good Dr. Hart here. It got me thinking, that's all. Philip being in the hospital at the time, I never got to talk to him. He looked so good at the stadium, I figured I'd look him up, have that little talk I wanted to have years ago——"

"Now you have. And I want that to be the last of it."

"Do you, now? And if Philip wants to play more chess?"

Amy shook her head, waiting until she could trust herself to speak. "Even if my father stole his own statue, which he didn't, you can't touch him now. What do you care anymore?"

"Care? Oh, I don't—not really. But you know how a thing catches your curiosity and just hangs on? For instance, did you know that the statue has never surfaced, not in twenty-plus years? That's a funny burglar, doesn't fence his take. But what the heck. That's the past, right?" Lenz's eyes glittered.

You care, Amy thought. You bastard. You care a lot. What is it? Do you want to prove my father's a crook? There's no time limit on ruining Winnie's reputation, is that it? Or do you want the statue for yourself?

"Amy, if I might?" Tom said.

She nodded, exasperated.

"Mr. Lenz, if you're hoping to get any information out of Philip about things that happened twenty years ago, you're wasting your time. His brain was severely damaged in that accident. He has very few memories of that time. Any fragmentary ones he might be able to dredge up would be very painful to him. And that's the bottom line here. Wasting your time is one thing, hurting my patient and Amy's brother is another. We can't allow that."

"You two seem to think you own Philip."

"Why, you——" Tom took a step toward Lenz, his face reddening. Yes, Amy thought fiercely, punch him, right in that smug, piggy face. A second later she was horrified at the thought; Lenz could break Tom in half. She put a restraining hand on Tom's arm, then saw he was still under control.

"Mr. Lenz," Tom said quietly, "you are not going to talk to Philip again. You are not going to see him. Just put it out of your mind."

Lenz stared at Tom. "Or what?"

"Or you will deal with me," Tom said softly. "And that won't be as easy as you might think."

Amy saw a flicker of uncertainty in Lenz's eyes. A tough, hardened man, but something in Tom had reached him, surprised him. He turned and walked away down the hall, the recessed ceiling lights shimmering along the snake-shiny fabric of his suit.

You won't give up, will you, Lenz? Amy thought. You'll keep after it, digging, prying into Philip's mind, trying to bring it all back. *Damn* you.

17

Amy sat on the edge of Eric Kraft's new office sofa, wishing he would drop the chitchat and get to the point. Emergency was still at capacity, and she needed to get back. She needed a plan for protecting Philip from Martin Lenz. Most important, she needed to ferret out some hard evidence on how the heart-attack murders were accomplished before it happened again—this time to Winnie or her.

She perked up as Eric walked from behind his desk and sat on one corner—his usual prelude to getting down to business.

"Amy, I know it hasn't been easy for you, facing the closing of ER—"

"It hasn't closed yet."

Eric smiled tolerantly. "It will."

"If the board sides with you and Burton."

Eric's smile slipped. "I'm confident that will happen, even though your father is, this very moment, wining and dining two board members. He put their entire families up in your chalet in the Catskills."

"I don't know anything about that." Amy did her best to hide her approval.

"Yes, well. I'm sure you do know that he's trying every-thing he can to stop us. I don't believe he'll succeed, but I didn't

call you up here to argue the point. In fact, I think I may have
fashioned a compromise that will please both sides in this."

Amy felt a small, wary hope. "I'm listening."

"After we talked last time, I felt I'd been a bit harsh about
that vagrant woman you treated free in ER. Actually, I admire
your humanitarian impulses. How would you like to head a
free clinic for the poor?"

Amy looked at him, startled and pleased, then skeptical. If
Eric wanted to close ER because of the costs, why would he
suggest replacing it with something that brought in *no* money?
She said, "A *free* clinic, here at Hudson?"

"Free," Eric said firmly. "As for being at Hudson, it might
work better if it were close to the neighborhoods it would
serve, don't you think?" His tone was all light and reason. Amy
could not quite believe what she was hearing. A free clinic was
a wonderful idea, but it was so out of character for Eric, she had
to be sure.

"There would be money for all necessary equipment," Eric
went on, "and a staff of, shall we say, four doctors. And a very
handsome salary for you as director, of course." He tossed the
last off in a very offhand way, as though unsure how she'd take
it. The fact was, she didn't know how to take any of this.

She said, "Where will all this money come from?"

"I've been talking to public-interest corporations that
might invest in something like this. I believe I have one lined
up to fund you into the foreseeable future."

The way he put it, keeping the corporation's name from
her, only inflamed her suspicions. "Eric, you used the word
'compromise.' What is the compromise? The poor get a free
clinic and I give up ER?"

"Amy, Hudson *must* close its ER or face financial ruin. It
is only fair to this hospital that you and your father accept that
unfortunate reality and stop fighting it."

"And if I don't, no clinic."

He gave her an uncomfortable smile. "Well, clearly you
can't run an ER and direct a free clinic as well."

"Eric, I'll help in any way I can to get a clinic like that
started, but my training and interest are in emergency medicine—"

"I understand. Name anyone you like to the post. But I still

think you'd be terrific at it, with your management experience."

Amy felt a weary disappointment. "A free clinic for poor
people is a wonderful idea," she said, "but not as a substitute
for the multimillion-dollar equipment and the full-range crisis
care of a top-notch ER. Our services here are, by law, available
to *everyone,* regardless of ability to pay. Take that away, and no
clinic could ever make up for the loss to low-income people.
If it comes to choosing, you know I have to go on fighting the
closing."

"And if you lose, the poor get nothing?"

"That would be your choice, not mine. You're the one
who says he can deliver corporate funding for the clinic. Will
you really withhold it if you lose and Hudson's ER stays open?"

Eric frowned. "It's not that simple."

"It isn't? Why not?"

"Damn it, Amy. Why won't you see reason?"

She looked closely at Eric, saw the sheen of sweat on his
forehead, the tension around his mouth. "I think I'm starting to
see the reason," she said with a sinking feeling. "Correct me if
I'm wrong. The public-spirited corporation that wants ER
closed? They want to buy Hudson—provided it is first stripped
of its most expensive and profitless service."

"You're quite wrong," Eric said.

"Am I?" Amy felt a wave of disgust as the full picture
dawned on her. "When you and Burton first sprang this on me,
Burton mentioned a preventive medicine clinic. I didn't get it
then, but now I do. What he really meant was a sports medicine
complex, like that one that crowded out a big ER in L.A. a few
years ago. Rich yuppies come in to have their shin splints
treated by guru doctors—a real moneymaker, unlike ER. But
Winnie and I are in the way, and you're feeling a little shaky
because he's fighting harder than you thought he could. So the
interested corporation makes this clinic offer so we'll back off."

Eric held up his hands. "Whoa, whoa. You're imagining
things. That's totally out of left field."

"I don't think so." Amy could feel her disgust growing,
making her angry. "What's your end of it, Eric? Do they make
you president and triple your salary? Why not? All you've sold
is Hudson General's good name. That'll be worth millions in

extra revenue when your corporate owners turn Hudson into a glorified health club for rich Manhattanites. If they have to fund a clinic in some low-rent, burned-out block of the city for a year or two to get it, the long-term profits will more than make up for it. Meanwhile, what happens to the kid who falls through a window and is bleeding to death, the grandpa that gets hit by a cab, the teenager shot for his athletic shoes? When you get a little older and keel over with a stroke from eating too well on your piece of this, are you going to take a cab to my free clinic? No, that's not for you. That's for the shoeshine man at Penn Station. I'll get to watch him die—*if* my clinic is still 'funded'—because I'm not approved for breaking up clots with TPA and don't have the equipment anyway."

"Damn it, Amy, you act like there are no other ERs in Manhattan—"

"Not enough others, and if you have your way, the number is about to shrink."

"I'm offering you a chance to do some real good in the poor community—"

"You're trying to buy me off, plain and simple."

"Don't make me laugh," he shot back. "You're too filthy rich already."

She turned away from him, furious, heard him stalk off in the opposite direction. When she turned back, he was standing at one of his high arched windows. The sun blazed on the glass, throwing him into black silhouette, like a fly embedded in amber. Over his shoulder, he said, "I would like your explanation of why Mr. Owen VanKleeck died."

Amy stared at him in surprise. "What?"

"Answer the question, please." His voice was cold.

"Cardiac arrest."

"Why did you badger Mrs. VanKleeck for an autopsy?"

"I asked her politely, twice. Hardly badgering."

"But why? If you already knew the cause of death—"

"When Mr. VanKleeck arrested," she said, "we were there in seconds with a full resuscitation effort. Usually we can get the heart beating again, even with massive attacks. With him, we couldn't. I wanted to know why."

"Are you saying it might not have been a heart attack that killed him?"

Suddenly she wanted very much to see Eric's face. What was this all about?

Eric said, "Mr. VanKleeck was from a very influential family. His widow is not happy with your treatment of him, and, quite frankly, neither am I. I'm afraid it's going to be my duty to turn this over to the hospital's morbidity and mortality board."

Amy was too amazed even for anger. "Get a grip, Eric. You tried the carrot and that didn't work, so now you're waving the stick. You figure that if I'm tied up defending my actions in ER, I won't be in any position to fight you on the closing. You can forget it. My staff and I did all that could be done for Mr. VanKleeck."

"ER is a busy place. Can you prove you didn't step away from him at the wrong time, get caught up in other work—"

"Of course I stepped away from him, but only when appropriate. And he was continuously monitored in the nurses' station . . ." Amy paused, thunderstruck.

The videotapes!

She felt a quick charge of excitement. That was the thing she'd been missing, the evidence she needed! When a patient died in the cardiac bay, the monitoring tape was automatically saved instead of being reused the next day. If anything lethal had been done to Mr. VanKleeck after he got to Hudson, it would be on that tape.

Eric paced toward her, jamming his hands into his pockets as though he needed to restrain them. "If you're smart, you'll reconsider my offer," he said. "Think what you like—you want to call it a carrot, fine. Take it, or I'll find a good stick, you can rely on that. Either way, you are not going to stop me from bringing this hospital into the black."

"Dragging it into the dark, you mean."

Eric flushed. "You think you're so clever. You're just smug. There you stand, blocking progress, pretending to care about ragamuffin street people who do no useful work and never put a tax dollar into this city—"

"Eric, I'd love to stay and get hysterical with you, but I have to get back to ER." And look at those tapes.

"Don't you speak to me like that," he snapped.

"Or you'll what? Close down ER? Get this through your

head, Eric. You don't scare me. If you get your way and ER is closed, I'll be gone. If you don't, you're stuck with me no matter how I talk to you—unless you think you can persuade the board to do without the millions my father donates and raises for this hospital every year."

"Wonderful," Eric sputtered. "You accuse me of waving a stick, then trot out your rich, powerful daddy—"

"There's no reason we shouldn't both have sticks, is there, Eric?" At the door, she turned. "If you call me up here again when I'm in the middle of a shift, I hope you'll have a better reason than trying to buy me or hang me out to dry."

Back in her office, with her anger and disgust cooling, Amy felt a deepening unease. Closing ER because it was draining money from the hospital was one thing—reasonable people could disagree about that. It was another matter entirely to shut it down for your own profit. Eric had admitted nothing, but it would explain his savage determination. How far would he go for money and its power? Would he kill?

Chilled, Amy considered it. The mysterious deaths of four rich and prominent men in Hudson's ER might help Eric close it down. But then the deaths would become public knowledge, and the scandal might well kill any sale. The hospital's good reputation was what a corporate buyer would most want and need for its profits.

Unless she was missing something, Eric did not make a very good suspect.

Too bad.

Amy looked at the four videocassettes stacked on her desk. VanKleeck, Jameson, Levesque, and Christiani, their last agonized minutes magnetized and reduced, wound tight in these flimsy black boxes. The legal department had put the procedure in place three years ago—not to catch murderers, but as insurance against lawsuits. As long as nothing bad happened, the tapes were recycled. If a patient worsened or died in the bay, the relevant tape or tapes would be pulled out by the charge nurse and saved. All very routine. No saved tape had ever been needed for any purpose. Which was why she hadn't thought of them.

Thank you, Eric.

Amy stuck the VanKleeck tape in the office VCR, switched on the TV, and closed her door. Using the remote controller, she started through it on fast forward, slowing only when there were people in the bay with Owen VanKleeck. There was Elaine, searching the crash cart for nitroglycerine, then turning when she couldn't find it to call for Philip. Philip appeared. Knowing what was coming, Amy fought the urge to look away. Elaine chastened him with just the right firmness for not keeping the cart properly stocked. The tape was not quite sharp enough to pick up the tears in his eyes.

Amy watched the rest of it. Herself leaving. VanKleeck alone, then Cathy DiGenova breezing in to adjust his blanket. Dr. Kellum from neurology stuck his head in. He had probably been called down on a consult and was looking into booths because he couldn't be bothered trying to find his case on the patient locator board. Amy felt herself tense as VanKleeck convulsed, grabbing his chest, making a strangled sound. Seconds later, Bernie hurried into the picture, calling for Elaine. Then Amy saw herself enter. The tape ran to its sad end, the removal of VanKleeck's body.

Stymied, Amy stopped the tape. There was no evidence of murder.

Or rather, none that she had noticed.

Amy put Jameson's tape into the machine. A handsome man with blue eyes, white hair tinged with yellow. He bore a vague resemblance to Winnie. Amy thrust the thought from her mind. She watched the tape through. It ended with Jameson dying in a way depressingly similar to VanKleeck—two doctors and a nurse, right there, coding him at once. Nothing had helped.

And nothing on the tape rang a bell.

Amy put Levesque into the machine, then Christiani. As she watched, she felt a headache starting up, working its way down her neck. Finishing the last tape, she looked at the names she'd jotted down of people who'd appeared on all four tapes. Nothing leapt out at her. Except for various doctors roaming through ER looking for consults, everyone on the four tapes had been in the booth for legitimate reasons—to treat the patient or tend the crash cart.

Amy watched the tapes again. Her headache worsened, silvery threads of pain welding her head and neck into one rigid piece. Yanking her desk drawer open, she shook out two aspirin and gulped them down with cold coffee.

I'm too close to it, she thought. Everything's too familiar to me. I need someone else—another doctor I can trust—to look at these with me.

Picking up her phone, she dialed Chris in pathology.

"Dr. Hunt."

"Chris, you doing anything?"

"Getting ready for happy hour at Carney's with pt's number-one hunk."

Amy looked at her wall clock, shocked to see that it was after four. She realized Chris was waiting for her to respond. "Jasper Eldridge—aka Jasper the grasper?"

"The very same."

The grinning brightness of Chris's voice made Amy smile, too. She saw Jasper in her mind, muscles like Schwarzenegger, sunny smile, thick blond hair. "Make sure he doesn't break anything."

"On me or on him?"

Amy hung up, laughing, then winced as the sullen pain of the headache speared briefly into her ear. Good for Chris. Half the women in the hospital had an eye on Jasper.

And I still need someone to look at these tapes with me, Amy thought dejectedly. Someone trained in medicine, with no preconceptions about ER's cardiac routines. Someone with a sharp eye and a fresh brain.

Someone I can trust.

Campy!

At once, the idea felt right to her. She could take the tapes to his place, get him to watch them with her.

And maybe, afterward, she could hear the rest of what he'd started to say to her in the park.

As she reached for the phone, Amy realized that her headache was gone.

18

As the cab pulled up to Campy's apartment building, Amy got a hollow feeling in her stomach. Was this such a good idea— setting herself up to be alone with Campy in his apartment?

How would he feel about her popping in unannounced?

It wasn't her fault, after all. He hadn't been in his office, and Personnel had no home phone listed yet, so she couldn't call.

Maybe he wouldn't even be there.

"Lady?" the cabbie said.

She paid him off and got out, the envelope with the video-tapes under her arm. At the building entrance, she hesitated. She needed a minute to think. Turning away, she walked up toward First Avenue. The sun shone full in her face, blazing above the buildings to the west, bright but not very warm.

Come on, it was perfectly reasonable to come to Campy. He knew medicine and could bring a fresh perspective to the tapes.

But that's not the only reason you're here. You want to know why he didn't come back. Why? Why can't you let it go, even after all these years?

At First Avenue, she turned around. A stiff wind, laced with the smell of diesel oil from the river, blew straight into her face. Pulling her collar tight, she leaned into the wind and

started resolutely back down the street. Ahead of her, she saw
Campy step from his building. She stopped, surprised, then
called out to him. The wind swept her voice back into her face.
Campy strode away from her toward York Avenue.

She hurried after him, curious. Not much but the river and
a little park lay that way. Most of the eating places were in the
other direction, but maybe he knew a little pub on York. That
would be nice—walk in and surprise him, explain about the
tapes over a drink.

Amy tried to close up, but Campy was walking too fast.
On York he turned right; at Seventy-sixth, right again, back up
toward First. Apparently he was just walking around the block,
stretching his legs. Keeping her eyes on him as she followed,
Amy almost missed the vagrant sprawled on a cushion of gar-
bage bags ahead of her. In anxious reflex she veered toward
the curb, speeding up to get past him. The vagrant tracked her
with bloodshot eyes. He raised his bottle. "Hey, baby!"

She hurried past, fear grabbing along her spine as he faded
back from her peripheral vision. Time to catch up with Campy,
even if she had to run—

Where *was* Campy?

Amy squinted into the sunlight up the empty sidewalk,
feeling a prickle of alarm. Half a block ahead, on First Avenue,
the cabs and trucks flowed past. Somehow, during the seconds
she'd been preoccupied with the vagrant, Campy had disappeared.

The vagrant called out behind her, spurring her forward.
Campy had to be up here somewhere—

A man stepped from an alley into her face, silhouetted
against the sun. She sucked a sharp breath.

"Amy?"

"Campy!" Relief flooded her. "You scared me!"

"Are you following me?"

"I called out when you left your apartment, but you didn't
hear." She moved around him so that his back was to the alley
and she could see his face better. He looked a little flustered,
definitely not pleased.

"Well . . ." He glanced up the alley. "Now that you're here,
you'd better stick with me. But stay back and don't talk till I
tell you."

Amy stared down the alley, feeling her stomach clench. It was narrow and dark in there, a dead end. Why did he want to go in there?

"If you'd rather wait out here—"

"And miss touring the Black Hole of Calcutta?"

He gave her a small, distracted smile and walked into the alley. She followed him in, staying close behind him. The alley was quite narrow, the chilly darkness almost absolute. She could smell urine. Something skittered behind her, making her stomach plunge. What in God's name was Campy *doing*?

A bird called in the darkness right in front of her, startling her, and then she realized Campy had made the sound. It was eerie and beautiful, a pure, liquid sound. A second later the same sound floated back from the end of the alley, followed by a harsh, metallic sound that she'd heard only in the movies: the bolt of a gun being eased.

The hairs stood up on her neck. A gun?

"James, I've brought a friend," Campy said softly.

James? He *knows* someone in here?

Amy looked over Campy's shoulder. As her eyes adjusted, she made out a pile of cardboard boxes in the near darkness. They were stacked into a low hut against the brick wall of the dead end. A shadowy figure crawled out from the crude hut and stood, gazing at Campy and her. He was quite tall, with wild hair and a beard down to his chest. A greatcoat hung loosely on him, as though his shoulders had once been bigger.

Campy said, "You remember I used to talk about Amy? This is Amy."

The man stopped backing up and stared at her. In the low light, she could see the moist glint of his eyeballs, and then the sheen of his teeth. "Amy St. Clair." His voice rasped, as though he hadn't used it for a long time.

"That's me," she said.

"So *this* is why we had to move here. I should have guessed. In country, Top used to show us your picture. You're even prettier now you've grown up."

"Thank you." In country—Vietnam. In her mind she saw Campy, young and lean, holding her high school class picture out to this man. The image touched her. But what had he meant, *we* had to move here?

"Don't get too close," James said. "I haven't had a bath since at least this morning." He laughed, and the laughter, too, sounded as if it hadn't been used for a long time. He was still looking at her, staring at her as though she were the most wonderful thing he had ever seen.

Silence stretched. Amy realized that her presence was keeping the men from talking. "Listen," she said, "I'll just go on back out so you two can talk."

"You don't need to do that," Campy said.

"It's all right," she said. "I'll wait at the alley entrance." She turned before he could protest again, and headed back to the street. Broken glass crunched under her soles. Back on the sidewalk, she stopped and looked around at them. They had squatted down facing each other. She could hear the bass murmur of Campy's voice. There was a soothing quality to it, even without the words. Their obvious rapport intrigued her. Clearly, James had soldiered with Campy. Campy had been his "top," army jargon for "top sergeant."

Amy heard James talking now. The raspy voice was flat, almost devoid of emotion, but there was a terrible sadness about him—Amy could feel it more strongly from out here. Children liked to play house in cardboard boxes, but at night they slept in warm beds. James might have had that once, too, but now he had only the boxes. How had his life unraveled to this?

Campy rose and walked toward her.

"James," she called, "I'm glad I got to meet you."

"Likewise."

As they left the alley, the sunlight slanting down the street blinded Amy. She blinked, feeling as if she'd just stepped through from another world. She walked with Campy up and around the corner with First Avenue. Campy turned down Seventy-seventh, still saying nothing as they headed back toward his apartment.

"So James *lives* there," Amy said.

"Yes."

"If we could get him into a shelter . . ."

"You won't. He's been living in alleys since we got back to the States. When I was in med school in Ann Arbor, I tried to get him to room with me. He lasted about a week in my apartment, then moved into an alley down the block."

"And now he's made the move here with you," Amy said.

"James feels, with some justification, that I need looking after. See, he's the guy I started to tell you about in the park. When I stepped on that pungi stick, he carried me out through forty miles of jungle. Without James, there would no longer be a Campy." Campy tossed the words off lightly.

"So that's how it happened," she said. "A sharpened stick planted in the ground."

He nodded.

"I read a lot about the war," she said, "including Viet Cong tactics, when you were over there."

"The NVA planted a few up north, too," Campy said, "after we started spooking them. The one with my name on it had feces on the point. So aside from the nice big puncture, I got infection, gangrene, so on. If I'd been nearer to any kind of medical help . . . But I wasn't."

She shuddered. "It must have been very hard for you."

"It's over now." He turned, and she realized they were back at his apartment.

"Will you come up?" he asked.

"Yes."

He unlocked the door and she followed him through into a small lobby, floored in gray marble and lushly tenanted with plants. A marble counter ran along the left wall, but no one stood behind it. Amy felt an air of safety and permanence here, as if it were a place outside of time. A wooden stairway ascended the right side of the lobby. An elevator waited behind ornate black grillwork. Disdaining it, Campy started up the steps. She followed him, watching the Du Pont foot, marveling at the easy way it flexed against its ankle.

At the second landing, he stopped, gripping the cap of the newel post. For a second she thought he was catching his balance, then he pulled the cap loose and dug a key out of the hollow it left in the newel post.

"This is for you," he said, "in case you drop by and I'm not here. I take walks, but I'm usually not gone long. Just let yourself in and I'll be back."

"What if a thief finds it?"

He dropped the key back into its hollow and knocked the cap home briskly with the heel of his hand. "There's always a chance of that. But I've decided to risk it." He paused. "Sometimes I forget my key when I go out." There was strain in his voice, as though forgetting his keys somehow shamed him.

"It's called advancing age," she said.

He groaned. "If you'll excuse me, I'll take out my teeth, see if your foot chipped any."

She laughed.

He unlocked his door and waved her through ahead of him. She stepped inside, eager for this first look at how he kept things. The perfume of lemon grass greeted her, drawing her first to the kitchenette, nestled beside a dining alcove at the back of the apartment. The sink and fridge looked old, the ceramic tile of the floor chipped in spots but very clean. No dishes in the sink, either. She joined Campy in the living room. The plain oak floor gleamed softly; there were no rugs. A tall central window looked out on Seventy-seventh. Rather than curtains, Campy had hung the window with a roll-down Roman blind made of bamboo. Beside the window sat a leather recliner turned not toward the middle of the living room, but out, toward the street. Amy imagined him sitting there alone, people-watching. He had chosen a good apartment, but the way he'd set it up, it was lonely, the whole room focused outward to somewhere else.

"Drink?" Campy said.

"Tiny bit of Scotch, lots of water."

"Have a seat." He pointed to a rattan couch in the corner away from the window and disappeared into the kitchen. The couch was pillowless and very new-looking. She put the envelope with the tapes on the seat beside her.

Campy returned with a very pale Scotch, just as she'd asked. His own looked even paler. She took a sip, savoring its mellow heat in her throat. As Campy started to shrug from his coat, something fell from an inside pocket and bounced heavily on the floor. When he picked it up, she saw with a little shock that it was a knife—a big military knife with an olive drab handle and a long, leather-sheathed blade.

"Your K-bar?"

"You *did* do your reading, didn't you?" Looking embarrassed, he tried to put it back in his jacket.

Amy's throat crawled with the memory of the other blade. Defiantly she suppressed the fear. "May I see it?"

He handed it across. She hefted it in her hand, chilled by its lethal weight, the perfect balance. "Actually," Campy said, "it's not mine. It belongs to James. I . . . lost mine. James prefers Kalashnikovs—that gun you no doubt noticed."

"You carry the knife around with you?"

"I used to. Now I just take it along to rough places." She handed the knife back and he put it away in the jacket. He said, "I knew a marine over there who survived some very heavy action. I ran into him in Washington, after the war. He had a nice home in the suburbs, a terrific wife. He was working as a consultant for Rosalyn Carter. A personable guy, laid back and funny. At night, he couldn't sleep without a baseball bat under his bed."

"A ball bat," she said, thinking of her hammer. "Now I could live with that."

"But bats have such dull points."

She smiled. He gazed at her, as if mentally recording every detail of her face. "I'm glad you're here, Amy. I've been wanting this. Just to sit here and talk with you."

She nodded, but felt her guard going up. The warmth in his voice drew her, but she was not sure she wanted warmth from him. What she wanted were answers. She saw that he was looking at the envelope beside her on the couch. "Videotapes," she explained. "From ER. I wanted your opinion on them. But I don't see a TV, much less a VCR."

"Is that the only reason you came?" He looked disappointed.

"No. I wanted to finish what we started in the park."

"Good."

"You were starting to tell me why you didn't come back after you lost your foot."

Campy met her gaze. "After the foot, James dragged me forty miles south until he located a temporary CIA LZ—landing zone. He got me onto a Company chopper. I was delirious. I didn't learn until later that James didn't come with me, that he went back into the jungle. To make a long story short, after I recovered, I had to go back in after James." Campy showed no sign of going on.

"Don't let's make the story quite *that* short."

He gave her a thin smile. "It did take me a while. The chopper took me back to Saigon. That period was a blur, partly from the painkillers, and partly from . . . what we'd been through up north. As soon as I was fit to travel, they shipped me stateside to Fort Bragg. When it really sank in that I'd lost my foot, I slid into a depression. They tried everything they knew to snap me out of it. Then a clever army shrink learned how James had saved me. He did some digging and found out James had disappeared back in country. The psychiatrist told me. It worked. I threw myself into rehab like a tiger. I was determined to find James and bring him out."

"And while you were doing all that rehab, you couldn't have written? You couldn't have called me, for God's sake?"

Campy looked at the floor. "And say what? Amy, I'm back—but I'm leaving again as soon as I can?"

"How about, 'Amy, I'm all right, and I still love you, please hold on and wait for me.' "

"Don't you think I wanted to say that?" His voice was suddenly intense, agonized. "What if I had, and you'd waited, maybe turned Bud away? And I'd got my stupid throat cut out there stumbling around on a tin leg with NVA all around me. That's how it *should* have ended and I . . . well, damn it, I knew that going in."

"You had to be a hero."

"That's not how I saw it. James had given me my life. I couldn't live it sitting back and letting him die."

"Surely there were others in your unit who—"

"No," Campy said. "By the time I stepped on the pungi stick, we were the only two left." His voice was very low.

She looked at him, appalled, feeling his pain. "All right. But Campy, no one with a shred of fairness—including yourself—could have held you responsible for James. You had been grievously wounded, lost a foot—"

"And bringing James out is what made me able to live with that. Knowing I had to try was the only thing that got me through rehab. When I actually pulled it off, I . . ."

"You felt like a man again," Amy said. She felt a sudden,

hopeless exasperation at men, quixotic, emotional, muddle-headed children in big strong bodies.

"It's damned foolish, isn't it?" Campy said wearily.

"Tell me about getting James."

"There isn't much to tell . . ."

Amy laughed in spite of herself.

"Well, there isn't. When I got to where I could use the foot pretty well, I tried to get the army to send me back over. They wouldn't, of course—for one thing, I was being medically discharged. But you could still get over there if you were with a newspaper or magazine. Believe it or not, I got myself accredited to the *Dallas Times Herald* as a free-lance journalist. It was a complete sham, but it got me back to 'Nam. James had a big start on me. I found out what this foot could do if it had to. I had an idea where James might be. I found him back where we'd been . . . operating, and coaxed him out."

With surprise Amy realized that, despite her fascination with the story, she also felt obscurely annoyed, in a strange way, even cheated. Here I sat, she thought, waiting for Campy, month after month with no word. And now I find that he had the best reasons in the world and it still makes me mad. Am I supposed to thank James for saving Campy's life, even though he also took it away from me?

Amy realized that she *did* feel grateful to James. I'm confused, she thought. She looked at Campy and felt herself wanting at last to let go of the past. He was here, now. She could not be anything but glad.

"What was it like," she said, "to be back in the place where you had lost your foot?"

"Terrible," Campy said.

"Only terrible?"

He was silent for a long time, his eyes distant, as if the question were totally new to him and he was considering it. "At night," he said, "the elephant grass looks silver in the moonlight. The crickets are so loud they sound like they are singing for the gods. You are alone. You know you might die that night. You have never been so alive."

She was struck by the intensity in his voice. A part of him had loved the danger, she realized. Why was it so hard for him to admit that?

He cleared his throat. "Anyway, after I got James back, I came to New York. That was in seventy-four . . . You were married to Bud. You had two young daughters."

Her throat felt hot and tight. "You . . . you mentioned that you had talked to Bud. Was it then?"

"Yes. I couldn't leave New York again without meeting him. I had to know if he . . . if he was right for you. You were at work—you'd just started at Hudson. I gave him a phony name, asked about him doing a painting for me. He said he never worked on commission, but would I like a beer? We sat up there in his studio and shot the bull. I didn't want to like him, but I did. I liked it that he painted what he wanted. I liked his face, his handshake. He was a big man in more ways than one. He talked about you and the girls. He loved you a lot. I could tell from his stories that you loved him, too."

Amy felt tears welling up.

Campy came over to her, putting his glass down, taking her by the forearms. "I loved you," he said, "I still wanted you so much, Bud or no Bud. But I knew what I'd done. I had all these reasons, sure, but they wouldn't take away what I'd done to you. Meeting Bud, I saw that I had not made a permanent hole in your life. It was the one thing I could be glad for." He let go of her arms and sat on the edge of the end table, as if suddenly exhausted.

Amy's body felt rigid. She was afraid to move. "So you just went away again."

"I had no right to do anything else," he said in a low voice.

Amy closed her eyes, feeling the fading trace of Bud inside her. "No."

"You know the rest," Campy said. "A few months ago, I saw the painting, found out Bud had died. It shocked me. I had formed an image of your life, of you being happy and content, you and Bud and your kids. Poor, dear Amy. What pain you've had."

Amy saw him through a blur of tears. She could not speak. She felt her heart would break.

Campy came to her, holding out a hand; she saw herself take it, felt her heart quicken as he drew her to him. "Is there still a chance for us?" he asked.

Amy felt the blood pounding, spinning through her head.

"Oh, Campy. How can I cut Tom off just like that? I care for him, too. I have to think about all this. I . . . need time."

"Take it. I'm not about to stop loving you now."

She became aware of a church bell tolling somewhere outside the window a few blocks away, five, six. Six o'clock. "I've got to get home," she said, startled, picking up the ER videos. "Joyce and the girls will be waiting dinner."

Campy nodded.

All of a sudden, she wanted desperately to feel his arms around her, the urge so strong it scared her.

He leaned into her, bowing his head to find her lips. She felt her face tilting up of its own will. The touch of his mouth seemed to awaken memories in her skin, so that her own lips trembled against his. She reached up and pulled his head to hers, kissing him hard.

Then backed away and ran to the door, down the steps, feeling the light and color and air swirling into her head as if she had just awakened from a very long dream.

19

The man made himself stroll through the night, looking confident and relaxed as he passed from darkness through the milky pool of a streetlight. He checked ahead to make sure the unmarked police car was really gone. Yes, thanks to a dead rapist.

As he walked the last few feet to Amy's front stoop, a savage determination filling him, threatening his charade of nonchalance. The key was already in his hand. He slipped it into the lock, trying not to think about the risk. If a neighbor should happen to be awake this time of night, and looking out the window—

They will see a harmless older gentleman dressed in a tuxedo, the man told himself. He held the laughter in his throat. It faded as the key refused to slide in. *Did Daddy's girl change the locks again?*

Sweating, the man forced himself to pause, to pull wearily at the black tie, untying it to dangle on his shirtfront. He liked the little touch—it was not the sort of thing an intruder would do.

He tried the key again, and this time it slid in and turned. Inside, he stood in the dark foyer a moment, holding his breath, listening. The town house was quiet, except for the hum of the refrigerator in the kitchen and the clack of the grandfather clock straight ahead. The clock annoyed him. How could Amy stand the morbid thing, relentlessly chopping away the seconds of her life?

The man pulled off the wig, the glasses, and the mustache, zipping them into one of the huge pockets he'd sewn inside the coat. He put on the dark knitted ski mask and a pair of rubber gloves and checked the new garrote. One looped end protruded an inch from his left coat sleeve and he could feel the other end beneath his armpit, held by a single stitch. It seemed a good solution and should keep him from repeating the earlier disaster. Now if Amy woke up, he could get to it *very* fast.

The man went to the foot of the stairs and peered up. The night light at the top spilled down, bright as a full moon. Leaning forward, he put both hands on the fifth step and started up on all fours, creeping with the slow care of a stalking cat through the sleeping house. The oak steps glowed like marbled gold in the soft light. His dress Rockports, well cushioned and wonderfully flexible, made no sound. He felt a dark exhilaration, a surge of confidence. This time he would get what he wanted. Amy had held out too long already, stubborn and willful even under the scopolamine. For a while he had found her resistance quite impressive, but now his patience was growing short.

A board creaked softly under him and he froze, his heart hammering. He listened for a minute, biting nervously at the insides of his lips, hoping the last time was not about to repeat itself. Kids normally slept like the dead. Denise must have already been awake that last time, or she'd never have heard the damned board creaking. He flushed, remembering how the fear had fountained in him, the way he'd scurried, without dignity, back down the steps. At the last second, before he'd turned out of the foyer, he had felt her at the top of the stairs, her eyes burning into his back. The memory crawled between his shoulder blades. Why hadn't she cried out? Had she somehow recognized him, even from behind, and simply accepted his presence? But that made no sense either; surely she'd have called out. Her silence would mystify him forever.

No sound from above. He relaxed a little. All right, slowly now, ignore your eyes, *feel* the steps, let your hands find the way for your feet.

He reached the top without making another sound, and paused to listen. There were no sounds from the bedrooms to his right, or Amy's to his left. He slipped into Amy's bedroom, easing the door shut and going straight around to the far side of the king-size bed, putting it between him and the door. She was lying on her back—good. The streetlight across from her town house bounced its silvery glow off the ceiling onto her face and neck. Easy to see. He took the Baggie with the dermal patches from his coat pocket. Carefully, with the lightest of touches, he stuck three of the adhesive patches behind her ear. Then he stretched out on the floor, out of Amy's sight, below the edge of the bed.

Now came the hardest part: waiting.

Dermal patches worked with agonizing slowness, compared to the instant strike of venous injection. He must give the scopolamine time to seep into the capillaries. He remembered the trouble he'd had at first, setting the dose for Cynthia. One patch—used by anesthetists to dry tissues—wasn't enough to sedate. He knew he'd need more than one patch to get Cynthia deep enough, but how many? That first time, the four patches had been too much. He'd missed her on the way down, then waited three hours, finally having to remove the patches and slip out without questioning her. He had prepared for that possibility by doing it on a Friday night; Cynthia had had plenty of time to sleep off the effects the next morning. But still, frustrating. The next time, with three patches, he seemed to have got it right. But on the final try he'd used the same dose and she'd awakened—a disaster almost as bad as leaving the garrote behind at Amy's. Fortunately, Cynthia lived twenty stories up and he could arrange her "suicide" easily. But it was maddening to think her death posed a risk to him when she'd given him nothing at all.

Amy would give him what he wanted, he could feel it. Tonight, *tonight*.

How much time had gone by? Not enough. The man waited, hearing the damned clock ticking, even through Amy's closed door. He practiced self-control, lying still and waiting as long as possible between checks on his watch. When half an hour had gone by, he raised his head, putting his mouth beside Amy's ear. "Can you hear me?" he murmured, watching her face. She made no response, but her eyebrows moved slightly.

Lying back down, he counted off five hundred ticks of the grandfather clock, then tried again.

"Can you hear me?"

"Mhmmm," she said in a lax, dreamlike voice.

Excitement swelled in him. "You are four years old," he murmured. "You are back home with Mommy and Daddy. It is late at night. You are walking in your sleep, out in the woods behind your house."

He saw Amy's forehead furrow, her mouth pull down. "Where are you?"

Her lips moved.

"Say it."

She frowned slightly. "Woods."

"Good. As you are walking, you begin to wake up. You see something. Do you see it?"

"Yes."

His excitement sharpened almost unbearably. *Yes, you do see it, don't you!* He saw Amy's forehead crease in a wince; she rolled her head away on the pillow.

"Don't be afraid," he soothed. "There is nothing to be afraid of—"

The man stopped as he heard the soft creak of Amy's doorknob turning. A cold shock went through him. Dropping below the side of the bed, he held his breath. Soft light washed into the room from the night light in the hall.

"Amy?" called a woman's voice. "Are you all right? I thought I heard someone talking."

The nanny—Joyce. The man cursed silently. Sweat poured again from his face into the knitted fabric of the ski mask. *Go away,* he thought.

But she did not go away. He heard her bare feet swishing across the carpet toward the bed, felt her steps throb closer through the wood beneath.

"Amy?"

A switch snapped, cracking along his nerves as the room flooded with light from her bed lamp.

"Amy, wake up."

The man felt the bed moving, heard the sheets rustling. Joyce was shaking Amy.

She's going to call an ambulance, the man realized with terrible certainty. The phone was on his side of the bed. *Quickly,* he thought. He grabbed the loop at his cuff, jerked hard, pulling the garrote from his sleeve, rolling as he heard Joyce coming around the bed. Bracing a hand on the side of the bed, he leaped up. Her head snapped back in surprise, and he could see her shoulders rise as he lunged, the wire looping tight around her throat, trapping the scream in her lungs. She struggled fiercely, clawing at his wrists, trying to tear his face with her nails. She kicked hard at his leg. Off balance, he fell toward the bed, twisting around, feeling the loops of the garrote dig into his hands as he pulled Joyce down on top of him. Not too hard, now. If he could just put her under—

One of her hands caught his ski mask and tore it up. He saw the shock of recognition in her eyes. A sick feeling plunged through his stomach. He tightened the garrote and rolled her off him, feeling his back bump Amy's side. Damn! now she'd wake up too. All right, Joyce first, and then he'd kill Amy— easy, with the drug in her.

Joyce's arms flopped, weak and uncoordinated. Gritting his teeth, the man pulled the garrote tighter. Her eyes rolled up and she went limp. He pushed her off him, pulled the ski mask back down, and unwrapped the garrote from her neck. Rolling the other way, he went for Amy's throat, then realized she was lying still, her eyes closed, her face relaxed.

Still under.

He found himself slipping the garrotte around Amy's neck anyway, starting to tighten it, rage boiling in his muscles. With a tremendous effort, he stopped himself. If he killed her now, he'd never know.

And he must take care of the nanny first.

As he moved away from the bed and bent over, he felt a surge of nausea. With a fierce effort, he kept from throwing up. What damnable luck, horrible, a complete disaster for him. A bitter fury burned through him. He bent over Joyce to make sure she was still unconscious. Lifting her, he carried her out into the hall. He moved very slowly, easing his back against the wall to steady himself, creeping along sideways, feeling trapped in a hellish nightmare in which the floor kept creaking softly and the hallway seemed to stretch on and on into infinity.

Passing a half-open doorway, he glimpsed a child's bed, a pajama-clad leg twined in the covers.

He paused, waiting to see if the leg moved. Was the kid lying in there faking it? Just one move and he'd have to take a little detour. The leg stayed still.

He inched farther down the hallway, thinking about Amy. Damn it to hell! He'd been on the verge of getting his answers from her.

Was there still a chance tonight?

No. She would be coming up too light by now. He must go back and remove the dermal patches, then get out.

The man felt his teeth clenching. He had really wanted to kill her just then. If Amy was really the one, she deserved to die. Could he stand to wait, come back for one more try?

The idea of killing her, rash as it was, filled him with a fierce sense of rightness.

Do it quietly, he thought. It could get messy if you have to kill the kids, too.

From a great distance, Amy heard Joyce calling to her: *Amy? Are you all right? I thought I heard someone talking.* Her voice seemed to puncture the woods, making them shimmer and fade away. Where am I? Amy thought. She struggled to open her eyes and could not.

"Amy?"

It *was* Joyce. Amy fought harder to open her eyes. Her arms and legs were impossibly heavy.

"Amy, wake up." She felt hands gripping her shoulders, shaking her. Her eyelids trembled apart a tiny slit. Joyce's face, creased with concern, swam against the ceiling above her, then pulled away before she could speak to it. Her eyes slipped shut again. She could hear Joyce walking around the foot of the bed, every sound sharp and clear, but still she could not move. She felt the bed push down at her side, heard feet rush across the floor. There was a terrible, choked sound and then she felt something jolting the foot of the bed. Someone fell on the bed beside her, sending a cold surge of fright through her. She forced her eyes open again and saw a man's back bouncing and jerking right in front of her. His back was almost at her shoulder, his hooded head straining sideways. Beyond him, Amy could see Joyce thrashing, her hand clawing at the man's shoulder. The hand grabbed at the hood, and Amy saw the pink of the man's ear as the hood wrinkled along the back of his head. He recoiled, tensed, then Joyce's hand at his shoulder stopped clawing and went limp, sliding away.

Horrified, Amy started to scream. *No, he'll kill you, lie still.*

She heard the man roll toward her, felt something slick and warm slide around her neck. It took all of her will to stay limp. The noose tightened on her neck, then loosened again. She felt the bed shift. Slitting an eye, she saw the man, his hood back in place, lift Joyce from the bed. Joyce's eyes were closed. She was limp, but not completely, not dead, *please, God, don't let her be dead.*

Amy felt sick with horror. She must do something, get up, try and save Joyce. She tried to move her arm. It slid a few inches, her fingers twitching impotently. Tears of frustration welled up. Through slitted eyes, she saw the man carry Joyce out the door. He moved slowly, seeming to take forever. He was headed past the girls' bedrooms. What if one of them heard him and cried out? He'd surely kill them.

Amy felt a cold rush of terror. She must get up, she *must*! She tried again to move her arm. This time she was able to draw it up to her face. It felt horribly numb, as though it had gone to sleep. She flexed her fingers, feeling prickles of sensation. Come on, Come *on*!

In an agony of desperation, she got the other arm moving, then the legs. She crawled to the edge of the bed. Her eyes kept slipping closed. *Am I dreaming? Please, God, let me be dreaming.* But she knew she was not.

She swung a leg out of bed, taking too long, she wouldn't be able to stand. The phone! She reached for it, watching her fingers, willing them to close around the receiver. She lifted it, pulled it along the bed toward her. The dial tone whined in her ear. She reached out to the buttons, walking her fingers to the zero. A board creaked in the hall behind her. She rolled onto her side, her hand knocking the phone from the stand. It fell to the floor with a loud crash. She gasped, appalled. The sound would wake the girls! They'd come into the hall and *he'd kill them!*

The air swam in little dots before her eyes. At the doorway, she saw the man, standing still, staring at her. His horrible black hood opened to pink circles around his eyes. She stared back, paralyzed, frozen in horror.

Then she saw a flicker of movement behind him.

"Mom, there's a man!"

Denise! The high, panicked voice struck through Amy like an electric shock. She lunged from the bed, screaming in a fury of terror and determination.

20

Amy staggered and almost fell. With a desperate effort she caught her balance. Standing, facing the man, took every ounce of strength in her legs. The room seemed to whirl around her—any second she would fall.

"I called the police." Her hoarse, growling voice shocked her. "They already had a car in the area."

The man took a step toward her, his eyes and mouth horrid slits inside the holes of the ski mask.

"You leave her alone," Denise screamed, beating on the man's back. Amy's heart stuttered with dread. The man wheeled around, pushed Denise aside, and ran from the room. Amy felt the ceiling swing down, the bed strike her back. The room spun, started to fade—

No, hang on.

With a fierce effort she rolled over and tried to push herself up. Her arms trembled; her hands slipped apart on the sheets and she sprawled flat. Twisting, she saw the doorway. Empty now. Denise got up and ran to her. "Mom, Mom!"

"Shhhh!" Amy heard the man lunging down the stairs. Hope burst in her. She fumbled for Denise, her arms heavy and awkward, holding her still in a tight hug. She heard the front door downstairs open and close. Relief surged through her.

Thank God! A second later, Ellie shuffled into her doorway, clutching her stuffed lion.

"What's the matter, Mommy?"

Amy saw that Denise was looking fearfully at her, too. "Hel' me up," she croaked. Her tongue felt thick and horribly dry. Denise pulled her to a sitting position. Her head felt very heavy; with a huge effort she held it up. "S'all right, now. We're fine. Come here t'your sisser."

Ellie did as she was told. "Denise . . ." Amy said. She felt her eyelids slipping shut, forced them open again. *Dear God, help me, I've got to get to Joyce, please let her be all right!*

"Mom, what's that behind your ear?"

Amy touched where Denise was pointing, feeling smooth dead spots. Had the feeling gone from her skin?

Dermal patches! Cold horror swirled in her. "Geddum off me!" She felt a light tug as Denise ripped the patches off. "No, don' throw away. Put 'em on bed." She fought a wave of dizziness. "Medical bag, desk, bring it."

Denise leaped from the bed. Amy felt herself sagging over, powerless to stop it. She lay on her side, the room blurring, swimming in and out of focus. She struggled to hang on to her thoughts. Dermal patches. What were they? Scopolamine? That would explain why her vision was screwed up and her mouth so dry. For a second she glimpsed Ellie's face peering anxiously at her, then it blurred again. Fragments of the dream swirled in her head: being in the woods again, hearing a man's voice, the questions, and Joyce calling her . . .

The man choking Joyce—that was real.

I'm coming, Joyce, hang on.

Denise's face swung into view. "Here's your bag, Mom."

Desperately, Amy tried to think. What was the antidote for scopolamine? She'd used it on the little boy who'd drunk some Donnatal . . . physostigmine. Denise tugged at her, helping her sit up again. Amy plunged a hand into the bag, feeling for the little vials, spilling a handful on the bed. "Phy-so-stig-mine," she said to Denise.

Denise sorted through the vials. "I don't see it."

Amy's heart sank. Hadn't she thrown a vial in her bag, when she'd brought Donnatal for Ellie's diarrhea?

"Do you spell it with a F?" Denise asked.

Laboriously, Amy spelled out the name.

"Here it is!"

"Good. Need syringe, too." Amy tried to help, saw that she was getting in Denise's way. With only a few words of instruction, Denise got the needle on the syringe and plunged it through the rubber seal of the vial.

"Pull back—that's it. More, more—stop."

Denise held the loaded syringe out to her. Gripping it in her fist, Amy plunged it into her own thigh, palming the plunger down with her other hand. Distant prick of pain, fluid fanning into the muscle. Faster if it was IV, but she couldn't help that. She breathed deeply. In seconds she felt her vision clearing. Her heart steadied; a chalky taste spread on her tongue.

"Ellie, a bad man was in here, but now he's gone. I'm just going to check and make sure Joyce is all right—"

"I'll do it!" Ellie said.

"No!"

Ellie's eyes started to tear.

"I didn't mean to shout, honey. But I want you stay here with your sister. I'll be right back and we'll call the police. Will you girls stay here, please, and not leave my bedroom, no matter what?"

Denise nodded. Her face was white, but she was not crying. Ellie was watching her closely, her mouth squeezed tight, ready to cry or not cry, whichever her sister did.

Amy felt a quick pride in both of them, and then she went out into the hall, feeling an artificial, jerky power in her legs, as though she'd drunk ten cups of coffee. Her eardrums throbbed. She hurried down to Joyce's room, fear clutching her chest. Joyce's body lay on the bed, terribly still. Sick with dread, Amy hurried to the bedside and groped for a pulse. A horrible purple line from the garrote ringed Joyce's neck. Her eyes were open, the pupils fixed and dilated.

"Oh God, no," Amy pleaded, feeling for a pulse. There was none.

Amy dropped to her knees, clutching Joyce's arm. It was still warm. Amy felt sobs tearing at her throat, scalding her eyes. She clenched her teeth, holding back with a furious effort. "I have to be strong now," she chanted, "be strong, be strong for Denise and Ellie. I'll cry later!"

She felt for the anger beneath the grief, letting it out, feeling it burn through her, boosting the chemical flames of the drugs in her. *Bastard! Bastard! Why did you kill her? You were after me!*

No, think about that later: Denise, Ellie—she must get back to them quickly. Amy looked at Joyce a last time and realized with a shock that her robe was open, exposing her body, as if it had been a sex crime. But it had not. Amy felt herself reaching for the robe.

Don't touch it, it's evidence.

False evidence, which the police would find all too easy to accept.

Amy closed and tied Joyce's robe and backed from the room, shutting the door. On the way back to her bedroom, she tried to compose her face for the girls. What was she going to tell them?

Denise, sitting on the edge of the bed, hugging Ellie, searched her mother's face as Amy came in, then burst into tears. Amy sat down on the bed, "She doesn't feel any pain," she said softly. She hugged Denise and Ellie to her as long as she could, then picked up the phone.

Detective Abraham Schumer of the NYPD sat with Amy in the parlor, his notebook on one knee. He wore a shapeless blue blazer, shiny at the elbows. His hair was still messed from his pillow. Amy had trouble focusing on him. She felt very jumpy, the drugs still battling in her system. I should be doing something, she thought. But there was nothing to be done.

"I know this is difficult for you, Doctor, but the more we can get from you right now, the quicker we can get on the trail of the killer."

"I understand."

"Now let me see if I've got this straight—you say the man had drugged you."

"Yes. He used scopolamine, I think. The patches are up-stairs on my bed. You can have them analyzed."

Schumer sent another policeman upstairs and continued his questioning. "These what you mean?" The cop returned with the plastic evidence bag.

"Yes." Seeing them curled like leeches in the bag, Amy felt a slow crawl of nausea in her throat. That was where the rash on her neck had come from, those things pouring their venom into her, sucking out her control.

Schumer gazed at her. "I have to say this. You don't look as though you've been drugged."

She told him about giving herself a shot. He wrote it in his notebook. "So he drugged you and was . . . questioning you. And you now believe he has been in your house several times before, doing the same thing."

"Yes. I thought it was a nightmare, a recurrent nightmare." Amy closed her eyes, feeling an icy coldness pass through her. Even though there was no other explanation, she still had trouble grasping it. Not a nightmare, there was never any nightmare—not the other times, either. This same man, this cold-blooded murderer, in her home before, creeping into her room, standing over her as she slept. Then drugging her, interrogating her.

And now Joyce was dead.

Schumer looked skeptical. "How was it that you didn't realize it? I mean, if he drugged you . . ."

"He must have done it soon after midnight. That gave my brain and nervous system time to throw off most of the effects before morning. I *do* remember feeling terribly tired and sluggish after the nightmares—and thirsty, which is a side effect of scopolamine."

Schumer nodded. Amy could read nothing in his homely face, the dark, defended eyes.

"What was he questioning you about, Doctor?"

As Amy told him, her thoughts were on Joyce: Oh, Joyce. I want us to be in the kitchen, drinking coffee, telling each other how lucky we are. You can't be dead.

Feeling the tears threaten again, she got up and turned her back on Schumer.

"If you want," Schumer said, "we can continue in a few minutes."

"Go ahead."

"Let me see . . . So you have no idea what it was the man was trying to get from you. What this . . . shape in the woods could be?"

"None."

"The man stood in your bedroom doorway a minute?"

Amy nodded, not trusting her voice. She could hear feet treading around in Joyce's room above her, the muffled voices of the police. "I need to get back with my daughters."

"Corporal Libretti is very good with kids, especially at times like this. Do you want me to call someone for you?"

"I already have."

"Good. Can you tell me anything else about the man you saw?"

"No. I'm sorry. Maybe more will come to me."

"Can you think of anyone else, besides your father and mother and the victim, whom you might have given a key to?"

Amy shook her head.

"What do you do with your purse while you're at work?"

"I don't carry a purse. I keep my keys in my pocket."

Schumer scribbled again, then looked up, his eyes intent. "Doctor, I don't want to alarm you, but based on what you've told me, this man is probably someone you know—possibly someone you know quite well."

Amy sat down again, stunned. She'd had the thought earlier. But was it really possible? Had she lost her best friend, and Denise and Ellie their second mother, to someone they *knew*? She felt a sinking sense of betrayal, then anger again, hotter than before.

Whoever he is, I'll get him, Joyce. For you and for me.

The front door opened. Amy heard a policeman telling someone to stop.

"Stand aside, young man, I'm Dr. St. Clair's mother."

Amy stood as her mother hurried into the parlor.

"Amy, Amy, poor dear." She held her arms out. Amy went to her. Victoria hugged Amy with fierce strength, surprising her. Just as the good of it, the comfort, started to flow into her, Victoria released her and stood back. Her hair was fraying around its barrettes—clearly she had barely taken time to run a comb through it. Amy remembered how Victoria had always been cool to Joyce because she disapproved of Amy leaving the girls at home.

Never mind. She was here now.

"I am Victoria Sturtevant," she said to Detective Schumer, who had stood when she entered. Schumer nodded, introducing himself. Amy saw in his face that he was impressed. Despite her frowsy hair, Victoria did look good, slim and straight. Her eyes, those beautiful green eyes, burned into Schumer.

"You cannot think of interrogating my daughter at a time like this."

"Mother, he wasn't interrogating me. And we have to catch this man."

Victoria glanced at her. "Yes, I know, dear. But you could not possibly be thinking clearly so soon. Tomorrow will do just as well. You'll all stay with me, of course."

Amy felt a surge of gratitude. She had not asked, but it was what she wanted more than anything. She could not stay in this house now. Perhaps never again. Despite the memories of Bud it held. The murder of Joyce would finish this house for all of them—even Bud's memory could no longer stay here.

"Where are my granddaughters?"

"With a policewoman in the kitchen," Amy said.

Victoria wheeled and stalked into the kitchen, her heels rapping out her disapproval.

Amy turned to find Schumer looking at her. "Quite a lady, your mother."

"Yes. If you need more . . ."

"Not for the moment. I imagine you'll want to pack some things. If you'll give me your mother's number, I'll call you tomorrow."

Amy nodded. She went upstairs. In the hall, she tried not to look at Joyce's room. A flash went off, cold, blue-white, behind the half-closed door. Amy gathered up clothes for Denise and Ellie, took toothbrushes from the bathrooms, some slacks and tops and a dress for herself. Her hands shook as she laid them out in the suitcase. Grabbing her medical bag, she hurried down the stairs, desperate to be away from this place.

Outside with the girls and her mother, she was surprised

to find Winnie's old Chrysler limo idling, the exhaust curling up in a ghostly plume in the cold night air. She did not recognize the chauffeur who held open the back door. The car was toasty warm inside. The chauffeur closed them in and hurried back to the driver's seat, pulling away at once. One of the backseats had been turned around to face the other. Amy settled into it, holding Denise against her. Denise sobbed quietly. Amy felt herself relax. The car's familiar old scents of leather and wood polish were somehow reassuring. Across from her and Denise, Ellie sat curled against Victoria's side in the regular seat, sniffling and sucking her thumb.

The significance of the car circled back on Amy. "You called Winnie?" she asked.

"I called the staff," Victoria corrected. Her face was invisible in the darkness of the car, her voice neutral. "Usually, I take cabs or the subway. But it seemed suitable."

"The subway?" Amy said, incredulous.

"That's right." Victoria's tone was forbidding.

Better let it drop. "Did you tell the staff why you wanted the car?"

"I'm sure they'll inform your father." Victoria hesitated, then said in a warmer voice, "I was surprised when you called me instead of him."

"Winnie can't stay with the girls during the day tomorrow," she explained. "I didn't want them with staff at the house."

"You did just right."

"Grandma," Denise said, "I don't ever want to go back there."

Victoria reached across and took Denise's hands. "You mustn't worry, dear. I'm sure your grandpa will be able to find you another house very quickly, and hire guards for you. Or perhaps find a penthouse in a place with good security."

Amy saw that Ellie had fallen asleep against Victoria's side. It surprised her, and then she reminded herself that she must be ready to spot the signs of grief in Ellie that would be different from an adult's. It did not mean she wouldn't miss Joyce horribly. I'll ask Tom what I should watch for, Amy decided. She leaned back in the seat, dizzied, closing her eyes. She had meant to call Tom after she called her mother. Why hadn't she? The confusion, police everywhere, Schumer asking her questions.

Amy had a sudden powerful urge to feel Tom's arms around her, then, in her mind, the arms became Campy's. Only a few hours ago, Campy *had* held her, kissed her. Was that why she had not called Tom? Her head swirled in confusion. She could not think about that now.

The chauffeur pulled up in front of Victoria's apartment building on Central Park West. Amy scooped Ellie up and followed Victoria and Denise into the building. Holding her daughter's vacant form as the elevator ascended, she found herself envying Ellie's sleep. It would be a long time before she fell asleep easily.

Amy helped her mother put the girls to bed together in the second bedroom. Denise was crying again, Ellie sobbing brokenly. Victoria put her arms around them, drawing them together, talking in a low voice. "It's all right to cry," she said softly. "You have to help each other now, all right? And Grandma will help too, all she can. So will your mother."

Amy's mother bundled the girls into bed. Amy leaned over, kissing their damp cheeks, her heart aching for them. "If you need me, just call. I'm right in the other room. You are safe now."

"Mom, are you sure he can't get in here?" Ellie asked.

"He doesn't even know where we are," Amy said, then realized it might not be true. She felt another surge of anger. She was not going to let this madman near her daughters, ever again. "He doesn't want to hurt you anyway," she said. "He had a chance to, and he didn't, remember?"

Denise nodded. "He wanted to hurt you, but I stopped him."

"You were very brave. I'm proud of you." Amy hugged her.

Ellie wiggled to the side of the bed, dropping her knees out to the floor. "I forgot my prayers, Mommy." She buried her face in the sheets. The muffled prayer Amy heard was not Ellie's usual rambling recital, but the old simple rhyme that every child seemed to know: "Now I lay me down to sleep,

I pray Thee, Lord, my soul to keep, if I should die before I wake . . ."

Amy felt a sudden pressure of grief in her throat. "I pray Thee, Lord," she prompted.

"I pray Thee, Lord, my soul to take."

Turning on the night light, Amy pulled the door to, slightly. She felt suddenly aimless, standing in the hall, not knowing what to do. Victoria steered her, hands on her shoulders, into the living room, sitting her on the couch while she made coffee.

Noticing the apartment for the first time, Amy felt a distracted surprise. It looked so bare. Where were her mother's prized paintings—the Sargents and the Corot? The parquet was bare of the big Persian rug, too. At the Waldorf, Winnie had worried that Victoria might fall under the spell of some slick young con man who preyed on wealthy older women. Amy had scoffed at the idea, but now it did not seem so remote. I must ask her about it, Amy told herself. But she thought instead of Joyce's murder. So unfair. The man had come for her, not Joyce. Come for her, to find out what she had seen in the woods. The nightmare had not been real at all, except as a drug-induced hypnotic suggestion.

So why did she feel so sure she *had* taken that walk in the woods so many years ago? That she had seen something terrible.

Victoria put a cup in her hand, wrapping her fingers around its heat, and then she sat down across from her. "I hope you will stay here as long as you wish. Once you're able to go back to work, you may rely on me to care for Denise and Ellie, of course."

"Thank you. You've been so good—"

"Nonsense. You're my daughter." Victoria's rebuking tone did not entirely rob the words of warmth. "The third bedroom is rather small. If you'd be more comfortable in mine . . ."

"I wouldn't hear of it." Amy sipped at her coffee. It was terrible—instant and much too weak. Come to think of it, she could not remember her mother ever making coffee before. It had always been done by one of the cooks.

"You must be tired," Amy said. "I woke you up in the middle of the night."

"Not at all. I'm fine." Victoria settled back and began sipping at her own coffee.

"Mother . . ."

"Yes?"

"I used to sleepwalk quite a bit, didn't I?"

"Yes, from time to time."

"Did I ever go outside?"

Victoria frowned. "Outside? Hmmm. I don't remember you doing that, I don't believe. Why do you ask?"

Amy hesitated, debating whether to tell her. As far as Victoria knew, the intruder had broken in tonight to rob them and had killed Joyce when she caught him. She had not told Victoria about the nightmares that were not nightmares but interrogations under scopolamine; that Joyce's killer had really been after her daughter. There was no point in frightening her mother more than she already must be.

"I've been having this . . . nightmare, lately," Amy said. "In it, I'm a little girl again at our place on Long Island. I go sleepwalking in the woods behind the house."

Victoria gazed into her cup. "The woods? How strange."

"In my nightmare, I see something terrible back there, but I can't remember what it is."

Victoria set her cup on the coffee table. Amy heard the saucer rattle briefly, but when her mother drew her hand back it seemed quite steady. "You poor dear. Nightmares, and then this horror tonight."

"When I was little, was there ever anything back in our woods that was dangerous?"

Victoria stared at her. "What do you mean?"

"I don't know. An old well shaft, a wolf, somebody getting mugged back there."

"Mugged? Certainly not. Amy, you must put this from your mind. It is only a dream, nothing more. You've suffered a terrible shock. You are the one who must be exhausted." Victoria stood, pulling her up, leading her into the small spare bedroom. "Lie down now and sleep. Your body needs rest— and so does your mind."

"Maybe you're right," Amy said.

"Would you like a sleeping pill?"

"You have sleeping pills?" Amy asked, surprised.

"Yes." Victoria looked defensive.

You never touch pills, Amy thought. For a second she saw into the sadness of her mother's life, saw also that her mother did not want to be confronted with it. She let it pass.

"It's a pretty mild dose," Victoria said, "but it might help you sleep."

"No, thanks. Anyway, I've got my medical bag along." Amy took off her shoes and lay back, letting her mother pull the blanket over her.

Victoria patted her shoulder. "You just rest now, dear. I'll call the hospital and tell them you'll not be in tomorrow—"

"I did that already. I have to be sure Ellie and Denise can handle it before I go back."

"You must also be sure *you* can handle it, my poor Amy."

Amy tried to think of something reassuring to say, but her mother had already turned out the lights and tiptoed out.

Lying in the darkness, Amy watched the glow of light from Central Park West ebb and flow on the curtains. A blower came on, masking the occasional blare of a cab horn that would never entirely cease in New York City, even at four in the morning. The bed was soft under her, but she could not seem to let herself relax into it. She ached with grief, as though her body had been bruised all over by a beating.

And now there was more to disturb her: Victoria, denying that she'd ever sleepwalked in the woods.

But I did, Amy thought. I'm sure of it.

And Mother remembers it, too.

21

Walking through the basement hall toward Pathology, Amy was painfully conscious what she had to do—tell a still unsuspecting Chris. Chris, happily studying dead people or dead bits of people; Chris, who knew the biology of death better than anyone else at the hospital, but still did not know how to stand it. Who does?

Amy paused in the dimness under the sweating pipes, formaldehyde stinging her eyes, burning in her throat. She did not want to tell Chris about Joyce. She wanted to walk away, let Chris's day continue in happiness. But it could not be.

The noxious smell of preservative strengthened as she approached Chris's lab. Looking through the round porthole in the door, Amy saw her perched on a stool, hunched over a microscope on the worktable, her curly red hair draped in a flaming mop around the eyepiece. As Amy entered, Chris raised a cautionary hand without looking up; Amy took up station behind her, admiring her concentration.

"I see you," Chris muttered, "nasty little *schweinhund*."

"I resent that."

"Amy!" Chris smiled, but kept her eye to the eyepiece. "Guess what I just found on this slide."

"A hotel continental breakfast?" Amy was surprised she was able to tease. To be with Chris was to joke—but that was about to change.

"A basosquamous cell," Chris said.

"That was going to be my next guess."

"No, really, they're fascinating. Histologically, they show characteristics of both basal and squamous cells."

"Are we talking carcinoma?"

"Yeah, but we're getting in real early on this one." Chris pushed back from the lab bench. Turning, she started to say something, then stopped, studying Amy. "I've got a fresh pot of coffee in my office."

"Good." Amy followed Chris through the tunnellike halls. Water dripped somewhere, monotonous pings jumping along Amy's nerves. You could tell you were below street level here, down with the necromancers. What a contrast to Eric's throne room, twelve stories above.

Following Chris into her office, Amy felt the upsurge of light, the sunny warmth that Chris's yellow paint job had given to the cinder-block walls. The aroma of rich, dark coffee filled the room with a cozy sense of well-being. Amy shut the door. Chris handed her a mug and she sipped gratefully, savoring the soothing spread of heat down her throat.

"Sit," Chris said, pointing to a folding chair facing her desk. She settled into the desk's swivel chair, shoving a stack of papers aside so she could see across. "So what gives, Amy? You look like you just lost your best friend."

Amy felt a small shock, the frivolity of the words turning heavy, sinking coldly inside her. "Oh, Chris. I . . . Someone broke into my house last night."

Chris leaned forward, staring at her. "You're kidding. You're not kidding. The girls—"

"They're all right . . ."

"But?"

"He . . . choked Joyce. She's dead, Chris." Amy felt tears welling up. Damn it, she had been determined not to cry.

Chris rolled her head back, stared at the ceiling. "Oh God. No."

Amy got up and rounded the desk, holding her arms out.

Chris grabbed at her wrist, her fingers clamping down hard. "No. *Damn it!*"

Amy buried her face on Chris's shoulder. Chris hugged her hard, her body shaking as she broke down and sobbed.

When the sobs ran out, Amy let her go. Chris looked at her with reddened eyes. "I can't believe it. How can you *stand* this?"

"I'll be all right," Amy said. "But already I feel . . . I just . . . miss her so much."

Chris got up and stalked to her blackboard, ramming the heel of her hand into it. She kicked her steel wastebasket over with a ringing blow, sending a sheaf of printouts cascading across the floor. Yes, Amy thought, feeling an answering anger inside herself. Circling back to her chair, Chris kicked it too. It twisted around with a squeal of casters. Chris caught it as it started to go over, yanking it back to the desk, dropping into it.

"Do you know who did it?" she said in a savage voice.

"Not yet."

"You're not staying there, are you?"

"No, we moved in with Mother. Chris, there's more. I need you to listen carefully now, put aside your feelings as much as you can, and think. I need you to help me *catch* this bastard."

Chris ripped a sheet of paper towel from a roll beside her coffeemaker and wiped her eyes, keeping the towel over her face a minute. "Putting my feelings aside is what I do best," she said in a hoarse voice. "Ordinarily."

"We'll cry at the funeral," Amy said. "We'll bawl our eyes out in the middle of the night. We'll go get drunk at Carney's for her. In the meantime, let's get him."

Chris cleared her throat. She wadded the paper towel into a ball and threw it away, settling her hands on the desk. "Tell me everything."

"Chris, the killer came for me, not Joyce. Joyce interrupted him and he killed her. Before Joyce walked in on him, he'd already drugged me—with scopolamine. Sound familiar?"

"Cynthia VanKleeck," Chris breathed.

"While I was under the drug, the killer questioned me, making it seem like a nightmare. Before she was killed, Cynthia told me about a recurrent nightmare she'd been having. It was the same as mine. Which means he was drugging and questioning her, too."

Chris shuddered. "God. That is so *creepy*."

"She must have awakened and caught him at it, so he threw her out her window. It has to be connected to her father's murder and those three other mysterious heart attacks I showed you on my office computer the other night. This man has at least six victims—so far. And, Chris, all four of the male victims are very like my father, from his height and age to his money, even to his blue eyes."

Chris paled. "Oh, Amy!"

"Chris, I'm terrified. If we can't catch this guy, I think Winnie and I are going to be next."

"You've warned your father, of course."

Amy nodded. "Before Joyce was killed, and again today—he rode along while his driver dropped me off here just now. I'm afraid he was too shaken up about Joyce—and the idea that the girls and I might have been killed—to listen very well. Even if he does take it seriously, I couldn't tell him what to be careful *of*. We have no idea how the murderer is causing the heart attacks."

"Some kind of cardiotoxin," Chris said.

"Right. But how is it being delivered? A glass of wine? Dissolved in the victim's after-shave?"

"Speaking of delivery, how did this bastard manage to get the scop into you without waking you up?"

"Dermal patches."

Chris pinched her eyes shut. "Smart. I should have thought of it. I might have, if he hadn't left those Ru-tuss samples on Cynthia's night table. I know scopolamine has a history as a truth serum, too—"

"Don't be hard on yourself," Amy said. "I didn't see it either."

Chris gave her a look of sympathy mixed with dread. "It must have been horrible."

"I keep thinking about it—him easing those patches onto my neck, then just sitting there beside my bed, looking at me, waiting." Amy shuddered. "Chris, part of my brain could hear him, but I was too sedated to grasp that it wasn't a dream. He . . . *controlled* me. I couldn't feel or see anything except what he told me to feel and see. And all the time, my girls were right down the hall . . ."

Chris stood and leaned across the desk, holding out her hand. Amy took it, squeezing hard, drawing comfort from the firm grip. She let go, and Chris sat back down. "Amy, this guy knows all about scop and dermal patches—do you think he might be a doctor or a nurse, someone from a hospital?"

"That's what I'm starting to think."

"The nightmare—describe that to me."

As Amy told her about it, Chris got up and righted the waste can, restoring its contents, wiping the shiny print of her palm from the dusky surface of the blackboard. She sat down again.

"The killer asked both Cynthia and me about walking in the woods," Amy finished. "Obviously he didn't know which of us had done it."

Chris looked at her. *"Was* it you?"

"I think so. Don't ask me how I know, I just do. What I don't know is what I saw—the thing the killer was trying to get me to say to him." Suddenly Amy felt rigid with tension. She got up, pacing to the door and back, trying to shake it off. Sitting again, she rubbed at the stiff muscles of her neck. "Maybe I can't remember because I was so young. Nobody remembers much of what happened to them from age four on back."

Chris shook her head. "A four-year-old, waking up alone in a dark woods—what *wouldn't* scare you?"

"True. And I never did like those woods . . ." Amy looked at Chris and realized they were both thinking the same thing: Maybe whatever had happened that night—the thing she could not remember—was the *reason* she had started hating the woods.

Chris opened her desk and took out a bottle of aspirin, shaking two out and washing them down with coffee.

"Headache?" Amy inquired.

Chris blushed. "You know when I kicked my chair a while ago?"

"I seem to remember that, yes."

"I think I broke my toe."

Amy burst out laughing, then groaned, ashamed of herself. How could she laugh at anything right now? But it had felt good.

Chris glared at her. "Oh, right. This is your bedside manner?"

"We should have it X-rayed," Amy said. "Do you want me to have ER send down a wheelchair?"

"No. I can walk. I'll take care of it when we're done here." Chris lifted her leg gingerly to her desk, elevating the foot, then leaned back and crossed her arms.

Amy got up again and stood still, realizing there was no real room to pace. "What should we do now, that's the question. We ought to try to find out if the other three men had children—and what, if anything, has happened to them."

"I have a friend at the *Times* who can look through their news morgue," Chris said. "These guys were prominent—their deaths and family details must have gotten full play in the paper."

"Good. While we're at it, let's check back over the obits for other heart-attack deaths who fit the profile—rich bankers, six-foot-one, so on."

Chris looked startled. "You think there are others?"

"I'm afraid there might be. I didn't think of this at first, but why should all four victims have low risk factors for heart attack? The answer is, they shouldn't. I doubt the killer cared about or even knew their risk factors. In a city of ten million people there must be some fat, cigar-chomping, diabetic bankers who are also six-foot-one and have blue eyes. If any of *them* got hit with a cardiotoxin, they'd be much more likely to die on the spot than to make it in to ER."

Chris looked at her admiringly. "That's a very nifty piece of forensic reasoning. It's interesting, too, that the ones who made it in had *second* attacks. Either this toxin hangs around in the system long enough to cause that, which seems unlikely to me, or our killer is able to hit them a second time, right in our ER, if he needs to. If we get another victim who fits the profile in here, we're going to have to watch him like a hawk."

"In a way," Amy said, "I've already done that." She told Chris about the videotapes. "If the killer *is* striking again inside the hospital, I haven't been able to spot it."

Chris chewed her lip thoughtfully. "It might be something very subtle."

"Yes."

Chris looked at her. "I can't believe she's dead. I just . . ."

"I know," Amy said softly.

Chris held another paper towel to her eyes. Amy looked away, at the ceiling, the coffeemaker. After a minute, Chris said, "Checking all city obits for other victims, even in the last few months, will be a huge job. We could get the police to do it—if we had some hard evidence to back all this up."

"What about the dermal patches?" Amy said. "I gave them to the police, and they link all this together."

"That might do it," Chris said. "We'll lay it all out for them, especially the nightmare link between you and Cynthia Van-Kleeck. Once they see that she was murdered under scopolamine, I'm betting they'll go for an exhumation order and autopsy on her dad, too. I still know a lot of people at the ME's office—I was one of their best forensic pathologists. Maybe I can get them to let me do it."

Amy almost smiled. Chris never would have said such a thing if she hadn't been swept up in the moment. But it was true. She had been a top-notch forensic pathologist before she joined Hudson. And on this case she had a stronger motivation than anyone currently working with the ME.

Chris said, "You'd better work this exhumation thing from your end, too. Use the family clout, do whatever you have to do. No guarantees, but if we get the exhumation, it'll give us at least a shot at finding out how the murderer kills. Then all we'll have to figure out is why."

"Chris, there may not be a 'why.' This is a very sick man—a murderer who steals blood and kills with extreme pain. There's no ER for his kind of sickness."

Chris shook her head firmly. "There's always a 'why,' Amy. Even if he's a psycho, he still has his *reason* for who he kills, however twisted it might be. I've seen what's left over after one of these animals strikes. Once I had four women on my table, one after another in a four-month period, physically alike enough to be sisters. I won't tell you what the filthy creep had done to them. But when you look at something like that, you see a lot deeper than you want to see into a very dark mind.

On the outside, our killer may a pathetic loser, or he may be attractive, even personable. But in his mind, along with all the horrors, there *will* be a very powerful reason for what he's doing. That reason may or may not make sense to us, but it's going to be there, I promise you."

"If he does have a motive," Amy said, "and we could figure it out, we'd be a lot closer to catching him."

Chris sat back with a speculative look. "We need to give some thought to this father-daughter linkage we see with the VanKleecks and you. Amy, when you told your father he might be in danger, how did he react?"

"What do you mean?"

"Was he surprised? Did he act like you might be onto something, or did he pooh-pooh it?"

"Neither one. He listened. He seemed skeptical that it had anything to do with him, but he promised he'd be extra careful. Today I got him to go further—he's going to add some new, top-line security people to the estate staff."

"Did you tell him the killer came to your house not to rob but to drug and question you?"

"No. It would just make him sick with worry, and there's nothing he could do about it."

Chris gave her a long, measuring look. "Here's the thing—I think you've got to do more than warn your father. You've got to question him."

Amy started to protest.

"Just listen a minute. All right, you love your dad. You think he couldn't possibly have any *guilty* knowledge of this. Fine. But maybe he has some other kind."

Amy felt anxiety building in her, filling her chest. Question Winnie? Why did that prospect disturb her so?

"Has anything strange involving your father come up lately?" Chris asked. "Something linked to the past?"

Amy flushed. *Martin Lenz!* Lenz was so sure, so damnably sure, that Winnie had stolen his own pre-Columbian statue twenty years ago—and hidden it . . .

But all that *had* been twenty years ago.

When the statue was stolen I was eighteen, Amy reminded herself. I was a little girl when I walked in the woods—*if* I walked in the woods. And, anyway, Winnie didn't do it!

"No," Amy said. "There's been nothing like that."

Chris looked unconvinced. "Amy, if your father *is* on this psycho's list, on some level he might know why. Maybe he doesn't want to talk about it. Maybe, like you, he doesn't even *know* what he knows—not consciously. But if it's there, you have to drag it out of him."

Amy nodded, but she felt a rebellious resistance to what Chris was saying. Chris was wrong about her father. He didn't know anything about this—he couldn't.

She eased the pent-up air from her lungs, but the anxiety clung. "Chris, I'm scared."

Chris stood, hobbling around the desk to her, pulling her into a hug. "He's not going to get you, my friend. Or your father either. We're going to stop him."

Amy squeezed her back. "Right," she said with a confidence she could not feel.

Chris didn't let her go. Holding on to her shoulders, she looked Amy in the eye. "Talk to your father," she insisted.

"I'll think about it."

"Don't just think about it, *do* it. I need my friend. Your girls need their mommy. And you need your father. The life you save may not just be yours, it may be his, too."

22

Amy, talking to Detective Schumer on the phone, felt Chris tugging on the cord, trying to get her attention. Chris pointed upstairs and hobbled to the door. Amy covered the receiver with her hand. "Wait till I'm finished—I'll help you."

"No way. X-ray's too near ER, and you'll end up working. I can walk fine. Keep on with what you're doing."

Schumer fired a question into Amy's other ear. She waved Chris out and finished filling Schumer in on what Chris and she had been able to piece together. Schumer kept stopping her to write things down.

"Getting an exhumation order will be difficult," he said.

"I know. But we've got to have that autopsy."

"What you've been telling me is bizarre, you realize that. You haven't even come up with a motive, only a theory. And why's the guy using heart attacks to knock these rich men off? Why so fancy? Why doesn't he just shoot them?"

"Come on, Detective Schumer. I can think of two reasons right off the top of my head. One, he didn't want anyone to know it was murder—especially with the victims being so similar. Two, he wanted them to suffer."

There was another silence on the line. "Christ, a psycho. Just what we need. All right. You haven't convinced me on any of this, but I can't prove you're wrong, either. *Something* damned strange is going on here. Maybe we can get some people plowing through the obits for the last six months. I'll go ahead and take a crack at the medical examiner."

Amy felt a surge of relief. "Good. Thank you."

"Exhumation is an ugly business, and if Mrs. VanKleeck resists, we may have to counterbalance that with some St. Clair family clout. Would your father be willing to weigh in, all the way up to the mayor if necessary?"

"I'm sure he would. We have to do whatever it takes, Detective. This killer isn't through yet."

"Yeah. Well, we know he's after you, and if what you say is true, your pop, too. I'll be in touch."

Amy hung up the phone and sat, feeling a small sense of accomplishment. At last she might have her shot at some real physical evidence—the kind she was better trained to interpret than even the police. For the first time she felt a degree of comfort at being forced to play detective. *We're a step closer, Joyce.*

Amy checked her watch: five-twenty. No use going up to Tom's office yet—he'd be with a client until five-fifty. She fidgeted in her chair, the silence of the office beginning to play on her nerves. How odd, this fear of being alone. How long would it be before she could take pleasure again in going off to her bedroom at night for a few hours of solitude with her journals or TV?

Bad question. She was looking too far ahead. She could start by getting a new bedroom to call her own.

Amy poured herself another cup of coffee and drank it. All it did was make her feel more jittery about being alone. I could run across and see Philip, she thought. The idea cheered her at once. Philip, with his sweet temperament and innocent detachment from all that had happened, would be just the tonic for her right now.

Amy left Chris a note summarizing her conversation with Detective Schumer and walked across Second Avenue to her brother's apartment.

Philip gave her a hug and led her into his living room—

And there sat Martin Lenz at the chessboard, just like last time. The blood rushed to Amy's face.

"Hiya, Doc," Lenz said.

"We're playing chess," Philip said happily.

She felt a huge frustration with him. Didn't he grasp after last time that Mr. Lenz was not here out of friendship?

"Get out," she said. She was so angry that the rest of the room looked red and blurred around Lenz's face.

Lenz gave her a smug hyena smile, spreading his hands, looking to Philip as if for guidance.

"But we haven't finished our game," Philip said.

Amy kept her eyes on Lenz. "I said get out. Now."

"Amy!" Philip said in a voice that was suddenly eerily low and powerful. "This is my apartment and Mr. Lenz is my guest. If you don't like that, then *you* can get out."

Amy stared at him, stunned. "Philip! You've never talked to me like that."

Philip looked as if he, too, were stunned.

The trouble is, she thought, he's right. I need help.

"I'll be right back," she said to Philip. Her face burned as she walked down the hallway. By the time she got back across the street to the hospital, it didn't seem such a bad thing, Philip's startling moment of independence. It hurt, but it was good, too—a new step forward.

But she still had to get Martin Lenz to leave Philip alone.

Tom's door was closed when she entered the waiting room. Before she could knock, it opened and he walked out, laughing, with his five-o'clock patient. When he saw her, his face sobered. "Amy." Ushering his patient out of the waiting room, he turned to her, holding out his arms. "I just heard about Joyce. I called your house before my last patient, and a policeman answered—"

"Tom," she said, "Martin Lenz is with Philip again."

"What?" Tom's face darkened.

"He won't leave. Philip ordered *me* out."

"We'll see about that," Tom said in a tight voice. "Come on."

In the elevator, Tom looked at her. He seemed rigid, almost frozen, and she realized he was torn between his anger and his desire to comfort her.

"I'm all right, Tom."

He nodded distractedly.

Outside, he ran across Second Avenue, crossing against

the light, waving off a honking cab. She had to wait for the light, and by the time she reached Philip's floor, Tom was fifty feet ahead of her down the hall. She hurried after him, catching up at Philip's door. "Tom, be careful. Lenz is a rough man. In his profession, he's been in plenty of tight spots. Don't provoke him."

"Don't worry." He gave her a savage grin, then plunged into Philip's room without knocking. Amy followed, exasperated, knowing she'd done the wrong thing in challenging Tom's male vanity.

Lenz rose from behind the chess table, squaring on Tom, who stopped a foot away.

"Out," Tom said. "Now."

"I thought Philip made it clear, Doc. I'm his guest. Maybe you and sister, here, are the ones who should leave."

Tom turned to Philip. "Is that how you feel?"

"No," Philip cried, his voice high and loud with emotion. "I wouldn't *ever* want you to leave."

"This man is your enemy," Tom said.

Philip looked at Lenz in shock, then his eyes narrowed. "I want you to leave, Mr. Lenz."

Lenz turned toward him. "Now Philip—"

Almost casually, Tom took Lenz's hand and bent and turned it, and suddenly Martin Lenz was lurching toward the door, Tom marching him out by the hand.

Amy stood in shock for a second, then hurried out behind them. Lenz glared at Tom, rubbing the bones on the back of his hand. His face was white. "So much for the Hippocratic oath."

"That's for M.D.'s," Tom said. "I'm a Ph.D."

"Don't ever put your hand on me again."

"Fair enough—as long as you stay away from Philip."

Lenz turned and walked off down the hall at a leisurely pace.

"Where did you learn that?" Amy said, amazed.

"I told you, I grew up in the Bronx." Tom looked with a wondering expression at his own hand. "I didn't know I could still do that!"

Amy turned as Philip came out behind her. He looked ashamed, dropping his head instead of meeting her eyes. He went to Tom, head down. She started after him, but Tom waved her off. Draping his arm across Philip's shoulders, he talked quietly to him.

She watched the two men together, glad again, so very glad that she had Tom.

A beautiful ceramic elephant stood on an etagere behind Winston St. Clair's desk. The man walked over to the stand, his feet whispering across the plush carpet in the midnight silence. He stroked the elephant's back, wishing he could take off his surgical gloves so that his fingertips could tell him what his eyes, in the dim security lighting, could not. Closing his eyes, he remembered that time in first grade when Mr. Howard had taken the class to the beach at Margate. They had stood looking at a huge wooden elephant. He could almost feel Mr. Howard's big, veined hand holding his, leading him up the spiral of steps through the warm, dim enclosure. The curving wall stroked one shoulder; his head swam with the sweet smell of sun-baked timber. They surfaced together into the magical, round room. Twin beams of honey-colored light slanted across in front of them, and he realized with delight that they had reached the head of the elephant. He could hear the surf now, murmuring in the distance. Mr. Howard held him up so he could gaze out one of the window eyes, seeing what the elephant saw. There, across a hundred yards of dazzling white sand, the Atlantic rolled and sparkled.

The man felt a twinge of longing. For a few minutes he'd had Mr. Howard all to himself. He smiled in the darkness. A good memory—one of the few.

What was Winston St. Clair doing with an elephant?

Probably a Republican.

The man gazed around the office, greedily gobbling up details, exasperated at his need and yet unable to help himself. What must it feel like to be this man—to walk into this grand office every day and sit down at this curving oak desk, twice the size of a grand piano? The sides of the desk, like the door, gleamed with inlaid squares of beaten gold—a fortune spent just to hide Winston's knees.

The man started for the executive bathroom then stopped,

frozen by a sound. *What was that?* He heard the outer door to St. Clair's office suite click again as it closed. Panic jolted him. *Hide!* Running to the bathroom, he stepped into the shower, easing the frosted doors shut along their tracks. His heart hammered wildly.

A moment later, feet scraped on the bathroom tiles only a yard from him. Water ran in the sink. The man held perfectly still, feeling the seconds stretch with agonizing slowness. A smell came to him—the frosty scent of expensive cologne.

"You won't miss this, will you, Mr. St. Clair? Rich man like you. You won't mind if old Jake takes a little." A male voice, barbed with the nasal vowels of Brooklyn.

The man smiled. A security guard, no doubt. *I like your thinking, Jake. Don't make me kill you.*

The medicine cabinet clicked shut and the footsteps retreated. The man let out a long breath, waiting until he heard the distant clap of the outer door closing. He stepped from the shower, removing from his jacket the small syringe of *Claviceps cyanidus.* The toothpaste was on the second shelf, next to a bottle of 4711 cologne. Unscrewing the cap, he eased the plunger of the syringe down so that the *Claviceps* would not penetrate farther than the top half-inch of paste. Winston would get it all the next time he brushed.

Screwing the cap back on, he returned the tube to its precise same spot on the shelf and pocketed the syringe.

Done.

The man walked out to the bathrooms by the elevators. He washed up and changed into the business suit he'd packed in the bag. Selecting one of the middle stalls, he settled on the toilet seat. A long wait until the bank opened in the morning.

Dare he try the stairs? Cameras on every landing. *Don't blow it now, after all you went through.*

He settled back on the toilet. At least with the cleaning crew gone he didn't have to return to the top of the elevator shaft. Taking the latest *New Yorker* from his bag, he paged through it, searching out the poetry.

He could not seem to concentrate on the lines.

Soon Winston St. Clair would die horribly.

He imagined it with relish—the crushing pains, the panic

and horror as the old bastard realized he wasn't going to make it.

And if Winston was not the one? He had to be. The list was getting very short.

And after Winston's beloved Amy had experienced the full pain of his death, she would die too.

The man put the *New Yorker* back in the bag, happier in the red reaches of his own mind.

23

Amy stood beside the open grave, hoping she could make it through this last part without breaking down. A cold wind bit at her face; her eyes felt swollen, her throat still thick from when they'd closed the lid on Joyce back at the funeral home. The tears had poured then; now she seemed able to glance at the bronze coffin without losing control. It hung on black straps over its hole, gleaming dully under a pewter sky. Amy smelled the fresh dirt, the bitter tang of torn grass. She felt Tom's hand soothing at her back, Denise's fingers digging into her coat on the other side. Ellie stood in front of her, chin quivering, refusing to let go.

" 'The Lord giveth and the Lord taketh away,' " the Lutheran minister said. " 'Blessed be the name of the Lord.' "

Amy started, her breath hitching in dismay as Philip stepped suddenly from the other side of Tom toward the open grave. The preacher faltered, then picked up again as Philip merely stood gazing down into the hole. Amy started to step over and get him, then realized it would only add to the disruption. What was he doing? She glanced at Joyce's parents on the other side of the grave, but their heads were down and they seemed not to have noticed Philip. Tom stared intensely at the back of Philip's head, as if trying to get through to him with telepathy. Uncannily, Philip looked around at him, then stepped back to his side. Amy saw with surprise that Philip's cheeks were wet with tears. Her mind flashed back to Bud's funeral, Philip smiling vacantly throughout the service, though he had loved Bud dearly. For months afterward, Philip had driven her to distraction asking when Bud was coming to visit him.

That was before Tom had started helping him.

" 'Comfort ye my people,' " the minister said, glancing at Joyce's parents. A short, tubby man and his tall wife, her hair restored in the little Manorville beauty parlor to a monochrome imitation of the blond it had been when Joyce was in high school. Amy's throat tightened at the way they huddled together, sheltering each other against the cold wind, their stricken, weeping faces only inches from each other. In their shared grief they had achieved a strange, unreachable beauty. Amy remembered when Joyce's father took the job managing Winnie's farm outside Manorville. Joyce had already moved from Connecticut to Long Island. She was still with Dwight then, helping him run his charters off Montauk. She'd been overjoyed to have her parents near her again.

Looking at them now, seeing their closeness, Amy felt a pang for her own parents, standing at opposite ends of the circle of mourners. It seemed suddenly incomprehensible that they could both be here and so far apart. How could they have let their love die? Bud was gone, but she knew she would still love him fifty years from now if she lived that long. People died and love survived, but when love died what was left?

" 'O death, where is thy sting,' " the minister said, " 'O grave, where is thy victory?' "

Right here, Amy thought.

She saw Detective Schumer near the back of the crowd in his rumpled blue blazer, ignoring the minister and surveying the mourners in front of him. He was here, she knew, in the hope that Joyce's killer might show up.

Maybe the killer *is* here, Amy thought, and we won't recognize him—not because we don't know him, but because we do.

The thought chilled her deeply. She looked at the familiar faces—Campy, standing behind Joyce's father, his head bowed. Tom, and beyond him Chris. Elaine Sikma, Bernie and his wife. Grace and Cinda, two neighborhood nannies who used to meet Joyce and the girls with their own young charges in the playground and at Eeyore's. Friends. Surely a murderer could not hide behind one of these faces. Amy wished with sudden desperation for the service to be over, then realized the minister was saying the final prayer. Bowing her head, she offered her own: Let us catch him before he kills again.

"Amen," the minister said.

Amy walked around the grave to embrace Joyce's parents. Joyce's mother bent to hug Denise and Ellie. "My Joyce sure loved you girls," she said.

At that, Ellie finally burst into tears. Amy steered her away from the crowd, holding her so she could weep in peace. She felt a tap on her shoulder and turned. It was Detective Schumer. "I'm sorry about your friend," he said.

"Thank you." Amy saw that Schumer wanted to say more, but was hesitating because of Ellie. Amy motioned her mother over. Victoria nodded at Schumer and turned back to Amy. "I'll just take the girls over there until you're ready. Are you still planning to go home with Winston?"

The frost in her voice pained and wearied Amy. "Just for a few hours, Mother. We're so close, it'd be a pity not to drop in. We'll be back in the city tonight. I do wish you'd come with us."

"No, thank you."

Mother herded the girls off toward Winnie's limo.

Amy turned back to Schumer to find his face impassive, as though he had seen and understood nothing. She liked him better for it.

He said, "I just wanted you to know that we got the exhumation order on Owen VanKleeck. Mrs. VanKleeck put up some resistance at first, but we were able to persuade her not to fight it."

Amy felt no satisfaction, but only pity for Mrs. VanKleeck. The autopsy was vitally important; the outcome might uncover four or more murders, but she could take no pleasure from her victory over a grieving woman.

"They'll find a cardiotoxin," she said, "you'll see."

"I hope you're right." Schumer started to say something

else, but stopped as Chris walked up. She was limping slightly from the toe she'd cracked kicking her chair. Amy introduced the two, then told Chris the news.

A fierce look came into Chris's eyes. "I'm going to do the autopsy if possible," she told Schumer.

"That's between you and the ME's office. I have one other thing to tell you: I got a man assigned to look through the *Times* obits for the last six months as you suggested. During that period, we found three other heart-attack deaths closely fitting the profile of the four in your ER. All three died before they could be taken to the hospital."

Nine people, Amy thought, chilled. He's killed at least nine people.

"Were any of them autopsied?" Chris asked.

"No."

Probably because they had higher risk factors, Amy thought. When they had heart attacks, no one questioned it.

"It will come down to Mr. VanKleeck," Schumer said. "Now please keep all this strictly to yourselves. The captain's convinced enough something might be going on that he's assigned two more detectives, but it won't help if the news gets out to the press. We've compiled rosters of the city's chief banking executives, and cross-referenced it with sources like *Forbes* to find the wealthiest ones. We're giving discreet warnings to any of that list who fit the age and physical profile of the victims."

"You forget he's killed two women, too—maybe more."

"Dr. Hunt, I'm forgetting nothing."

"Chris," Amy said, "he's right. We don't want the entire population of this city afraid to go to the best cardiac ER in Manhattan if they have chest pains."

Chris gave a grudging nod. "Good point."

Amy turned back to Schumer. "Did any of the three men have children?"

"All of them did, though only one had a daughter. She's a schoolteacher in Chattanooga, in her early twenties. She's fine—so far. We've warned her too."

Amy shook her head, baffled. "Just Cynthia and me. Why? It doesn't fit."

"Let us worry about that," Schumer said. "You've done your duty. I appreciate it. Now let us do ours. You just concentrate on staying out of harm's way."

Amy nodded.

Detective Schumer excused himself and Chris followed him, asking him more questions. Amy searched for Tom, and found him standing off a bit by himself. But before she could go to him, Campy walked up to her. "I'm sorry about Joyce," he said. "She was a fine person. I always liked her. It must have hurt you terribly."

"Thanks for coming."

He nodded. She felt strangely awkward with him. The last time they'd stood this close, they'd ended up in each other's arms. That seemed an eternity ago now.

"I want to see you," he said.

She smiled. "What happened to giving me time?"

"Not a thing. I still want to see you, be with you. I'll be home all afternoon tomorrow, unpacking my books."

Amy tried to focus on the idea. She couldn't, not here. "I don't know . . . I'll call you."

He wrote down his number and handed it to her.

She looked at Winnie's car, saw him seated in the back with the girls, waiting. Mother and Philip were standing a good distance from the car, probably waiting to say good-bye to her, and Tom was coming over toward her and Campy.

"I've got to go now," she said quickly. "Thanks again for coming. It meant a lot to me."

"You've had too much of this," Campy said.

"Yes, I have."

He took her hand briefly in both of his, gave it a gentle squeeze, and then he left, going over to offer his hand to Joyce's father.

"Nice of him to come."

Amy turned to find Tom at her shoulder. "He went to high school with Joyce," she said. "Listen, I'm taking the girls out to the estate for a few hours. Can you come with me?"

Tom looked doubtful. "I think I'd better take Philip back. As you noticed, he's a bit upset."

"He'll be fine with Mother. If he goes with you, she'll have no one to ride back with. Come on, you've never seen the estate." Amy tried to put lightness into her voice. "Winnie will spend some time with the girls. You and I can build a fire . . ."

Seeing his eyes crinkle, she poked him in the ribs. "Not that kind of fire, Romeo, a real fire."

"I really wish I could. But I've got a patient in crisis right now, and I'm worried about being so far away. I'm afraid I'd better get back."

Amy felt a powerful disappointment. She wanted to tell him that she needed him. Instead she said, "If you're sure."

"Sorry. I'll drive out with you some other time," he said.

"All right. Thanks for all you've done. You've been tremendous. I'll see you back in the city."

Tom kissed her and walked away quickly, glancing at his watch. Beyond him she saw Campy getting into his rental car. She felt suddenly very alone.

Amy sat with her father on the old camelback sofa in the west den. The heat of the fire felt wonderful on her face. At her feet, both girls dozed on the huge bearskin rug, exhausted from their tears. She knew now was the time to talk to Winnie, and yet she hesitated. I don't want to, she thought. *Why* don't I want to?

"Are you all right?"

She saw that he was looking intently at her.

"I'm all right. It's you I'm worried about."

"Me?" Winnie spread his hands. "I'm fine."

"So was Owen VanKleeck." She kept her voice low, afraid to wake the girls.

"I'm not going to die."

"I'm sure the others believed that, too."

Winnie reached across and patted her hand.

She said, "I . . . I haven't told you everything about this, and I think it's time I did."

"All right." He turned on the couch. As she explained that the killer had actually come for her, his expression tightened, his face growing pale in the light of the fire.

"God in heaven, Amy. You should have told me this before."

"I didn't want to worry you."

Winnie looked pained. "Worry me? You are the most precious thing in the world to me. You must tell me if you are in danger, whether it will worry me or not." He sat back, staring bleakly into the fire. "We have to do something about this, get some guards for you."

"The best thing we can do is try to figure out what this man is after. *Did* I ever go sleepwalking here in the woods at night when I was little?"

Her father continued to gaze into the fire. It took him a long time to answer. "No," he finally said, and she knew with a sinking feeling that he, like Victoria, was lying. It stunned her. How could he lie to her when he knew both their lives might be at stake?

She felt suddenly furious at him. Mother was one thing, but she was not going to let Winnie lie to her. She must confront him here and now, make him tell her the truth.

She opened her mouth, but the words would not come.

"What's the matter?" he said.

"I . . . nothing. Were you ever . . . Did *you* ever go out in the woods late at night. Did something happen to you there?"

His eyes grew distant. For a moment he did not answer. Her palms felt damp with sweat.

"No," he said, "I can't remember anything."

Can't—or won't?

Amy looked at Winnie. He had turned away from her again to look at the fire. She felt ill. She had never doubted Winnie before. It was an awful feeling.

The woods, she thought with dread. Nothing, not even Winnie, was going to save her from going out there. She could feel it out there waiting, not a hundred yards away from this cozy fire.

She stood, saying, "I need some exercise. I think I'll go out for a walk. Do you mind staying with the girls?"

"Of course not. But Mrs. Blanchard would be happy to look after them if you want me to come along."

"No," she said. "No, thanks. I think I need to be alone now."

He looked a little hurt, but nodded. Standing with her, he

pulled her into a hug. She patted his back mechanically, then pulled away, walking out through the foyer.

Outside, she felt the cold seeping through her overcoat. The sky was starting to lose light, the sun sliding down behind the massive gray blanket of clouds. The light would last another hour—time enough.

She walked around the west wing, fear swelling inside her with each step, and headed across the back lawn toward the woods.

24

Amy felt uneasy as she skirted the edge of the woods, looking for the old paths. Fading silvery light poured across the meadow, painting the trunks and vines beside her with a skeletal pallor. In the gaps between, darkness waited.

Amy felt her shoulders knotting. Maybe this wasn't such a good idea so soon after Joyce's death. It was getting too late in the day anyway, the light fading faster than she'd expected, maybe she ought to do this some other time.

Except that night was when whatever happened here before had happened. If she really meant to remember, darkness would be a help. And with all the guards her father had added, it ought to be safe. The new man at the gate had seemed quite sharp. And she'd seen another guard walking along the east wing. The whole estate was like a fortress now. She had nothing to fear in these woods—

Except the past.

There—up ahead, a break in the trees. She made herself stride forward to it, feeling the wind tugging through her coattails, scouring the backs of her legs. Turning around, she stared back across the meadow at the rear of the house. On the second floor, the window of her old bedroom gazed emptily back at her.

She saw the meadow as it had once been, with a bare dirt

path right about here, beaten through it by generations of St. Clair feet. In her mind, a blank-eyed little girl walked along it toward her, her nightgown fluttering like moth wings under a gibbous moon.

Amy shuddered and turned back toward the woods. This is the path, she thought. Go.

As she stepped into the darkness of the woods, she felt a sudden drop in temperature, smelled the moldy bite of fallen leaves. When her eyes adjusted, she was surprised to see a fallen tree, long dead, blocking the path ahead. Either the groundskeepers were getting lax, or someone had told them not to bother with this part of the estate. That someone could only be Winnie, but why would he do that?

Why would he lie about her sleepwalking back here?

As she stepped across the tree trunk, a bird fluttered above her, disturbed just as it was settling in for the night. Hugging her coat about her, Amy continued, her feet crunching through the matted floor of twigs and leaves.

For a second she thought she heard other steps, behind her. Stopping, she held her breath and listened. Nothing.

She walked on, letting her mind drift. Memories began to emerge. When she'd walked this path as a child it had been smooth dirt, unobstructed. And it had been warmer— either later in the spring, or maybe an unseasonably warm day in April. What else? Nothing. She couldn't remember. Why had she always hated these woods? Avoided them for years?

She had the sudden prickly feeling of being watched. Turning, she peered back through the trees. The tangled overlays of branches cut the failing light of the meadow beyond into creamy tatters. Was someone standing back there?

No. Stop trying to chicken out.

Resolutely she picked her way deeper along the fading path. She smelled a faint, sweet fragrance, growing stronger as she walked. The woods opened and she stepped into a clearing. At its center was a circle of tall bushes, indistinct under the dying sapphire sky. The sweet smell was strong now—

Lilacs!

Amy felt goosebumps rise on her arms. When she'd been under scopolamine she'd smelled lilacs—or, rather, imagined their scent. The smell now must be coming from that big grove in the middle of the clearing.

Amy heard a foot hiss through leaves behind her. She whirled in alarm. There *was* someone back there. She strained to see. Too dark.

The footsteps drew closer. Her heart began to race.

Maybe it was just her father or one of the guards.

But what if it wasn't? What if the killer *had* been at the cemetery and followed her here?

But he couldn't get past the guards, Amy thought.

Unless I know him. Then all he'd have to do was to call Winnie from the gate and they'd let him in.

Hide!

Amy hurried toward the clump of lilacs, pushing her way between two bushes, grunting in surprise as her hip hit something straight and hard. She climbed over it and crouched, feeling smooth boards beneath her. Footsteps slashed closer through the leaves, then stopped.

She waited, terrified. The silence stretched.

Gingerly she prodded the boards, feeling a few weeds between the cracks. What *was* this place?

Still no sound. Carefully she rose to a crouch on the boards and looked out through a gap in the bushes. A man stood in dark silhouette in the clearing. His head turned slowly.

Searching for her.

She felt a burst of fear in her chest, but resisted the urge to drop again, afraid the movement would catch his eye.

"Amy?"

Her fear broke. "Tom!"

He hurried across the clearing. She stepped back over the barrier and wormed her way through the lilacs to meet him, grabbing his arms—half in relief and half in anger at him for scaring her. Relief won out, and she pulled him into a tight hug.

"You're trembling."

"You scared me half to death!"

"I'm sorry! Your dad said you'd gone for a walk. I was looking for you behind the house and then I saw the woods and it hit me. Of course—you'd come here."

"But what are *you* doing here?" she said.

"I was halfway to the city when it sank in that I'd let you

down. I turned around and came back. Hope I did right."

"Of course you did."

He hugged her to him. She smelled the sandalwood of his cologne, felt the strength of his arms around her. She eased back from him, too jittery to be held.

"You came out here to remember." His voice was gentle.

"Yes."

"Any luck?"

"I'm not sure. Come look at this." Amy led him through the bushes, climbing the barrier, which she realized was a railing. Inside it and below was a seat. Bending over, she walked her hands along it in the twilight gloom, feeling it curve, curve. "This is a gazebo!" she said, stunned.

"Well, yes," Tom said in a baffled voice. "Didn't you realize that when you came in here?"

"It just looked like a clump of lilac bushes."

She felt Tom's hand clasp hers in the darkness. "Incredible." His voice was full of wonder. "Here, sit with me."

He pulled her down on the bench with him. "You study Freud," he said. "You fill your head with the theories of the unconscious and defense mechanisms. Then you see patients year after year, and sooner or later you get that rare case, a person so blocked with rage or fear that he can look right at something and not see it. But I have never run across a case this extreme." He sounded quite amazed.

Amy was stunned. "Are you saying you could plainly see that this was a gazebo?"

"Yes. It would never occur to me that you couldn't."

Amy shivered. "This has to be it. This has to be the dark shape. This is what the murderer was trying to get me to remember."

"I would say so, yes."

"Tom, I'm scared."

He hugged her, stroking her cheek. His hand was warm, the fingers tender. Through her fear, she felt a stir of arousal. She pulled away, not wanting that now.

"Do you remember anything else?"

"I don't even remember this. But I *know* this is right. I came here when I was a little girl one night. I saw this gazebo. Something about it scared me so badly that I can't remember."

Amy got up, pacing across the center of the gazebo, straining to bring back the buried memories. Her foot sank suddenly, pushing one end of a board down. At the last second, she saw the far end swinging up through the murk at her. She jerked her foot up, dodging, and dropped to one knee as the sprung board winged her shoulder and clattered to the deck.

"Are you all right?" Tom asked.

"Yes." She groped for the board, slipping it back into the gap, shaken by the close call. She could have broken an ankle. Still on her knees, she probed the boards around her, determined to find any other loose ones before she tried to walk back. They seemed securely nailed into place.

Odd . . .

"What are you doing?" Tom said in the darkness.

"Have you got a match?"

"A lighter."

"Better yet. Light it and come over here."

Tom knelt beside her. In the flickering glow of the lighter, she examined the floor of the gazebo. Nailheads, protected from rust by the roof overhead, glinted dully in the light—everywhere but the one board. She could see the holes where they once had been. Someone had pulled the nails out. Amy prodded the board, intrigued. "Watch out, I'm going to spring this board again." She found the end of the board and pushed down. The board popped up and clattered to the side.

In the black crease, Amy saw a glint of gold. Her breath caught in her throat. "Here, hold the light closer!"

Tom lowered the lighter over the narrow black gap left by the board. Against the dirt, the five-hundred-year-old face of the Aztec funeral figure gazed up at them through protective layers of clear plastic. The statuette was half buried. She dug it out, brushing the dirt off the plastic bags to reveal the familiar odd proportions—the head large compared to the body, hands out as if to hold something. Reverently she eased it from the doubled plastic bags that had protected it for so many years. The gold necklace and eye inlays glowed in the flickering flame.

Amy heard Tom's sharp intake of breath beside her.

"This is the statuette," he said, "that that sleaze Lenz is looking for."

"Yes." Her mind whirled. How had this gotten out here? Had Winnie, in fact, stolen the statuette from himself and hidden it here?

No, it made no sense. He had loved this statuette dearly, spent hours in his trophy room admiring it. The insurance money had been very poor compensation for its loss, something Martin Lenz could never understand. So why would Winnie hide it out here all these years and deprive himself of it when he could have moved it somewhere much safer—his office safe, for example—and looked at it every day?

Clearly, *someone* had hidden it out here. Then left it for twenty years.

"I don't understand this," she said.

Tom lifted the statuette from its resting place. It was covered with spiderwebs. He brushed them off. "Is this the thing in your nightmare, Amy?" His voice was very gentle now; in a rush, she realized what he must be thinking.

"*I* didn't take it."

"Perhaps you saw who did."

"No. I'm as surprised as you are. Whatever I couldn't remember about this place, this isn't it. I have no idea who would steal the statuette, then leave it here."

Tom was quiet for a minute, then said, "I have a theory, but you may not like it."

"If you're going to say that my father—"

"No, no. Not your father. Your brother."

Amy looked at him, astonished. His face was grim in the soft, wavering light. "Philip? But why?"

Tom took her arm, pulling her up. Holding the light out, he led them to the encircling bench and sat down. She settled beside him, filled with a dread fascination.

"Before his accident," Tom said, "do you remember how Philip felt about your father?"

"There were some problems and tensions here and there, but Philip loved him, of course."

"I'm sure he did. Otherwise he could not have hated him, too."

"*Hated* him? Oh, come on, Tom—"

"From what you've told me," Tom said, "the statuette turned up missing shortly before Philip's accident. No alarms were triggered—other valuables were left. Even the family dog raised no alarm. Of all the things in the display cases, your father prized this most, didn't he?"

"Yes," Amy said. She felt angry at Tom, but knew it wasn't fair. His analysis was all too close to the mark. Philip and Winnie *had* been at each other's throats more and more in the months leading up to the accident. Not just tensions here and there, but furious arguments followed by walls of silence between father and son. They fought about everything and nothing. Philip's choice of college major at Harvard was the main sticking point. Winnie wanted Philip to go for pre-law or, better yet, a business degree. Philip, who had ambitions to be a writer, picked the one major Winnie considered most useless—English Lit. They sniped at each other constantly about it. And then there was the war. Philip would goad Winnie, threatening to drop his student deferment and head for Vietnam, the way Winnie had marched off to World War II. Winnie would get furious, claiming that it wasn't the same, that Philip must finish school first if he expected to be an officer. Philip would then accuse Winnie of being elitist, of caring nothing for the foot soldiers, the sons of common men. Those were fighting words to a former brigade commander, and Winnie would start shouting. Amy remembered the sly smile that would come across Philip's face before he began shouting too, both of them yelling at the same time, neither listening, neither realizing how much he was *scaring* the other.

She felt the statuette warming to her hand. Its surface felt oddly soft, buttery, and she realized her hands were sweating despite the chill.

"In my early sessions with Philip," Tom said, "I would occasionally see flashes of anger and resentment at his father, which seemed connected to nothing current. Over time, I formed a theory that Philip and your father had had quite an . . . unsatisfactory relationship."

"I know that my dad loves—and loved—Philip."

"But you were always his favorite."

Amy bristled. "We just got along better. And Philip got along better with Mother than I did—a *lot* better. If I was Winnie's favorite, Philip was Mother's. And I never stole my mother's things."

"At the risk of sounding sexist, maybe that was because you were a girl. Who knows what you might have done to your mother with a couple of shots of testosterone in you."

Despite herself, Amy laughed. "Don't, Tom. This is serious." She groaned. "What must you think of our family?"

"Philip's grudges are not my grudges," Tom said. "In a way, it's ironic. If he *did* steal this, the same injury that made him forget it also made him forget why. He now thinks your father makes the sun rise and set. With all that he lost, at least he gained that."

Amy stared at the pre-Columbian figure, wishing that she could put it back into its grave beneath the gazebo. To Winnie, the pain of its return would exceed the pain of its loss. "Why would Philip bring the statuette here, of all places?" she asked. "Did this place have significance for him, too?"

"An interesting thought."

"Suppose Philip did steal the statue. At least he didn't destroy it. He knew how much it meant to Winnie, and he took care to preserve it, putting it in the plastic bags. That's worth something, don't you think?"

"Yes," Tom said. "But you are my main concern right now. If this gazebo was the shape in your dream, the next question is, what happened here?"

Amy closed her eyes. "I . . . just can't remember."

"Maybe nothing."

"No. I wish you were right. But something did happen here, something very bad. I'm sure of it." A chill ran up her spine, making her shudder. She had the sudden powerful urge to be away from this place. She leaned into Tom, but when he put an arm around her, she felt herself stiffen. *What's wrong with me?* She tried to relax, feeling his cheek against hers, smelling his hair. His arm squeezed her gently.

"No, Tom." It came out in a near gasp.

At once, he released her. "Are you all right?" he asked in a baffled voice.

"I . . . no. I feel terrible."

He took her hands.

Her stomach heaved. She felt a huge rush of anxiety. Her mind was suddenly blank; she could not think. The anxiety turned to panic, clutching in her chest. She must get away from here, *now!*

Tearing her hands free of Tom's, she got up. The rough wood of the bench caught at her coat. She jumped off the platform and, clawing her way through the lilac bushes, bolted into the dark woods toward the house. She was dimly aware of the ground jolting unevenly under her feet, vines and creepers tugging at her ankles. A leafy branch slapped her face, stinging. Her lungs began to burn with effort. Which way out? She zigzagged through the trees, staring around in the darkness, her throat tight with fear.

Arms enfolded her from behind, held her. She screamed and bucked.

"Amy, Amy, Amy . . . Amy."

After a minute, she stopped struggling.

"We're far away now," Tom said gently. "No more gazebo. You can relax."

She stood rigid, panting. She made herself relax a little in his arms. "Crazy," she said.

"No. You saw something once. It scared or troubled you so much you drove it far down in your mind."

"How can that happen?" Amy said desperately. "I want to remember. Why can't I?"

"Let's get out of here," Tom said.

"The statue—"

"I've got it. You dropped it in the gazebo, but it's right here." He formed her hand around the statuette in the darkness. "Hold this a second," he said, "while I get my lighter out." She heard the flint striking repeatedly, but no light flared. "Must be out of fluid," Tom said. "Never mind—I can see well enough."

Amy gave him her hand, letting him lead. A suffocating pressure remained in her chest, easing as the trees thinned, dropping away as they walked from the woods. The meadow glowed softly under a fat moon. The wind had dropped off, leaving her warm from her run. As Tom started across toward the house, she held back, tugging at his hand. "Let's stop a minute."

"Of course."

She stood in the tall grass, taking deep, calming breaths,

smelling the clean straw and dirt scent of the field. He moved to her side, the moonlight outlining his head and shoulders from behind.

"What would make me panic like that?" Amy asked.

"If you were molested sexually in that gazebo," Tom said quietly.

Amy let the idea settle through her. Ugly words, but they held no extra weight for her, created no surge of anxiety. "I don't think that was it," she said.

"Neither do I. Your panic came when I hugged you—if I were your therapist, I would suspect a sexual attack. But as your lover, I would have seen the signs many times already, and they're not there."

"No. So what else might you suspect?"

"That you saw a murder, perhaps."

Amy closed her eyes, feeling the woods, dangerous at her back, but again the words brought no extra charge of fright. "No," she said. "Whatever it is, it's more complicated than that."

"I agree. You were quite young. It was something you knew was bad, but had difficulty understanding. Your confusion then makes remembering now that much harder."

Amy took the statuette from him. It was very heavy. Her fingertip traced the gold eyes. What would those have witnessed, if they could see? If the slit mouth, smiling enigmatically for centuries, could speak, what would it report?

Oppressed, Amy lifted her finger from the mouth. Even Philip no longer knew, the memory destroyed, along with his bitterness against his father and so much else.

"I think you're very close to remembering," Tom said gently. "If you want, I can help you."

Beyond his shoulder, Amy saw movement in the field. "Someone's coming." She watched the dark figure walk toward them. She could not make out his face but recognized the graceful stride, the squared shoulders, the way his long coat furled and flared with each step. "It's Winnie," she said. "Tom, it would hurt him very much to think Philip stole the statue. Let's not tell him that."

"I agree," Tom said. "If he doesn't figure it out himself, there's no reason for us to tell him."

25

The drawn curtains in room 11 boxed Amy in with the smell of urine and sweat. Looking down at the sleeping woman, she tried not to feel frustrated. Tracey, Tracey, the face too familiar. Five prior admissions; a real mess this time, trembling, agitated, sobbing about being chased by a white deer with bloody teeth and red, human eyes. Amy shuddered, feeling a new connection to the woman. This time around, your doctor knows what a bad trip feels like, Tracey. But at least I didn't give the drugs to myself.

She laid the back of her hand on Tracey's forehead, feeling a small relief at its coolness. The fever had broken—they'd headed off convulsions.

But when Tracey felt better and went back out on the street, crack would be there waiting. *Step on crack, break your own back.*

And the next time you OD, we might not be here.

Dread swelled in Amy's chest. She fought it off with a deep breath, slipping from the room, pulling the curtain shut behind her.

Bernie Wickham was waiting for her, his round face filled with concern. "Amy, you shouldn't be here."

"Now don't you start."

"We're fully covered, it's all under control. Go home to your kids."

"They're at Carnegie Hall with Mother—a matinee of *Peter and the Wolf*. Besides," she added, thinking of the autopsy, "I'm expecting a call."

"I'll put them through to your mother's or anywhere you say. Anywhere but here. I'm serious, Amy. I shouldn't have to tell you this, but this ain't Ob/Gyn or Dermatology. The last thing you need right now is a DOA or, God forbid, a knife victim."

Amy knew that Bernie was right. "I'll just go back to my office."

He sighed heavily.

"Call me if you need me."

He mumbled something that sounded like assent but included the word "stubborn."

Back in her office, Amy stared at the phone, then the clock, wondering if Chris was done with the VanKleeck autopsy yet. Four-thirty, so probably not. She had said she'd call, and she would.

I should be there, Amy thought crossly.

But no, Chris had been even more adamant than Bernie. Did they think she was fragile?

No. They care about you. So just grin and bear it.

She looked for paperwork, then remembered that she'd done it all, completely caught up, first time ever. It sat in a neat stack in the outer office, waiting to ruin tomorrow for Doris.

Frustrated, Amy tried to think of something to do until Chris called. Tom would be in his apartment, right next door, seeing his private patients. She could go over and wait for a break. But he'd want to fish around in her brain. The memory was down there, she could feel it cruising the bottom caves of her mind like some huge, carnivorous fish. She felt her teeth clenching, her shoulders tensing with dread. Maybe later, after the autopsy. She must keep trying, but if she couldn't remember yesterday evening in the gazebo, what chance did she have today?

Campy had invited her to come help him unpack his books. But that was no good. She wanted to be right here when

Chris called. And unpacking books could too easily turn to something else. Amy felt a pleasant tingle in her stomach. No, she thought.

But I did promise to call him.

She dialed the number he'd given her yesterday and waited through five rings. As she was about to hang up, the phone was picked up. She waited a few seconds. "Campy?"

"Yes?"

His voice had a strange, drawn-out slowness. There was no recognition in it.

"It's me," she said, "Amy."

"Hello."

Still no real recognition, as though he were deeply preoc- cupied. She began to feel uneasy. "I said I'd call you today—"

"Yes?"

Her uneasiness bloomed suddenly into real concern. "Are you all right?"

"Yes."

His voice was still slow, otherworldly. Drugs? No, not Campy. "What are you doing right now?" she asked.

There was a long silence.

"Campy?" The line was open, she could tell, though she could hear nothing but the slight hiss of a not quite perfect connection. "Campy, are you there?"

Nothing. And then a loud thump, like the receiver drop- ping to the floor. The hair stood up on Amy's neck. "Hang on," she said in a loud, firm voice. "I'm coming."

Amy paid the cabbie off and hurried to Campy's apart- ment door, clutching her medical bag. She was very worried. Campy's speech—those strange, detached monosyllables. He'd sounded as if he'd suffered a concussion. If so, he might collapse and lapse into unconsciousness or even a coma at any moment. He might be lying on the floor beside his phone right now. She had to get to him as fast as she could.

Inside the entry, she tugged at the second set of doors. Locked. Turning to the row of call buttons beside the doors, she pushed Campy's buzzer. Nothing happened. The speaker beside the buttons remained silent. She pushed again, over and over. Silence.

Frustrated, she went back outside and peered up at his window, three stories up. The Roman shades were down, blinding the apartment to the gray daylight outside. The windows were all closed. She shouted his name several times, hoping he'd come to the window. He did not.

Amy felt the air catching high in her lungs. She went inside again and pounded at the inner doors as hard as she could. The tempered glass took the blows with solid indifference. The lobby beyond them was still and deserted.

She began pushing other call buttons. None answered, and she realized her shouting out in the street and hammering on the doors must have frightened whatever tenants were inside.

She ran back out in the street. Empty—no, there was a cab sitting at the corner. She could see the cabbie and, dimly, a passenger in the backseat. If she told them she was a doctor and that a man needed help in this building, they might help her break in. She waved at the cab. It sat there. Neither the cabbie nor the man in back moved. Maybe they didn't see her.

She whistled, waving wildly at the cab, holding up her medical bag and pointing to it. She saw the cabbie move slightly, and knew that he saw her. Still the cab sat there.

In an agony of frustration, she started toward it, then heard the apartment building door open behind her. Turning back, she felt a surge of relief as she saw an old man stretching awkwardly between the outer and inner doors. Oblivious to her, the man was trying to hold both doors open for his Scottish terrier. The dog tottered along with the slow, stiff waddle of age and arthritis. Amy slipped past the man, holding the inside door open for the second it took the dog to finish getting through.

"Thank you, young lady."

"You're welcome." And thank you.

Amy ran up the steps two at a time. She wasted no time knocking, but grabbed the key from its hiding place in the newel post and let herself in.

She went first to the phone in the kitchen. It lay on the floor. She hung up the dead receiver and ran out, looking in each room, careful to disturb nothing.

Campy wasn't there.

There were no signs of a struggle, or of anything abnormal—not counting the phone.

Amy paced around the apartment, reluctant to touch anything, feeling uncomfortably like an intruder in the spartan order of the place. What should she do now? Call the police? And tell them what? That a grown man was missing from his apartment on a Sunday afternoon?

She realized suddenly that it was almost dark, the whole apartment sunken in gloom. Going to the window by the easy chair, she rolled up the shade. The uncovered window barely raised the level of light in the apartment. Another April shower was brewing, the sky very dark—only five o'clock, but it looked like twilight outside. She searched the street below, hoping to see Campy wandering along. Pressing her cheek against the window, she was able to see all the way to the corner.

The cab was still sitting there. Odd.

Amy lowered the shade back to where it had been, went to the couch and sat, trying to collect her thoughts. She decided to search the apartment once more, then head down to the street. Maybe Campy had wandered over to see James in the alley.

She got up and went toward the bathroom, pausing at the entry to the apartment's back hallway. The light had sunk so low that it was hard to see now. She groped the wall for a light switch. Behind her, the living room floor creaked. Startled, she'd begun to turn when something fanned her eyes and thudded into the wall right in front of her face. She screamed and jumped back.

Light flooded the apartment. Inches from her eyes, a knife stuck out from the wall. She turned with a gasp, and there, behind her, stood Campy.

26

He ran to her, throwing his arms around her. "Amy, Amy!"

She stood rigid, too stunned to push him away. She could feel him trembling. Turning her head, she saw the knife sticking from the wall, gleaming with a murderous light.

Her fright ignited suddenly into fury. She pushed him away, punching him hard in the chest. Pain shot up her wrist—it was like hitting a truck tire. She clamped her teeth to keep from crying out. "You almost *killed* me." Her voice shook.

"I'm sorry. I was letting myself in, and I heard you in here. I thought it might be him."

"What?"

"Someone got in here yesterday while I was gone."

"You would kill someone for breaking into your apartment?"

"Not kill, warn."

"Warn? That knife missed me by an inch."

"Not much of a warning if it missed by a yard."

"An inch, Campy! No one's that good!" She realized she had shouted it, her nerves still jangling with fright and anger.

Grabbing the handle of the knife, Campy yanked it from the wall and switched it, blade downward, to his right hand. "Left jamb, next to the switch," he said as if calling a pool shot.

Turning, he hurled the knife across the apartment. It stuck in the wooden jamb of the door.

She walked over to it, dumbfounded. The knife had stuck an inch from the light switch. She tried to pull it out of the jamb and couldn't.

He pulled the K-bar from the wall and tossed it on the couch. "Amy, I'm so sorry I frightened you. I swear, I had no idea it *was* you in here."

Amy's anger drained away, leaving her shaky in the knees. She remembered why she'd come, and her fear for him returned in a rush. "You don't remember me calling you?"

"You called?" His face went terribly pale.

Amy's heart sank. She moved to him. "Hold still, Campy." She scanned his forehead while she probed gently around in his hair with both hands. There were no bumps.

"I didn't have a concussion."

"I think you'd better tell me," she said.

"I've had a few blackouts." His voice sounded hoarse. She went to the kitchen and got him a glass of water. He drank it quickly, his throat convulsing as he swallowed, then stared at the empty glass in his hand. "I'll be doing something," he said, "and suddenly I'm somewhere else. Half an hour has passed and I remember none of it."

"Fugues," she said.

"Yes. Unfortunately, these fugues have no prelude. I can't feel them coming. I had one a little while ago. It must have been while you called. When I came out of it, I took a walk. I had no memory of you calling. When I realize it's happened again, I usually want to just go out and walk somewhere as fast as I can. Trying to get away, I suppose." He gave a bleak laugh.

"Have you had a checkup?"

"You mean a psychiatrist?"

"I mean a neurologist."

"It's not epilepsy," Campy said.

"How do you know it isn't?"

"The lack of any prodrome—no auras, no odd smells."

"Epileptics don't always have prodromes. And a doctor who diagnoses himself has a fool for a patient."

He gave her a fleeting smile. "I believe that goes 'a doctor who *treats* himself . . .' "

"What about your surgeries?"

"I told Eric Kraft I needed two weeks off to finish getting settled. He didn't like it, but I was able to persuade Halvorson to come back in."

"That's just buying time."

"I know." Campy rubbed his forehead, the fingers probing hard, as though he hoped to dislodge the sickness.

"Campy, you have to go to a neurologist. We have several fine ones at Hudson. If it's epilepsy, chances are it can be completely controlled with medication."

"And if it's not epilepsy? They'll sit me down, Amy. I might never work again. They might . . ."

He trailed off. Amy heard real fear in his voice. "What, Campy? They might what?"

"Have you looked in a locked ward? Have you seen that mesh they put over the windows?"

"Campy, no one's going to commit you—"

"No? The grounds for involuntary commitment are if the patient is 'a danger to himself or others.' When I'm in these states, I don't know what I'm doing. They could put me away, you know they could. And I can't allow that."

The hard edge in his voice made her uneasy. "You're getting ahead of yourself, Campy. If this isn't epilepsy, it could be multiple infarcts or some other cause. It could be diabetes or possibly a tumor. Even if it's a tumor, it might be small and low-grade—"

"Amy. None of those scares me—not compared to going crazy. Turning psycho, that's what scares me."

She laughed before she could stop herself. "I'm sorry. There's nothing funny about this. But psycho is the one thing you're not."

"You can't know that."

"I know *you.*"

"You *used* to know me." Campy took a deep breath, let it out.

"What do you think, you're some crazy Vietnam vet, like in the movies? That's a stereotype, not a diagnosis. You don't want to be examined at Hudson—fine. Go upstate somewhere. Give a false name and pay cash for the workup. But do it. Then you can stop worrying and start getting treated."

He gave her a speculative look. "I could wear a wig and call myself Alfred E. Newman. Or Mr. P. Mac Sito."

"Is that a yes? Promise me, right now."

"Yes, all right. I'll go to a neurologist."

"Good," she said, relieved.

"So I'm off the hook for not knowing you were here?" He tried to smile and didn't quite manage it.

"Yes. But not for throwing the knife."

"I know 'I'm sorry,' doesn't help much, but it's all I can say and keep saying."

"What if I *had* been a burglar and I'd had a gun?"

"You mean like this?" Campy reached into his coat and pulled out a huge handgun.

She stared at it, her mouth falling open. "If you had that, why did you bother with the knife?"

"I told you. The knife was a warning. This was what the knife was warning about." Campy gave her a thin smile. "Still think I'm not crazy?"

"*It* is crazy to go around New York with a handgun inside your coat."

"If you don't know exactly how to use it—and when *not* to, yes."

"Campy, even if it's not foolish, it's illegal!"

"I know. I don't usually carry it. The fact is, I don't like guns. But I can't let this one go. It . . . belonged to the Major. It's been in my footlocker for fifteen years. I took it out with me because there's no place to hide anything here that a burglar can't find. And someone definitely got in here yesterday. As soon as I can get a good safe in here, I'll keep the forty-five there."

Amy took the gun from him and, holding the handle by two fingers, put it on the table. "Tell me about yesterday," she said. "Was anything taken?"

"That's what's strange. That gun was in my footlocker, the first place any savvy burglar would look. But he didn't take it—didn't take a thing, in fact."

"Then how can you be sure anyone's been in here?"

"You won't believe it," Campy said with resignation.

"Try me."

"I smelled him."

She looked at him.

"It's something you pick up," he said defensively. "The Cong were very good at it. We learned it, too. This guy was easy. He wore cologne."

Amy felt a chill. It seemed so primitive, like a wild animal. She realized that Campy was right: she had no idea, no idea at all, of all the changes he had gone through.

But that did not make him crazy.

She said, "What do you think he wanted in here?"

"I don't know. But he searched my things."

Amy felt a sudden, strange sense of kinship to him. She, too, had had an intruder, a man who'd slipped in and out of her house almost at will. He hadn't taken anything either, except her control of herself and Joyce's life.

"I wonder if there's any connection," she said.

"To what?"

She told Campy the whole story about Joyce's murder—that the killer had slipped into her house at least twice before to interrogate her under scopolamine.

When she finished, she realized that Campy was holding her hands. His face was grim. "I want you to move in here with me," he said.

"Campy, I can't do that. I'm fine—I'm staying with Mother. She's helping take care of the girls."

"Marry me. Say yes, Amy."

She pulled her hands away, flustered. He did not mean it, not just like that—he couldn't. There was too much to think about. They had a lot more talking to do before she could think of anything like that. "Thank you, Campy," she said. "For wanting to protect me. But the only thing that's going to protect me or my father is catching this killer. If I could just remember what happened in the gazebo. That's what the killer is after. But I can't. Tom tried his best to help me and still I couldn't—*wouldn't.*"

"Maybe you shouldn't be trying," Campy said.

"I have to remember."

"You have to forget," he said gently. "That's why you have."

"But if I knew what happened back there in the woods all those years ago, maybe I'd know who's doing this."

"Maybe. And maybe you'd just be more scared, more hurt. Amy dear, give yourself some credit. This world is full of people who need to forget and can't. They go over and over things, they stay in a permanent funk. They tell their shrinks and sink them into a funk, too. You and I have a different method from the shrinks'. We stitch people up so their wounds can heal. Only when we know the wound won't open again do we pull the stitches out. We don't tell people to keep ripping at their stitches, clawing at their scars. You don't need to remember why some gazebo in the woods terrified you when you were little, any more than you need to remember the day Bud died or I need to remember how Gordon Silvestre looked after they'd cut his throat. What you need is for us to nail this murdering psycho."

He took one of her hands and stroked the back of it with his other hand. His touch, so full of love, warmed her. "Look at you," he said. "All that's happened—you've lost the brother you looked up to, then a husband, then your close friend is murdered. Are you lying in bed with a cold compress on your head? Are you popping Valiums? No one would blame you. But no, you've made yourself strong. You've taken the blows and moved on, leaving your grief, anger, and bitterness behind. The day I met you, all those years ago, I knew that you were special, and I was more right than I knew. Do you think I love you just because you're beautiful?"

She tried to find the flaw in his logic. How could it be right to go on repressing? Some therapist Campy would make—and yet the inner allure of it enthralled her.

"It can't be so simple," she murmured.

Still holding her hand, he looked into her eyes, the way he had so many years ago. She gazed back, feeling herself slipping toward him, unwilling to look away. "Move in with me, Amy," he said. "The fugues are fairly far apart. I'll go to a doctor, get medication, whatever I need. I'll be here in this place whenever you are. I'll protect you and your girls until this is over. That's what you need. And I need you. Marry me."

She felt the blood surging through her head. Her fingers hurt. She realized she was clenching Campy's hands very hard. She did not want to let go. Marry Campy? Just like that? What about Tom? She cared deeply for Tom, owed him so much.

But did she love him? Did Tom love her? He had never said so . . .

"I went to war," Campy said, "because I felt there was something there that I had to learn. What I learned was that I should never have gone to war. I should have asked you to marry me. That was a long time ago. I hurt you. You have every right to be angry with me—"

"Not after I heard why—"

"Doesn't matter. You still have the right. Any psychologist would tell you that—not just Tom. You also have the right to put it behind you, as you have so much else. I pray to God that you will. I love you more than ever. We're here now, alive now. We can't have the years that are gone, but we can the ones that are left. If we—"

"Yes."

"What?"

"Yes, I'll marry you."

He looked at her, his eyes wide. A tear spilled and rolled down his cheek. She leaned forward and kissed it away.

"Amy." He pulled her to him, covering her face with kisses, holding her tight. Her mind felt clear suddenly—at peace. Joy filled her like a sweet breath after a long and desperate swim under water.

"Make love to me, Campy."

He looked at her, his eyes glistening. He stood and pulled her to him. She felt his hands sliding around to the small of her back, pulling her against his flat, hard stomach. She smelled him—a tang of sweat and after-shave.

"I love you," he said. "For twenty years I've loved you, and now I'm going to make love to you."

She looked up at him. His face was a blur. She could feel her heart pounding against him. He fitted his mouth to hers, his tongue gently exploring inside her mouth, greeting the places it had left so long ago. She could feel his hands working up inside the back of her blouse, his strong, deft fingertips probing into the creases of her back, his thumbs entering the warmth under her arms. She felt him rock-hard against her now. She groaned around his tongue, feeling a soaring lightness, a pain as invisible as the weight of her bones, leaving her at last.

She let him hold her against him as he walked her slowly

backward, and then they were in his bedroom and she could
hear the rain starting to pelt against the gray window beyond
him. She saw the narrow bed behind him. He backed against
it and she floated weightlessly down on top of him, laughing,
rolling to her side and easing back to pluck at the buttons of his
shirt. She ran her fingers over his chest, finding it matted with
fine, curly hair that had not been there when he was a boy.
Letting her palms descend to his hard stomach, she rubbed at
the rippled muscles beneath the skin.

He struggled out of his pants, revealing strong thighs,
bunched with muscle. She let him work his hands up under her
skirt, moving to help him slide her panties and panty hose off
in one long movement. He rolled into her, cradling her face,
and then she felt him against her.

She guided him to her, glorying in the springing weight of
his desire. She straightened on her side, pulling him into her.
"I love you so much," he whispered. He stroked down her
sides, gripping her buttocks, helping her into a smooth, gliding
rhythm with him. She felt his heat reaching up inside her,
torching golden waves of warmth that swelled through her
belly. He kissed her mouth again, then bent to kiss her breasts,
and the glow swept up her, tingling out into her fingers. He
rocked with her in the soothing patter of the rain, slowly,
slowly. She heard herself gasping half-formed whispers; he
followed them, each movement and hesitation perfect, easing
her inch by inch, higher, higher, oh yes, oh yes, oh OH OH. She
shouted into the rough blanket, rocking with the climax.

She drifted in the patter of rain, tears of release rolling
down her cheeks, his arms around her.

After a while, she realized he was still inside her, still hard.
"Oh," she breathed. "Sorry." She moved around him, experi-
mentally, finding she could bear it. He gasped. She moved
again, ever so slightly, teasing him, goading him the same
wonderful way he'd done her. Watching his face, that rugged,
centurion's face with the scars, the broad, intelligent forehead.
The fine, even teeth showed now in a silent grimace of rapture.
She moved her hips again, seeing the movement reflected in
his face, as though it were another part of her own body.

"Don't come, Campy," she whispered, then moved her
hips again.

"Ah—sadist."

She laughed, feeling his trembling contractions, just short, just on the edge. Languidly she tilted her hips a last time, giving him release, feeling him shudder and explode as his back arched, holding him in her, cradling his head as he slumped.

"God in heaven," he whispered. He wrapped her in his arms, holding her gently against him. It felt so right to her, like something they had perfected over the years in the life that had never happened.

The rain gurgled down a drainpipe outside the window, soothing and hypnotic. After a long time, Amy raised herself on one elbow. She could make his face out dimly in the shimmering, rain-patterned light from his window.

"I'm going to marry you," she said with a sense of wonder.

"Say it again."

She did.

Campy closed his eyes, smiling. "I can't wait to meet your daughters. They look great. I know I'll love them."

"You might not find them so lovable. Denise, especially, still misses Bud terribly. She might resent you."

"I expect she will. I respect that. She is Denise Thurman-St. Clair. She doesn't need another name. I know I can't replace her father, and I'll make sure she knows I'm not trying to. What I *can* do is love her for herself and because she's a piece of you. I can love her for the man I met and liked in that studio."

Amy kissed him, loving him, feeling the old Campy still deep within him—everything she had fallen in love with at the start, his clear way of seeing things, his humor and kindness, his strength. He talked about what she had endured, but look at him. To see all but one of his friends die horribly, to lose a part of his body—and the woman he loved . . .

But he's found me again, she thought. And I've found him.

How will I tell Tom? she wondered. The thought pained her deeply. She put it away. Now was not the time to think about that.

Campy gave her another long kiss, then got up and ambled out of the bedroom, the wavering light from the window winking along the false foot as he turned out of sight. She heard water running in the bathroom. She rose, full of all that had happened, the wonderful comfort of knowing again that she loved and was loved. Campy needed her and she would help him.

She smoothed her skirt and put her blouse back on. Campy returned, pulling on his trousers, sitting on the edge of the bed. His back was so broad at the shoulders, narrowing down to a compact waist. What would it be like to get up each morning and see that strong back at the edge of her bed—*our bed?* It would be wonderful.

As he was pulling his shirt on, someone began pounding fiercely on the apartment door. Campy gave her a perplexed look. The knocking stopped for a second, then resumed, louder and more rapid.

He rose and headed for the door.

There was a scary arrogance in the pounding. Worried, Amy got up and hurried after Campy, saw him sweep up the gun from the table and cock his arm behind his back to hide it. He eased the door open a crack, then tossed the gun onto the couch beside the knife and pulled the door wide. A man in a rumpled blue blazer stepped through.

Detective Schumer! Amy thought, startled. Behind Schumer, she could see two uniformed cops. Schumer saw her and looked momentarily off balance. He returned his attention to Campy. "Are you Dr. Otis Camp?" he asked.

Campy said, "What's this about?"

"You're under arrest for the murder of Owen VanKleeck."

27

Amy stood rooted, stunned. When Detective Schumer started reading Campy his rights, she could stand it no longer. "This is ridiculous. Dr. Camp is not a murderer."

Schumer did not look at her, keeping his eyes on the small Miranda card. "Excuse me, Doctor, but I have to finish this. Then I'll listen to whatever you have to say."

Amy waited, feeling sick, while Schumer told Campy that he had the right to an attorney and that anything he said could be used against him. *Oh God, what is this?*

"Would you put your hands behind your back, please, Doctor?"

"Before you do that," Campy said, "I need to change the padding in my prosthesis. Otherwise the stump could become infected, and if I'm going to jail—"

Schumer looked a little squeamish. "How long will it take?"

"Ten minutes, tops. I promise not to run off."

Schumer turned to one of the uniformed cops. "Go with him, Bertelli."

Bertelli grabbed Campy's arm, walking him past Amy. Campy's face was pale, expressionless. All at once Amy was terribly frightened. Why didn't he protest, tell these men they were wrong?

The fugues! Was he afraid he might actually have done it? Amy's stomach plunged with horror. Was it possible? It might be.

"Are you all right, Doctor?" Schumer asked, looking at her with concern.

"Yes. Thank you."

Campy and the cop rounded the corner into the bedroom. Amy felt dazed. Campy wasn't guilty, *please, God, he can't be.* "This is a terrible mistake," she said. "Campy would never kill anyone."

"Look, Doctor. I assume you are friends, and I know how you feel. But how much do you know about him?"

"I once knew him better than anyone. And everything I know about him now says he's not a murderer."

"That knife and gun—didn't they bother you?"

Amy thought of Campy throwing the knife at her and suppressed a groan. Thank God Schumer didn't know about that. She said, "those are just his service weapons. He had them out because someone had broken into his apartment and he was trying to decide what to do with them to keep them from being stolen. Don't you think if he was guilty of murder, he'd have tried to use them on you instead of turning them over to you?"

"Not necessarily. He might have been afraid you'd be hurt if he started firing." Schumer nodded to the other patrolman. "Try the medicine cabinet first."

"Do you have a warrant?" Amy said.

Schumer held it out to her. Amy saw with surprise that it was dated today, signed by the judge only an hour ago.

"What are your grounds for arresting him?"

"I'm not sure I should be discussing that with you. That's between him and his attorney."

"He'll be using one of my family's attorneys."

Schumer looked a bit annoyed. "Even the sharpest lawyer isn't going to get him off."

"Detective Schumer, I brought the heart-attack murders to your attention in the first place, and I've cooperated fully since. Don't you think you could tell me what your evidence is?"

"We found a scalpel blade," he said, "locked away in a

drawer of Dr. Camp's desk at the hospital. It had some obscure heart toxin on it—enough to kill with a scratch."

Amy felt a cold rush in her veins. "What . . . what were you doing looking in his desk in the first place?"

Campy's phone rang. Schumer started toward the kitchen; Amy stepped past him, picking up. "Hello?"

"Amy?" Chris said. "Thank God. Are the police there?"

"Yes." Amy kept her face impassive.

"Are they where they can hear you?"

"Yes."

"Then you'd better pretend I'm a casual friend of Campy's. If they know it's me, they might think I'm calling to warn you. Which I guess I am."

"He can't come to the phone right now," Amy said. "Can I take a message?"

"Good. Listen—*Claviceps cyanidus*. Deadly stuff. We found traces of it inside the eyeballs, barely enough to register. It's an alkaloid derived from a plant, like digitalis, but a microgram suspended in the right vehicle is enough to cause cardiac arrest. And get this—it grows only in the Amazon and Southeast Asia."

Vietnam, Amy thought, her heart sinking. *That's* why they looked in Campy's desk.

"We gave a verbal report to the police right away," Chris said. "And then I got to thinking about the Vietnam angle and realized they'd go straight after Campy."

Conscious of Schumer watching her, Amy groped for something innocuous to say. "So you can't play golf on Tuesday." Her voice seemed to belong to someone else.

"Have they arrested him?" Chris asked.

"Yes."

"I'm sorry. I know you . . . liked him."

The way Chris put it, in the past tense, filled Amy with dread. "I'll tell him," she said. "Good-bye." She hung up the phone, watching her hand move in slow motion, turning to find Detective Schumer looking at her.

"Dr. Camp can play golf with that foot?"

"He does a lot of things that might surprise you, but one of them isn't murder. Listen, Detective Schumer, these heart-

attack murders go back half a year. Campy just moved here. He
lived in Ann Arbor until just a week or so ago."

"Yes, but he made a lot of flights here in the past six
months. They fit with the deaths."

"He was looking for a position at a hospital here. Did he
make any flights when there were no deaths?"

"Irrelevant."

"No, it's not!"

The cop came out of the bathroom. "Look at this!" He held
up a plastic evidence bag. Inside was a small vial with half a
gram of brownish powder. "Found it inside the plastic toilet
paper roller. You know how the two pieces come apart and
there's a spring——"

"That's fine, Rasmussen. Give it here."

Amy looked at the little vial as it changed hands. The
powder was very fine. Half a gram was plenty for analysis. Her
mind spun, grasping for answers.

"The ME said it should be a brown powder," Schumer
noted with obvious satisfaction.

"Campy was framed," Amy said. "Who told you about the
scalpel in his desk?"

Schumer sighed. "Really, Doctor——"

"I told you, someone got in here when he was gone. They
didn't take anything. Campy couldn't understand it, but *this* is
why. They didn't come to steal. They came to leave that vial."
Amy felt her hopes rising. It made sense.

Schumer looked unimpressed. "Rasmussen, go see if Bertelli needs any help." He turned back to her. "Dr. Camp spent
a couple of years in the jungle where this plant grows——"

"I'm aware of that."

"Are you also aware that, while he was over there, he did
some killing the old-fashioned way?"

Amy felt a desperate desire to turn away, silence Schumer
somehow. She did *not* want to hear this, it did not matter——

"Thirty-seven NVA and Viet Cong," Schumer said. "That's
how many he killed, according to the CIA boys who were
running his unit."

Amy felt the kitchen wall against her back, felt herself
leaning rigidly against it.

"I'm sorry, Doctor, but facts are facts. And these are pretty grim. War can unleash the killer in a man. He was very seriously crippled. That can do things to the mind, too. Maybe after 'Nam, he missed killing. Over there, he always killed quietly and at close quarters with that big knife of his. That's not so easy once you're crippled. So maybe he switched to a little knife with an exotic poison on it that he learned about in Vietnam. Isn't that reasonable, Doctor?"

"No." But she knew that it was.

Rasmussen ran in, his face pale. "He's gone! He knocked Bertelli cold and got away out the window."

Amy's heart leapt.

"What!" Schumer started forward. "We're three stories up. There's no fire escape out there."

"He shimmied down a drainpipe. I don't know what he did to Bertelli—there ain't a mark on him."

Campy, escaped! Amy felt a surge of fear for him. They would hunt him now, shoot him if he gave them the slightest excuse. She watched Schumer run into the bedroom. A moment later he came back out, his face grim.

"Detective Schumer," Amy said, "this should show you that your theory is wrong. Campy is not a cripple, in any sense of the word. He wouldn't need a little knife and a sly poison if he still wanted to kill people—"

"What this shows me," Schumer said, "is that I have a murder suspect on the loose and he's armed and dangerous." He brushed past her to the phone. "But don't worry, Dr. St. Clair. We'll get him."

Amy's fear for Campy deepened. "Alive, Detective Schumer. You must not harm him!"

"That will be up to him," Schumer said.

28

Amy peered nervously into the black mouth of the alley. It seemed to breathe on her, a tide of cold, humid air that smelled of damp dirt and oil. She shivered. Please be in there, James. You're my only hope.

A siren wailed in the distance, filling her with foreboding. The hunt was ranging far and wide, thanks to a witness—a woman in the apartment across the street. She'd told Schumer she'd seen Campy climbing down the drainpipe, a gun stuck in the back of his belt. The woman had seen him run up to First Avenue and get into a cab that had stopped at the light. By now, Campy, armed with Officer Bertelli's service revolver, could be anywhere in the city—or outside New York entirely.

Amy had a feeling he was not. Campy had never run from trouble. In fact, she thought with pained exasperation, he seemed always to run toward it.

I have to get to him, she thought, before the police do. After what he did to Bertelli, they'll shoot him if they even *think* he's trying to resist.

Amy called out to James. There was no answer. If he was in there, he meant for her to come to him.

Her stomach squirmed at the thought. She glanced up and down the street to see if anyone was watching. At the York Avenue end, a man leaned against a building. He had not been there when she'd passed, but he seemed to be paying no attention to her. Except for him, the street was still empty.

"James, I'm coming in, all right?" Her neck prickled as she stepped into the darkness; she forced herself forward. Broken glass crunched under her shoes. She remembered it from last time, and wondered if James had spread it there deliberately as an alarm system. She felt her way along the gritty brick wall, barely able to see. A thin glow found its way down from a window high up in the back wall of the alley. She made out the shanty of boxes and stopped—

Then saw the man standing to the side, a dark form so still it wavered on her retinas. She froze, feeling her heart lurch.

"Hello, Amy," said the raspy voice.

Cool relief rushed through her. "James."

"You didn't put on that nice perfume today."

"James, I need your help. The police are after Campy."

Finally he moved, the barest shimmer in the darkness.

"They tried to arrest him, but he got away—"

James laughed, an utterly cold sound that sent a chill up her spine. "Of course he did. Did he have his K-bar?"

"No. But he took a gun from the cop he knocked out."

"Bad," James said, but his voice held admiration, too. "They know he has that gun, they'll shoot a lot faster."

"If he surrenders—"

"No chance of that," James said.

Amy felt a sick dread. "Campy's a sensible man," she said. "Surely if he sees he can't get away . . ."

"Top won't let 'em lock him up." James sighed in the darkness. "One time they caught the Major. We couldn't get him to keep his brass butt back in camp. 'Course, our unit was a little different than most, or we wouldn't have had a major at the wheel. Anyway, the Major went out at night with Van and Borger. Got separated, made a noise, and the Cong bagged him. Campy and the other two went looking for him. The Cong were waiting, of course. They put Campy in a bamboo cage a little bigger than that crate there. Kept him in there eight weeks. Let the rats at him. Poked him with sticks when he tried to sleep . . ."

Amy felt the strength draining from her legs. She was dimly aware of James's hand on her arm, steadying her, helping her to a seat on a crate. She felt his hand move to the back of her neck. Gently he pushed her head forward and down until the blood flowed back in.

"Sorry," James said.

"Finish the story."

"Well, we kept looking for Campy, but we just couldn't find him. Finally he chewed through a few tongs and got out. Cong tried to stop him, so he killed them and brought the Major back to base. Major wasn't much good after that, and Campy, well, he'd changed too. Kept his back to the shower so he could see anyone who came in, things like that. Top won't ever walk into any kind of cage under his own power again."

Amy fought a wave of despair. "Do you know where he might go?"

James said nothing.

"I just found him again. I can't lose him, I *can't*. But if they catch up to him, I will."

James patted her shoulder. "Don't worry. He's pretty good at not being caught by the wrong people."

"I hope you're right. They think he's been killing people here in the city—"

"He didn't."

She stopped, heartened by the conviction in his voice. "I don't think he did either, but—"

"You don't think? Don't you know?"

"James, be reasonable. The police say he killed thirty-seven people in Vietnam."

James grunted. "Don't know where they got that number, but even if it's right, every one of them was trying to kill us first. We were just trying to stay out of sight, do our mission, but we were right in the middle of them. It was war, and Campy was a soldier. People just don't understand." James's voice turned harsh with disgust. "Once you've had to kill, you know what it is and you don't ever do it again unless there's no choice. The only crazy killers that came out of 'Nam were crazy killers in their hearts before they went in. Campy has killed, but he's not a killer."

The passion in his voice braced her. She felt the strength and will flowing back into her. "I love him, James."

"I know it. But you've got to leave this to me, Amy. I didn't

hear anyone else out there with you, but the police'll be following you before long, watching you. You go near Campy, you're
likely to cause the thing you're scared of."

Amy's mind went to the man she'd seen at the corner,
leaning against the wall. Was he a policeman? She felt a rush
of anxiety. She had to get out of here before they got onto
James, too.

She stood. "Be careful, James."

"If I weren't careful, there wouldn't be any James anymore. Before you go, have you got any money? Top might not
need it. But then again, he might."

She dug out her money from her pocket, leaving the gold
clip on it, and handed it all to James. He touched her shoulder.
"All right. Go."

Turning, she felt her way out of the alley into the street.
The man still stood at the corner, leaning against the building.
A cop? He seemed to be paying her no attention. Turning away,
she hurried up toward First Avenue. As she rounded the corner,
she glanced back. The man was walking up the street now. She
felt a stab of alarm for James, then relief as the man passed the
alley without a sideways glance.

Which was probably luckier for him than for James.

Turning down First Avenue, Amy saw plenty of people
and felt better about the man behind her. But she kept him in
mind as she walked past a row of homey little restaurants,
looking for a cab. Couples strolled together, stopping to gaze
at the menus posted in the restaurant windows. She longed
suddenly for such safe serenity, nothing more pressing than
"Should we have chalupas or chicken Kiev?"

Instead, she was in love with a man who had certainly
once killed, and might have again. James had been so sure that
Campy hadn't killed since Vietnam, but did he know about the
fugues? Might Campy be capable of murder while in a state of
mental blackout?

Amy felt her jaw clenching. No, she thought. Campy may
have killed as a soldier, but he was no murderer. If James can
be positive of that, so can I.

She saw a cab coming and started to hail it, then remembered with a start that she'd given all her money to James. She
still had change and tokens in her other pocket. Where was the

nearest subway? Seventy-seventh and Lexington—a block north and three long ones west.

Amy paused at a public phone, using its small plastic shield as a mirror to check the man behind her. He was still there, strolling now, apparently interested in a restaurant menu. In the light from the restaurant window she could see him better, but there wasn't much to see. He wore a stocking cap and dark glasses. A mop of dark hair flowed from under the stocking cap to his shoulders. His mouth was hidden by a full Zapata mustache. He kept his hands jammed in his jacket pockets, shoulders slumped, making his belly stick out a little. He reminded her of that undercover cop, Belker, in "Hill Street Blues," except he was taller.

She turned left at Seventy-seventh and walked up the first long block toward Lexington, relieved to see a few other people on the sidewalk with her. Lengthening her stride, she worked out her next moves. The best way to keep Campy from being cornered and shot was to clear him. She remembered the videotapes back in her office. Maybe a fresh look at them would help. The toxin was too concentrated to give orally. Most likely, it was applied to the skin—Schumer probably had that much right. This time, when she looked at the tapes, she'd concentrate on each instance of anyone touching one of the victims.

At Lexington Avenue, Amy paused at the subway entrance to check behind her. She couldn't see the man in the stocking cap. Relief filled her. She heard the faint rumble of a train below. With luck, it was going her way.

She hurried down the steps. As she neared the turnstile, she heard the train screeching to a stop. She fumbled in her pocket for a subway token. *Hurry.* She slid the token in and butted up against the turnstile, running through, slowing as she saw that the train was at the uptown platform. Its doors hissed shut and it pulled away. She scanned the station. Across the way, a small knot of people that had gotten off the train were now headed for the exits. On her side, there was one man, waiting down near the end. He looked about fifty. He was wearing an outdoor jacket that looked as though it had just arrived from L.L. Bean. Amy walked down to him, stopping a few feet away. Glancing back, she saw the man in the stocking cap. A cold shock ran up her spine. He was back, standing down the platform from her, looking at her now, staring at her, his silvered sunglasses as blank as a bug's eyes.

Amy felt a stab of alarm. Who was he?

Suddenly she remembered the cab she'd seen when she'd first gotten to Campy's. It had idled there at the corner, a passenger sitting still in the backseat. When she'd tried to call the cab, it and its passenger had stayed put. Later, when she'd looked out Campy's window, the cab had still been there. Could the man behind her now have been the passenger? If so, he'd followed her not just from Campy's but all the way from the hospital, maybe even before that.

Amy thought of Strickney following her in the park, only to be killed by someone who'd been following him. At least that was the police theory. But what if the killer had not been following Strickney? What if he'd been following *her*?

What if that was him, behind her now?

Amy's uneasiness deepened. She cursed her luck. Sunday evening—one of the few times the subway was ever deserted, and here she was with only one person to help her. She edged closer to the man in the L.L. Bean coat. He glanced at her, looking annoyed and a little nervous. She smiled, trying to establish eye contact. He frowned and moved a few steps away, toward the man in the stocking cap. Reluctantly, Amy followed. The man in the coat turned and mumbled, "Look, I'm not interested."

"What?" she said, then realized with amazement that he thought she was a prostitute.

The rumble of another train reverberated down the tunnel. Relief filled her; she put a hand on the man's arm to explain. He jerked away from her and scurried down the platform past the man in the stocking cap and out of the station. Amy almost laughed. Was she that unappealing? Or did the man just have a real problem with women? It didn't matter now, the train would take her away. With luck, there would even be a transit cop on board.

Amy walked toward the edge of the track, glancing at the man in the stocking cap, feeling a shock in her stomach as she saw, instead, a man in a ski mask—he'd rolled it down to cover his face. Amy stared at him, frozen with shock. That mask—it was the man who'd drugged her and killed Joyce.

And now he meant to kill her too.

Amy's paralysis broke. She ran, terrified, along the platform toward the approaching train, seeing the light grow in the tunnel, *come on, come ON.* She was almost to the end wall of the platform now, but the train was almost there. Its front appeared inside the tunnel. She saw the words OUT OF SERVICE on its front, and her heart stuttered with panic because the train wasn't going to stop—

Hands grabbed her arms from behind, muscling her forward. She screamed, knowing in a terrible instant that the man meant to push her in front of the train.

She jammed a foot back between his ankles, twisting her body, feeling him lurch and stumble. A bow wave of grit and fumes hit her face, and she felt she was very near the platform edge. She screamed again, hearing nothing but the roar of the train. She threw herself backward, pushing the man down. As he fell, he dragged her down with him. The edge of the platform slammed her side. She twisted toward the man, facing him, both of them on their sides. Jerky strobe flashes of light from the passing empty cars winked on the horrid masked face. She could feel her shoulder hanging out over the edge, inches from the train. He tried to shove her, but she clung to him, forcing him to drag her with him as he scrabbled backward. She let go and sprang up, but he kicked her back toward the speeding train. She teetered on the edge of the platform, feeling the compression of air whip along her back as the train roared past.

The man sprang up as she struggled desperately for balance, but lost it, twisting in the air toward the train as the last car flashed by. She flung a hand out as she fell, catching the edge of the platform. Landing hard on her feet, she sprawled backward, sitting down on the ties. Her head swam with the stink of hot grease; she saw the man looking down at her from the platform, pulling a garrote from his sleeve.

She scrambled up, but before she could run past him along the tracks, he jumped down to block her path. Turning back, she ran into the train tunnel, feeling the ties slap against her feet.

She heard him behind her, his feet pounding the ties. Terror filled her. Seeing the black maw of a side tunnel, she swerved into it.

The darkness deepened, forcing her to slow. Veering left, she found the wall of the tunnel with an outstretched hand as she heard the man running in behind her. She felt her way deeper along the wall, unable to see a thing now, hearing his footsteps falter behind her as the darkness swallowed him completely too.

She stopped, keeping her hand planted on the wall. The gritty sludge of soot and condensation was so thick she could not feel the surface beneath. She could hear the steady plink of water deeper in the tunnel.

Why was it so dark in here? Not that she was complaining, but didn't they usually light the tunnels between the stations, even if it was only a dim bulb every fifty yards? Maybe this tunnel was never used. She wondered if there was a stair down to the express tracks somewhere along here.

It might be a side spur for storing subway cars. In which case the power rail would be live. A touch of one toe, and she would be dead before she could draw a breath. She'd be all right as long as she kept to the wall.

Amy listened. She heard the man's shoes, a faint crackle on the railroad ties, *close!* The hackles rose on her neck as she realized he was working up the same wall toward her. She must keep moving, or he would run into her. The garrote would find her throat and she would die, choking, in the blackness. He would leave her here in this filthy place, and Denise and Ellie would never know what had happened to her.

Amy closed her eyes a second, her stomach swooping as she fought off the panic. She tried to keep her mind focused on the task of setting her feet down carefully in the darkness. If she could get to the other side of the tunnel, she could wait for him to pass her and run back out. But that would mean crossing the power rail.

Amy heard his foot scrape again, closer.

She stepped away from the wall. As she lost contact, a

wave of dizziness swept her. She held herself still until it passed, then took two more steps across the tie, lifting her feet high with each step. The power rail should have a board bracketed above it, a precaution in case some fool decided to run across the tracks. She must make sure she stepped down on top of it.

Just another few steps now—

A horrid thought struck her: What if there was no bracket in here? This wasn't a station, no one would be running across these tracks.

She heard the man again, *closer!*

Foot high, ease it down, *careful,* back onto the tie.

She crept along, terrified of making a sound, knowing he was listening for her. Her eyes itched and crawled, the darkness coiling and swimming in her brain as she tried to make him out.

Another high step, letting her foot coast down like a ballerina's, sweating as an image flashed of her toe hitting the rail. Something solid and flat stopped her foot high up. This was it—the protective board. If the rail was still hot, death waited only two fingers below. She stretched her leg well over the board, feeling the wooden tie on the other side with her toes, rolling her weight forward and over the rail. She hurried straight to the far wall, arms outstretched, hands finding the solid haven. Her eyes watered and stung from straining to see. She leaned against the grime, sweating, feeling her heart pound in her chest.

All right, now where was he?

She listened, hearing the water, nothing else. If she could see him now, would she know him? That thought frightened her worse than anything. Detective Schumer had believed he was probably someone she knew. He might have worn the disguise to keep witnesses from identifying him later.

Or to keep her from knowing him, in case he failed to kill her.

Amy heard a quick tappity-tap along the tie. Something with claws ran over her foot. *A rat!* Biting her lips, she stifled a scream. She heard the man step toward her from across the tunnel, and then he halted and she could almost *feel* him thinking about the power rail, see his anxiety flaring redly around him in the darkness.

A small, gnarled paw stepped on her foot. She felt the rat's whiskers nuzzling her through her panty hose. It was going to bite her! She flexed her foot and the rat squeaked and ran away, and she heard the man sigh across the rail from her as he dismissed the sound. Only rats.

Amy's knees trembled. She sank into a squat, feeling the sweat pour into her eyes. She could plainly hear the whisper of his feet now. He was finding his way back to the far wall. Would he go deeper now?

No, he was standing there across the tunnel from her, waiting for her to make a sound. She realized that she now knew something new about the killer: he was not a smoker. If he had a match or a lighter, she would have been dead minutes ago. Amy shuddered, imagining him over there, looking for her, his eyes useless now, his ears everything.

Go on, she thought. I'm farther in, I'm getting away.

He did not move. She counted off sixty seconds. Another sixty. No sound from him.

Her nerves jangled with fear. The urge to scream welled in her throat and passed. She must do something. Groping the cinders at her feet, she found a rock and hurled it deeper into the tunnel, hearing it ping against the tracks.

She heard him hurry toward the sound.

All right, go! Rising from her crouch, she headed the other way, back out of the tunnel. Her feet got the measure of the gap between ties, and she sped up. Then she felt a vibration. *A train!* A second later, she heard it—a faint rumble, silence, another rumble, and then the sound swelled steadily.

The train sounded like it was coming down *this* tunnel.

Panic seized her. She began to run along the ties, the slap of her feet swallowed up in the horrid, rumbling crescendo of the train. Light speared across the mouth of the side tunnel ahead, the backwash showing her the ties and rails. She felt an instant of relief, knowing the train was on the other track, and then she realized that the man would be able to see her now against the light of the train, and that the train was going to cut her off, blocking that last few feet to the platform.

She ran all out now, hearing nothing but the deafening roar of the train, knowing the man must be closing up behind her now, chasing her. If she could just beat the train to where the tracks converged, cover those last few yards of common track, she could vault up onto the platform.

She grabbed her skirt, lifting it high, racing for the opening. Her throat hurt, screaming, she was screaming, the sound lost in the squeal of the train's brakes, and then she realized that it was slowing as it neared the station. Hope sprang up in her. *I can make it!*

Amy found a last burst of speed, the ties hammering her feet as she saw the light, blinding white ahead of her. The common wall of the two tunnels hid the train; she would not know how close it was until the last second.

Amy ran the last few feet of wall, the train screeching to her left.

GO!

She raced out onto the common track, feeling the ties vibrating under her feet. Glancing back, she saw that the train was right there, hurtling down on her.

Screaming, she ran toward the corner of the platform, hearing the tortured squeal as the train's brakes grabbed at the rails. The train's horn blasted a warning, deafening her as she planted her hands and scrambled onto the edge of the platform.

SAFE!

But he was right behind her.

She screamed and kicked at him and he almost fell off the platform into the path of the skidding train. He grabbed a post and hauled himself back, and then she was up and running.

People's faces flashing past.

Up the steps to the street, his footsteps pounding up behind her, and then she burst out onto the sidewalk and there was a mounted policeman. She ran over, grabbing one of the reins and the cop's stirruped boot before she sank to her knees with the smell of horse, sweet again, in her head.

29

Amy sat in her office with the door shut, waiting for the trembling to stop. She was safe now, people all around her, but her body didn't buy it yet.

He won't give up trying to kill me now, she thought. The only way to stop him is to find out who he is.

She was worried about Campy. Was he hiding in some alley with James, waiting for the police to close in? Or maybe he was still alone, keeping the cop's pistol close at hand, determined to die rather than be locked in a cage again—

Horrified, she cut the thought off.

So *cold* in here. She saw three medical coats, back from the laundry, hanging on the door hook. She put another one on over the one she was wearing, tugging the sleeves to get them right. Her hand and knees hurt where she had scraped them scrabbling up the platform. In a few minutes she must examine her scrapes, clean and disinfect them, but first there were more pressing things to do.

Amy picked up the phone and dialed her mother.

"Where in heaven's name are you?" her mother demanded.

"The hospital. How are Denise and Ellie doing?"

"They're fine, of course. But I'm sure they'd like to see their mother. I can't imagine why—"

"Mother, please listen—some policemen are on their way over. They are going to guard your apartment tonight. Lock your doors now, and don't let anyone in until they get there. Make sure they're in uniform, and make them show you ID. Whatever you do, don't go out. Stay right there, and you'll be safe."

There was a short silence at the other end. "I understand. Can you tell me why?"

"The man who killed Joyce is after me. I'm safe now, and I want to make sure he doesn't go after you or the girls instead."

"I see. Don't worry. I'll take care of everything here." Victoria's voice was firm, strong. Amy felt herself relax a fraction. *Thank you, Mother, for your strength.* She smiled, struck by the irony—she'd spent her life disliking Victoria's ironwoman image.

"Let me talk to Denise and Ellie for a minute."

"Of course."

Ellie came on first, telling her excitedly about how they'd gotten Grandma to take Joyce's place in their Sunday Monopoly game, and now Ellie had hotels on Boardwalk and Park Place, and it was Grandma's move and she was only seven and nine squares from dis*a*ster. Amy discussed the game with her, lingering as long as she could in the wonderful illusion of normalcy. Denise came on next, sounding a little sullen as she asked when Amy was coming home. "I'll see you as soon as I can," Amy said. "I love you very much."

"Me too," Denise said a bit grudgingly.

"Please put Grandma back on."

"Amy?" Victoria said.

"Don't say anything to alarm the girls."

"Of course not."

"I really don't think he'll move against you or them, but we have to be sure."

"And what about you, dear?"

"I think I'll stay here in the hospital for now. I've got staff all around me and the hospital has its own security people, of course."

"If you go out, you'll get a police escort?"

"Yes," Amy said, meaning it.

"Call us, no matter the time," Mother said. "Keep us posted."

"I will. Mother, thank you."

"Be careful, Amy dear. We . . . need you. All of us."

A lump rose in Amy's throat. "I love you."

"And I love you," her mother said softly.

Amy hung up the phone, feeling the burn of dammed-up tears in her throat. They would have to stay dammed up.

Amy picked up the first videotape and put it in the machine. She watched it and the second tape and the third, starting to feel frustrated. No single staffer had touched every one of the victims.

She watched Philip walking into the cardiac bay with John Levesque, not going near the patient, just stocking the crash cart—

And just like that, Amy knew with a sinking feeling what she had been seeing but not letting herself see:

Philip was there on every tape.

Amy turned the VCR off and sat, stricken with a sense of foreboding. Surely it meant nothing. On the VanKleeck tape, Elaine had chewed Philip out and he'd tearfully brought her the missing nitroglycerine paste. On the other tapes he showed up on his own to restock some item. In two of the tapes his back was to the camera. On another, he was stocking the cart with the electrode paste used on the chest to increase contact for electrocardiograms.

It was his job to keep the crash cart stocked with all minor, non-drug supplies. Each tape ran for hours—you'd expect to see him doing it here and there.

But all four times?

Amy felt sick. From what Chris and Detective Schumer had said, *Claviceps cyanidus* was potent enough to kill by absorption, even through unbroken skin. There were dozens of innocuous things on the crash cart that would touch the skin if used in treatment—cotton swabs, alcohol . . .

Nitroglycerine and electrode paste.

But how *could* it be Philip? Amy slapped her desk in consternation, rebelling against the idea. It was impossible, ridiculous, which was *why* she'd thought nothing of seeing Philip on all four tapes.

What motive could he possibly have?

For years, Victoria had bitterly blamed Winnie's neglect for Philip's terrible injury. That was Victoria's problem, but the statuette buried under the gazebo said that it might be Philip's problem too. How deep was his anger against his father? Had it, despite Tom's observation, somehow survived in the injured cells of Philip's brain? Had it grown into the kind of twisted rage that could do this? Even if it had, surely he wasn't capable, mentally, of murdering so many people in such a clever, almost undetectable way.

Unless he had been pretending for some time.

Amy remembered Philip's flash of temper when she'd tried to run Martin Lenz out of his room. What if that had been the real Philip, angry and forceful, darting out for an instant from behind his mask of dull, sweet innocence?

Amy's skin crawled.

She realized someone was knocking at her door, had been knocking for several seconds. "Yes?"

Elaine Sikma entered, coming to her, putting a hand on her shoulder. "Now take it easy, they just brought your father in."

"What?" Amy's throat clenched with dread.

Elaine said, "He may be having a heart attack—but don't worry, it looks fairly mild—"

Cold with horror, Amy sprang up and ran past Elaine toward ER.

30

Amy tried to pull away from Bernie, feeling the fear beating in her chest. Bernie held on, Elaine Sikma on the other side, easing her out of the cardiac bay. She burned with frustration. They didn't understand. Someone had already tried to kill Winnie, and he would try again, and she must watch every second.

"Come on, Amy," Bernie said in a low, worried voice. "You know better than this. Ken Shepherd is the best cardiologist in this hospital. You're getting in his hair. I know it's your father, but you've got to give Ken room to work."

"I'm going to watch," she said stubbornly.

Bernie shook his head. "This isn't like you." He stopped, looking her up and down. "Are you aware that you're wearing two coats?"

"Oh, stop it, Bernie. It was cold back in my office. Now . . . let . . . me . . . past!"

Bernie held onto her arm, glancing helplessly at Elaine, giving her a look that said, *You're a woman, can't you do something?*

"What if we keep the curtain open a few feet?" Elaine suggested. "You can sit out here and keep an eye on your dad."

Amy thought briefly of telling them why it was so important, why she must stay with Winnie every second. No—Winnie would hear, and he didn't need the extra stress of being reminded that someone was trying to murder him. And she dared not leave him alone while she tried to convince Bernie and Elaine he was in danger. The way Bernie and Elaine were looking at her now, she wasn't going to be able to convince them of anything.

"All right," Amy said to Elaine. "A chair would be nice. I'm bushed. Maybe that's why I'm so cold." A spasm of shivering shook her. With a huge effort, she held herself still.

Elaine hurried off. Bernie kept hold of her arm. Amy wondered why they were being so insistent. All she'd done was . . .

Jump every time Ken touched Winnie, ask him at every step what he intended to do, and get in his and Elaine's way whenever they made a move toward the supply cart. Amy suppressed a groan.

Bernie leaned close to her ear. "I don't get this," he whispered urgently. "I might have expected behavior like this from Philip—I'm sorry, I didn't mean that the way it sounded. Hell, the fact is he's being a lot more adult about this than you are—and it's his father, too."

Amy looked at Philip. He stood ten or so feet from the cardiac bay, his face grave, his hands jammed into his pockets, looking as though he'd lost his best friend. His desolate expression heartened her. How could she have suspected him?

On the other hand, he *was* being very adult about it—a little *too* adult?

Bernie put the back of his hand to her forehead. "You've got a fever."

"I'm all right, really."

"I'm getting you some aspirin right now."

But he waited until Elaine brought the folding chair, then walked off, shaking his head. Amy sank gratefully into the chair, never taking her eyes off Ken. He had his stethoscope pressed to Winnie's chest right now. That might be it—anything that touched Winnie might be it. Amy fought the urge to get up and charge back into the cardiac bay. What could she do? Tell Ken not to listen to Winnie's heartbeat?

Bernie brought her the aspirin. She started to swallow them dry. He pressed a glass of water into her hand. The water felt gloriously good flowing down her throat. She hadn't realized how parched she was.

Fred Bascomb called Bernie. "Go," Amy said. "I'm fine."

He hurried off. Elaine stayed with her instead of going back in with Ken, who didn't seem to need her at the moment. "Did you hear on the radio?" Elaine said. "The police are looking for a doctor from this hospital—a surgeon, I think."

"I heard." Amy's stomach tightened with fear.

"Did you catch his name? I wasn't really listening until they mentioned Hudson."

"No."

"I think the radio said he was wanted for questioning in a possible murder."

"Did they say who he was supposed to have murdered?"

"If they did, I didn't catch it. Murder! You might know it would be a surgeon—"

"Nurse Sikma!" Ken called.

"Excuse me." Elaine patted her shoulder and stepped inside with him. Amy saw Winnie raise his head and wink at her. His face was pale, frightened. She mustered a smile and waved at him, hoping he could not see how afraid she was. It could happen, right here, right while she was watching—

Amy realized Elaine was searching the cart, a confused frown on her face. "The paste was right here," she was saying. "Dr. Wickham used it when he did the initial EKG. I must have laid it down somewhere." Ken said something Amy could not hear, his voice heavy with forced patience. Amy felt a strange, horrified calm descending on her. She knew exactly what was going to happen next: Elaine was going to ask Philip to bring more paste. The paste would be laced with toxin. Amy got up as she saw Elaine tug the curtain on Philip's side away and motion to him.

Amy took off for the supply room as fast as she could walk, careful not to draw Philip's attention. Her bruised feet hurt her, but she managed not to limp as she passed Bernie, giving him a serene nod, turning into the short hall. She ran, wincing, into the supply room, closing the door again, positioning herself so she would be hidden behind it when Philip came in.

Time seemed to stretch. Her anxiety deepened. Had she guessed wrong? All the electrode paste—as well as the nitroglycerine that Philip had brought for VanKleeck—was kept here, and here was where a nurse asking for paste would expect Philip to come. But there was still a chance he might keep the doctored paste somewhere else. Philip might, this moment, be handing a tube to Elaine.

Amy hesitated in an agony of indecision, then flattened herself against the wall as she heard footsteps outside in the hall. The door opened. She held her breath, watching the carton of electrode paste at eye level on an upper shelf. If Philip was not implicated in this, he would take a tube from that box.

If he was, he'd take it from somewhere else, some hiding place in here.

Amy saw part of her brother's head and shoulders lean toward the shelf. His hand started for the box of electrode paste, then he pulled it back as if slapped.

"Huh?" he said.

A chill ran up Amy's spine. What did he think he had heard? No one had said anything.

Philip stood a moment in apparent indecision, then knelt on the floor. Amy saw the one-inch gap between the bottom shelf and the floor. Her heart sped up. Philip ran his fingers under the edge of the bottom shelf, teasing out a tube of electrode paste.

As he straightened, Amy stepped from behind the door, sick at heart. "Philip."

"Sissy!" he squeaked, jumping comically.

She stifled a hysterical urge to laugh. "Give me that tube," she said.

"You *scared* me, Sissy."

"Give me the tube, Philip."

He looked down at the tube in his hand as if he'd forgotten it was there. "Well, all right—but Nurse Sikma wants me to bring her some paste." He handed it over.

Amy felt a burst of hope. He had not resisted at all. Was he involved in this without knowing it? *God, let it be so.*

"Take her this." Amy plucked a tube from the regular box and handed it to him.

"Okay."

She wanted to grab him, shake him, ask him if his innocence was an act, but she knew Elaine was waiting for the
paste, and Ken needed the EKG on Winnie. Now was not the
time—and she still had some thinking to do.

"Go ahead, Philip."

He looked at her. "Sissy, are you all right?"

"Fine. How about you?"

"I'm scared. What if Dad dies?"

"He won't." *Not if I can help it.* "Nurse Sikma is waiting for
the paste, Philip."

He nodded and hurried out. Amy slipped the other tube
of electrode paste into her pocket and hurried out after him, her
mind reeling in confusion. She was sure of only one thing:
whether Philip was behind this or only a cat's-paw for someone
else, she must get back to Winnie before someone tried again.

Campy walked into the lobby of Tom Hart's apartment,
hoping he would not be recognized. With his mug being
broadcast all over the city, all it would take to cook his goose
was one sharp-eyed citizen, eager to be a hero.

He took the elevator to the fourteenth floor, glad he'd
already checked out where Tom lived before this afternoon.
Walking down the hall, Campy counted off the numbers on the
doorways. He found Tom's apartment at the end, next to a
dramatic floor-to-ceiling window that finished off the hallway.
Campy looked out the window. The roof of Hudson General
was only ten feet down, a narrow gap between it and the
apartment building. On the other side of the hospital, the Sky-
Tek building soared up another twenty stories. A great loca-
tion, Campy thought. Right next to the hospital. It must cost
Tom a pretty penny, but then, at a hundred twenty an hour for
his private patients, he could afford it.

What would happen, Campy wondered, if I asked Tom to
help me with my problem? *Tell me, Doctor. Could a man
having blackouts kill while he was away from himself and
have no memory of it later?*

Campy felt a wave of fear trapping the air in his chest,
making it hard to breathe. He stood at Tom's door, waiting for

the attack of nerves to pass. He thought about what he wanted
to do now, just how to play it.

As he raised his hand to knock, he hoped that, if push
came to shove, Tom was not as strong as he looked.

Amy sat by Winnie's bed in the cardiac bay, watching him
sleep. He was doing well, the EKG was almost normal now.
She tried to think. She could feel the tube of electrode paste in
her pocket, a small but malignant weight. She must get it to
Chris, have it analyzed. Where *was* Chris, anyway? Probably
out somewhere with Jasper the Grasper, her beeper buried in
the bottom of her lingerie drawer. Amy contained her frustration. Elaine had promised to keep trying. Sooner or later, Chris
would answer her phone.

Amy yawned, her jaws cracking. Her eyes swam with
fatigue. She was exhausted, the adrenaline from the subway
long gone. A long night ahead. If no ICU beds were available,
Winnie would be staying right here. Somehow she must stay
alert. If only she could sneak herself a hit of epinephrine. There
was some in the crash cart, but it was locked away, and Elaine
had the key, and everyone in ER was already too suspicious of
her because she'd acted so strange earlier.

Amy fumbled her coffee cup from the bed table. Empty.
So was the Diet Coke. Philip would get her another, but she'd
had too much caffeine already—everything looked too bright,
searing her eyes. Amy felt her head nodding. She fished some
ice from the spent cup of Diet Coke on the floor and rubbed
it on her face. For a minute she felt wide awake, then her eyes
started to close. She thought of Philip again. Did he know what
he was involved in? Why had he hesitated in the storeroom
tonight? He'd started to reach for the regular electrode paste,
then stopped and said, "Huh?" It was almost as if someone had
been instructing him—which would fit, if Philip *was* only a
cat's-paw.

But I didn't hear anything, Amy thought.

Could he have heard something I didn't?

Unlikely—his hearing aids aren't *that* good—

Hearing aids!

Amy sat up straighter in her chair, thinking suddenly of those little radios you could wear on your ears while you jogged. What if the killer was giving Philip instructions through his hearing aids? Telling him first to remove the regular nitro or EKG paste—whatever—from the cart, probably shortly before the victim was brought in. Then, when the killer was sure his intended victim was in cardiac bay, telling Philip which tube to bring when the physician asked for it. It was possible. It would mean that the killer was not someone who normally worked in ER—which also made sense, because if the killer worked in ER he wouldn't need Philip; he could do the killing himself.

There was only one problem: to give Philip instructions from outside ER, the killer would have to know what was going on in the cardiac bay—

Amy felt her mouth dropping open. Stunned, she looked up into the red eye of the monitoring camera. If a videocam could send images to the nurses' station while it made tapes, it could certainly be modified to send them somewhere else at the same time.

Suddenly Amy was wide awake. She could feel her heart pounding. She stood staring at the camera. Had someone monitored the images of this camera tonight, waiting for Ken to ask for the paste? Had that same someone told Philip, through his hearing aid, to get the paste from beneath the bottom shelf?

If so, the voice in Philip's hearing aid would have to be very familiar. So familiar it would sound to Philip like the normal cross-talk people subconsciously heard in their own minds. A voice so familiar he could scarcely distinguish it from his own thoughts. A voice he was intimately acquainted with, one he trusted totally . . .

Amy sank into her chair, breathless with shock. Oh God, no, she thought. *Not Tom, please God, not Tom.*

31

Tom sat in his easy chair across from Campy, laughing at his joke and wondering what the hell he was doing here.

It was such an intriguing question that, when he'd seen Campy's face on the security monitor, he'd been unable to resist answering the door. A minute earlier, in the middle of instructing Philip, he would have had to ignore the buzzer. But now there was nothing left to do except wait for Winston St. Clair to die. He'd prefer to see it happen, but he would be watching it over and over on the tape anyway.

And he could not afford to let Campy walk away from his door without knowing why he'd risked capture by surfacing here.

"I know you care a lot for Amy," Campy said, "and I'm an old friend of hers, too. So I thought we might get our heads together about what's been happening to her."

"Sounds good." He's relaxing a little, Tom observed with clinical interest. He's decided I didn't catch him on the evening news. I did better than that, my man. I was there when you shinnied down that drainpipe. And the question is, do you still have that gun tucked away in the back of your belt?

"I understand you tried to help her remember the shape in the woods," Campy said.

"Yes. But she just couldn't do it. It's buried too deep. Have you had any luck with that?"

"No." Campy leaned forward in his chair. "The police seem to think that the man who killed Joyce knows Amy—is perhaps even a friend."

"So I understand." A friend! Tom felt a flash of inspiration. Regardless of why Campy had come here, it was a stroke of luck. You don't know it, Campy, Tom thought with relish, but *you* are going to kill Amy.

"You know her current friends a lot better than I do," Campy said. "Do any of them strike you as possible suspects?"

Tom made a show of considering the question. Instead, he studied Campy, planning how to take him. What he saw made him uneasy. Campy only seemed to be relaxing. There was something in his eyes . . .

"No," Tom said. "I've given her friends a lot of thought, but none seems remotely possible as a suspect."

Campy sagged back in his chair, rubbing his eyes, as if he were tired. As well you might be, Tom thought. But you're also up to something, aren't you?

Tom decided to take the initiative. "When you say you're an old friend of Amy's, do you by any chance mean old *boy*-friend?"

Campy nodded matter-of-factly. "High school flame."

"Interesting that you should end up working at the same hospital."

Campy gave him a weary smile. "You're a pretty good psychologist, aren't you?"

"I do my best."

"So you've probably figured out I came back here to be near Amy."

Tom felt a twinge of jealousy—absurd, but there it was. He gave Campy a disarming smile. "Yes, I figured that out. Listen, as long as we're talking man to man, how about a drink?"

"Not for me, thanks. I'm dead on my feet."

"Been working pretty hard?" Tom was starting to enjoy this.

"I think you could say that, yes."

Tom got up and walked to the china closet behind Campy's chair, noting how Campy swiveled to keep an eye on him. He took out the Waterford tumbler with the heavy leaded base and poured two fingers of Irish into it. "Sure you won't have one?"

Campy waved him off. "You know how sometimes a smell can trigger a memory—a perfume, for example? Or cologne?"

Something in his voice—Tom whirled to smash the tumbler against Campy's temple, but Campy ducked. The bottle grazed the top of his head instead. Slipping out of Tom's hand, it crashed to the floor and broke. Campy sprawled forward, off balance, into the shards on the floor. Tom jumped on him, grabbing his right ankle and twisting, then realizing he'd got the real foot. Campy kicked him off. Tom felt a surge of fury— he was not going to let this cripple wreck all his plans. Campy shook his head, looking dazed. He started to stagger up. Tom aimed a vicious kick at his left ankle. The blow connected squarely, tearing the artificial foot half off. Campy fell onto his back, then reared up, reaching one arm behind him—

The gun—

Tom dove on top of him. He sat on Campy, straddling his chest and right arm, pinning the arm to the floor behind his back. Campy jabbed at Tom's eyes with his other hand. Tom dodged and caught the thick wrist in both hands. He wrenched hard, trying to sprain the elbow, but Campy held him off, his biceps bulging. God, the man was *strong!*

Tom let go and slammed a fist down on Campy's right collarbone. He heard the bone crack, saw Campy's face twist in pain, but not a sound escaped him. Tom felt a flicker of amazement, and then Campy bucked him off and rolled, trying to get his left hand on the gun. Tom beat him to it, flicking the gun away to spin across the floor, feeling a searing pain in his palm as a shard of glass knifed him. Campy kicked him in the thigh, and Tom gasped in agony. Enraged, he lunged across the floor for the gun. *Got it!* He whirled to find Campy crawling toward him.

He aimed the .38 at Campy's head, half out of his mind with rage and fear. He started to pull the trigger, but realized, *No, he can't die before Amy.*

"Hold it," Tom said, easing his finger back on the trigger.

"Right," Campy said, and stopped crawling toward him.

"I know you . . . killed all those men," Tom said. Panting, he had to pause, catch his breath before he could go on. His thigh hurt horribly. His palm was slick with blood where the glass had cut him. "If you move, I'll kill you."

"Fair enough," Campy said reasonably. His face was gray with pain; the broken collarbone must be agonizing. And yet his voice sounded calm as death. Tom felt a grudging admiration for him. You're a strong one, he thought. Just like me.

Tom knelt beside Campy and hit him hard on the head with the gun. Campy's eyes rolled up and he went limp. Tom stared at his palm, feeling a little sick at all the blood. The cut stung like hell, but the bleeding looked worse than it was. It was already slowing.

Tom took Campy's pulse. It was slow and regular. A thick skull, fortunately.

Tom stood and rubbed at his thigh, still out of breath. The smell of the spilled whiskey hit him. No time to worry about that. Keeping an eye on Campy, he went into the kitchenette, got some filament tape, and bound Campy's wrists behind him. The artificial foot was hanging by a strap. The sight of it made him vaguely uncomfortable. Going into his den, he unlocked the utility closet. Inside, he felt the dark, blank TV screen drawing him. In a minute, he thought. He opened the safe beside the monitor and counted out five scopolamine patches. That ought to do it, at least for now.

Tom went back to Campy and put the patches on the back of his neck.

Sorry I can't end it for you right now, Campy. You earned it. But you can't die until after Amy. And if you're going to kill her, you need your rest. So sweet dreams.

Tom hurried back to his monitoring room, extremely pleased with himself. Campy would be out for a good long while now. And if he needed to extend it, he could just keep sticking fresh patches on. No one would miss Campy, since he was on the run. And there was plenty of time to kill Amy.

Right now he wanted to check in on Winston St. Clair.

Tom went back into the utility closet, locked the door behind him, and flipped on the monitor. The screen gave him the usual clear view of cardiac bay. Winston lay still in his bed, his eyes closed. Amy sat beside him, her face pale with shock.

Tom felt a savage glee. "Yes! Dead, you bastard! And I killed you, I *killed*—"

Winston's arm moved.

Tom stopped, his heart plunging in horror. Winston's eyes fluttered open briefly as he rolled to his side, then closed again.

Not dead. Asleep.

Tom stared at the screen, dumbfounded. How could it be? Philip had gone for the paste. By now, Winston should be dead. What had happened? Had Philip screwed up?

Cursing, Tom punched the onscreen rewind, watching the picture reverse until Philip brought the tube in. He ran it forward again. There was Elaine, smearing the paste, with its load of *Claviceps,* on Winnie's chest.

Tom shook his head. He must be dead, he *must* be!

Sweat began to stream down Tom's forehead. He rewound the tape farther, to the point where Elaine had called Philip over. Movement in the corner of the picture caught his eye—Amy, beyond the curtain, getting up suddenly, leaving the bay, going in the direction of the storeroom.

Tom's blood ran cold.

He raced the tape forward. There was Philip, bringing the paste to Elaine. A moment later, Amy sat down again. She was gone just a little longer than Philip. Long enough to intercept him.

"Amy?" Tom groaned. He could not believe it.

He punched the tape off, returning to a live picture.

Amy's face filled the screen. She was standing on her chair, looking just below the lens, examining the videocam. Her eyes focused suddenly on the lens, gazing straight into his. Tom edged back from the screen, struck by a superstitious dread. Her expression—almost as if she could see him now. He shuddered, flipped the monitor off.

She *knows!* he thought.

I have to kill her right now. Her and Winston.

But how? There are people all around them.

Rage filled him as he thought about her escape in the subway. That would have been so perfect. He could not believe his luck when she went down there. But then she'd managed to get away. She kept doing it, frustrating him, slipping away from him at every turn.

Had she already called the police?

The thought sent a surge of panic through him. He must hide the evidence, clear out this room—

But what if Amy did *not* know he was the one?

Tom forced himself to be still and think: There was a chance Amy had figured out *how,* but not *who.* It wouldn't take her long to decide it was him. If he took time to clean up here, he might miss his last chance to kill her before she could expose him. It was double or nothing now.

Tom ran from his control room. He put the gun that Campy had stolen from the cop inside his coat. Kneeling beside Campy, he felt for the pulse in his neck. It was very slow. He was completely under now.

Tom stayed on his knees a minute, controlling the urge to bolt, trying to make sure he had thought of everything. Another, smaller inspiration hit him. He got a gym bag from his closet, unstrapped Campy's foot, and stuffed it into the bag. With it gone, Campy would be all the more helpless.

And it would be perfect if, when Campy shot Amy with the gun he'd stolen from the cop, some of her blood got on his foot.

Amy's mind spun with panic. *Tom*—she could not believe it. Tom, who had done so much for Philip, Tom, whom she had trusted, with whom she had almost fallen in love—

Stop it. I've got to be calm and think now.

Amy sat down beside Winnie's bed. By now, she thought, Tom knows that Winnie isn't dead. He probably saw me run out when Philip went to get the paste. He knows that I know.

Which means he'll try to kill us both, as soon as he can.

Cold horror filled Amy. I have to get us out of here, she thought. But how? If I try to just wheel Winnie out, someone on the staff will stop me. They already think I've gone crazy.

She heard sirens pulling up out front. She saw Elaine hurrying out. An ambulance! If she could get it to take her and Winnie away . . .

Amy ran to catch Elaine, ignoring the shooting pains in her feet. "What gives?"

"Another gang fight," Elaine said disgustedly. "Two kids shot up. I long for the days when they used to go after each other with switchblades and brass knuckles."

"You'll need space," Amy said. "Winnie's doing fine. I'll wheel him out of cardiac bay."

Elaine hesitated.

"I can take care of him in the hall till they find a room. God knows I'm not good for much else tonight."

"You're all right now?"

"Absolutely."

"Fine. It would be a help."

Amy hurried back to Winnie's gurney. She pushed him out of the cardiac bay and down the hall, steering to the side as paramedics rolled in two kids. She caught a glimpse of dangling arms hooked to IVs, blood-soaked chests. She recognized one of the paramedics—the tall guy with the little ponytail who'd tried to flirt with her a few days ago. Good!

She waited until all the hubbub was past, then wheeled Winnie out to the ambulance, positioning the gurney behind the open rear doors. She would need help to get it up inside. She waited, fretting. A breeze from the street swept between the big round columns of the concrete overhang, ruffling the blanket on Winnie's chest. He stirred and moaned in his sleep. Amy tucked the blanket up around his chin, worried about his chances. The heart attack had drained him—not just the physical onslaught, which was enough to exhaust anyone, but the fear he must have felt along with it, the knowledge that someone was trying to murder him.

I won't let him get you, Amy thought. Or me!

The big paramedic sauntered out, leaving his partner at the triage desk to fill out forms. Amy waved him over. "Help me get this man in."

"Whoa, whoa, Doc. We got no dispatch orders on him."

"I know, but your gang fight just displaced him. He's stable and resting, but we need to get him to another hospital. I'm going to ride along and make sure he's admitted."

The big attendant looked at her. "This is not standard operating procedure, Doc."

Amy wanted to scream with frustration. She resisted the urge to push him down to the other end of the gurney, wrap his fingers around the lift bar. "This is a special case," she said. "This man is my father. You can run us over to Cornell, that's just ten minutes this time of night. What is the normal charge now, a hundred bucks for a ride? I don't have the cash on me, but I'll make sure you get it, no red tape, no ugly forms for the home office to fill out."

The paramedic smiled. "Doc, I'd do it just for your eyes— not that I dislike the idea of money, you understand. But my partner in there, he's the uptight type, and I just don't think it would work."

"I'll take care of it when we get back. I'll take full responsibility, tell him it was an emergency. Which it is!" Her throat felt tight with desperation. "Come on, help me out." Without waiting for an answer, Amy started lifting her end of the gurney. The paramedic sighed and walked to the other end, picking it up easily. With the strength of desperation, Amy hoisted her end level with the deck and helped roll it in. She clambered up into the ambulance, feeling the paramedic's hand on her haunch, welcoming the push.

The paramedic stood a moment in the doorway. "If I get a call—"

"You have room for a couple more in here. And I think I've got enough medical training to fill in for your friend."

"Tell you what, Doc. Forget the hundred and go dancing with me."

"Deal," she said, feeling a giddy sense of unreality. What could this big kid possibly see in her right now? Her hair was a wild tangle, her eyes must be bloodshot, and she'd sweat her makeup off in the subway. But if he wanted to dance with her, she'd dance all night.

With a happy grin, the paramedic slammed the doors. Amy settled in beside Winnie, making sure he was comfortable. It seemed to take the attendant quite a while to get to the cab. Just when she was about to check on him, she heard the front door open, and felt the subtle shift of the ambulance on its shocks.

The ambulance started up and rolled out of the bay, and Amy let out a long breath. Safe! Relief flooded her. Let Tom come to the hospital now. He'd find her and Winnie gone, and he'd have no idea where.

Amy sat down on the bench beside Winnie, a terrible weariness welling up in her now that she was safe. But she must not go to sleep yet. She still had to get Winnie admitted at Cornell. And then she must call Detective Schumer, get the hunt for Tom started.

And the hunt for Campy called off.

Tears sprang to her eyes. Tom, *why?*

She thought about it, putting together what she knew the killer had done with what she knew about Tom.

The smooth glide of the ambulance lulled her. So sleepy. She pinched her cheeks and bit down on her lip to stay awake. She checked her watch in the dim light. One o'clock. It was now Monday morning. They should be at Cornell in another five minutes . . .

Amy jerked awake, feeling a dull pain in her head. She'd slumped forward, banging her forehead on the rail of Winnie's gurney.

Before she'd dozed off, she'd been thinking about Tom and the stolen blood. Why had Tom done that? It certainly wasn't for some voodoo ceremony.

Suddenly she had it.

And at the same time realized that something was wrong. She checked her watch again. *One-twenty!* Amy felt a surge of alarm. They should have been at Cornell long before now. She scrambled to the ambulance's rear window and looked out. Grimy yellow-tiled walls rolled past. She stared at them, not believing her eyes. They were leaving the Holland Tunnel, heading for the New Jersey swamps and landfills that ringed the southeast approach to New York.

She hurried to the hatch that sealed off the cab and rapped on the glass. The driver pulled the hatch open. She leaned through to ask the paramedic what the hell he was doing, and then she saw that the paramedic was lying slumped across the passenger seat beneath her, his eyes open, his head twisted so far that his chin rested behind his shoulder. She stared at him, her mind blank with horror, and then she felt the muzzle of a gun pressing against her temple.

"Hello, Amy," Tom said. "Why don't you come up and join me?"

32

Amy sat beside Tom in the front of the ambulance, between him and the dead paramedic, feeling numb. There was a lulling falseness to the darkness of the cab, Tom driving with one hand as if they were coasting home after dinner and drinks in the country. But she could feel the gun in his left hand pressing against her ribs. On her other side, the paramedic's head lolled on her shoulder, nudging her cheek each time the ambulance went over a bump. She could smell breath freshener on his lips. There was no room to pull away from him, even if she had the strength.

In a minute, Amy thought, I'll be just like him.

A suffocating dread filled her. She would not be with Campy, would not see Denise and Ellie grow up . . .

She felt a spark of anger. Who was Tom to do this to her?

"You're very quiet," Tom said, and laughed.

"Why are you doing this now?" she asked. "There hasn't been time for a genetics lab to analyze the blood you stole. What if the report proves that Winnie *isn't* your father?"

He glanced at her. "Very good. I'm impressed."

"Winnie isn't your father. He can't be."

"He fits."

"Just like the other men you killed. Were they all your father, too?"

"I did the best I could with what I had. All my mother told me was that my father worked in a bank and had blue eyes and was tall—she made a mark on our door to show me how tall. And once she told me his age. I pestered her all the time about it. I had fantasies that he hadn't really left us on purpose, that there was some explanation."

Amy was chilled by Tom's voice. So calm. What a horrible, insane fury must lie beneath that voice. The force of habit was still keeping it hidden. And oh, how much practice he'd had. *My God, he was a master at hiding himself.*

In the back of the ambulance, Winnie groaned. Hush, Amy thought, afraid for him. "I'm sorry your father abandoned you," she said, "but your father is not my father."

"You're wrong. *Our* father murdered my mother."

"Murdered? Tom, that's absurd." Amy felt indignant. Why was Tom saying these awful things? Winnie *had* lied to her, but he was a good and kind man, a loving father. He was not a murderer.

"You told me your mother died in a subway accident."

"She was pushed in front of the train. One instant she was standing in a crowd, the next she was on the tracks. The train tore her in half."

Amy stared at him, appalled. In her mind she heard again the deafening roar of the train, felt the shock wave of grit and fumes, the terrifying certainty that she was going to die. "If that's true, how could you even think of doing it to someone else?"

"Not someone else—*you.*" Tom's voice was suddenly harsh, a hint of rage showing through. "It would have been so sweet if that train had hit you, Amy. I might even have let your father live. It would be worth it to have him feel what I felt, live with it—" Tom stopped. "It doesn't matter. I've got you now." The gun jabbed into her ribs, sending a cold rush of fright through her. A wash of approaching headlights bathed Tom's face. His murderous expression terrified her. She realized that he was insane, and had been the whole time she'd known and admired him. Crazy with a madness not of the mind, which worked brilliantly, but of the heart. He had one real emotion— hate. All the others were only masks.

Terror ripped through her. Could she jump against him

now, drive him off the road? No. A wreck would kill Winnie in his condition. And Tom would probably just keep hold of the wheel and shoot her. It would have to be something else.

Slowly the pressure of the gun on her ribs eased. "Why were you following me?" she asked.

"It was getting time for you to die. And spare me your outrage—you'd have been dead already if I hadn't been keeping an eye on you."

Amy tried to understand what he was saying, but her mind stayed stuck on the one thing: He's going to kill me. "What?"

"I warned you not to go running in the park."

"You killed Strickney," Amy said. Her throat was very dry.

"Fortunately for you, I wasn't ready for you to die. You hadn't laid the golden egg yet. What I do to you will be merciful compared to Mr. Strickney's plans. So you see, you really have nothing to complain about. Your life is already mine."

Something soft and heavy slipped onto Amy's foot—the gym bag on the floor. She tried to nudge it away, but the dead paramedic's legs blocked it.

"I thought I knew you," she said, "but I can't begin to fathom you. You killed seven men, just because they *might* have been your father?"

"They were all smug, rich bastards. Don't waste your pity on them. If I had known my father's name, they'd be alive, but the world would be no better off."

Hearing the madness in his voice again, Amy edged away from Tom, pushing against the dead paramedic in her revulsion. How will he kill us? she wondered. The gun, or does he have some of the toxin with him—

The toxin! I have some of the toxin!

She slipped both hands into the pockets of her medical coat, as though she were cold. Tom was maneuvering around a truck, and she used the moment to locate and grasp the tube of electrode paste in her left pocket. "How many more men are you going to kill?"

"The original list was thirteen. My lucky number."

Amy shifted her fingers to the cap of the tube. "My father is number eight, not counting Cynthia and Joyce. So you have six murders to go."

"No. I'll stop with your father. He's the one."

"What makes you so sure?" She forced herself to relax, working at the cap, unscrewing it slowly between a thumb and forefinger.

"About a month ago," Tom said, "I was moving in on number seven—not VanKleeck but a man named Hammill. Then I located a woman I'd been searching for for a long time—my mother's best friend. She was living in the barrio in L.A. As I'd hoped, she knew more about my father—some things my mother would never have told me." Tom paused and Amy saw him glance at her, just as the top of the tube came off. *Careful!* She rubbed her fingers inside the pocket, terrified that she might have gotten some of the paste on her skin.

Never mind. If I don't use the paste, I'm dead anyway.

Tom said, "She told me about that night in the gazebo."

Amy's hand froze in her pocket. She felt her throat closing in sudden panic. She lowered her head, pulling in a deep breath. "Stop it, Tom. I don't want to hear it."

"I'm sure you don't. But it happens that I want very much to tell you. Think, Amy. Why did you panic when I put my hands on you in that gazebo? Why did you run, just like you must have that night when you were a little girl. Surely you remember now. You walked out there in your sleep, then you woke up and saw . . . *them.*"

Amy gasped, feeling her stomach twist. She pinched her eyes shut, but the images broke through at last, scalding her brain: Winnie and a woman, naked—

NO!

She stood barefoot on the cool dirt path, scared and confused. What was she doing out here? There was Daddy and the woman who cleaned downstairs for Mommy. Why had they taken off their clothes? The woman sat naked on Daddy's lap, facing him, her legs around his tummy, rocking back and forth, crying as if Daddy was hurting her. Amy started to cry too. The woman looked at her and screamed.

And then Daddy saw me, and he jumped up and pushed the woman away and she started to cry, and then he cried too, and I ran and ran . . .

Tears poured down Amy's cheeks. She sat, rigid, remembering. Afterwards, for days and days, there had been a terrible silence in the house.

And I caused it.

"The woman in the gazebo was my mother," Tom said. "Her name was Honora—not that a rich brat like you would remember the name of a mere maid."

"I was only a little girl." Amy became aware again of the tube, still in her hand. She eased it from her pocket, moved the nozzle against his leg in the darkness, and started squeezing. She held her breath, terrified that he would feel it.

"Only a little girl." Tom's voice was scornful, ragged. "It's your fault, too. You've always known it. You ran back and told your mother and it drove your parents apart—that's why you wouldn't let yourself remember. But look what you did to my mother. If you hadn't stumbled upon them like that, humiliated him, she might still be alive. After all, that night in the gazebo was not the first. He had . . . had *taken* her there many times." Tom's voice thinned in disgust. "Only when his darling little daughter caught him with her did he feel any shame. But did he take that shame out on himself? Oh no."

Amy wanted to scream. What Tom had said about the gazebo was true, she could not deny it. How much else was true? Could her father really have abandoned the woman, let alone killed the mother of his child? There must be some other explanation. "You know about the gazebo," she said, "but you can't know what happened after—"

"Oh no? That night a lawyer came to my mother's quarters with a note from your father dismissing her. She was to clean out her things at once and never come back. She was not to see or contact him again. If she did, he would have her deported. And if she spread vicious lies about being pregnant by him, she would be very, very sorry. My mother was not from this country. She was terrified. He was a man of wealth and power. In her country, such men could have her killed while the police looked the other way."

Amy felt torn by a vast, terrible confusion. How could everything she believed about Winnie be wrong? Fury began to build in her at Tom. How he must have longed to tell her this, to rub her face in it. He was trying to make her hate Winnie as he did. If he couldn't have his father's love, no one could. How hard it must have been to hold this in all the time, acting nice to her, making love to her . . .

My own brother.

Amy squeezed the tube savagely, flattening it between her fingers until it had emptied completely on his leg. She eased it down the crack in the seat. "You *bastard!*"

"I see it's finally sinking in, *sister.*" His voice was filled with a grotesque pleasure.

"If I'm your sister, you're the one who knew it and you made love to me."

"It wasn't easy, believe me."

She wanted to slap him, to scream at him that he had *enjoyed* it—

—and so did I, oh God, so did I.

"Nothing that happened between us meant anything to you, did it," she said. Tom did not answer.

She heard a stir from the back again. *Please, Winnie, don't move.* She had to keep Tom from hearing him.

"Why did you kill Owen VanKleeck?"

"VanKleeck had a daughter and an estate with woods in back, just like your father. He and your father were the only two out of those left who did."

"But how did you get the original toxin into Winnie?"

"Simple. The toothpaste in his office," Tom said. He glanced out the window again, and she realized he was looking for a place to get off the expressway. So he can kill us and dump our bodies, Amy thought. Her stomach lurched. Bearing down, she got control of her fear. "So you drugged us both, to see which one would remember that night. But neither of us could. She because it didn't happen to her, and I because I had repressed it so deeply."

"You're stubborn, Amy. Even your unconscious is stubborn. If you had only told me, Cynthia and her father would still be alive."

His taunting voice infuriated her. "Everyone's to blame but you, aren't they, Tom? How you suffered. That's what this is really about. You didn't murder seven men and two women to avenge your mother. All you really care about is yourself—how wronged *you* were."

"You have no idea," Tom said softly. "Tell me, what is it like to be loved by your father? Why did he choose you and reject me?"

"No, no, listen, I . . ." Winnie gasped from the back of the ambulance.

Amy turned, startled.

Tom raised the gun to her head, where Winnie could see it. "If you move, I'll kill her right now."

"Relax, son. I . . . I can't even make it off this cot, or I'd have been all over you before now." His voice was weak, hoarse with anguish.

"Don't call me 'son.' " Tom's voice rose in pitch, giving Amy the sudden, eerie feeling that she was hearing the child still buried in him

"I didn't kill your mother," Winnie said. "I cared very deeply for her."

"You used her and threw her away," Tom said. "You destroyed her life whether you pushed her in the subway or not. You broke her heart and she died."

Amy realized with astonishment that Tom didn't even know for certain that his mother had been murdered. It might have been an accident. He had believed what he wanted to believe—and killed his "father" over and over.

"I tried to find you," Winnie said. "I searched for you for a long time."

"Liar!"

"Listen to me," Winnie said. "That night in the gazebo, I was ashamed, yes. My daughter should not have seen me being unfaithful to her mother. But I did not send your mother away. I expected to see her the next day—"

"Filthy liar. Your own lawyer ran her out."

"That is true," Winnie said. "But I didn't order it."

Amy sensed a sudden reluctance in his voice, a careful choosing of words. An awful suspicion began to dawn on her.

"When she wasn't at work that day or the next," Winnie said quickly, "I went looking for her in the city, Spanish Harlem, all the Hispanic neighborhoods, but no one knew her, or else they weren't willing to tell me anything about her."

"Because you'd threatened her."

"No. She was carrying my child. I was desperate to find her. I searched everywhere, but she was an illegal with no paper trail. It was as though she had never existed. I wanted to see her and I wanted to raise my child."

"Shut up! It's too late for your lies." The child voice was high and furious now, the madness at full gallop.

Amy looked at him, transfixed with horror as she understood at last, understood it all. "But don't you see, he isn't lying," she said. "He didn't send your mother away."

"Of course he did. She was terrified—"

"Yes, but not of my father. Of my mother. My mother sent the lawyer to threaten your mother. I'm sure she wrote the note and signed Winnie's name to it."

Tom glanced at her. There was no comprehension in his eyes, only insanity and death. Why hadn't his heart arrested? The paste had had time to work if it was going to. With a terrible certainty, Amy knew that she and Winnie would die now—

And all she could think about was the fact that it wasn't Philip's injury her mother held against her father. Oh no. She held Tom's mother against him. And it's my fault, Amy thought brokenly. Tom's right. I must have gone back that night and told Mother what I'd seen. If it weren't for me, my parents would still be together.

A terrible weariness settled over her. Dimly she felt the ambulance bumping down a dirt road. Tom stopped in a vast, marshy landfill, the highway hidden now behind a towering mound of scarred and pitted rock. In the distance, she could see the smokestacks of Newark, black against a reddish sky. She gazed at them. They seemed oddly beautiful.

"Tom," Winnie said from the back, "if you shoot us, the police will know it's murder."

"I didn't shoot you," Tom said. "Campy did. And then he shot himself."

"You're crazy," Amy said wearily.

"You think so? Take a look in that bag."

Amy leaned over and zipped open the bag. Inside lay Campy's foot. She doubled over, her stomach heaving.

Campy, he's killed Campy, too—

No, she thought. If he's going to blame this on Campy, then Campy has to still be alive. But not for long.

Amy turned against the gun, determined to fight, then saw that Tom was holding his right hand up to the window, staring at it. "What the hell is this?" He sounded baffled.

He was looking at a gleaming wet smear on his palm. The electrode paste! He must have felt the wetness on his trouser leg and reflexively touched it.

In the middle of his palm, Amy saw a cut. I've got him! she thought exultantly.

"You bitch!" Tom said, horror dawning on his face. He raised the gun toward her face. She leaped on him, terrified, grabbing his wrist, holding it away with all her strength. She heard a crash in the back of the ambulance and knew with dread that Winnie had fallen in an effort to get out to help her. Tom forced her hands back, back, the mouth of the gun inching around to her head—

And then his face went rigid with pain. His gun arm yielded suddenly; she pushed the gun away as he pulled the trigger over and over, loud explosions blowing out the windshield, glass clattering along the hood.

Tom fell back against the door. His eyes stared at her accusingly.

She realized he was dead.

"What happened?" Winnie cried out.

"He had a heart attack," Amy said. Her voice seemed to come from far away. "Lie down, Dad. I'll drive us back."

Winnie groaned. "I was such a fool," he said softly. "I have always loved your mother. I would never have left her. But I cared deeply for Honora too. And I would have loved Tom. If only I could have found them."

Amy tried to find an answer. She could not. She could only think about Campy—the foot in the bag. She crawled over Tom's body, pushing him until he fell on top of the paramedic. Starting the ambulance, she drove up out of the landfill.

EPILOGUE

Amy sat with Campy in their old booth at Frenchie's, almost unable to believe that she was there. On the table she traced the words carved so long ago: *Campy loves Amy*. She ran a finger over the grooves, darkened almost to invisibility by twenty years of cooking grease and cigarette smoke.

Campy said, "Are you sure we should have left the girls at the playground?"

"Now don't start that," Amy said. "They'll be fine with Philip. And Frenchie's isn't a healthy atmosphere for young girls."

He gave her a slow, understanding smile. "They might meet a guy like me."

"Exactly." Then she ruined it by smiling too.

"I think Philip's doing better," Campy said.

"He still misses Tom, but yes, I think so. You've had a lot to do with his accepting Tom's loss, you know. Taking him to baseball games, playing chess with him—he really appreciates that."

"He ought to. He beats me every time."

"Do you think he has any idea of how Tom used him?"

"I doubt it. Tom wouldn't have wanted Philip to have any inkling that he was involved in murder, for fear he might blurt it out to someone."

Amy was only partly satisfied by Campy's answer. She knew she was fretting, but how could she not? "Something else worries me," she said. "Tom saw himself in Philip. In his twisted way, he identified with him, I think. I dread the thought that Tom might have tried to bring back Philip's resentment of Dad."

"I think you're right about the first part," Campy said. "I'm sure Tom *did* see some of himself in Philip. He may even have harbored the conceit that Philip, if he were his old self before the brain injury, would *want* to help him get revenge on your father. But actually stirring up Philip's old resentments would have been the last thing Tom needed. Tom wanted a tool, pure and simple. An innocent, sweet, tranquil guy that no one would suspect of murder."

Amy shuddered. "Tom was a monster, a pure sociopath."

"He fooled us all," Campy agreed. "Until the end."

"It's horrible to think this, but if only my mother hadn't sent Honora away, everything would have been different. Mother didn't mean to, but she helped create the murderer in Tom."

"Other boys have grown up orphans without killing anyone. Tom created himself."

"I know. You're right, of course."

"She's doing her best to make amends."

Amy smiled. "You're sweet to stick up for her."

"I admire her. That group home for boys she's been funding over on the West Side is doing a world of good."

"Yes, isn't that something? When she sold the Park Avenue place and most of her paintings, Winnie was afraid she'd gotten taken in by some young stud. I knew it wasn't that, but I had no idea she'd turned so philanthropic."

"It's penance, you know. That home is going to save some kid who might otherwise end up like Tom."

"I think that's stretching it a little, Campy. When she helped to establish the place, she didn't even know what had become of Honora's child."

"No, but it did torment her, especially after the tragedy with Philip. Philip's injury changed a lot of things in your mother. She didn't just blame your father, she blamed herself. She knows she's not a warm person. She's sorry that she never showed enough affection to either you or Philip. She would give you a nod when you should have had a pat on the shoulder, a pat when you should have had a hug."

Amy looked at Campy, astonished. "Where do you get all this?"

"We talk," Campy said.

"I can't believe this. Mother never liked you."

"Your mother has changed, Amy. If you got to know her now, I think you'd like her better."

Amy felt a quick pressure of tears and blinked them away. "Maybe I would."

He grinned. She studied him, loving his face, his eyes, the humor and kindness that all the terrible times had not erased. His hair was growing back where the neurosurgeon had cut. She remembered exactly how the tumor had looked in Chris's lab—grayish and quite smooth, the size of a small grape. Chris said it had not metastasized, and Chris was very good. Thank God.

And Campy and I should both be dead now anyway.

The knowledge had a curiously relaxing effect on her. Every day of their lives together was a bonus now, to be reveled in without fear. The tumor might come back someday, Eric might get his way next time and close ER. But this was now.

And now was good.

Still gazing at Campy, Amy saw at the bottom of her vision that he was rolling up one of his sleeves. In a minute she would look down and find that he had inked a tattoo onto his arm. She leaned back in the booth and inhaled, savoring the old familiar smells of french fries and coffee.

After a while she looked down at his arm.

The tattoo said: *Déjà Tattoo*

She laughed and leaned over to kiss him.

He said, "Let's go to the playground."